THE END,
AS IT HAPPENS TO THEM

RANDY DOLPH

Order this book online at www.trafford.com
or email orders@trafford.com

Most Trafford titles are also available at major online book retailers.

© Copyright 2016 Randy Dolph.

All rights reserved. No part of this publication may be reproduced, stored in a retrieval system, or transmitted, in any form or by any means, electronic, mechanical, photocopying, recording, or otherwise, without the written prior permission of the author.

Print information available on the last page.

ISBN: 978-1-4907-6958-5 (sc)
ISBN: 978-1-4907-6959-2 (hc)
ISBN: 978-1-4907-6957-8 (e)

Because of the dynamic nature of the Internet, any web addresses or links contained in this book may have changed since publication and may no longer be valid. The views expressed in this work are solely those of the author and do not necessarily reflect the views of the publisher, and the publisher hereby disclaims any responsibility for them.

Any people depicted in stock imagery provided by Thinkstock are models, and such images are being used for illustrative purposes only.
Certain stock imagery © Thinkstock.

Trafford rev. 01/29/2016

 www.trafford.com

North America & international
toll-free: 1 888 232 4444 (USA & Canada)
fax: 812 355 4082

This Book is dedicated to;

My awesome Wife, who will forever be on my mind and in my heart. You know I love you more and that you are the greatest. Thank you so much for all you've done both with my writings and in all our lives together.
To my two wonderful children, you make my heart so full.
To Wanda, thanks again, for all you do and for being my friend.
To everyone that encouraged me through all this, and who played a part in this book. Your personalities have made some of these characters easy to think up. (You know who you are.)

Other Books
By Randy Dolph

The End Trilogy:
Book 1: The End, As It Happens To Me
Book 2: The End, As It Happens To Us

A Break-out Book To 'The End Trilogy':
The End, As It Happens To Quade

Western:
The Old Drake Place

CHAPTER 1

I had longed to be home, much as everyone would who has been on such trips as we had just experienced. My thoughts of home were always full of warmth and they brought with them the ideas of a peaceful place. The faces there always say safety and comfort are now ready to envelope you. As we raced through the foothills and made it onto the plains and as we searched our compound from top to bottom such thoughts still pushed in and said that everything was going to be alright. I hoped that the recent events we had been through did not rob me of such things, as I feared they had already robbed me somewhat of my personality. I will write on now then, in even more hope, that maybe someday I can look back over these writings, (I'm hoping they are forever stacked in the bottom drawer of my office desk) and find that together we have been through so much and still live on as the people we once were. Yes, I will yet give hope to remaining sane. And so I write again:

As the two of us walked back to my group, this unwelcomed man with a hillside of Humvees to back him and I up, everyone was still standing there with nerves on end. They looked at me and then back to the man walking beside me as though that would tell them everything. I stopped just before we got to them.

"Sounds like they may know where he's headed," I told everyone.

"Who the hell are they and what the hell is going on," Jadee asked, stepping out in front of everyone. The man beside me did not flinch or give any indication that her movement toward him mattered. That concerned me a little. I hoped I did not show it.

"We are what's left of America," the man said. "It's not the same word for America that it was before the war, with all of its political mess. We separated long before that and worked beneath the surface to keep the true America alive. This disease came along before the political America could collapse on its own, though we had been trying to help it on its way for quite a while. We are the ones that would stand up for the way things should have been in America, ma'am. We still stand and America still lives on." We looked around at each other. I think he saw we were not in the mood for small talk.

"Why come here then if you knew that Kevin was gone?" I asked him.

"It was my orders," he said flatly and looked at me straight. "I guess, to see for ourselves that you are not part of his team. Kevin never was the kind to be able to recruit real well so we figured he had just fallen in with whoever would take him in. We did not expect to find a group like you in a place like you have there. We needed to check it out. Usually we would be on our way but it seems like you all are a much different type than we've seen. We needed to be sure. We thought Kevin was going to be retrieving the data from Site 823. That's why we were there waiting to take him out and whoever might be with him." The admission that they were the ones that fired on us and knowing we had fired back played on my nerves a little. "And now, quite frankly, we need help." I looked at him a little sideways. Here again was someone asking for our help when all we were looking for was the peace to live out our lives.

"We will get our people back," I told the man. "Don't take this the wrong way but we're not real interested in whatever group thing you're part of. I would much appreciate the information that you have but we don't want to join your organization or whatever you are." The man smiled.

"That's just the type of people that can help us," he said. "We are not looking for people to join us. We are only trying to make it so those who survived can do just what you are taking about. Kevin, and those like him, threatens that. We need you to find him and I think we can help you do that. I and my men are truly needed elsewhere. I'll give you all the information we have and when you take him out I'm sure we'll never see each other again. I will say here, live on in peace when it's done and bring back what America was, just like you are wanting to."

"The sales pitch sounds great," I told him. "Maybe I'm just a little skeptical. It concerns me that you guys were the ones that we ran into down below Colorado Springs. You nearly killed one of us and I'm sure I saw a few of you fall."

"I'm not in charge of this whole operation," he said. "I was down there for a damn good reason. One of my corporals fired on you without me telling him to. He lost a man because of it and I'm still kicking his ass daily. But I'm not here to smooch up to your ass either, pardon me saying it like that. My orders here are to check you out and retrieve whatever data you took from Site 823. I understand your position in what's going on, that's the only reason we're talking." The man paused and seemed to want to switch gears. "Think of it this way, if we weren't here what would you be doing, looking through your satellites and combing the countryside from above. I'm sorry to say Kevin knows that and won't be so stupid as to be seen. I'm offering you some information on where he may be going and then we're out of here. If you don't want that information, still we are out of here. There are other men that need to be had just as bad, though I must say I'd love the privilege of capturing yours. That's just not my orders this time. Only thing is, I really need that info you got." I looked around then and nodded my head to him.

"Okay, where is he?" I asked.

"We didn't find him here until just a few days ago, though we knew he was somewhere close around here. He was looking for the group we are after, trying to join up with them." The man looked over at me. "We have been looking for the rest of his team too. The other one we're after, put together with Kevin, are pretty dangerous. That's why we need to see what was sent to you guys down there. Maybe I'm playing it down a little. The other one is just as bad as Kevin really. But my guy must have something new as they are preferring his capture over Kevin's. This is where you come in if you're interested and we give you the help you need to do it."

"That seems hard to believe," I told him. "He said he had The Monk's blood and DNA which was what he needed to complete some research program."

"You must be talking about Steve. Maybe we should sit down for the rest of this?" the man asked. "We won't make any trouble. My lieutenant will come with me if that's okay and he will disarm. He's really the professional on all of the science stuff. I have extensive knowledge on what's going on but really my job is just to find Kevin or others like him." I looked around at my family. I was not sure how to get us out of this thing we had become part of but I figured we should gather as much information as possible while we could. I knew I would not commit us to anything, however.

"Okay," I told him. The man gave me a nod and spoke into the radio at his shoulder.

"Send Charles over and tell him to leave his side arm," he said. "Everyone else at ease. I'm going inside with Charles. This shouldn't take long so stand ready to move out. No firing." I heard them respond and the man looked back at me.

"What's your name?" I asked him.

"Name's McQueen," he said. I reached out and took his outstretched hand. With the other hand I reached in and retrieved the pin drive from my vest pocket. I threw it to him and gave him a shrug.

"Didn't seem like a lot of stuff on there that could be of any help now," I told him. "It was all the whys and what fors."

"I was only told to get it," McQueen told me.

"Maybe I didn't see it all," I said with a little wonder. I was just glad we had made two copies.

"It's not for me to decide what's usable," he said. "I just hope headquarters finds something on it that makes my job easier." I saw a man coming down the hill from the Humvees.

"Where you headed from here?" I asked him.

"California I am pretty sure they said," McQueen replied, seeming to be disappointed about that. "But it changes a lot, obviously."

Charles walked up to us and looked to be a little unsure what to say. He had the look of a scientist, though his fatigues were starting to fit him well. He tried to smile like a dutiful soldier but you could tell he was the wrong kind as he introduced himself.

"My name's Randy," I told him. "McQueen here says you may be able to tell us a little plainer what's been going on."

"Yes sir," Charles said matter of factly. He seemed to calm a little, seeing we were not all that bad. "What did you want to know, sir?"

"Wouldn't mind taking you up on that offer to sit down a bit," McQueen said.

"Follow me," I told him.

I started toward the door to the water tanks. I wondered at letting them into our home but figured they could not do much to all of us with their forces outside. We were probably the safest inside.

"I'll stay out here and keep an eye on things," Chris said from behind us all. Laura said she would as well. I gave him a nod and they moved over to the horse corrals.

"Really haven't seen inside one of these since I toured one in my cadet days," McQueen told me, taking in the water tanks. "How'd you guys come to be here?"

"I bought some government land before the war and moved my family out here. My son found the entrance under an old pile of what used to be the entrance shack," I told him. "Took a little bit to open the door but now we have a mansion down there."

"Wow!" he told me. He looked at everything as we got closer.

We walked into the tanks and I am sure I heard Charles catch his breath. They were both looking at the garden with mouths open. I also took some time then and looked at all of the ripe fruit and vegetables hanging everywhere. Vince and Mary had been busy. They turned and looked at the satellite dish and the caged area underneath, eyes wide.

"Oh, I see there, the control room," Charles said.

"No, that's inside," Davina told him. "We haven't much figured out what most of that stuff is."

"It's a secondary transmitting station for tactical strikes or whatever else they needed them for," McQueen said. He saw us all turn toward him. "These types of bunkers were set up to control everything if they had to. The government could give sites like these the keys to everything and they would be able to take care of it all. These sites were set up in case everything went wrong. There were only three of them in the nation. They became obsolete when sites like NORAD were built." We all continued to watch him until I heard him clear his throat.

"Right this way," I told him and led the way through the inner door and down the steps.

We made it into the hallway and down to the Control Room. They both kept up and looking around, I saw that everyone was following close behind them. I made the turn into the room and led the way to the large table we used as our meeting place there. Without taking his eyes off the screens, McQueen pulled out a chair and sat down. Charles sat down beside him.

"That is amazing," McQueen said. I let him be amazed for a moment but was really still feeling the stress of our people being kidnapped and now intruders inside our home.

"So anything you can tell us about where Kevin might have taken them will be a huge help to us," I told McQueen. I looked also at Charles. "What do you know about him taking them somewhere particular?" McQueen nodded at Charles.

"I can tell you what I know of his experiments," Charles started.

"I think I've seen that on that pin drive," I told him. "Human experiments and the like. Yeah we know about that. I just want to know where he's headed."

"Kevin took some of their people and left here," McQueen told him.

"I see," Charles said. "I guess that's why we didn't attack you guys right off." I looked hard at McQueen but he just looked at Charles.

"He has a pregnant one," McQueen told him.

"And my teenage daughter," Jadee put in harshly.

"Of course, ma'am," McQueen said softly.

"He also told us that he had his serum and The Monk's DNA," I told him. Charles looked at McQueen.

"He means Steve's DNA," McQueen told him. Charles nodded grimly.

"Then theoretically, he has everything he needs," Charles said slowly.

"Everything for what?" George asked.

"I don't want to be callous here but embryos make the perfect test subjects," Charles said. "Most of Kevin's leaps forward in research were done on the unborn subjects. Yeah, he experimented on adults but when he found something new or unusual he'd test it on pregnant women and their fetuses. It gives more perfect results in young cells and the pathogenic shift is smaller in such a sterile environment. In science it's called narrowing the field." My rage was starting to boil and I think Charles saw that.

"You think we are at all interested in the science, asshole?" Jadee asked, standing up. "We need to know where he's going." I saw tears welling up in her eyes.

"I'm sorry, ma'am, but I don't know that," Charles told her, looking at McQueen with some concern in his eyes.

"I think I can be of some help with that," McQueen said. "I mean, my people can be of some help with that." Jadee glared at him. "Ma'am, won't you sit down. We're only trying to help here." Jadee sat heavily down in her chair. "The kind of things that Kevin is going to need can't be found easily anymore. He is going to need power. He's going to need laboratories and equipment. Most hospitals will have a lot of what he needs but the power to them, almost nationwide, has been cut off. So he'll be looking for government compounds as they are often separate from public power grids. He'll be looking for something close I'm sure. The less travel with hostages the better. There is a facility in far western Kansas that would be perfect for the kind of setup he would need if he's looking to continue his research. He will have known all about it."

"What kind of government facilities are we going to be looking for?" Neil asked.

"Anything with a research department in it," Charles said first. "I know it will seem like a needle in a haystack at first but there's just places that won't work for him."

"What is he looking to do?" Mary asked and we all looked at her and then back to Charles.

"We intercepted the call you guys made here on your radio," McQueen said. "It sounds like he is wanting to complete what he started, though some don't know if he can."

"What he started?" Neil asked.

"Looks like Kevin was a lead scientist on the research that lead to an antidote for the Chinese virus," I told everyone. "He did all kinds of human experiments and The Monk was one of his worst. The Monk escaped and the virus spread around the world from there. I think they came this way from California. It turned out to be its own virus which reacted with the real Chinese virus. That's why they all died. They released a deadly virus that most of the world had already been immune to. If you got the Kevin's thing first, you could survive it. The Chinese were immune to it already as well, only they didn't know it. When they gave all their citizens what they had already made as an antidote, it was really another form of the virus. That's what took them out while we all remained immune. Well, some of us I guess. None of it worked like it should have."

"You seem to understand it pretty well," Charles told me.

"Was all that on the pin drive?' McQueen asked. I nodded.

"And Kevin was studying it?" Vince asked.

"Not studying it," McQueen said. "Kevin, and others like him, made the antidote from the original Chinese virus. But he found something or created something more, we still don't know which, during his experiments and now he is wanting to get it all the way figured out."

"You must know something of what he found," Vince said plainly.

"We know for sure he created something of a new virus." Charles said. "But what we don't know, if what was in the virus he is looking to create will hurt what in some patients causes regenerative properties that react with human cells. The mitochondria got huge but sent out enzymes that kept the cell walls from breaking down. They divide into new healthy cells that actually replace existing cells with a slower rate of decay and could stand up to fatigue better, almost invincibly better. In some cases there were some large side effects in blood production which caused...," Charles trailed off, seeing everyone looking at him blankly. He shrugged, though I wish he would have continued. "That's when the big guys stepped in and the testing really got scary. Sorry, ma'am." He looked at Jadee apologetically. "We are sure he is looking to separate the regeneration properties from the harmful effects of the disease. He'll need to do lots more DNA sequencing and the like so he'll need a fairly sophisticated facility."

"What is he going to do to Olivia?" April asked him. Charles looked at Jadee.

"Is she the pregnant one?" he asked. Jadee nodded. "One of the biggest problems with these kinds of experiments is that they take so long for the results.

The woman should not be in any immediate danger. He will probably start whatever testing he has in mind soon, though. The fetus will be experimented on inside the womb. It will probably not survive." We all stayed still then for some time.

We had all cared so much for Luke. When we had found out that Olivia was pregnant it had seemed that not all of him was gone. I remembered seeing Olivia holding her stomach so tenderly and the way she whispered to it made me hurt to think about. It made me rage now to think of it.

"Do you have some sort of list of possible sites that Kevin could be going to?" Neil asked McQueen.

"I will have them sent to your system," he told him. "He headed east from here, staying on the road. We think Kansas or eastern Colorado. He made it at least an hour east before we lost him. They lost him in the cloud cover and they haven't reported seeing him again."

"So who are you after?" I asked and Charles looked at him hard.

"A different group of know it all's in the old government found out what was going on with the new virus we got from China, secretly of course," McQueen started. "They tried to take over but it was too widespread then. They took some of the antidote and did their own studies. Some of the samples the team got were from Steve himself. Seems they became fast friends with Kevin. We have a lead on the whole group of them. The higher ups say we can't pass up taking them out and getting the virus they contained."

"What a freakin' mess," I said in disgust.

"You said it," McQueen said.

"How many people are left out there?" Vince asked.

"We don't know," McQueen said.

"I mean how many soldiers and all are left?" he asked. "What's left of this new America you talked about?"

"A few hundred, spread so thin I haven't seen any of them in months," McQueen said and Charles nodded. "There isn't much to fight for any more, so a lot of them just end up packing it up and taking off. Can't say I blame them much. A lot of them don't know much about what's exactly going on."

"So why tell us so much?" Marla asked. We all looked at her. "I mean what's so important about us, that we get the full rundown?"

"We need the help," McQueen said flatly. "I don't think we should be going in on this group they say is in California. Kevin is the real target for me but I don't make the orders. It's hard finding someone who understands the importance of chasing some guys to who knows where. Our teams down here are falling apart. The truth is we need the help. I think we should be going after him ourselves but truly I don't know everything either. I'm told to go west and capture the other part of this problem. Maybe they don't see Kevin being as big of a threat. It seems to work out best so far to just follow the orders given. We are headed in the opposite direction and he'll get away if you all don't find him. That's all I've got." At this he stood up and Charles did likewise. We all followed suit. "Our biggest hope is that Kevin thinks that we wanted to take you all out and that by now you're all gone. He may not expect you all to be following him. He may expect us but he'll think we are following in a military manner. He's a science genius but not a strategist. Maybe keep that in mind as you all go looking. He knows our tactics which is why he's been able to hide for so long. He screwed up communicating but he must have been planning on leaving here before he did. He may not know some of what you guys do as far as his friends, not that it isn't effective. Whatever you do he's running hard."

"We are heading out right now," I told McQueen. "His lead is already big enough." He nodded his head.

"Like I said, I wouldn't mind keeping in contact," McQueen said as we started for the door.

"Our radio took a bullet on the way out of that compound down south," I told him. "It isn't real reliable. Got something you can spare?"

"I do in fact," he told me. "And I'll get whatever information we have on possible Sites sent to you right away. If we can be of help to you let us know. Whatever you need, we'll do it. I'll send you all you'll need to contact us."

We all followed them out and McQueen keyed the radio at his shoulder. He told someone to bring over one of the radios and he heard the response he was looking for. Looking around we saw everything was as we had left it. Chris, I saw, was still sitting on the fence around the horse corral with Laura leaning against one of the posts. We all watched as a man with a large pack with a long antenna sticking out of it made it over to us. McQueen indicated me and the man tried to hand me the pack. I pointed to Jake and he handed it to him instead. I saw Jake crack a big smile as he looked at it and I felt some familiar annoyance. The man left with Charles following.

McQueen put out his hand and smiled. I shook it and returned the smile the best I could. He started to walk off and then stopped. He turned to look at me. He gave me a salute and promptly turned and rushed to a waiting Humvee. As one, they all moved off and over the hill. In only a few moments we could not hear them anymore.

CHAPTER 2

No one really knew what to say as we all stood there and watched the hillside. The wind still blew the tall grass there as it always did, though now we could see vehicle tracks going all over it. Another storm looked to be coming in soon and I was hoping for it to be the fast moving kind. I pointed at it and told Jake I wanted him to have a look at it from the Control Room. He and April left together, heading back inside.

"Looks like it's time for a meeting, huh?" Neil asked me, bringing me out of my own head. "I think everyone is a little concerned, to say the least. I know you know that."

"Yeah, let's all head into the Control Room," I said aloud and heard the words echoing in my ears. "And someone please inform Dan at the other compound what's going on."

I knew this thing was going to take a lot to get done. I saw how far away from home it could take us and wondered at the world around us. It had not done so well for itself in the recent years and I was sure things must have gotten worse. I thought on for a while but finally came to a conclusion. This was going to take more than a brutish outlook. I could not let the darker parts of me push in and allow negativity to cloud things. I knew that was going to take some willpower.

I turned and saw only my wife still standing there. She smiled at me and moved over to be beside me. I took her hand and looked into her eyes. I loved doing that and felt the calm of her gentle spirit flood over me.

"Let's get this done," I told her and moved around her, still holding her hand.

We made it inside and saw most everyone sitting around the table. Jadee was standing over Jake at the computers, pointing at different things, most of which I had no idea about. They took turns looking at the screens.

"So what's the plan?" Neil asked. I came and sat down and Davina sat next to me.

"Well, obviously we are heading out on another uncertain trip," I told them all. "I know it's not what we all were wanting, but it's got to happen. I know we are all ready to go right now. We just need to figure out the best way to do that. And I need to know if any of us aren't up for this, though I think I know the answer."

"I guess we did pretty well on the last one," Chris said and everyone agreed.

"I think we made a pretty great team out there," I said. I was not sure how to broach the next part of what I had in mind.

"I think the best thing is to leave right now," Jadee said from below us at the computers, her now more interested in the meeting than helping Jake. Everyone looked at me.

"We should wait to see what McQueen sends us," Neil said.

"We can't wait!" Jadee yelled and then seemed to understand she was starting to lose control. "Let's just head east on the highway and maybe we'll catch him. Maybe Tara or Olivia are leaving some sort of trail." I was glad to see she was now speaking more calmly.

"I don't think he is going to stay on the highway for long," I told her. I did not know what to say about the other part of what she said. I hoped it was true. "How are the clouds looking over everything east of here?" I asked Jake. We all turned and looked at the screens. We could see only clouds from overhead.

"Not sure yet," Jake told us. "The satellite is out of range. These clouds are what is ahead for us. The next three days look to be mostly cloudy."

"Okay, so the satellites aren't going to be much help with that," I said, a little disappointed. "Jadee can you see if we are getting anything sent to us from McQueen?"

"I will," she said and went to another set of computers. We all watched her for a few minutes until we figured it was not going to be a quick thing.

"Do we know of any close by military compounds?" I asked Neil, turning back to the table.

"Not like a research kind of thing," he told me. "There is an air force base in Aurora just outside of Denver." I put my elbows on the table and ran my hands through my hair. How were we ever going to find them?

"Looks like I'm getting something," Jadee yelled with some excitement. "No, it may not be anything. No, wait, it's a file. No, wow, it looks like they are sending us a whole new operating system! Its got NASA all over it. I hope this system can handle it. This thing is going to take these computers forever to download."

"I guess NASA is the right place to look for satellite images," Neil said.

"Why would NASA have info on military compound stuff," April asked. I took some time and told them everything that Kevin had told us and all that we had seen on the pin drive.

"Speaking of the pin drive, can I see that other one?" I asked Davina. She produced it from down her shirt and I tried not to smile. "Jadee can you copy this onto another pin drive and download it into our computer system? I want you to be able to cross-reference everything." I got up and brought it to her.

She took it and plugged it into a laptop that was connected several different ways to others and what looked like the old computer system. She told me not to ask and I was happy to comply. She explained a little how she had been slowly trying to upgrade everything since we had been there. I smiled at her and sat back down.

"Did someone talk to the other compound?" I asked.

"Yeah I told them most of what was going on," Sterling said. "Dan's headed over here."

"Did he say if his screens were working?" Neil asked.

"He said they have been off and on for a while," Sterling told him. "He said he called here when the trouble with them started and everyone just figured it was a new bug to work out."

"This sure isn't anyone's fault," I told Sterling. "There is no way of knowing sometimes what might be an emergency." I thought I should talk to April about getting a system in place to figure that out.

"Wow, okay!" Jadee said from where she was working. Everyone looked at her. "Looks like whatever they sent is already uploaded and ready to look at."

"Wait!" I yelled a little too loud. "Is there a way of keeping whatever they sent alienated from the rest of our system? Not sure it's a good idea to just let them into everything." Everyone seemed to agree with that.

"It will take a while to figure that out," Jadee said with a little disappointment. "I guess you're right. Not sure what they could do but it might be safer."

"I don't think we should just let these people know everything," I said flatly. "We really don't know who they are or really what their agenda is. It's all pretty confusing right now so let's just move slowly for now."

"Can you download whatever they sent onto one of those laptops there and then open it from there?" George asked.

"I guess I could," Jadee told him. "It doesn't look like a live stream so it's downloadable."

As we were talking the upper right screen came on and a man's face showed there. You could see the older screen did not have the resolution to make his face show up crisp. The symbol on his coat I did not recognize. I could see that he was trying to say something.

"What the heck is that?" Jake asked and stood up. Everyone saw it then.

Jadee ran over to yet another set of computers and started typing away. We could see the man was typing away on his end and then still trying to say something. The screen went blank then and everyone looked at Jadee. She frowned and typed away again. I saw she was trying to reboot some part of the system. I for one had never remembered that screen coming on.

"I don't think we are going to be able to keep them out of our system," she told me. "It's either we use their help or block them all the way out."

"Can we separate the armory computer before they make it in?" I asked and Laura jumped in. "I'd like to have a little privacy."

"I can do that," she said. "I'll need to do it from down below. Sorry, I don't know how exactly these ones work up here."

"No, that's fine," I told her. "Just hurry and get it done." She ran off and Chris followed. We all looked back at the blank screen above Jadee.

"Sorry this system takes a while to reboot," she told us.

"I leave all things to do with that monster to you," I told her. She tried a smile.

"What is it you are trying to do?" George asked.

"I guess there are a couple of different systems at work here," I told him. "It would be nice to be able to have one without them in it."

"Good idea," he told me. "That McQueen seemed trustworthy enough but then again all the bad ones do." I heard agreements all around the table.

We watched as the screen blinked several times but did not do anything else. Jadee walked back to her other computers and started typing something. I seemed the meeting was resting now on the idea of what we would see on the computer screen. We all wanted to know what would be our closest lead. Feeling the pressure of all that needed done, I stood up.

"Jadee, keep me posted on everything here," I told her. "I'm sorry Jadee that we can't just leave right now. I think the best thing to do is to wait to see where he might have gone. Otherwise we are just taking guesses." She nodded her head, but did not seem happy about it. "I'm sure everyone has something to do. We need to get ready for another trip. Let's do that and no one move away from a radio. As soon as we know where we're headed, we are outta here."

Everyone stood up then. I stood there looking at the screen and willed it to come back on, complete with a large X that told us where Kevin had gone. Out of the corner of my eye I saw George and Margie coming over to me.

"I think I'll go get things ready for our soon departure," George said. I started to speak.

"Please don't tell us that we don't have to help and that we have done enough," Margie said with a tired smile. "We are going and the quickest way of getting there is the train." I smiled as George agreed.

"Okay, how's it doing on oil?" I asked.

"I'll be over there in a minute and let you know," George told me. "We may need some water. Anything close by the tracks around here?"

"They had some windmills in that town north of the tracks you're on," I told him. "It didn't look like the tracks got close to the lake down south there and the river here is pretty far back."

"No, the wells in that town should do fine," George said and Margie nodded.

"It was walled in so I'm not sure how easy it will be to get to them," I told them.

"Is that the one you said got burned?" George asked softly. I looked at the floor and nodded. "Well, we'll see how she looks first. I think we'll take a ride over there anyway."

"Take someone with you, will ya," I told them and they agreed.

"We'll take Sterling and Ramon," George said and they moved off to ask them.

I walked down to where Jadee was and I saw Neil was standing beside her. Jake was writing something down on a note pad but I could not see what it was. I looked for April but I did not see her. Quickly finding we had nothing to offer, Neil and I walked back up to the table.

"Doesn't look like you are going to be home for long," Neil told me when we stopped.

"Yeah, it kind of looks that way," I told him. "How're those generators running?"

"Just like new," he told me.

"Looks like Dan and some others just showed up," I heard Sterling say at the radio on my shoulder. I saw Jessie turn and head for the door. I smiled, thinking of how much he must have missed his wife and daughter.

"Vince said they came over once while you guys were gone," Neil told me. "I was mostly down in the bowels of this place. I guess I missed everything."

"Just like you like it," I told him with a smile. He returned it. I saw Vince and Mary standing by the table and looking ready to leave. "Anything you need help with?" I asked them both. They looked at me and wondered. "I'm sure you guys had a pretty good routine around here while we were gone. I don't want to come back and mess up the way things were going. Is there anything I can do to make that happen?"

"No, but I wouldn't mind taking some time with getting things looked at in the garden," Mary said. "We were in the middle of harvesting when... well when Kevin came at us."

"Okay I think that's a great idea," I told them. "I'll keep you all posted on whatever news we get." They started off. "Vince, I'd like to talk to you after a while." He nodded and walked out behind Mary.

"I'm sure he's taking what happened here pretty hard," Neil told me. "He took his responsibility here while you were gone pretty seriously."

"I know," I told him. "I hope he can get back on the horse."

"You plan on leaving him here again?" Neil asked, lowering his voice.

"Yeah, I think bringing more out there is just going to make things harder. I don't think everyone is going to like it either." I moved my head toward where Jadee was sitting at a line of computers. Neil nodded and raised his eyebrows high.

"Yeah, that might not go over so well," he told me, seeming to know he was stating the obvious.

"Maybe with all this new crap here to figure out, she'll have to agree," I told him.

"Well, good luck on that one Buddy," he told me. He started to turn to leave.

"Make any more interesting finds down there?" I asked him. I saw him smile.

"No, just never-ending tunnels and large, empty tombs," he told me. "The chess board is waiting for us whenever you are ready."

"I hope I get the chance," I told him. "You going to be okay with staying here? I think with this new military stuff in the mix I'd like you up here a lot more."

"I can stay up here and I'll give them whatever help I can," he told me. "I hope I can be of some help with this stuff. It's a bit out of my zone but I'll do anything.

And I'm sorry brother, but I don't think I'd be much good out there, unless you're bringing that tank." He said the last part with a smile, until he saw me starting to think about it. "I'll talk you through it again," he said with a smile and turned and walked away.

As he left I saw Dan and Jean coming through the door. Davina came up as I yelled a greeting to them. Jean came over and gave us both a hug. Dan shook my hand and then gave Davina a hug. They both stood there then and gave us a frown.

"So sorry about what happened here," Dan started and seemed not to know what else to say. "Sterling gave us a bit more of the rundown. I brought Jessie's wife and daughter. I think if I would have agreed to it, everyone from over there would have wanted to come. None of us can believe it. Everyone feels for you guys."

"I'm sure, and we appreciate it," I said, not knowing what else to say. "Neil told me you came by. I'm glad you're looking out for us."

"I wish I could have done more," he told me. Jean agreed.

"No, there is nothing anyone could have done," Davina said before I could. "We just have to figure out what to do now."

"We tried not to think the worst when we heard you guys got surrounded down there in Colorado Springs," Dan said.

"Yeah, sorry Jessie took one as we stood and fought for all of two seconds," I told him. "He did great."

"Sounds like you all did," Jean said.

"Then to come home to this," Dan added, shaking his head. "So they really showed up at your front door, huh?"

"Yeah, I thought that was it for us," I told him. "There had been too much of that lately." We all thought back over the last month and nodded. "Looks like those guys are wanting to be of some help, though." I spent some time and told them what we had been doing. They stood amazed.

"I wonder if we are getting the same thing at home," Dan said out loud. I looked down at April.

"April, will you go call Dan's compound and see what they are getting over there?" I asked. "Maybe it will help." She agreed and ran to the Com Room. I watched her put her cat down beside her as she tried on the head phones.

"How's our bet working out?" Dan asked with a sideways grin. I looked at him and had to think hard about what he was talking about.

"Oh, yeah, neither one has made a move yet," I told him. "I think I saw Sterling weakening a little though. Shay will never let me down." I smiled. "I better head outside," I told everyone. "George is looking up at the town there for some water. I better be outside in case he's trying to call me."

"I'll help out April up there if you don't mind," Dan told me. "Our new man over there on coms isn't the greatest."

"Understood," I told him with a smile.

"I'm going to hang out here and see if I can help," Davina told me with a peck on the cheek. I smiled at Jean and walked up to the Com Room. Dan moved aside as he saw me come in behind him. April saw me and moved the headphones off of one ear.

"When you get a second I need you to tell Chris and Laura to get us resupplied with everything out of the armory that we are going to need," I told April. "Have them put it up by the horse corral." She nodded. "And have Marla get us some MRIs ready, please. Have Chris stop by and grab them." She nodded again.

I saw her roll her chair over to the other end of the table to where the mics were that could call anywhere in the facility. She turned switches expertly and turned dials without even looking at them. I left before I heard her say anything.

There was a lot to still figure out before we left, I knew, and I could already feel the stress of things piling up. I knew I needed to delegate them as soon as possible or I would not be of much help to anyone. I consciously slowed my walk down along the hallway that led outside. I took the steps at a snail's pace and breathed deep. At the top I opened the doors that led into the Water Tanks and felt ready to take on this responsibility.

The scent of a ripe garden hit my nose and it brought back the memories of the early mornings I would come in there and search the garden before anyone was awake. It reminded me of my dog Simon and I could not believe that I had forgotten about him. I moved quickly outside. I turned and grabbed my rifle as I heard someone behind me. I saw Vince stop suddenly, worry in his eyes.

"Sorry, you startled me there a little," I told him.

"No problem," he told me as I took my hand away from the trigger. "Up for a few tomatoes?" I saw that he carried two, large, fully red ones.

"Wow, those look great!" I told him. He handed them both to me and refused it when I tried to hand him back one.

"I've had my fill, believe me," he told me.

I smiled and bit into one of the juicy vegetables. It squirted all over my beard and vest but I did not really care. The taste that exploded in my mouth took everything away for a few seconds. I bit again and do not remember finishing it and moving on to the other one. I guess I had been pretty hungry. Vince still watched, obviously enjoying someone liking the fruit of his labor.

"You said you wanted to talk to me?" he asked when I had finished them both.

"Yeah, mind following me to the top?" I asked him. "Wouldn't mind looking around atop these again. The air is a little fresher up there." He agreed and followed me to the top. I was glad that someone had fixed a few of the rungs that had recently worn loose.

I had not seen Shay or Sterling, I thought, as I moved across the wide tanks. I had also figured to run into Jessie and his family but I did not see anyone. I mentioned it to Vince and he said they had all gone inside.

"They were following Shay," Vince told me. "Maybe they were going to the Med Center."

"Yeah, I guess that makes sense," I told him. "Jessie took a bullet as we were leaving that compound down there."

"It must have been pretty scary, walking out and finding that," he said. I nodded my head and put the thoughts out of my mind.

I looked around then and watched the soft wind play with the upper limps of the trees by the pond that we made in the side of the river so long ago. They were all moving to some unknowable rhythm. The river was still flowing well and the small pond was still crystal clear. I looked but I did not see any fish moving around the surface. I looked far over and saw the beautiful range of Rocky Mountains that made the spot I chose so nice. I watched the clouds pushing in everywhere but still admired the splendor of it all.

"Wow, I don't think I have ever come up here," Vince told me. "I can see now why you do."

"My family and I spent our first night up here, watching the sunset," I told him. "We definitely fell in love with the place right then."

We both stayed quiet for a while and looked around some more, leaning hard on the railing that encircled the top of the tanks. I listened to the different sounds the wind made as it moved around our complex. I saw the geese were still flying overhead and I had to smile. I looked far off and tried to see if some cattle were on the hills close by. I saw them there as they always were. I heard the soft bleating of our two goats and it brought me back to where I was.

"Have you seen Simon?" I asked. "I guess with all of the rush and worry I didn't think to look for him." I saw Vince look away. "What is it?" He still would not say anything. "Tell me Vince.."

"A few of us found him when we were searching down below," he told me. "He was in one of the small rooms off of the cafeteria."

"Why didn't you let him out?" I wondered and saw the seriousness and something else in Vince's eyes.

"Kevin must have....must have killed him," he told me. "We didn't want you to see so we closed the door. I'm so sorry. I know how much you loved that dog."

I could not believe him at first. I thought it was a stupid joke to be playing on someone at a time like that. I then realized Vince was not like that. Then anger filled me for many reasons, not the least of which was someone touching something that was mine.

"I'm going to kill that worthless man," I said, though I am quite sure I used a lot more colorful language than that.

"I'm sorry I couldn't keep this all from happening. I can't get over the feeling that I let everyone down. This is our home and you all left it in my care," he said. He turned and walked away a little.

"I need you to get past that, because I'm going to need you to do it again," I told him.

"Do what?" he asked, turning back.

"We are leaving, probably within the hour," I told him. "I need someone I can trust here, watching over everything and making sure that things are getting done." I saw him start to shake his head. I could see that he was telling himself no. "Don't even think of doing that."

"What?" he asked, looking at me.

"Doing the whole it's my fault thing," I told him. "The best we can do is hit what's pitched. No one could have foreseen any of this and that's really the last I want to talk about it. I need you here. All of you here, without doubts and worries that make us sloppy or afraid of everything. I need you Vince, now more than ever." I watched him stand up a little bit. "You did a great job here and you shouldn't bully yourself about the unpredictable stuff we can't do anything about. No one can do anything when someone you trust turns on you."

"I'll do everything to keep this place safe," he said with every fiber of his being.

"I know you will," I told him. "And that makes it so I can do what I have to out there without any worries of what's going on back here."

We smiled at each other then. It almost turned into a laugh with us needing to release some of our pent-up tension. We looked out over the side and became distracted with the landscape instead.

"I think I'll be up here a bit more while you're gone," he told me.

"That slightly bent rail over there is the best place to watch the sunset," I told him as I pointed a bit to our left.

"I'll keep that in mind," he said.

"No women up here while I'm away," I teased. "And no wild parties." We both laughed a little and then watched the stream for a while.

"I'll bury Simon when you're gone and clean everything up," he told me. "I'll make a nice place up there by Luke." He turned then and walked back down the ladder. I grabbed the radio at my shoulder.

"George, come in," I keyed the mic and said. It only took a few seconds to get a response.

"Yeah, George here," I heard. "Looks like we are doing fine on oil. Could use some before we travel the whole world but we should make it pretty far. Our water's looking about half full. I think we can leave now if you are wanting to but I'd sure like to fill up given the chance."

"Yeah go ahead," I told him. "We aren't going to be ready for a little bit, I'm sure. Did you check out that town yet?"

"No but we are about ready to head that way," he told me. "If it doesn't look too easy, I'll let you know. We can make it far on down the line with what we got."

"I read you. Either way just come on back when you're done. I'll be inside and I'm not sure if my radio will reach you from there. We'll be getting ourselves ready."

"I will do it," he said with some assurance. "Getting anything on those computers yet?"

"They hadn't a while ago," I said with some sorrow. "But I'm headed there now to see what help they will be in getting us started somewhere. Can you make it back in an hour either way?"

"I will make that happen," he told me.

"We might just be ready to head out by then," I told him and putting the radio back on my shoulder, I headed for the ladder.

CHAPTER 3

I went back inside and saw that little progress had been made. I saw everyone hard at work, however and was not looking to complain about it. I wondered to myself if those old computers were going to be of much help.

Dan came up to me as I walked in. He tried a smile and I returned it. I think I was still thinking far away at that time and I was sure I was not going to be good company.

"How're things over at your place?" I asked him.

"Looks like they are okay," he told me. "We are getting the same thing over there. Looks like these NASA guys are trying any way they can to get into your system."

"Yeah, just that is scary," I said and immediately wished I had not. It was not a time to spread worry. "I'm sure they will be of help once they get through."

"Pretty weird, working with NASA," he told me.

"True," I said with a smile. "Never would have thought that would happen, talking to someone in outer space."

"I wonder if we get the cool jumpsuits," he said with a smile. I could see he was trying to bring me out of my own head. I appreciated that and told him so. "I think I'd like to go with you guys on this one."

"I don't think you should go, Dan," I told him. "I really need to know things are okay back here. Bringing more along really won't help us." I hoped I said that last part with some tact.

"I don't think Jessie's wife is going to let him go," he said. "She was a nervous wreck the whole time he was gone and she literally almost lost it when we couldn't get you all on the radio."

"Yeah, he did great out there," I told him. "He stood and fought when he could have been running for cover. It's what got him shot. But even then he didn't roll over."

"I think he feels indebted to you for getting his family back," he told me. "But I do think that's only part of it. He seems like the honorable type that will do anything for others."

"Yeah, I think it's just the kind of person he is," I said. "He's one of those understanding fellows that I like being around." We paused here and turned and watched the screens for a while. Nothing seemed to be changing. "I think I'll go visit Jessie. I think they're in the Med Center."

"Yeah, Sara wanted him to get checked out," Dan said. "I guess that's what good women do."

"How's that coming along for you?" I asked him. I saw him smile.

"Yeah, I think I found the one" he said. "Never thought I would but it just kind of falls on ya."

"Sterling will be happy for sure," I told him. "He said he saw it heading that way."

"I guess there aren't any secrets in our little neighborhood," he frowned.

"Yeah, I just hope to keep from hearing the details," I told him with a wink. He nodded and moved off down below to the computers.

I went out of the room and headed across the hall. I bumped into Chris and Laura on the way over. Laura assured me all was separated with the computer system down in the armory. I saw they had an armload of something and I really did not want to get in their way. I told them good job and moved over to the Med Center.

I saw Shay talking to Sara, Jessie's wife. She looked to have just completed an examination and he was looking a little annoyed. Shay did not look to be enjoying the situation either. I walked over with a smile and looked at Jessie.

"How you feeling?" I asked him. "This guy here is one of the brave ones. Stopped a bullet with his sheer will." I tried a smile.

"Hi Randy," Sara said. "Shay here says there is an infection." I looked over at him with some concern. Shay was starting to show her annoyance a little more.

"It's a small skin infection where I closed at," she said. "I gave him some antibiotics and everything should be fine." I saw Jessie's daughter smiling at her mother's worry.

"Everything okay inside?" I asked Shay, now myself a little concerned.

"Yeah, everything looks good," she told me. "No fever and the color is good. He's eating fine."

"Good," I told him. I paused a little to figure the easiest way to bring up what I wanted to tell him. He looked at me.

"What is it?" he wondered. Then they all looked at me.

"I think you should stay home and take care of yourself and your family," I told him. I saw an immediate smile on Sara's face.

"No, I'm in this," he said.

"You're hurt," Sara said in protest.

"It's not about any of that," I told them. "You're hurt but you kept going out there. I know you could do it. It's just we need to move fast and we are not needing a large team. I'm sorry, but say we are out there and something turns on your wound there. We can't afford the down time. Seriously, stay here and heal up. Take care of your family. Get ready for winter. We'll use you on the next one."

"Please stay home," Sara asked tenderly. He looked down at her then over to me. I gave him a nod and a smile.

"You've done enough," I told him. "Sit this one out." I gave him some time to think about it. "Will you hang out over here for a few days while we're gone? I'd feel a lot better with someone of your caliber watching out for my home while I'm gone." I gave him a smile.

He looked over at his wife and then over at his daughter Leah. Leah had been sitting a bit away but when she heard that her father may be staying home she had moved in close and her eyes looked to be filled with hope. Sara hugged him and pushed her head into his chest. Leah came over and joined them. I gave him a wink and a nod. He returned the nod and gave me a smile.

"Okay, I'll stay and watch your home," he told me. I even saw Shay smile. "But if we lose contact with you guys, I'm heading out of here to find you."

"Deal," I told him and went to shake his hand. "Whenever you are ready can you check in with Vince? I put him in charge around here while I'm away and he might know of a good post that needs manned."

"I'll do it first thing," he promised. I did feel a sense of relief.

Sara came over and gave me a hug then. She started to say something but then did not. I am sure I understood her feelings and was glad to see them all together again. With a smile I left the room, asking Shay to follow.

"Back in business already, huh?" I asked her when we had gotten into her office. I saw her roll her eyes.

"I know she's just being protective, but wow, that woman would drive me crazy," she told me as she sat down at her desk. "That's why surgery was my field." I had lots of funny things to say here but I kept them to myself.

"Are you wanting to go with us on this one?" I asked her. She looked up at me suddenly. "I'm just asking."

"I'm coming," she said matter of factly. "I'll have everything ready in just a few minutes."

"You did great out there and I don't think we could have done it without you," I told her.

"Yeah, well thanks," she told me with a smile that said she did not know how to take compliments. "I really hope I'm not needed out there again but if Kevin is going to do something to Olivia or Tara I'd better be there when we find them." I totally agreed.

"Is there anything big from here we need to bring?" I asked her.

"No," she replied, shaking her head. "I'll just have my trusted doctors' bag." She started thinking then. "I should bring some sterilization tabs and a fetal monitor." She mumbled some more stuff and I smiled and found my way out of the Med Center.

I wondered where Sterling had gone and thought about finding him. I was also wanting to know how Chris and Laura were doing but I knew they would be taking care of everything. As I stood there in the hallway junction Jean came out of the Control Room.

"Anything good going on in there?" I asked her.

"No, just more of the same," she told me. "I saw the screen come on where that guy was trying to talk. It flashed off though."

"A little frustrating I'm sure," I told her. "I'm sure Jadee will get it figured out, though."

"Yeah, she's working up a sweat in there," she said, looking back over her shoulder.

"How's life over at the other compound?" I asked her. "Feeling like home yet?"

"Oh yeah, it feels like we should have been there from the beginning," she said warmly. "I really wish Dan would calm down on the sheep thing. I think he's starting to get some people on board with him though. That's all they talk about." I smiled and hoped much for her in the future.

"Sounds like they may be taking over from what I remember," I told her.

"Yeah, I wouldn't mind a day without hearing their bleating," she rolled her eyes to add to her shaking head.

"Well, if it gets too much we can always need you over here for a few days for something," I told her with a smile. She returned it.

"You're really doing a great thing in all of this," she said, turning serious. "All of you are."

"Just what we have to," I told her. "If Kevin didn't get too far we should be able to find him." We both nodded our heads.

I saw Dan running out of the Control Room door, a look of excitement on his face. He would have ran right into me if I had not moved as he sprinted into the hallway. He pulled up on seeing me.

"We got the feed hooked in from that NASA guy," he told me.

I turned and ran into the Control Room ahead of him. I jumped down the small set of steps and ran to the railing that overlooked the computers. I heard Jadee asking her laptop something technical.

"It should feed through just fine on that laptop," a man's voice came back over some speakers in the wall. "And I can have a continuous stream to you. I will jump to whatever satellite I need to keep us connected." I watched the man talking on the large screen on the far wall.

"Did we get the info on where he may be headed?" I asked. I saw Sterling nodding his head.

"Do you want me to open it?" Jadee asked. I nodded back to her.

"Are you still hearing me okay?" I hear the speaker ask.

"Yes, we are hearing you," Jadee told him.

"Okay, sorry, those are just some old systems," he said. "Good idea plugging in some laptops."

"Yeah, that gets us out of the 80s I guess," Jadee said from in front of her laptop.

"Can he see us?" I asked. Sterling shook his head.

"Just through the camera on the laptop," he told me.

"My name is Mackenzie," I saw the man on the screen say. "But please, call me Mack."

"I'm Jadee, Mack," Jadee told him. "Nice to meet you."

"Great, a soft voice to work with," Mack said. "It's nice to meet you too. Now, I know you guys are needing some help and I'm here to do everything I can. Did you get the files of where all of the primary experimentations were going on?"

"I got a file but it was huge," Jadee told him. "I have a few laptops here and I loaded everything into all of them. I can look up different stuff and cross-reference whatever you tell me."

"Wow, and a brain, that's going to be nice," Mack said. "Great, now can you find the file for 'Core project'?"

"I'll look," Jadee said and turned to one of the laptops. I heard her typing away. "Found it!" she yelled and moved down several lines. We were all reading as she went.

"Can you put those up on the big screen?" Jean asked.

Jadee moved one hand over and typed something on one of the old computers. Another of the screens on the wall went on and we saw everything she was seeing on her laptop. I definitely liked that better.

"Now you are looking for 'Region 6'," Mack told her. "That should tell you about what went on at which facility. Sorry, but some of it may get a little disturbing."

"Not as disturbing as Kevin himself," Jadee told him. "What the hell does he want with my daughter?"

"Oh, you're the one," he said. "Sorry, you must be pretty upset."

"Yeah, I am," she told him.

"Don't worry," Mack said softly. "Jadee, don't worry." He waited for her to look at the camera on the laptop. "We will find where he took her. It can't be too many places. We are monitoring all of the sites he could be going to. McQueen said Kevin is looking to hook up with some of his other group. When he tries to contact them, we'll know right where he is. And if he doesn't try to contact them, I'm sure when McQueen finds the ones he's after, they'll tell him where to find him."

"Has Kevin been able to contact them?" I asked.

"Yes, we think so," Mack said. "We don't think for very long, though. It was yesterday. McQueen is headed for where that signal came from."

"What is 'Region 6'?" I asked.

"No, 'Region 6' is all of the Colorado, well mostly Colorado, sites," Mack told me. "It runs over a little east and some north. It will cover anything within two hundred miles of where you guys presently are; farther than that east. That's where they think Kevin is headed."

"Why east?" I asked.

"Well, sorry, more southeast," Mack told us. "That's where he started later. We found out, when he was recruited, he was looking to move on and take his research long before Steve escaped with him in California. He was directing supplies and equipment to several different research labs in western Kansas. There's little chance he knows that we know that. It took some digging and he used plenty of back channels."

"I'd like to know what kind of stuff he's looking to do," I told Mack, still feeling like I was talking to the air. "Is what he's planning going to take days or months?"

"I have not heard anything about that, sir," Mack said apologetically. "I was told to give you guys anything you needed. I can ask one of the scientists to give us a meeting."

"I'd very much like that information, Mack," I told him. "But first, where is the facility that most of these supplies were headed for?"

"It's Site c-9 4039," he said. "It's just into Kansas about fifteen miles, and a little south of the Nebraska line. I'm looking it up now." I could see him looking off to the side of the computer and doing some typing. "Looks like it's before a town called Goodland on Interstate 70. The site isn't close to the interstate though. It's north a few miles, looks like close to Beaver Creek, just east of Highway 27. I'll send you exact coordinates." He was still looking off the screen somewhere.

The screen that Jake had been looking at the weather on came on and showed an overhead view of something. We could all see it was partly cloudy but we could see most of the ground. I heard Jadee's laptop receive a message. It was weird hearing such a sound.

"Got the coordinates," Jadee told him.

"Jake, Davina, Sterling, it's time," I told the two of them. Jadee looked up at me. I shook my head at her.

"There's no way I ain't going," she told me standing up.

"There's no one here that can run this system like you," I told her. "If you really think about it, you know you have to stay."

She wanted to say something but I could tell she knew her argument had better be a good one. I knew she was forming a powerful one in her mind. I also knew all that she said, no matter how heartfelt and reasonable, would have to be overruled.

"There's no one else," I told her. "We desperately need you here telling us where to go if this place turns out to be a decoy. I know it's bitter right now but learn everything you can about what they sent. Find him for us and we'll be out there ready to get him. We'll bring them back to you, and him." I paused here to let her say something but she didn't. I looked her deep in the eyes and walked over to her. "I can't let you go Jadee."

She put her face in her hands and I saw her start to sob. Davina was there in an instant and put her arm around her. Jadee turned into her and sobbed with some pent-up emotions. I heard Davina telling her that we would find her daughter.

"We might as well get this over with," I said to no one. I turned and saw April looking at me from out of the Communication Room. I shook my head at her too. "I know you are probably wanting to come but we need you here too."

She looked at Jake. I looked over at him too and saw him smiling at her and softly shaking his head. Looking back at her I saw my daughter fighting to contain her anger. She tried a realistic looking smile but I knew her too well to see it as anything besides what it was. She took a deep breath and shook her head.

"Okay, I'll do whatever I can here," she said.

She moved back into the Com Room. I wondered at that having been easier than I thought it would be. I saw Jake looking over and smiling at me but I turned and walked down to Jadee, not liking his face for some reason.

I saw Jadee was still a bit of a mess. I figured to pull her out of that by getting her on some task that would keep her busy. I knew I needed her at her best. I also knew she would step up and do a great job.

"I need those coordinates for my GPS, Jadee," I told her. She looked up at me with tears on her face. I tried a smile that told her I understood her pain. "I also need either a copy of that pin drive or the one I gave you."

"I downloaded it all onto that laptop over there," she told me. "I'll put it on a pin drive later. You can take yours back."

She moved away from Davina and grabbed the pin drive. She typed a few things and I saw some files come onto the screen. She nodded to herself and walked back over to me. As she handed it to me I pulled her in for a hug.

"I'll find her, Jadee," I told her. When I pulled away she smiled at me and nodded.

"I know if anyone can find her, it will be you guys," she said.

"Tara's tough," I told her. "Kevin might be in mortal danger even before we get there, seriously." I gave her a smile and turned and walked toward the door. "Send me those coordinates, Jadee."

I walked over to the Com Room and walked inside. I saw Jake holding my daughter and my hands balled into fists. The man had no respect.

"Time to go," I told him, barely able to keep from ripping his head off. The two pushed apart. "I'll meet you at the corrals. Make sure you check that you have everything you are going to need."

"Yes sir," he told me as he brushed by me.

My daughter looked at me angrily. I knew she really wanted to go. I hoped her anger about that would ease.

"Sorry I haven't gotten much time to talk to you since we've gotten back," I told her.

"No problem dad," she said, picking up her new kitten and sitting in one of the chairs. "And I know I need to stay." She did not sound too convinced to me as she looked into the eyes of the cat and petted its head.

"I hope you'll understand sometime," I told her. "I'll try to keep in contact more."

"I'll be ready for anything here and keep you posted," she told me, getting up and coming over to me. "Jake is a nice guy, dad." She said it with such seriousness.

"I know he is," I said. It was so hard not to see my daughter as a little girl. For some weird reason I just blurted out, "I'll bring him back safe." It felt silly saying it. It got a smile from my daughter and that is all that mattered.

"Thanks dad," she said.

"So, what are you naming that thing?" I asked her.

"Disco," she told me. I furrowed my eyebrows.

"Maybe we should take a vote on that," I told her.

"No, she's mine," she said, pretending to be hurt.

"Fine," I told her, petting it between the ears. "Maybe I'll bring it back a big rat."

"Yuck dad," she said. "Just bring yourself back and let's get on with life."

"I second that, kid," I told her and gave her a kiss on the head. "Later."

"Later," she said and gave me a sideways wink that meant for me a daughter's love. I turned and walked out.

I made it into the Med Center but I did not see anyone in there. I looked around there more but finally went outside. I saw everyone was gathered around the corral.

"George hasn't made it back from town yet," I told them all.

"I called him and he just made it back to where he dropped us off," Davina said.

"Okay, sounds like I'm the one holding us up," I said.

I went over to my horse and saw a pack was sitting on the ground next to it. I looked at it and then over to Davina who gave me thumbs up. Neil came over to me and looked nervous and a little sad. I stood up and looked at him and Marla who was right behind him.

"We'll be back soon, my friend," I told him. He held out his hand and I took it. Marla came around and gave me a hug and walked back over by the door saying something in Spanish. Dan walked over to me then. I saw every one of the ones going were on their horses.

"I'll be over here more than I am at home," he told me. I smiled.

"I'm sure you have a lot to do at home with all of your sheep and all," I told him. "Make sure you take care of what needs done there too, okay." He nodded his head and we shook hands.

Looking over I saw Jessie and he gave me a salute which I returned. Jean waved and I gave her a nod. As I climbed on my horse I heard Chris clearing his throat.

"Hey Dad, didn't you lose some bet recently?" he asked me. I heard a few laughs.

"Oh yeah, I almost forgot," I told him. "Hey Marla, just wanted to tell you we've always loved all your doing for us down there in the kitchen. Jake there though, he's not so appreciative. He says you shouldn't cook no more geese."

Everyone looked wide-eyed at Jake and barely held back laughing at him. I saw Marla's evil eyes turn on him and I watched Jake's face plead innocence. I heard a few of the Spanish words I often got myself and I had to grin a little. I turned my horse and walked him down the hill and onto the start of yet another undesirable journey.

CHAPTER 4

We all made it to the road outside the gate and started into a trot to make it to where the other road headed north at the T-junction. We slowed and went straight from there, reaching the train with no trouble. I tried not to think of anything but finding the place in Kansas. I saw George oiling away at parts in amongst the wheels of the large locomotive at the head of the train. Looking up, I saw the steam coming from the stack and was glad that he had the thing running.

We steered the horses to our boxcar and I was glad that someone had put down the ramp for us. Riding up we all dismounted and started unsaddling our horses. It was a quick ride for them and they were still stomping around wanting more. I calmed mine with some long strokes down his neck. I put him in the end of the box car that Chris and Laura had sectioned off for them.

"I don't think that's exactly how the bet went," Jake told me from across the boxcar as I started to leave. I turned to look at him.

"Don't ever let me see you touching my daughter again," I told him as I turned and looked into his eyes.

"But, sir...," he started.

"Ever," I told him again.

"Yes sir," he replied and looked past me.

"Now it's time to get mission ready...again," I told everyone. "I know this is not what we were expecting but let's get right back at it. We didn't get a break which means we didn't have time to get sloppy. I told Jessie to stay home and heal up. I know home is right there and it pisses us all off that we have to be away again. Let's just think about what we have to get done and get on it. We'll be back here in no time." I heard encouraging acknowledgements all around. "Jake please give me regular reports on that radio. And I need to know what kind of weather we are expecting. Shay and Sterling, can you guys ask George for one of his laptops and look over every inch of this pin drive." I threw it to them. "Try to find out everything and look for any hints at all. I'm hoping your medical knowledge might hit on something there, Shay. I know the rest of us have stuff to do and some of it is just sitting tight and waiting for the action. Chris, could you get us set up a little better in here? I still don't want to be a burden on George and Margie."

"No problem," he told me. "I brought some stuff from the armory that I think will help that a lot." I saw cheer on his face. I could only guess what he was going to do to our boxcar but I knew it was going to be a big improvement over the way it was.

"Dinner and the like too?" I asked him.

"I got that covered," he said.

"I'm going to go talk to George about where we're headed," I said to everyone. "Jake, Jadee should have some coordinates for me by now. Could you get them and bring them to me?"

"I will, right away," he said.

"We will get this over and be home before we know it," I told them. "But let's keep it sharp. We never know what we could run into. Everyone is armed at all times. Code word is 'cozy'. The response to that is 'valley'." Everyone nodded. "Cozy," I tried.

"Valley," everyone said in unison.

"Looks like we are right back into it guys," I told them. "Let's make it work."

We all split up then. I went to find George and waved at Margie in the caboose as I passed. I found him on the opposite side of the engine, hips deep inside a compartment under one of the wheels toward the back. He jumped on seeing me.

"Sorry, didn't mean to startle you there," I told him.

"No, I just get so involved in what I'm doing with ol' Rusty here that I forget anyone else is around," he told me. "You must know where we're going."

"I should have the coordinates in a few minutes," I told him. "The place is in eastern Kansas."

"Oh?" he asked. "I think we can be there in four or five hours or so. There's usually lots of water to be had out there in the flat stuff. How far into Kansas are we going?"

"Fifteen miles in or so," I told him. "I'll show you when you're done."

"Well I'm done now," he told me. "I ran out of grease for my grease gun here. I figure I grease too much anyways. The whole thing will probably outlast us with what they got in 'em now." He laughed to himself at that. "Maybe you should show me on the map."

"I think we are loaded and ready when you are," I told him. "I guess we just need to know which way to go. I saw the general area so I can show you pretty much on your atlas, I think. Jake should be getting me the exact spot."

"Well then, I'm keeping us from moving out," he told me. "I'll put this away and meet you in the cab."

He moved out from under the engine and hurried to the front of it. He went around to the other side and I knew he was going to put away his grease gun in the compartment over on that side that I had seen him take it out of so many times. I climbed the ladder at the front of the locomotive and walked down the short catwalk. I yanked on the door there as it had started sticking a little and went into the front of the cab. I stepped over the pile of fur that lay just inside the door.

I went to the small table at the back of the cab that often held the Freight Interchange Map which worked for us as a road atlas. Not seeing it there, I sat on the chair at the window opposite of George's position and looked around outside. It did not take long for George to come in followed by Sterling and Jake. Jake walked over to me.

"I have the coordinates you asked for," he said plainly.

"Okay, George should need them, I think," I told him and he turned to George, who was at his chair in the driver's seat. I saw him take out the familiar map.

"Let's see what we've got here," George said, moving over toward the table at the back. "I grabbed this old road atlas from Margie. We have a ton of them in the back. We should be able to get pretty close with these." He laid out the maps on the table.

Jake told us the coordinates and it did not mean much to me. George looked around at us and seemed to be as confused as I was. He seemed a bit embarrassed.

"Sorry y'all, but I'm going to need a global positioning map for those coordinates," he told us. "There's no longitude or latitude on these things." I looked at him a little concerned. "Don't worry, I have one of those too. I'll get it from Margie. Only she knows where things are in this train." He started to move as though he was going to leave.

"George!" I said a little too loud. "I think we have a general idea of where the place is. Is there a way of just figuring how to get moving in that general direction and then after we're on the road find the exact spot?"

"I think that sounds best," he admitted. "Sorry, just so used to working off of the destination first. Show me where we're headed and we'll see if we can leave without making a decision on which tracks to take."

We all turned then and looked at the Freight Interchange Map laid out flat on the table. We looked through eastern Colorado and found a variety of tracks leading almost anywhere we would want to go. George turned it over to Kansas then and I pointed to the area which we needed to go. I was relieved to see that there were still just as many rails crisscrossing there.

"Looks like no matter which way we take it should be easy to get to," George said. My relief was plain, I am sure. He flipped back to Colorado and ran his finger around a bit. "Looks like this line here will give us the most options in case something gets in the way or we need to find a different direction; that happens now and again. Plus it will keep us close to the mainline running east and west through south Nebraska so we can jump on that if we have to." I was feeling good about George's ability. "Time to move out," he said as he looked up with a smile. "One thing left to talk about. We are going to need some oil sometime during this trip."

"How long before that's necessary?" I asked as we all looked at him.

"Well, if we keep our eyes open I'm sure we'll find plenty of oil pumps out in the plains we're headed for. It shouldn't slow us down much at all," he told us. "We'll be looking for the storage tanks somewhere close by them with a specific type of exhaust attached to them. Those are small refineries which is what we'll have to have. We can't use the stuff right out of the ground. Also, call out if you see some close by water along the way. Chances are I've seen it and we can keep going but it's worth mentioning. We won't be in any urgent need, probably until we get there but if something shows itself easy along the way we might as well take advantage." We all agreed and he smiled. "We are ready when you are."

"Jake, will you let everyone know that we are ready?" I asked him.

"Will do," he said as he started to leave the cabin.

"From now on, if we are in a safe area, I'll just toot this whistle and that will give the signal," George told him. "Two soft, short blows will say we are close and one a minute later will mean hold on cause we are moving out." I saw Jake smile and I too liked the idea.

"I'll let everyone know," Jake told him and left the cabin.

"Looks like he's liking the responsibility," George told me as he went to sit in his chair.

"Yeah, I think he'll do well," I told him, going and sitting in the opposite chair. "Which way we headed from here?"

"Looks like the tracks head out east just a few miles north of that town up ahead," he said. "We can turn a little southeast after that and then back east again from there."

"I guess you found all the water you could want," I told him, forgetting to ask.

"Yeah, it took a little doing but windmills really crank the stuff out," he said, starting to switch levers. I heard the low rumbling go deeper.

"Everyone on back there?" I asked the small, handheld radio at my shoulder.

I got affirmatives from everyone. I gave George a nod and he flipped a few more levers. He pushed hard forward on the lever I always saw his hand on. I felt the power of the engine ripple through my body and then with one more movement from George's feet, we moved forward and slowly picked up speed.

It felt significant, us finally moving forward. It felt like we just stopped in for a fill-up and now we were on our way again. I breathed deeply and watched the tall grass and short shrubs begin to move past us. I was trying not to think of all that could be going on with Olivia and Tara and what we were also leaving behind.

There was a small hill that was blocking the site of the town to our north but as we picked up speed it quickly came into view. Several times it disappeared again as we got closer to some other hill that rose to hide the town. Finally, however, we came close enough to where it was laid out in front of us. I saw The Monks gang had done their job well.

Of course the sugar buildings had been burned to the ground, though still the tall, metal ladders jutted up and created a gnarled knot. The wall of semitrailers had been pulled away as several piles of burned remains dotted the area. Some train cars were also torched though little of them were flammable; I could see where debris from the collapsing sugar buildings landed mostly on top of them. It seems the structures had somehow kept from falling on the tracks on their other side, which is where we looked to be driving past.

"Is the way through clear?" I asked George.

"Yeah I checked that and we are fine," he told me.

I looked at Sterling. He was looking intently out of the side window behind me. His face was expressionless. As we passed it he went to sit at the table and began to look over the atlas left there.

"Sorry to see it so trashed," I told him.

"I'm not really," Sterling told me as he gave me a frown. "I thought it would be hard to see again but really, it's okay. The place we all moved to is far better. I know Greg loved that place but I always felt a little out in the open. I'm glad we have that other compound and I'm sure Greg would have to agree." I gave him a grin and was happy to see that attitude in him.

After some time George slowed and told me that the switch track was just ahead. He pulled out some binoculars and looked intently for a while. He put them back into some side compartment and pushed forward again on his trusty lever.

"Looks like the sign says we are turning in the right direction," he told me.

"Wow, nice," I told him. "How can you tell?"

"The lever signs tell you sometimes, if you know how to read them," he told me. "You'll see as we go by that the sign says TL. That tells us which track the switch is leading us on. That's the one we want."

"Someday you'll have to show me how all this works," I told him.

"Any time," he told me and turned back to looking outside.

I looked for the switch lever that he was talking about and saw it coming up. It did in fact say TL and as we passed it I felt us move onto the other line and curve east. As I felt the last bump of the switch tracks I saw George push more on the throttle. The motion of the train smoothed out and I saw George pull out his pipe and start to pack it with tobacco. I nodded in admiration.

After a few minutes Sterling asked George if he might barrow one of his laptops to do some research. George looked a little offended and told him that anything he needed was his to use. Sterling thanked him and moved out of the cab. I settled into the motion of the train and tried not to let my mind wander.

"Coffee should be ready in a few if you are up for some," George told me.

"Sure," I told him. "I can go back and get it when it's ready."

"No we have it right here," he said, pointing in front of him.

I went over and looked and saw a kettle sitting on a part of the lump in the middle of the cabin that got hot. A small piece of pipe had been added that made it wedged in where it sat and was not in danger of falling with the many bumps and turns that the train took on. I must have worn a large grin.

"I didn't have the coffee up here on our last trip," George told me as smoke billowed around his head. "But I made us a bit more ready this time. Should be coming right up." I saw steam coming from the kettle.

"Well, I think that is just what I need," I told him.

"Hard to get out of your head at times like these, I imagine," he said. I nodded and went to sit back down. "I love your home. I would have never thought to be able to find a place like that. Oh, looks like the coffees percolating." He produced two cups from somewhere and poured us both some as I told him the story of my son stumbling upon the entrance. "And that proved to be the main one for the whole area, huh? Lucky you." He smiled and I went over and got my coffee from him.

"Yeah, but I'm starting to think I would prefer some well-fortified canyon to some of these troubles," I told him. I immediately rebuked myself. "I guess I shouldn't say such things. Really, finding friends in the town north of us has been good. It restored a bit of something for us. And we would never have known what was going on there nor found you guys, which I would regret. The place has been the best thing for us and I shouldn't say anything otherwise."

"I think I know what you're getting at, though," he told me. "I think we all just want to go on with our lives the best we can find a way. Looks like you all are real comfortable there. This kind of stuff is getting in the way of that." I nodded agreement. "What was it exactly that FDR said about those going off to fight in WWII? 'These men fight not for lust of conquest. They fight to end conquest. They yearn but for the end of battle, for their return to the haven of home'."

"What truth in that saying for us," I told him. "I had no idea you liked history." I blow on my hot coffee.

"Never could read in school but I loved the way that lady teacher would talk about it," he said, looking far off.

"Sounds like someone had a crush," I told him from behind my cup. I saw him smile.

"Indeed I did," he said, puffing on his pipe. "When I was in junior high I went to a private school that was too hard for me. I took the same grade a couple of times, though I told myself it was because I was in love with Ms. Harding. I'm pretty sure she wanted me too." He gave me a grin. "She would walk back and forth along the front of the class and just read from those history books. She would make it seem like the best story you ever heard as she would march into some battle or talk softly of some hero of old. Boy, she would make you want to get things wrong just so she would come around and lean over your shoulder, long hair hanging down and playing with your neck. I loved that teacher."

"Sounds like it," I said, barely able to hold back a chuckle. He looked at me.

"Broke my heart when Daddy took me out of school," he said with a frown. "Said he wasn't paying for no school if I couldn't keep up. He put me to work in the factory and that was the end of that romance. Still loved history though."

"Any boy would," I told him with assurance.

We talked on then about history and let it take us where it would. George still turned levers as I slowly sipped at my coffee, refilling the cup several times. It was exactly what I needed.

"Switch track ahead," George told me as he brought out his binoculars. "It's the one that brings us straight east now. Looks like this one will need changing." I got up out of my seat.

The train slowed and I looked out in front of us. There was nothing but flat land for miles. It was beautiful to me. I turned the handle on the front cabin door as we almost stopped. I was back in under a minute with us now headed in the right direction.

"I haven't seen Roman since he went with you to get us ready," I told George, thinking of everyone's role in whatever was up and coming.

"Yeah, he did great in helping us get everything ready," George told me. "He really helped with getting the water. Last I saw he was in the cave." I looked at him sideways. "Oh, sorry, that's what Margie calls our boxcar. She says I stay in there to get away from her. It just became to be known as that over time."

"Just when I thought I knew everything about you all," I told him. "Maybe I'll go back that way and see what's going on. We need water any time soon?"

"Yeah, I've been keeping an eye out," he told me. "Haven't seen any real close. We're just getting started yet and we're pretty full."

"Sorry, I kind of spaced it," I told him, looking again at the plains around us.

"No problem. I've gotten so used to it by now, I do it without even thinking."

"Could you give me a shout when we get within an hour or so?" I asked him.

"Will do," he said. "I'll need that map from Margie but that will be after a while. Maybe we should plan to stop an hour away or so and come up with what's next."

"I think that sounds great," I told him.

He smiled and poured himself another cup of coffee. I moved then out of the rear door of the cabin. I made it to the burn chamber room and looked at the flame and the level of oil inside the burner. It being where it needed to be, I pushed on a lever and sent sand blasting through the exhaust system, hearing it land on us from overhead. With little else to do in there I continued on. As I did, I saw we were again up to top speed.

I saw Margie in the caboose and thought to sit and talk to her for a few minutes. She seemed to be cleaning the entire caboose, everything being pulled out from under everywhere, the beds being covered with containers. I figured maybe I should keep going through.

"Need some help?" I asked instead. "I'm actually pretty good at dishes." I saw her concentration take a break.

"If you are willing then I will never turn that away," she said with a smile. She pointed to the sink and I walked to it.

I saw a large tall pot in each sink and on looking inside, found they were both filled with dishes. I smiled and got right to work on them, taking what hot water there was on the stove. I looked at Margie to make sure it was okay and she only pretended not to notice me.

"This looks like it could be a full-time job," I said, thinking of Mary back home.

"It feels that way sometimes, but only when I get lazy and let them stack up," she told me.

"We'll have to keep an eye out for a large supply of paper plates," I told her over my shoulder. "Then we can just throw those out as we fly on down the tracks."

"That would work nicely," she said. We stayed quiet then as we both continued to clean.

"So, George won't tell me how you guys got together," I told her when I could think of nothing else to bring up.

"Oh?" she said coyly. "I see." I waited for more but she did not offer any.

"Really?" I asked, stopping the dishes. "I know you guys met when he started driving a train up somewhere at a tourist area you were working at." I waited for her to add more. "Really? Oh, there must be a good story there I'm betting." I waited again and still she only stuffed boxes here and there. "Come on, tell me something," I tried. She ignored me altogether then. "Oh, now I have to get to the bottom of this. I must have stumbled onto some scandal." That made her smile. I turned and started back at the dishes, wondering how to make one of them talk.

With the dishes well on their way to being finished, Margie brought up the beauty of the plains. I told her of my childhood playing in them and she told me of her own in the mountains on the Reservation. We smiled often to each other as one or the other story needed it. I looked at her as she was doing some more cleaning and was so glad to know her and George. As our conversation ended and the dishes were done, I turned and with a smile started toward the back of the caboose.

"There will be more of those after dinner here in a little while," she told me.

"Any time," I told here. Looking at my watch I frowned. "It should only take us a couple of more hours to get there."

"I will start on it right away then, so that we have time to eat before we need to set out again." I left her there with a smile.

I made it to George's boxcar with no trouble and saw Jake talking on the radio on a chair by the fireplace. It kind of reminded me that it was still a little cold outside. He stood up as I came in and looked a little nervous. I walked over to him.

"Has Jadee figured anything out on what they sent yet?" I asked him.

"She is looking through them," he told me. "She said there is a lot of stuff. She also said that Mack has been keeping some kind of channels open over the area just in case Kevin tries to call anyone." I nodded and started to ask him a question. "The thick clouds are giving way a little bit and it may break up in the morning. Some current is moving in from the south and it should warm up some. It may change though if the Jet Stream coming in from the north gets some force behind it. It could bring rain or snow. Sorry, there is no way to know for sure. Three or so hours should tell us better."

I looked at him, standing there almost like he was at attention. He had changed his clothes and looked to have showered and shaved. He wore a pleased look on his face that seemed to be fading the more I looked at him. Looking hard I saw an AK47 round stuffed in with the rest of the bullets that fit his gun in a belt he wore around his chest. I scoffed and moved off.

I saw Roman sitting at the far left of the bench that I always saw George sitting at. (Sterling and Shay were watching a laptop screen at the other end.) He was doing something with our old radio. Rummaging through a box I saw him find something he was looking for. I walked over to him.

"What are you doing with this old thing?" I asked him.

"I asked George if he would mind if I got it fixed if I could permanently mount it in here," he told me. "I don't think it will be any good as a portable one but it should work well in here. I think I may be onto something but I can't be sure. Just keeping myself busy, I guess."

"I can understand that," I told him. "I guess we never did find you a good stop. I know you were just wanting a ride out of the mountains."

"No, I think I signed on with you guys," he told me. "I'm pretty sure I'll see the world." He said the last part with a smile and I had to laugh.

"Yeah, I guess it seems that way," I told him. "Really, I can't wait to get back home though."

"I can understand that," he said. "I wasn't meaning to be callous. I do know this pretty much sucks for everyone."

"No, I didn't think you meant anything by it," I told him. "I really appreciate you helping as much as you have already."

"Please, count me in on whatever happens here," he said. "I'm not looking to crowd in but I am looking to help if I can."

"I'll keep you in the loop," I told him. "So what's it going to take to fix this thing?"

"It's mostly fixed. I mean, it will send out and receive. It's just figuring out frequency stuff, of course, that's the hard thing. I am trying a few different dials but nothing so far. It would work fine without the dial if we want it to just stay on a channel, like to just call home. I'm also trying to make it so you don't have to crank it. Once it gets permanently installed it should work off of a battery. I'm planning on still leaving the crank option open though, and I do want to find a dial."

"Good idea. Never know when the juice will run out or when we'll need to find another frequency. It would be nice to see what we're doing."

"Randy, this is George, come in," I heard a box say at the middle of the bench. I looked around. "Randy, you in the Cave?" I still looked around. Roman pointed me to an old telephone-looking thing. I felt the train slow.

"He hooked up an old com system," he told me. I picked up the receiver.

"Yeah, what's up George?' I asked and felt everyone looking at me.

"Found some water," he told me. "We aren't desperate yet but I'd like to fill up all the way before we head into some trouble."

"Agreed, and I'll be there as soon as we stop," I told him and hung up the receiver. I looked around the boxcar, wondering what other things I was missing.

I called everyone on the radio and told them we were stopping for water. They all said they would be ready to set a perimeter. I hoped it would not be necessary to use but I always wanted it there just in case. As I finished the thought we came to a halt.

I jumped to the ground and watched everyone else do the same. I walked up to where George was getting off and saw him go up to where they stored the long hoses and pumps. As he opened the compartment I was there to help. Looking around I did not see any water, however.

"It's on the other side," George told me as I pulled on some length of hose. "A damn lot of it too."

"Enough to get us through the next few days if this isn't the place?" I asked with some hope.

"I'm sorry but I can't rightly answer that one," he told me and we both moved around to the front of the train. "I do think we will get plenty far if we top it off." I took that answer to mean yes.

As we moved to where George usually climbed up to fill the tank, I looked around. I did see the water he was talking about. There was a lake that came all the way up to the tracks. I smiled and got back to helping George, though he little needed it.

He took the rolled up hose from me and with his pump, went down to the water's edge. I watched as he adjusted the bobber to keep it from sinking to the bottom. As he moved about doing other things having to do with the process, I turned back to looking around. I saw only the lonely plains.

I tried at first to find any sign of humans, either past or present. There was none so I started looking for something of interest in the landscape. I always found beauty there and I let my mind flow with the low waves of the horizon.

"All's still clear here," I heard Chris check in. Everyone else followed.

"I read you," I told them. "Doesn't look like much has been happening around here."

"Yeah, no kidding," Chris said.

"Well this shouldn't take long so let's just keep a sharp eye and make sure," I said and they all agreed.

I watched a large herd of cattle come over the hill then. It looked like they were headed for one last drink from the lake, before bedding down for the evening. We had taken some time a while back and studied some of the movements of the herds around our home. It seemed you could almost set your watch to some of their behavior. I wondered then about going and shooting one for some fresh meat but thought I would much rather be on the tracks sooner.

I saw George had managed to get the hose into the intake hole at the top of the engine and was now helping the electric pump by giving it a few cranks now and then. It was interesting to watch but for some reason I just could not settle into a relaxed mood. I hoped to have it under control by the time we got to where it mattered.

It took about twenty minutes and several trips to the top of the engine before George stopped the pump and started the long process of putting things away. I wanted to help but he had a way of doing things by himself that made you feel like you were hindering more than doing any good. Instead, I kept an eye on the landscape and waited. I was glad that I did.

"Movement," I heard Jake say.

"I see it," Chris said. "Northwest, behind the cattle, right?"

"Affirmative," Jake said.

"Got it, three riders, moving slow a quarter mile off," Chris said. "They see us."

I looked to where George was just starting to roll his hose. He had moved a little down the hill beside the tracks. I saw him trying to throw the portion ahead of him in the water so he could roll it up clean. He looked up when I yelled to him. I pointed northwest and he looked that way. I saw him roll in haste.

"Looks like they are headed our way," Davina said behind me and up the hill some. "I hope they don't want trouble."

"Yeah, that would be nice," I told her. "As long as they aren't some other government organization with bad news I'll take them." She laughed and I grinned to hear it.

George finished with his work quickly. He scrambled up the hill and walked around the front of the train. I saw the three people on horseback were not in any rush to come up to something so unfamiliar as us. I suggested everyone get back on the train.

"We should be able to get out of here before they get close enough to do anything," Margie said over the radio to my surprise. She seemed not to like those things.

I saw movement at the window above me and saw George poking his head out. He was looking at the approaching people with his binoculars. He put them down and looked at me.

"Looks like three men," he told me. "They are pretty heavily armed. They ain't holding anything though." I looked over at where they were coming from.

"I guess maybe we should just move along," I told him. He agreed and moved back inside.

I heard the engine rumble and heard the wheels squeal. I looked back and saw the ladder at the rear of the engine drawing closer. I tried to keep an eye on the horsemen and get on board at the same time. It worked mildly. They watched us moving away and stopped. I saw one of them lift his hand and wave. I returned it and watched them turn around and head back toward the cattle.

I thought about them a little as we went on down the tracks. They seemed friendly and I hoped so, but I am sure they understood our taking off without waiting to find out. Notwithstanding, the wave was a kindness, I thought. It actually did my heart well to see that longtime symbol of friendship so easily given.

"You doing okay?" George asked me and I guessed I must have been looking a little weird somehow, so deep in thought about it.

"Yeah, I think I'm actually doing better," I told him.

"It is amazing what stretching your legs can do for you," he said and turned back to his levers.

"I would agree with you there," I told him and leaned back in the chair, looking outside as the hills rolled by.

CHAPTER 5

We seemed to have gone forever down the tracks when I saw George pull back on the levers some. We noticeably slowed and he got out of his chair. He walked to the back of the cabin and turned to look at me.

"I'll be right back with that map we need to find your coordinates," he told me. "Keep an eye on her."

As he walked out of the cabin I stood up in some excitement. I had not yet been in charge of the cabin and here I was all by myself as we moved down the tracks. I, of course, knew nothing of stopping if we needed to, though. I could see for miles in front of us and saw nothing of interest on the tracks or beside them. I knew nothing of most any of what was in there. I did not let that stop me but went over and sat in George's chair.

The scenery was the same over on that side of the cabin, though I am not sure why I thought it would be different. The chair was a little more cushioned and had a very nice sheepskin pad on it. Looking around, I saw all of the levers that George so expertly maneuvered. With a smile, I put my hand on the one he always held and turned and looked out the front window, feeling quite important. The feeling however, too quickly passed and soon I just felt silly. I got up then and moved back over to the other side of the cabin, seeing I had been closely watch by the hairy lump on the floor in the corner.

"I didn't break anything if that's what you're wondering," I told the dog as I sat down. It turned once again to ignoring me.

George came back in with Sterling and Jake in tow. George looked out front and with some silent nod of satisfaction went over to the table and laid out a large map. We all surrounded him as he turned through the pages.

"Okay, this should be where we need to go from what you were telling me earlier," he said and pointed to an area on the map.

I could see that the map was well-lined in every direction. It was broken down several different times into grids with corresponding numbers at the margins. Roads were under the lines as were streams and rivers. Cities were marked plainly but that was it. Looking hard, I saw no railroads on the map. We all watched George go and get his Interchange map and come back to the table.

"Let's see what we can do now," he said as he sat the other map down beside the first.

Here Jake gave him the exact coordinates. We all looked intently to find what we would be up against. I followed the lines on the map twice and nothing seemed to be of interest in the spot I was coming to. I figured that made sense with all of the secrets the government kept. I looked up at the others and we all kind of shrugged.

"How far out are we from it?" I asked George.

"We are about right here," he told us. We all looked at the map and tried to see how close the tracks we were on would get us. "We should move into Kansas in not too long. Sorry, but I think we are forty-five minutes away. I wouldn't mind holding up right here." He pointed to the Interchange map and we all saw that there was nothing special about the spot. He looked up at me. "Sorry to just rush straight for the place but I saw there weren't any other rails that ran in this area. This one we are on is it."

"No problem," I told him. "We didn't know exactly where we were headed so this is what we get. It's nice having someone taking care of this stuff. Seems you know just what we need."

"Why stop there?" Sterling asked. I looked and saw the spot he indicated would put us about five miles north of the coordinates we were looking at.

"No particular reason," he said. "It just seems equal distance between these two roads on the map there, which puts it in the middle of nowhere. If problems arise, it looks like from the topography here that it is a downhill run out of there. It's not a very steep run but it may help. And there does seem to indicate some flatland just after that so we can pick up speed quick. These maps aren't always right but it's the best we can go by for now." We all agreed and I found I had a lot to learn about looking at maps.

"I have a weird question," Jake stated dryly. We all looked at him and waited. "What if he hasn't made it there yet?"

"Yeah I was kind of wondering the same thing," I admitted.

"What if he's holed up somewhere and taking his time moving?" Jake asked as he walked toward the window. "Maybe he's watching this place and us going in scares him off." I did not like where this was going but I knew it was a true possibility. "It's not like we can hide that we are coming here in this thing." I looked at George but he seemed to be thinking along with the rest of us.

"You're right on that," he said. "There ain't no sneaking in with this thing, although we are pretty far north."

"I had been thinking about that as well," I told him. "I think though, if we get there ahead of him we can hide out somewhere and wait. It should be real obvious, once we get inside I guess, if this is where he's coming. Not sure what to do about this train being out in the open. It looks like any roads are pretty far off. I'm thinking we shouldn't be seen way out like that."

"Oh, I think that's easy enough to do something about," George said. "There are plenty of hills out here to hide at the bottom of."

"Okay, that will work," I told him. "And really, I think we can guarantee that we will be there ahead of him. Let's not leave him any sign that we are here though.

We'll have to watch how we move in and look to see which way he would be coming from." I looked at Sterling. "You guys finding anything of interest back there?"

"Not yet," Sterling said. "We are just getting into it though." I nodded understandingly.

"Any idea what kind of facility we are coming up on?" George asked.

"I am not sure," I told him and could see he did not like that answer. "I don't like it either."

"They said Kevin was sending stuff to medical facilities, right?" Sterling wondered aloud. "Sounds like we should be careful what we do. We could be entering some study facility that still has experiments left turned on." I had not thought of that.

"I wonder why they thought he would come to this one?" Jake asked and we all looked at him. This was not making me feel better.

"Let's curb the curiosity for now and see what we find when we get there," I told them. "We will definitely be on high alert for whatever we find and with some luck we can find a good spot for Kevin to walk right up to us. And you're right Sterling, we should be careful with whatever we find, especially if we are walking into a research lab. I hope there isn't any experiments left on but we should be ready for that."

We looked at the map some more and I tried to find a good place to stop the train with what the topography was telling me. I knew George would pick the perfect spot but I just needed something to do. I was glad for the distraction and was glad for how familiar I was becoming with the area already.

"We will need some oil eventually," George told me after a few minutes. I looked up at him. "Not right away but before too awful long."

"Can we do something with all of those big oil pumps we've been passing?" I asked him.

"No, that stuff is pretty crude," he told me. "For the kind of burning we are doing it needs to be refined. Not totally refined but a little. None of the ones we've passed so far have the refineries with them. It's not actually that hard to make a simple refinery if you plan on staying in one place for a while. I mean if you're planning on staying for a week." He could see I was not interested. "Something to look into when we get back home."

"Anything we should be doing for now?" I asked him. "I mean what is it going to take?"

"Usually we look for a large town that has a bunch of cars or large trucks," he told me. "Now and again we fill up pretty good at a refinery. We drain them and move on down the line. We always need to look out for any oil tanker cars. If we can find one of those even half full we'll be on easy street. We don't find those very often. I know it's not what you want to hear."

"No, I'm sorry George," I told him. "If I seem distracted, it's just because of all that's going on. I know we need to take care of our ride. You tell us what we need to do and that's what will happen."

"I saw a bigger town up ahead of where we are headed," he told me. "We may need to stop there and fuel up before we go much farther. More than that and we may have to worry about getting stranded for a while. We can always take out the wagon but it takes a while that way."

"Okay, let's plan on stopping before we need to do that," I told him.

"Sounds perfect. Half an hour until we are in position," he told me and turned and went back to his chair.

I got on the radio and told everyone we were getting close. I heard back from everyone and Laura said she and Chris would get the horses ready. Sterling moved out of the cabin. I asked Jake to have a weather report ready when we stopped and anything else he could get me. He said he would and moved out of the cabin as well. I went over and sat down by the window, looking through my vest and trying not to overthink what was ahead.

"I like that com system you have back there in your boxcar," I told George. "The old phone thing is pretty cool."

"Yeah, that was one of the easiest things I've done," he told me. "It was part of this engine and I just extended it. It hadn't worked for a while though."

"How old is it?" I asked him. "Looks like it belongs beside an old telegraph machine."

"Yeah, it is a pretty old system," he admitted. "All the old trains used to have them. It's a pretty simple thing to do. And really, simple is best."

"I can see that," I told him. "I wonder if they thought it was simple or was it kind of a cutting edge technology for them back then."

"I'm sure it was all pretty technical back when. I bet the electrician felt like a magician when he just made the wire loop together and everyone thought he was a genius."

"Well, I guess it's that way again for most," I said with a smile. George nodded agreement. "I guess you're the new Geek Squad." He laughed at that.

We stayed silent then as George smoked another pipe-full of tobacco. I had never seen him smoke so much which I took to mean he too was a little nervous about what was up and coming. The plains rushed by outside and I let the long, swaying grass take me far away to a childhood that saw great adventures just over every low hill. It was a hypnotic feeling as the warm air flowed inside the cabin.

I must have been well lost in thought as I felt the train come to a complete stop and I focused outside to see that we had in fact come to a halt. The plains outside carried on forever but the place we were parked was at the bottom of a small hill. It was in a spot that kept us well hidden where a hill had been cut in half and the tracks lay in the middle. All of the other hills around us were slightly taller than where we were. It was the best that we could have hoped for.

"Great spot here," I told George. "I shall be always impressed with what you can do with these rails and this train."

It got a chuckle from him and he moved to leave the cabin. I followed and left him shutting down everything in the burn chamber. I shouldered my small pack and took the ladder to the ground.

I saw that most everyone was on the ground except Chris and Laura, though I did see they had lowered the ramp to our boxcar. I saw Davina walking toward me and I headed for her. Sterling and Shay were walking back to the horses.

As I met up with Davina, we too started toward the horses, I saw Margie moving in an odd way. She was almost dancing and I stopped for a second to see what she was doing. As she did a slow turn I saw that she had two streaks of paint on her face, a green line down her right cheek and a red squiggly line down her left. I saw she was chanting something and she continued her slow dance that moved her farther in a small circle. Davina and I walked past and into our boxcar.

It took a few minutes to get things ready and then to recheck everything. I had been trying to think of everything that I would need. When I was satisfied that I had all in its place, I led my horse to the ground. I saw everyone else double checking their things as well. Margie and George were both there now, as well, with the horses we had given them.

I had put the coordinates into my small handheld GPS and looked to see that it was working. Glad to see all was good there, I looked over at Jake. He was atop his horse with the large radio strapped to his shoulders. I nodded as I looked at everyone. Looking at the sky I saw the clouds were breaking up.

"How far from here?" Chris asked. I looked at George.

"About five miles southeast of here," he told us. I looked at my GPS and nodded.

"It's been brought up that Kevin probably isn't here yet," I stated. "I'm sure we got here before he could have, so let's ride in a way that leaves little trace of our passing by. It seems he should be coming in from the west, if this is where he's coming. A road should be back west a little from here." I looked at George to confirm that, which he did with a nod. (I must have been daydreaming pretty hard to have missed it.) "It may be that Kevin travels right down it. Maybe we should go have a look around at the compound first before we decide what to do. Let's ride up to where we can get a good view of what's going on around here before we leave the train behind." Everyone looked around then and it was pointed out where that could best be done.

We rode to almost the top of a nearby hill and dismounted. Our horses were well enough trained to stay where we left their reins, so we moved without them to the top. I was glad to see the train mostly disappear behind the small hill we had stopped at. It would be impossible to see if we moved just over the crest of the hill we were at and that would be true of every small hill that surrounded us. I was glad we would not have to worry about that, though I knew that was only mostly true.

When we topped the hill, we could see for miles, everything in the surrounding area being a little below us. The plains stretched on for miles with only hints of large changes in elevation spotted here and there, though small hills were constant. Trees tried to grow at the bottoms of the low-flowing hills and were only barely hanging on. Shrubs and long grasses made up most of what we saw. I did see the train tracks disappear at the horizons both east and west.

"Looks like no one could see us coming for miles," Chris said. "How'd you find this place to park?" We all looked at George.

"It doesn't look like it but there is a lot more hollows and small canyons out there," George told us. "You won't even know it and you'll walk right up to a gully that will run deep and stretch for miles." I remembered many such ditches when I was a kid. "The road is about two miles back that way." He pointed west. "Looks like, by the map, if we take the road, the compound will be about five miles south and a half mile back east of it."

"I thought it was going to be ten miles south?' I asked George and looked again at my GPS. Sure enough it said five miles.

"That's what the maps seemed to say," he told me. "But it's only about five miles south of where we are right now. That latitude and longitude map don't lie."

"Okay then, I'd say we look for a way of coming at it from the northeast," I said. "It will keep us from spreading out our tracks and making it obvious we're here. Also, I think we should follow the tracks for about a mile east and then turn south. If someone does spot our tracks it won't lead them right back to the train." We all turned and looked southeast past the train.

There were a lot more of the elevation changes in that direction, of course. I was hoping that would help us in the long run. There was a hint of some structures directly south about four miles off, which we all agreed was probably a farm; we would miss that if we went a mile farther down the tracks before we turned south.

"I agree with going farther but we should head back southwest from there and check out that farm," George said. "It would be nice to see if someone was close by and it may have some things we need. Either way it would be nice to know if there's someone between us on our way out of here. And it's got to be close to the facility we're looking for."

"I think that sounds good," I told him. "If it's only a mile or so from the facility then maybe we leave our horses there and walk in. It will make it easier to sneak around." There were shrugs all around.

I looked at the sky. We were going to have a mild storm coming up, Jake had said, and it looked like that was going to be true. Whatever came, the clouds overhead now and up and coming meant that Jadee would not be able to help us see what we were walking into. The clouds rolled and I hoped for a quick rainstorm.

We all got on our horses and started at a slow trot. The saddle was comfortable, though the stirrups were going to take a day to get used to again. We went back to the train and started down the tracks in front of it, walking off the side in a grassy ditch that ran along with it. As we all made it into the ditch, Chris, who was in the lead, started us off at a run.

It did not take long to get a mile farther down the tracks and we looked for the best way to head south. It mostly looked the same there so we turned in that direction and saw the wide plains in front of us, though hills plagued the horizon. Again, we soon got into a run and quickly moved through the grass.

We topped yet another small rolling hill and saw an old windmill at the bottom about ten feet lower than we were. The recessed area was entirely covered with a herd of black cattle, looking to be done with the day. A few of them moved off a little as the rest wondered at our intentions. We circled around the hollow and, leaving them behind, quickly got back into a run.

"Them were some Black Angus cows," Roman told me as he rode up close. "Sure good eatin' in winter time."

"Maybe we'll slaughter some on the way back to take with us," I yelled as we traveled. That got a broad smile from him.

After another couple of miles, having stopped twice to cut fences, we all drew up and looked at the farm drawing closer. (Looking farther on, we could still not see the facility, though it made sense as the hills there grew taller.) We could better make it out as it was just about a mile away then. Trees surrounded a large farmhouse at the top of a hill that had a long, dirt driveway running to a single mailbox and small overgrown dirt road which headed north-south kind of and disappeared among the surrounding hills. One of the biggest oak trees I've ever seen stood beside a tall, proud, faded, red barn. A few white corrals were spread out, we could see and a tall fence surrounded the barn and narrowed as it led into the back. Several other outbuildings were evenly spaced. Two, large, grain silos were on the far side of the barn.

"Looks like every other farm we've seen," Laura said as her horse moved around under her, it still wanting to run. "We should be able to get pretty close if we use that ravine there."

She pointed out a small, low, spot full of shrubs off to the left of the farm that led up to the barn. I looked at it and saw it would get us somewhere close to the barn. The tall sides of it would keep us well below any view of the barn if we were to stay among the shrubs and tall bushes. (I knew there must have been a small stream there to support such vegetation.) I could see it would get us all the way to one of the corrals but that we would still have to cross some open area to get to the barn. It looked about the best we could hope for.

"Okay, let's move over southeast there and come over that little hill," I said. "It should get us closest to the end of the ravine. It looks like we will be open for a few seconds as we move into the bushes at the bottom but I think it's doable. Chris, you and Laura flank and find somewhere to cover us once we're there. We'll move to the barn and then watch the house for a few minutes. If it's clear we'll move there and secure it." Everyone looked to understand. "Let's make this take as little time as possible. We need to clear this and be moving on."

"How long do you think before Kevin gets to that facility?" Davina asked.

"I don't think it could be before tomorrow, late," I said and looked at George. He seemed to agree as did everyone. "Let's get this done."

Chris led us again in a direction that would put us over the hill from the ravine. The gentle hill we needed to come over in order to get into it was long and had a gentle slope. I signaled Chris and he held up. With a swift kick to my horses haunches, I topped the hill and ran down to the bottom of the other side.

I moved along a small trickle of water that sometimes spread out and made a shallow pool. I stopped a few times to look around and my horse took advantage and drank deeply. I saw we were all moving one at a time into the ravine so I moved farther up toward the barn. A large pheasant flew out of some short shrub and spooked me and my horse. An old, rotten, wooden fence made it so I had to move out of the bottom a couple of times but I was mostly able to stay in cover.

When I got to the end of the brush I saw a large pipe coming out of the ground that was letting out the small amount of water. It was just outside of one of the many corrals that were at the farm. The large barn was about a hundred feet in front of me with the corral beside me and it. Looking, I saw several large skeletons that surely must have been those of the horses trapped inside long ago. I moved to watching for movement from the buildings.

The barn was the two-story kind and had a large hayloft whose door swung in the wind that was starting to pick up. A haze had moved in with all of the moisture that was hanging in the air. A set of huge doors was opened at the back side of the barn we could see, and wired to the fence that ran up to them, the fencing of the corral in front of me running up to one side of the doors. A smaller sliding door that most likely led to a tack room was the only other door on that side and it was closed.

When several minutes passed without seeing anything, and seeing Davina right beside me also looking, I moved along the corral and headed for the backside of the barn where the two doors stood open. I went in the direction that would keep the barn between me and the house, every nerve on end as I slowly made my way. It felt good at least knowing that Chris and Laura would be watching me from somewhere safe, ready to take out any threat.

I made it to the barn fine and saw Davina start from the brush at the end of the ravine. I looked inside the barn and saw several empty stalls. A large open area that allowed the animals to come in out of the weather was well-fertilized. An empty watering trough sat in the middle of the area. Railing made it so that the animals could only take up about half of the barn whereas the rest was filled with stacked hay and far off a large tractor and an old looking flatbed trailer. Riding inside of the barn, I got off of my horse and led him to one of the empty stalls.

I saw the stairs that led to the loft and looked for the gate in the railed fence that would allow me to move farther into the barn. Seeing Davina coming in, I waited and shouldered my rifle to cover her. As she got off I saw George coming in and then Margie. I looked and found the gate and moved toward it. As I made there, I saw Shay and Sterling come in and Roman shortly after. Jake brought up the rear and I opened the gate and moved in around the tall stack of hay.

We all moved easily through the barn and went up the stairs to the loft. Moving through the old farm equipment and all else that was left over from farming and had became obsolete, we cleared the loft. Several cats ran off as we came to where they were hiding. We moved back out of the top story and made it through the barn to where we could look outside and see where the house was. Finding some windows on that side we all held up and took some time to watch.

"The barn is all clear," I told my radio.

"Copy that," Chris said.

"I can see the house from where I am," Laura said. "I haven't seen any movement."

"Great," I told them. "We're moving out."

I gave the sign that had come to mean we should move out. I saw everyone shoulder their weapons and adjust packs, getting ready for whatever was ahead. I was glad to see them all so ready as I led the way through the door.

I moved outside and along the wall of the barn. I went down toward the corner about ten feet away and stopped. Jake came out next and moved straight for the house. I moved across some open area to a tree that was next to a white, picket fence that surrounded the house. Jake moved through the gate as we all made our move toward different areas of the home. When Jake was on one side of the door and I came up to the other, we stopped and listened. I looked around and found us all in position.

Hearing nothing, Jake moved to open the screen door. I saw we were at a porch connected to the front of the house. Margie came in behind us and walked up to the door. She opened it and walked right in. Jake and I shrugged and moved in behind her.

We walked into a large living room that looked to be decorated to look like an old, log cabin. A big couch sat in the middle of the floor covered by a huge cowhide. Well-cushioned chairs with some western pattern were in front of the couch. Oversized lamps made out of cowboy boots were on the end tables at either side of the couch. The wooden floor was well swept and nothing on the many shelves seemed out of its place.

Margie pointed to her left and we followed, entering a long kitchen that ended at a huge dining room. There was a long table filled with chairs in the middle of the room there. Several hutches filled the far walls and were packed with beautiful dishes and pitchers. A long, lace, tablecloth covered the table. The back door was in the right side of the room.

We went back through the kitchen and went the other way off the living room. It took us to a small bathroom and a hallway that led to a basement. Several more of the team had come inside and were aiming at the whole inside of the house. We went downstairs and found a small tornado shelter and various different shelves of canned foods. I saw lots of clear mason cars with what looked like different fruits and vegetables. I smiled as we left the basement, leaving the food behind.

We easily cleared the top floor of the house, finding another well-decorated bathroom and three small bedrooms, one with a balcony that held two chairs and faced west. (I was sure the sunsets there would have been awesome.) Making it back downstairs to the ground floor we stood looking around the living room. I was glad all had been empty of people.

"We should call in Chris and Laura and stash the horses in the barn," I told everyone.

We moved outside then and I radioed the two of them. I looked around some more at the other small buildings and saw a few with a small fence coming from one side of them. There were screens over the fence, most of which had been blown to shreds. I figured this farm must have raised quail or pheasant at one time. Seeing nothing else of interest I moved along with the rest into the barn.

I thought of unsaddling my horse but figured it would be better to have him ready in case we needed to race out of there on the way back. I did put him into one of the bigger stalls and Davina put her horse in with mine. I took the bridle out of his mouth and went and looked at the large stack of hay in the barn. Spilling several bails, and digging to the middle of them, I found some good hay for him and Davina's as well. I saw all of the others following suit.

We were ready to move out in only a few minutes which pleased me very much. I saw everyone gather and I told Jake to let them know what we were doing back at home. He moved outside to do that and we all moved there with him. A small rain started and the breeze picked up almost immediately. I was not so happy about that, though all of it could help us move in on the facility. We all just watched Jake and as he put the radio back on his shoulders we started south.

"They say still too much cloud cover to see us and more of the same expected," Jake told us. "A current is moving in from the south that looks strong enough to move it out though." I looked down the way and did see some tumultuous-looking clouds. "They haven't gotten anything from Kevin yet."

"Okay, could you ask them about keeping us posted on that McQueen guy? I'd like you to keep on top of that." I told him. "I'd like to know if he's finding anything or if he's striking out. Maybe he'll get done and can come our way."

"I'll ask them that on the next check in, if that's okay," he told me.

"Yeah, that will work," I told him.

I looked ahead of us and saw that we were walking in a field of pumpkins. They were everywhere. I could have guessed at least a hundred acres of them. And they were not the small kind. Most were up to my knees. As we walked, the stalks of them pulled at our pants.

"This is not going to be fun," Roman said, stepping high over some broad leaves.

"Let's turn around and head out along the fence there," I said. "I guess we can walk along the driveway until we get past this field." I was still amazed at seeing so many pumpkins, the entire hillside dotted orange.

We walked down the driveway and I constantly looked for evidence of any human activity. No tracks were anywhere and the drive was starting to become fully grown over with goat-heads and other pesky plants. Making it to the road at the end of the driveway and seeing the field of pumpkins end on our left, we walked into the ditch and turned south.

I saw the road was starting to become fully grown over. I was not sure how long it would take to fully be so, but it was obvious to all that no one had passed there for some time. The ditch was a little hard to walk in with all of its tall grass but I preferred to leave the road untouched.

We quickly came to a paved road that came from the west and curved south as the dirt road ended. A sign nearby said we were coming to a dead-end if we went south. The road sign on the road heading east was... (Well, I won't here tell you exactly as I do not want to lead you to such places.) Up ahead we saw a very official looking sign as well.

We moved along the road, looking far ahead but still seeing nothing. A large hill raised up in front of us and hid everything from view that was over half mile away. We could see that the pavement only led about a hundred yards and then went back to gravel. A large sign sat in the middle of the road at the end of the pavement. At the top of the hill just beyond the sign a tall, chain-link fence stood with barbed wire at the top. As we walked up to the sign, Chris read it aloud.

"Private property," he said. "Weapon use authorized. Do not enter. No parking." A smaller sign was attached to the post at the bottom. "Do not litter. One hundred dollar fine enforced."

"Wow, sounds serious," George said.

"Looks like our facility is just ahead," Roman said as the rain started to gain strength.

We all passed the sign, anxious to get to the fence. Tumbleweeds ruled the area and were stacked quite high up against the chain-link. We slowed as we drew closer and peeped up over the weeds to get our first look at the facility.

The place was entirely fenced in and huge. It must have been at least two miles across. There were three large separate buildings set long-ways in a north-south direction. Their tops were covered with solar panels. Two long and tall greenhouses were attached to the south side of the building farthest away from us. Tall lights set everywhere in pavement were between each building which were about twenty yards apart. A parking lot was on the entire north side of the facility. To my amazement, a short runway was on the south part of the fenced in area. A short watchtower was at the east side of the runway close to the fence there. A hanger was next to it with two, large doors facing into the facility. A large, paved road led to an entrance gate at the southeast side of the compound. I looked over the small shack there.

"I don't see any movement," I told everyone.

"Kind of hard to see what's going on with this rain," Sterling said.

"Look like a research facility, Shay?" I asked. She only looked at me and shrugged.

"Maybe we should go check out those hangers over there," Chris said. "That tower would be a great place to cover you all from." I heard Laura concur.

"Looks like that will get us the closest to the buildings too," Davina put in.

"Anyone see any vehicles?" I asked. The rain really was getting bad.

Looks like there's some down there on the far west side," George said. "They were probably here from before. Who knows?"

"Okay, let's move back down behind this hill and circle around over to the tower," I told everyone. "We'll see what we can and decide when we get there."

We moved as one, only a little spread out and in a pretty big hurry. The rain did not let up and it was the cold kind that gets inside of you quickly. I think we made record time on that short maneuver and soon we stood overlooking the watchtower.

The facility looked the same from the other side which we could now see. We got a closer view of the greenhouses which did not tell us anything. The south side of the buildings were all brick, just like the north side. I looked down at the tower.

There was a door to the tower on the north side. The hanger was about thirty feet away from it and ran long-ways in front of us, all inside the fence of course. Behind the hanger were old oil drums and crates of different parts. A few military boxes of various sizes littered the area. The place looked abandoned.

"The power is still on," Chris said and pointed to the greenhouse. We all saw the lights were on inside.

"A little early in the day for those lights to be on," George noticed.

"Must mean there's no one around to turn them off and on," Laura said. I figured that could be one reason.

I turned my attention to getting us inside without making it known to anyone that came after. I figured cutting through was out. It looked like some hard climbing and a few scrapes were soon to be had. I nodded to everyone and made the motion.

Sterling moved down first and I shortly followed, heading down about fifty feet from where he was starting to climb. I hurried the best I could and with some difficulty made it over the overhanging barbed wire. Hitting the ground, I ran to the backside of the hanger. There were several doors there and I moved up to one of them and waited until everyone was inside the fence and up to the building.

With a nod, I tried the door I was standing at and found it locked. Shay tried the one she was standing at when she saw mine did not open. Hers opened at her hand and Sterling moved inside. We all hurried down to where Shay was standing and made it inside the hanger.

We were in a long hallway that had several doors lining it. Pictures of different aircraft covered the walls on both sides. Trying one door, I found it was locked; so far that was zero for two. Looking, I saw Roman listening at the door at the end of the hallway. He looked back at me and shrugged. I moved to come up next to him but shook my head so he would wait until we were all ready.

He pushed open the door and walked in just before I got to him. Coming through the door as well, we both moved quickly, trying to find something for cover. I saw a row of bikes to our left on the far side of the building in front of one of the large hanger doors. Tool boxes and work benches were everywhere. Shelves lined the back wall and parts of various sizes were dripping off of them. The lights in the shop were left on which surprised me. It looked like someone had just put down their tools and ran away. I could not, however, believe what I saw to our right.

It was a fighter jet that looked so shiny, it could have been freshly polished the day before. The top glass dome that came down over the pilot was in the up position, making it so we could go look inside if we could get to it. A rolling platform ladder was close by, I saw, and I immediately got excited.

"What the hell!" I heard from behind us.

I circled around but could not see past Roman to see who had spoken. Shots from an automatic rifle rang out before I could do anything and I saw Roman fall. Chris came through the doorway behind where Roman had come in and I heard the distinct sound of his rifle being fired. Other shots rang out from somewhere and I turned around to see the glass dome on the fighter jet shatter. A bullet hit the floor at my feet and several more traveled up the door frame beside me. I fired at nothing as I yelled the call for getting us out of there.

As I continued to fire, I saw Jake pulling an unconscious Roman out of the doorway we came in at. George fired at something and then stood with me and bravely reloaded his double-barreled shotgun. I fired at someone taking aim at him and continued to pepper the room. I am not sure if I got anyone. I pushed George out of the room after he again fired both barrels.

I quickly moved with him out the doorway and closed it. We sprinted down the hallway and I closed the door behind us as we all made it outside. I remember the rain stinging my eyes for some reason more than I remember exactly what happened next. I saw Jake cutting the fence as Roman laid at his feet, everyone else covering him. Bullets came through the back walls of the hanger, I know, and I took one to the leg which did not even seem real. Turning around, I fired back through the wall. I remember hearing a loud alarm going off and finally seeing a hole in the fence large enough for us to fit through. We all ran with some haste through, although Jake and Sterling entirely carried Roman. We all made it over the top of the short hill.

I looked back as we made it to the safety the hill provided. Now able to see over the hanger building, I saw at least twenty people, dressed in different apparel, running toward the hanger. No one came out of the back doors there. I ducked down and we all turned and ran quickly north. My disappointment at the way this campaign started filled every part of me.

CHAPTER 6

The hills around the compound were not the kind that were going to give us much to hide in. We did move as fast as we could back to the farm to gather our horses but we did slow up a bit having to carry Roman. We switched off, two of us carrying him entirely and me losing hope for his survival.

I told Chris to break off and flank us, trying to give us a chance if the people from the compound followed. I also told him not to go too far and watched him and Laura move to our left, still keeping up with us. I hoped for nothing more than to be on horseback.

Looking back, I only saw the hills with the fence at the top that we had seen on the way there. I figured if they were going to come after us, it most likely would be from a different way than we had escaped from. I had no doubt they would come fast. I turned and concentrated on running with Roman and tried to ignore the small ache coming from my leg.

We made it over another hill and looked down on the pumpkin patch that we had avoided earlier. I was glad to see it and ran headlong into it. I watched the barn, not too far off that held our horses, getting closer and my heart lifted a bit. Nothing moved there and I tried all that I could to keep from thinking about the pain tearing at my calves and ankles from the prickly pumpkin vines.

I was surprised and more than a little relieved when we raced through the yard of the farmhouse and made it back to the barn. Sterling and I put Roman down inside one of the empty stalls. Shay ran in behind us and looked at him with some worry. She pulled at his buckled-on vest and could not find a way of getting it off quickly. I came to help her but she was already looking at something else. I watched her put her fingers on his neck. Looking up at me, she shook her head.

"What!?" I asked her.

She shook her head again. I ripped at the buckles and got his vest open. I looked at her, willing her to now move in and do her work. I ripped open his shirt and still she did not move.

"They got him right in the neck," she told me. "He was gone the second it happened."

Looking at his throat, I saw where the bullet had entered. Moving his head to the side, I looked at where the bullet exited through the vertebrates at the back of his neck and knew immediately that she was right. I knew, though I did not want to acknowledge it. This man we had barely gotten to know was already gone.

"How's your leg?" she asked.

I looked down at it and saw blood streaking my lower right calf. I shrugged and Shay came in for a closer look. I moved off and she stood up and watched me go.

THE END, AS IT HAPPENS TO THEM

"Anyone else hit," she asked. No one answered.

I checked my rifle as I moved over to the stall that held my horse. I saw Davina had already gotten our horses ready and had mounted hers. She handed me the reins as I came in. I led him slowly out of the stall.

"What are we going to do with Roman?" Chris asked me.

"Grab some rope," I told him. "Someone grab his horse and make it quick."

I ran over to him and with Sterling's help, we lifted him into the saddle of the horse Laura brought in. Chris tied his hands and feet together under the horse. I told him to tie him tight and Chris added a couple of more loops. Everyone else ran to their horse then and Laura led Roman's horse behind her and got on hers.

I jumped into the saddle and rode outside. I looked at the hills toward the compound. I did not see any movement and was glad for that at least. I was not sure how much longer that would be true so I called to everyone and kicked my horse into action. He moved rapidly under me and pulled us both back north, the rest of the team following.

We slowed after a few miles. I thought I had taken about the same way and looked at my GPS several times. However, we did not pass the watering hole that held all of the cows from earlier. With a shrug at that I again kicked my horse and we ran on at a full gallop. I looked several times and found that Roman was still tied on tight.

The tracks finally materialized ahead and we slowed as we neared. We turned west and before too long we came to the train. We loaded up in silence and I felt us start off before a full minute passed. I made it to the burn chamber room and sat looking out over the plains flowing by. I held my rifle to my shoulder and watched the tops of the hills and willed there to be no movement.

I calmed down from the sheer rush of excitement that we had just gone through. I played over how we could have done a few things differently but then pulled away from doing that to myself. The danger faded away behind us and I sat down in the doorway of the burn chamber room. I pulled out pen and paper and wrote a bit of this manuscript. I am sorry if the disappointment I felt then found its way a bit into the first part of these writings though in truth I did not get very far.

Time barely passed and the sun started to dip a bit lower, though I only knew that because the light was beginning to fade. It was easy to see that nighttime would soon be upon us. I wondered if I felt hungry but found that for some reason I was not. I watched George open the back door of the cabin and welcomed the coffee that he brought.

He leaned over the rail and looked out over the plains with me. We did not talk for a while and I found I liked the companionship of him standing there. As I sipped about half of my coffee down I stood up and leaned against the door frame.

"Sorry, but we better not think we are out of this yet," he told me.

"What do you mean?" I asked.

"We should get off this track as fast as we can," he said. "There's a switch track about ten minutes ahead of us. It will turn us south a little but we don't have to stay that way for long. There's one just a few minutes after that which can get us heading east again. I think that should throw anyone off that's looking to follow us."

I acknowledged what he said and told him I would do whatever he needed me to do. He said he could take care of it but I insisted on helping. He told me when and where to throw the levers as we made it to them and before too long we were again heading east and past any worry of pursuit, having taken four different turns. I made a mental note to check and see where we had gone. I made it back to the burn chamber room and sat down again. George came over and stood at the railing of the catwalk. We both said nothing for some time, letting the small mist of moister that was left of the storm, that had finally passed, clean one side of our faces.

"Hell of a thing," he said finally.

"Yeah, sure is," I said, not knowing if there was more I needed to say. "I'd love to blame someone but that kind of stuff is just going to happen no matter what we do."

"It ain't no one's fault, that's for sure," he said softly, looking over at me and then back over the rail.

"I know," I told him. "We'll just have to move on and get this done so that we can all go home."

"I got a little scotch up there if you're interested," he told me, leaning a little closer.

"Well I think that would be just the thing," I told him.

He moved off to the cabin and brought back two tin cups and an almost empty bottle of some fine-named scotch. He told me when he saw me reading the label that it was not exactly what the bottle said it was. I smiled and took it as he handed it to me. We made some toast to our fallen comrade that I remember meant a lot at the time but now I cannot quite remember how it went. It really only mattered to me that we sent our deepest respects to Roman and wished him well on his journey. We threw the bottle overboard and heard it break among the rocks that flew by under us. George turned with a smile.

"Right here," I told George.

We stopped then and dug Roman a grave. We all pitched in and made quick work of it. We lowered him in and covered him up. I looked at the hills and tried to remember the exact look of the area.

"I'll find us a safe place for the night somewhere up ahead," George told me and moved back up into the cabin.

I climbed aboard behind him and sat down in the doorway again. Everyone slowly got on board and I saw Davina give me a smile and head back into George's boxcar. I watched the night grow closer and again let my thoughts carry me through our mission ahead, slowing down and replaying the part where we found Kevin and tore him limb from limb. It did not help, however, and I stood up and thought of how to better spend my time.

I made my way back to George's boxcar, passing through the caboose and Margie cooking. She smiled and I patted her shoulder as I moved on. I found Jake, as I always did in the boxcar, talking on the radio. Shay and Sterling, I was glad to see were again at the work bench, looking over a laptop. I went to Jake and asked for a report. Davina moved up beside me and her hand found mine.

"Weather looks to be like this for the whole night," Jake told me. "They told NASA what we found and it didn't sound like they were too happy about it. Sounded like they had high hopes of that being the place."

"Yeah, there's a lot of that going around," I told him and tried to keep a lid on my anger over the situation. He nodded.

"April said they are going to find another likely place for us to check out," he said.

"Not sure I'm liking this guinea pig, goose chase crap," I said. "Tell them I'd want to know what kind of information they are going off of that tells them what place is next. It sounded like they knew what they were talking about on this last one. I don't think we'll walk in so easily on the next one. They had the information, that's why we're out here, but I'll be damned if we're risking our lives to clear out facilities that are someone else's homes. They need to get their crap straight." I paused here in the tirade I was on. "It ain't you, Jake. I just needed to say that and you were listening. Let's see what they can tell us before we head into whatever else they think they know."

"I'll get on that and have some answers for you," he told me. "I'll tell home not to put it to them nicely like either."

"That's why you're on that thing, Jake," I told him.

I moved over to where Shay and Sterling were looking at the laptop. They looked up as Davina and I came over and seemed to be wondering what to say. I looked to see what part they were watching on the computer and saw some nurse talking. I lifted my head to them and they only shrugged.

"Nothing yet," they both said. "I think we are kind of getting a clear picture though."

"Well, I appreciate you guys going through it," I told them. "I know some of it's pretty bad."

"No problem," Shay said. "We're looking at everything, including patient sheets when we can get a clear view. We're hoping they will tell us where they came from. We may come across something."

"I think that's all a great idea," Davina told them and I agreed.

We moved out of the boxcar and back up to the engine. We talked to Margie in the caboose a bit but really the conversation was pretty dry, probably because all of our minds were on something else. We sat together looking out over the plains and watched the darkness begin to wax stronger. The rain had basically stopped, though we could tell the wind was blowing pretty hard. Davina laid her head on my chest as I leaned against the frame of the window. The sky changed colors beautifully.

We finally slowed when the light had mostly faded. I did see us pass a small river and I remembered seeing on the map one called Beaver Creek. It did not flow much but it did add to the landscape. We also passed a very old ghost town that had several buildings, all of which were falling apart. None of these must have caught George's eye as we zoomed right passed them. Now it seemed, however, he had found something a short distance ahead.

We finally stopped and I saw the place George chose for us to spend the night was beside another train. There was nothing special about the spot, save that it was in a bit of a low spot. I saw an irrigation ditch running not too far away. Pulling alongside of that train, however, felt a little weird. (I guess I was not used to something being so close like it was.) Davina and I stood up and left the caboose with Margie. We stepped to the ground just as George did.

"What do you think?" he asked. I took a second to respond and he must have noticed. "There's a hill behind us and this train here is blocking our other side. What could be better?"

"I think it will do just fine," Davina told him before I could put the words together. I nodded agreement.

"Looks like an old grain carrier," George told me. "We'll have to check some of the cars before we go. They could be full of corn flour. They ain't oil tankers but that would just be too much to ask."

"That would be cool," I told him, warming to the spot a little.

"Hey, I saw that irrigation ditch was running," George said. "Now that's just plain miraculous. I think I'll go have a look at it. We'll fill up before we head out in the morning." Davina and I smiled at each other.

We watched George walk around the front of the engine and we decided to walk alongside of our new neighbor. We had come to about the middle of that train before we stopped but I was interested in what the engine looked like. I figured to take a stroll to have a look, seeing everyone already taking care of our security needs. I got a wink from Chris as we got close.

"The horses are a little skittish for some reason," he told me. "I brought some long corral panels from home this time. I think I'll set them up on the other side and keep them penned in close tonight."

"Need some help?" Davina asked.

"No, we can get it," he told us.

"No, we'll help," I told him. "It'll go faster that way."

We opened the door on the other side of our boxcar and that felt odd; we had not ever opened it before. Laura and Davina handed us the eight foot panels and

THE END, AS IT HAPPENS TO THEM

Chris and I set them beside the ditch that was just down a little slope beside the train. It did not take long and we soon had about a twenty by thirty foot corral hooked together for the horses.

Davina and I moved on then and went to look at the engine at the front of the other train. Shay and Sterling wanted to come so we all went. It seemed to take a while but finally we saw it just ahead.

Actually there were three engines. They were the modern kind so I really was not sure what to expect inside. As we got closer to climbing the rear ladder I grew excited. I did, however, let the ladies go first. Looking at the small group I saw we were all pretty excited. It seemed silly but we were ready for a little bit of that.

We walked along the catwalk that led to the cabin of the engine. Shay was first and opened the door. She had pulled out a flashlight and used it to look inside. I pushed from behind and Sterling helped, piling everyone inside of the cabin. Grabbing my flashlight I looked around as well.

The cabin was smaller than I would have thought, maybe because I was used to ours. There were two swivel chairs each at the far side window and one at the right side window where the driver sat. The driver's side chair was up close to a set of computer screens and switch panels. There were even small screens overhead for the drivers and paddles of some sort on the floor. A CB mic dangled from where it was supposed to be hooked. I was surprised also that there was no table at the back of the cabin, just different sized panels.

It immediately felt crowded in there. I saw in the middle of the cabin there was a little stairwell that headed down about four steps and ended at a door. My wonder grew but Sterling beat me to the railing there, though I tried hard to push him out of the way. He was however, in the better position and took his sweet time in going down, acting like everything on the walls in the well were something to look at. We all watched him with some annoyance. Finally, he turned to the door and opened it.

We could see it opened to a small room at the very front of the engine. I pushed my way past Sterling with the help of Davina, Shay coming in behind her. This room was much tighter than the cabin though it had a lot more of the pipes and tubes that I was used to seeing in George's train. I did see a set of lockers before anyone else and opened the first one I could reach.

I saw a pair of coveralls that had the name Carter on them. An old pair of oily boots sat in the bottom of the locker beside a tool bag. A lunch box was laying sideways on a top shelf and I pulled it down. Removing the thermos from the top of it and feeling that it was full, I set it back on the top shelf and opened the lunch box.

I saw the melted nutty bar first and grinned. Some type of sandwich on what looked like dark rye had long since shriveled to half its original size. I opened a small container and saw that it was a mass of something unrecognizable. A small bag of chips rounded out the discovery. Taking them I closed the box and put it back.

I opened the bag of chips and tried one. It was still crispy and I got several groans. I turned and offered the rest some and only Sterling took one. With a look of delight he dived in for another.

"What, they're sour cream and onion?" I asked the ladies. They only shook their heads and opened the other locker.

They did not seem excited with anything they found and I turned to the thermos. It was a nice type and immediately I knew I would keep it. Opening it I could not tell what it had once been, though I think I had gotten a small whiff of coffee. I did not brave a close smell but dumped it in the corner. With the place fully explored, Davina opened the front door of the small room and we all made it out to the front catwalk of the engine. I left my empty bag of chips back inside the room and closed the door behind us.

We made it to the ground and started back toward our train. We caught site of George coming and gave him a wave. He smiled and looked to be wondering if we had found anything of interest. He pulled up in front of us.

"I definitely like our ride better," I told him.

"Without a doubt," Sterling helped.

"Yeah, there isn't much to these newer ones," George told us. "But they do carry a lot of oil." I had not thought of that. "They're diesel engines so the oil isn't much better than sludge but it is refined a bit which is all we'll need."

"Well, if you'll get out the wagon, I'll help," I told him.

"No, Margie just put the burrow out to chew on some grass. I'll go get him after a while and take care of this. It's pretty easy stuff." He started to move past us. "I think I'll have a look-see anyways, just in case we can use something they have."

"Sounds good," I told him. "I think we are going to see how dinner is coming and if we can help. I think I volunteered for dishes afterwards so I'm hoping for finger food."

"I think Margie has it already done," he said. "You all get started. I may be a bit."

"I think someone should be with you," I told him.

"I'll stay with him," Sterling said. "I'm not all that hungry anyway and I'd like to get a better look at those things." I did not know he was that interested.

"Okay, check in every now and then," I told him and he nodded as he turned and started talking to George. "Looks like we have our future engineer."

"Yeah, I guess so," Shay said and I could not tell if there was something more in her tone. I waited to hear more from her but nothing came.

"Well, I'm going to go check in with Jake," I said as we got close to the train.

"I'll bring you some dinner," Davina said and I kissed her cheek.

I climbed into George's boxcar and looked for Jake. Not seeing him I started to get a little annoyed. I went back outside and went to our boxcar. Not seeing him there either I took some deep breaths to calm myself. Looking where the horses were corralled, I saw him sitting in the grass next to the small ditch, of course talking on the radio. I climbed to the ground and walked over to him.

"Finding out anything good?" I asked and watched him jump a little. He got to his feet and turned to face me, almost coming to attention.

"NASA told them some new coordinates which Jadee said is kind of far from here, maybe fifty miles or so," he told me. "I wrote them down and figured I could give them to you when I saw you."

"Okay, fine," I told him. "George is looking through that train engine back there but he may want to know that too."

"Really? I wonder what that looks like," he said and immediately seemed embarrassed at his excitement.

"Yeah, I know," I told him. "I looked and it's not very cool at all. Go check it out if you want. Sterling and George are there now. Maybe grab some dinner before you head that way. Sounds like Margie has it ready."

"Yes sir, I'll do that," he said and started to walk off.

"I'll take that radio for a bit," I told him and he turned. "Show me how you've been working it though."

He took it off his shoulders and did a quick run through on what he found everything did. He told me which channels he had been using and how he had been switching them three turns up the dial every new contact. I thought that smart and told him so. I also told him to spend some time and find everyone when they were not doing something else and teach them how to use the thing. He agreed and still stood there.

"That will be all," I told him. He grudgingly moved off.

I looked around and was glad again that the rain had stopped. The wind was still a bit chilly but endurable. The horses seemed to like the freedom from confinement that the boxcar held them in as well as the fresh grass they were now feasting on. I turned back to the radio and turned it on.

"Come in, home base," I told the headset as I put it on. I liked the newer style that fit over your ears like headphones with the mic that came down to your mouth.

"Is that you, dad?" I heard April ask.

"Yeah, it's me, how's it going?" I asked her.

"It's going good," she told me. "Jadee still hasn't stopped. She's pretty intent on going over everything NASA is sending. I think they are sending a lot too."

"Well, let's hope that it's worth something," I told her.

"I'm really sorry to hear about Roman," she told me. "I only met him for a little while but he was funny." I did not remember that about him.

"Thanks," I told her.

"Sorry too to hear about that not being the right compound."

"No, those were definitely not doctors and researches that came at us," I told her a little annoyed. "They weren't military either. They looked like just a group put together from all over, kind of like us." I took a few deep breaths.

"Sorry, it sounds rough out there," she told me.

"It doesn't seem like it has to be," I told her, thinking of the horsemen we had seen along the way. "Is there anything they are coming up with that sounds worth looking at?"

"Mack told Jadee that Kevin sent a ton of stuff secretly to that facility you guys were just at," April said. "They are talking about some places in Nebraska and there is a place they are looking at pretty hard that is about fifty miles east of the other place you just left. It seems pretty far north too. Jadee keeps bringing that one up. Really it sounds like there are places all over down there. Sorry to say that."

"I wonder why they think so strongly that Kevin would head this way?" I asked.

"They are pretty intent on it," she said. "Sounds like he started out there or something. They're talking so strong about it. His home town must have been out there."

"Has that McQueen guy gotten anywhere on what he was doing?" I asked.

"They aren't talking about him. Sounded like it was supposed to be a while before he got to where he was going, I thought."

"Yeah, I was just hoping."

"I can understand that," April said softly.

"I still want to talk about why we are out in Kansas of all places," I told her.

"Jake kept asking that and Jadee has been too. They said there are no real medical sites of any significance in Colorado, at least within two hundred miles. They keep saying that Kevin sent supplies to only a few places. Jadee thinks that Kevin must have been leading The Monk, I guess we're calling him Steve now, out this way from California in order to get him to one of those facilities."

"But why did they stop before they got there?" I asked.

"Maybe Steve got tired of listening to him and wanted to stop at that compound we found them in," she said. "At least that's what the discussion is sounding like here. NASA is saying they followed them through a couple of states, looking through different compounds. Steve joined up somewhere and got run off or something like that. Sounds like they were collecting supplies along the way after that but more for survival. They are pretty convinced he's headed out there. They keep saying they are sure he doesn't know they found out about his shipments."

"They told me that too but I wonder how they are so sure."

"I don't know. They told Jadee they found a lot of stuff when Steve kidnapped Kevin and made him go with him. Sounds like they found a lot of pretty bad stuff. Jadee has been looking over a lot of it."

"So what's going on with this facility east of us?" I asked, feeling a little spent as my mind was trying to put everything in place.

"Sounds like it's a smaller facility but more of an underground one," she told me. "They said it was always kind of a back burner kind of one, something that never really got used much. They said it would fit Kevin's style to choose something like it. They said too that he sent some weird stuff to an Army Reserve unit in the area. They are talking about him sending stuff that would have just sat on a shelf and seemed innocent enough but that he would definitely need now."

"Sounds like we should visit this reserve unit first," I told her.

"They were not sure if the stuff would still be there," she said. "They figure he could have contacted them directly and had them send it to the facility and that would not show up anywhere. There would be no way of them knowing if he did that or not."

"Okay, I think fifty more miles isn't too far out of our way," I told her. "Did you give Jake the coordinates?"

"I did," she said.

"Great," I told her. "Tell Jadee to get some rest before she burns out."

"I will tell her," she said.

"Just make sure she eats something then," I said.

"Will do. Dan and some other guys are here. They brought some tents and set them up outside."

"That's awesome," I told her. "That kind of makes me feel better."

"We'll be fine here," she told me. "Vince is going crazy trying to figure out what to do. He has that Jessie guy walking around the perimeter."

"Hopefully that goes away soon," I said and she agreed. "Go have some dinner."

"I already did," she said. "Marla made beef stew."

"Where'd you get that?" I asked.

"One of the guys that came with Dan brought it for her to make," she said. "It was delicious. It almost melted in your mouth and with a little bit of the fresh veggies from the garden, steamed to perfection."

"You are an evil daughter," I told her. "I've always liked Chris best."

"Yeah, sure," she laughed. "Take care out there. Are you going to try to make it to that place tonight?"

"No, I think we will move on from here in the morning," I told her. "George is getting some fuel from these engines we stopped by."

"I guess I would not have thought of that, needing fuel all the time I mean. Okay, well I'll be here whenever you need me."

"That makes me feel good kiddo," I told her. "Night, Honey."

"Good night, dad," she said and I turned off the radio.

I sat there for a while. Things were going pretty fast and not much was in our control. We could only hope for the outcome we wanted. It was not a good feeling to have but I knew I had to make the best of what it was. I sorted out some of my thoughts before I went back to join the others. I stood up and shouldered the radio. It was heavier than it looked.

I met Davina in our boxcar and saw that she had waited to eat with me. It was a stew of some kind and I figured it would probably not be as good as what April had eaten. It was a bit cold but did hit the spot. Looking up at my wife I saw her looking at me sideways.

"What?" I asked her.

"A little hungry were we?" she asked and pointed to my bowl. It was entirely clean and I barely remembered what it tasted like. I smiled back at her, seeing her bowl only half gone.

"Sorry," I told her.

"No problem," she laughed. "Hear anything good from home?"

"They think they have a place for us to try," I told her. "It's about fifty miles east. I think we should all sit down and see what we come up with."

"That sounds good," she said. "Jake and George are probably still in the caboose," she told me. "They came back a few minutes ago. It seems Sterling has found a new passion." I was glad to hear that.

"Maybe we should move in there and see what everyone wants to do," I told her.

She drank down the rest of her stew and we walked slowly to the caboose. I turned and kissed her deeply before we climbed the steps. She seemed to want more and held me there for some time. She indicated the engine and I smiled.

"Definitely later," I told her. She nodded and we entered the caboose together.

I smelled more of the stew that was still cooking as I entered. I had my bowl in hand and, walking over to the stove, I refilled it. Seeing Jake, I brought him back the radio and he scooted it under his legs. I sat down across from him and Margie at the table by the entrance and Davina slid in beside me. Looking around I saw everyone inside.

"I was just heading out for a watch," Chris told me.

"No, maybe we should talk a bit," I said, putting down my spoon. "It looks like they have another place for us to look at."

"What's so special about this one?" Laura asked and everyone mumbled something that said they wanted to know as well.

"I guess Kevin was sending stuff close by during his research in California," I told them. "He sent it to some Reserve Unit and they said he could have easily sent it to the nearby facility without anyone thinking twice about it."

"Sounds like a good enough reason to give it a try," George said.

"I agree," Sterling said and everyone seemed to concur.

"Okay, it's about fifty miles ahead, something like northeast of here," I told them. "I don't think we need to rush in and I don't think we should move out in the open much anymore."

"We leaving in the morning then?" Chris asked.

"I think that would be best," I told him. "How long will it take you to get the oil out of those engines?" I looked at George.

"I'll get right on it," he told me. "I'll have it all sewed up in an hour."

"I wouldn't mind helping you with that!" Sterling said a little too excited. "It would be good for some of us to know a bit more about this train stuff." I saw George barely give a sign of annoyance and wished I had a way to help him.

"Okay, let's set a watch and be ready before the sun's up to move out of here," I told everyone.

"I wouldn't mind looking over those coordinates if you got 'em," George said.

"I'll get them to you and look over your shoulder at your maps if you don't mind," I told him.

"Sure thing," he said and, getting up, refilled his bowl with hot stew.

"Any more rain on the way?" Shay asked Jake.

"Looks like none overnight but a good chance tomorrow," he said over his shoulder.

I went back to my bowl and finished it off. George and Sterling headed out as did Chris and Laura. Jake took the radio and left. Davina stayed sitting beside me. We all talked and Shay soon joined in. I think we laughed easily for the first time in a while and I was not sure why. We found out different things about each other, including the fact that Margie once worked as a bartender. She would not go into many details. She would not say anything when I asked if that was before George or after. We moved on from there as the others too grew interested in what Margie may be hiding. We found out Shay took a Belly Dancing class on a dare and even did a stage performance afterward. She said that was not part of the class but she did it when she was out with her friends and had drank a little too much. (I told her I would not write that part but she will never know.) The night wore on as we laughed but we eventually got quiet.

With little else to do I took Davina's hand and excused myself. We headed back to our boxcar. I will not here mention how we passed the first hour of the evening.

CHAPTER 7

There were many sounds coming from outside. I laid there and tried to figure them all out and was glad that they were all some sort of animal or insect. The horses did move around a bit but it seemed they were just moving to get more grass. Davina's soft breathing told me she was asleep and brought a calm over me. I thought about staying there but finally I had to get up.

George had gotten his donkey hooked up to the small trailer that held the small oil tank they used to transport any volume of oil they found back to the train. I wondered at how much oil those other engines held but knew that George was already getting enough questions from Sterling. I figured I would go see how Shay was getting on with the computer, if she was still up.

I walked into the other boxcar and saw a small light on at the workbench. Shay was in fact still awake and leaning back in her chair with the laptop in her lap. The light from its screen reflected on her face. I made some sound as I came in so as not to scare her.

"Finding anything good?" I asked her.

"Not really," she said looking over at me. "Mostly stuff I've already heard about and now am having to look at."

"Sorry about that," I told her.

"No, I'm not complaining about the assignment," she said defensively. "It's just a lot of sick stuff to go through and I've been rewinding it to be able to look at everything. Everything so far is California stuff."

"I think I can understand that getting a little old," I told her and came and found a stool at the work bench.

"How's the leg feeling?" she asked with some concern.

"It's fine," I told her and really, it barely felt injured at all.

"You should stay off of it for a while," she said.

"I will," I lied and she knew it. She looked back at the computer screen.

"I did open some stuff about some of the other scientists I think McQueen is looking for," she said.

"What?" I asked with earnest, jumping up and coming around her. "I haven't seen any of that."

"Really? It was in a folder but kind of hard to get to. I can go back there if you want to see some of it."

"Is it going to mess up what you are doing now?" I asked, probably showing some weird excitement at this new information.

"No, I could use the break," she said and turned the laptop so I could sit and both of us could see. "I'll just close this down." Her hands moved around the keyboard quickly. "Pretty cool being able to work on a laptop again. I even saw he had a few tablets in there. I think that would spoil me though." We both smiled. "Here's the file right here. It's this one that says 'research teams'. If we click on that it brings us to 'solutions' and then we click 'file browser'. It's almost like they tried to delete these files but didn't empty them out of the hard drive so that whatever they downloaded, this got attached to it. Whoever did this was not very good with computers."

"Like me," I said. "Whenever someone wanted me to send them something in an email or whatever I'd just yell for Davina. She'd have to make everything so easy for me. I couldn't even turn the TV on. Those damn remotes got pretty complex." She looked at me and I think raised her eyebrows a little.

"Well, this was something like that," she said and clicked on different headlines. "This here is where Kevin and some other science guys are talking about some findings. I've looked over every inch of the background and watched every paper that got turned over. Nothing real obvious as to where they are or who they are? Kevin and them seem to be close friends though. They talk like drinking buddies."

"Why do you think it's the guys McQueen is going after?" I asked her.

"Just a guess," she said. "They show up quite a bit in some of this stuff. Everyone else, Kevin just talks down to and seems to not even listen to what they are saying. These guys are working off of the same research stuff as Kevin too."

"That makes sense," I told her. "Anything that would explain what we already know but also give us a clue we need?" I asked and hoped.

"Not yet," she said, taking in a deep breath and letting it out slowly. "I do think I found those guys that signaled us from Kenya though."

"No way!" I told her. "What did they have on them?"

"I'll pull that up," she said and played the keyboard again. "It's a research lab in Kenya is all. It's kind of a small one too. They didn't seem real interested in carrying the research anywhere close to what Kevin was doing. They did some gross stuff to apes and all but it pretty much stopped there. It looks like they were scared and sent the research as a last request to some team they were supposed to be working with here. There's some video of them ready to disappear and never tell anyone where they were going. Sounded like they were done being a part of the research stuff long before they sent us anything. It sounds like they were trying to tell someone about the research Kevin and the others were doing. Sounded like only two of them were real serious about not letting some of the findings get to the wrong places. The guy even wrote on here a little note that said he was willing to die getting the info safely where it belonged. He specifically mentions us and says where we're to get it to in Missouri. There's door codes and everything. There's coordinates to the lab there."

"We should look at that a lot closer," I told her.

"I looked at every inch of that, a bunch of times," she said. "Here's the file." She clicked on it.

We both watched it and she had not left out telling me anything. She gave a commentary all the way through which was a perfect synopsis of the whole thing. We watched it to the end.

"There really does seem to be nothing there that could help us," she told me. "I really should have thought to bring it up earlier. We should report that to NASA maybe. They may know where that guy was headed. Maybe he in turn knows a little more about what we need to know." I saw her shrug. "I know it's grasping at straws but it may be worth a try."

"You're right, it may," I said. "You saw how they were, though. They definitely were not the brutal type. You may just be bringing them down on the guy. It sounded like they were more the whistle blowers. They weren't trying to communicate with Kevin, that's for sure. They kinda seemed amazed at what the information was. Sounds like it got to them by accident. Their stuff is on there too and they were trying to show someone they weren't part of any of it. Maybe we should tread lightly and see if NASA already has seen this stuff. Maybe we play a little dumb and see if NASA will tell us what they think it all means. Maybe we head to Missouri next, if we have to. I wouldn't mind hearing their answer."

"Me either," she said. "But I'm sure they've seen this."

"Maybe you should get some sleep and take another crack at it in the morning," I told her. "We'll talk to Jake and see what we come up with from NASA."

"No, I'm up for a little bit more," she said. "It's just like my old days studying for some test. The late hours is when it all starts coming together." I smiled.

"Mind showing me some of the stuff with the ones showing who Kevin is getting along with so well?" I asked her.

"Sure let's just click on this one here and go from there," she said. She backed quickly out to the start and hit some more keys.

I watched a video start that had Kevin and another scientist talking back and forth, though it only showed Kevin's face. They talked about something that must have only meant something to themselves as far as some patient or other. They seemed to laugh at different ideas in their research. That seemed to get us nowhere so Shay moved on.

We went through several different files and there seemed to be no end in sight, with us getting nothing that would even seem to help. The screen showed different faces several times and only a few of which Kevin seemed to acknowledge. It did seem however, that there was an inner circle.

"They seem to be talking in some code," I finally said. "I don't really know what they are saying with a lot of this stuff. Is it some sort of medical way of talking?"

"Some of it is but a lot seems to be from them knowing what the other one is talking about, like knowing the results of a test and talking about what the test was about," she said. "We don't even know what subject the test was about let alone the answers to the questions. They're talking in some doctor jargon no doubt, but more in research terms. It seems to be going nowhere."

"Do you think that could be what we're looking for?" I asked, wondering if we stumbled onto something.

"You mean like a code kind of thing?" Shay asked and wasn't really talking to me. She pulled up closer to the screen. "Does that say 'Kenya Research' there on the clipboard that nurse is holding?"

I looked as she pointed. She rewound the footage a little and then let it play again. I watched as a nurse came into the screen and started adding some information to a computer. Sure enough it said 'Kenya' on one of the sheets. My heart leapt and then I wondered why.

"What does that mean?" I asked.

"I don't know," she told me. I felt a little silly. "I have seen where that facility and where those people are. That nurse there is in a California facility. They must be using something that Kenya published or sent in as part of their research documenting. That happens a lot." She pulled back and looked over at me. "I do like what you were saying about them saying something but kind of hiding it in some doctor code kind of thing. I think I'll look more into these files and keep an eye out for that. It looks like Kenya was researching and sending info to these guys without knowing what the results were getting used for. They must have found out and tried to shut down the lab there. I wonder if NASA will understand it that way."

"Well, maybe that's something we can help with," I told her and knew the enormous job ahead for her. "Keep me in the loop on this stuff. And Shay, don't go crazy in here on us."

"That is a very good possibility," she said with a laugh. "Maybe you should get some rest. I'll keep you posted."

"Sounds good," I told her. "Sounds like Sterling is liking this train stuff."

"Yeah that seemed to come out of nowhere, didn't it," she said with furrowed forehead.

"I think he's getting on George's nerves a little," I told her and we both chuckled. We must have been getting tired. "I'll talk to you in the morning." She gave me a small wave and went back to her laptop.

I left the boxcar and headed for the burn chamber to see if George and Sterling were done with the oil transporting. I found them finished and both sitting in some collapsible chairs. Coming up to them I heard them talking easily about something to do with welding. It seems I came in at the part where George had asked some technical question and Sterling was explaining the principles of metal expansion.

"Sounds pretty deep," I said as I found a place to sit on the backside of the small trailer they had used to transport the oil.

"Yeah, Sterling here was a union welder at one time," George said. "I've needed some of that done on a project or two with ol' Rusty there. I think my friend here is just the ticket." I was wondering if he was just being nice as I had seen lots of welding already done all over the train.

"Well, it sounds like something to keep you out of trouble," I told him.

"Yeah, I think I could work for twenty years on this thing before I get everything where I want it," George said, looking off and thinking about something.

"What are you thinking you need welded?" I asked him.

"I'm wanting to permanently install an oil pump that will fit into the lower side of the tanker there," he said, pointing to some spot. "It sure would make things easier."

"And we were thinking of something that will make getting the hoses out a lot more efficient," Sterling said. "It's the kind of stuff that I could think about all of the time." I was glad to hear that.

"Did you guys empty those engines of all of their oil then?" I asked.

"Every last drop," George told me. "It got us back into the safe zone for a while."

"That sounds great," I told him and felt one burden come off of my shoulders.

We talked on then about nothing in particular. We did talk long about welding and the like, though I knew little on the subject. (I think I knew even less about it when we moved on to talking about other things.) Nothing came up about the mission we were on and I was happy about that. Looking at my watch I saw it was time for me to take watch.

I relieved Chris and Laura and got the report that nothing was moving though a badger had been spotted by Laura. She told me that Margie had wanted to know when such things were found. She said Margie had gone out with her bow and killed it. She said something about badgers being good medicine, I was told and had to hold back a smirk.

"She went out there with some cool night vision scope thing and came back with the thing over her shoulder," Chris said. "It's cool. She's like this real Indian and also like a modern warrior with tech all rolled into one." Laura and I both smiled at him.

I took over the watch and did a few wide circles around the area. Several times I heard thunder rolling and saw some lightning in the background. The storm seemed to be passing around us which I was glad about. I was also glad for a quiet watch and after a few hours I called Jake to take over.

I went and laid beside Davina and passed a couple of hours thinking. It did not help me much and I did not come to any conclusions. I did however feel some energy return and had to be happy with that.

I heard Jake call Sterling to take over the watch. It was an hour before the sun would start to lighten the horizon. I got up and decided to go for a run. I went to tell Sterling that I would be going ahead of us and he looked at me a little weird but shrugged.

I set out at a jog, giving my leg a chance to hurt if it was going to. When it felt okay, I finally started racing down the tracks. It felt good and also seemed like something I had not done in quite a while. I felt my legs burn but then energy returned to them and filled me. I was not sure how far I got before I slowed and did some walking.

I saw the ditch beside the tracks divide a couple of times and finally dry up. A few times I passed some groves of stunted trees. I did also manage to scare a few cows along the way. It was pretty dark out though, and nothing seemed of interest.

I made it back to the train and went into the irrigation ditch to bathe. It was pretty cold but it felt good. I made my way dripping back into our boxcar and found the extra pair of clothes Davina had packed for me. I thought of going back and shaving when I found my razor in one of the pockets of my bag. I frowned and put it back, thinking to do it sometime later. When I walked out of the car I saw the eastern horizon starting to glow.

I found Sterling and told him to go get some coffee. He said he was okay and I left him there to go get some for myself. I instead asked him to wake everyone up as I moved off.

I got some water from the irrigation ditch and set it on the grill that had been put on the fifty gallon drum George had given us to heat our car. I tossed in some wood and paper and started the fire going. I went over to the door and watched the horizon getting brighter. The light that played with the colors there was beautiful.

Soon my coffee water was ready and I got myself a cup and stirred in my instant coffee. I saw Chris and Laura moving around. We said our pleasantries, though they looked ill ready for the day. I took some coffee to Davina and got a gorgeous smile for my effort. I always thought she looked beautiful as she turned over in the morning and I took some time to enjoy it. She looked at me weird as she took her coffee and sat up. I caught sight of her nakedness before she had time to pull a blanket high enough to cover herself. It was amazing what coffee could do in the morning.

"We should get moving soon," I told her. She looked and saw the soft glow of morning coming through the door beyond the curtain that worked to separate a small area for us from the rest of the car.

I took some time then and looked around at what Chris and Laura had done with our boxcar, sorry I had not taken the time before. They had hung some of the long canvas, they had found in the armory storage area, from the ceiling of the boxcar and made one entire side into several rooms, complete with a hallway that went down the center. The canvas hung to the floor and was fastened somehow there. A small flap had been expertly made to make an easy entranceway that could be tied back or secured for privacy. Our room was right next to the large doorway with the flap pulled open now to the morning. Inside our small room I saw had been placed three military air mattresses somehow joined together. I went then and looked at the fold-up table that had been placed in the corner of our room. I saw it was screwed to the floor. Two folding chairs had also been screwed to the floor on each side to the table and pushing on them I found them quite secure. Two footlockers were secured next to the flap that worked as a door. I was well pleased with what they had done so far.

I left our room and looked at the fifty gallon drum that worked as our heater/stove. I saw a chain hooked to the two points at the top of it and those connected to hooks in the floor. A frame to hold wood was off to the side and full of small pieces of two-by-fours and other various remnants of wood. I moved over to the side the horses took up.

I saw immediately that I had missed much of what my son and Laura had done. They had basically made the place there into a mini-barn, with a small stall for each horse and even a section toward the front to store some hay and grain. A bucket of water hung from the front of each stall. It was a quick job of cutting the boards and screwing them together but what they had done was very impressive and I was again sorry I had not noticed it earlier. They both deserved to be well praised.

I turned and saw Davina coming out of our room. She looked ready for battle though her eyes did not agree with that. She walked slowly over to me and then looked outside.

"So are we heading out now or what?" she asked.

"I think we are," I told her. As I said it I saw a tired looking Chris coming down the curtained hallway, followed not too far behind by a fully awake Laura. "Looking like we are about ready to start burning some daylight." I only got an "ugh" from Chris as he sat down on a close by footlocker and started putting his socks on.

"I'll start getting the horses inside," Laura told me.

"Hey, you guys did an awesome job in here by the way," I told them both. "I'm real sorry I didn't notice before."

"Thanks dad," I heard said in a tired voice from Chris.

"Need some coffee son?" Davina asked him. I heard some affirmative reply.

"There's a lot more we want to do," Laura said. "I know the stalls aren't much yet but they work for now."

"No, I think they are great!" I told her.

"Well, we'll make them a lot better," she said and turned to go outside.

THE END, AS IT HAPPENS TO THEM

I followed her and helped round up the horses. She was pretty good at getting them in the corner to get their lead ropes on, even the ones that were not excited about going back inside so soon. She would hand me the ropes and I would take them inside and put them in the stalls and I am quite sure they were not the right ones. It seemed to work well, though I quickly saw she had the harder job.

When we were all loaded up, with the metal corral pieces nicely stowed in a place designed for that very thing, I went to see how George was getting along with us moving on. I found him inside the cabin and felt the low rumble of the locomotive that said we were ready to go. I cleared my throat and watched him turn.

"I think we were just waiting for you all to load the horses," he told me. "They all set?"

"Yeah, we are ready to get out of here," I told him. "Need me to do anything?"

"No, I think we got it," he said, "but much appreciated."

"Did you get the coordinates of where we are headed?" I asked him. "I think Jake was going to get them."

"Yeah, he gave them to me," George said and walked over to the map. He pointed to the opened Interchange map and, stepping up to it, ran his fingers along some lines there. "I think these are the best tracks to take. Right here is where they said the place was."

"Did Jake say if NASA said where the Reserve Base was that Kevin sent the stuff to?" I asked, looking at where George had pointed.

"Yeah, he said they told him at the town southwest of there," he told me as he walked back to his chair and blew a soft blast through the whistle by pulling a string overhead.

"This town here called Colby?" I asked.

"Jake told me Jadee was getting some info on it now," he said. He blew the whistle again two short times. "Sounded like it wasn't a huge town but big enough." I nodded and looked outside. He made the final whistle.

"It's weird seeing this train right up against us like that but it's good cover," I told him.

"There's a bypass track that runs along this one for a couple of miles," he told me.

He pushed on the lever and we moved ahead slowly. He pushed it a little more and we picked up speed. I went and sat down.

"I took a little jog this morning and I came to the end of the train but there were still tracks beside ours."

"These grain cars aren't very long most of the time. The front two we checked and they are full to the top with grain. Wheat was all the way to the top. It was the unground kind, perfect for storing. Margie had a heyday filling every container we got."

"Wow, sounds like a gold mine if we were to stay anywhere close by."

"Maybe we'll come back this way and pick them up on the way back. We'll just hook right onto them and drag them home."

"That's perfect, George," I told him. "Should we mark where this place is at?"

"Already did," he said and smiled broadly to me.

"I like you running things up here," I smiled back.

"You know what's funny is that train rolled here," he told me as he pushed harder at the levers. I took a second as everyone checked in.

"What does that mean?" I asked him when I heard from everyone.

"Not sure, really," he said. "It was a runaway train is all I know. Nothing to worry about. Trains can roll for miles without a driver. They pick up speed on the downhills that can take them a state away." I calmed a little at hearing that.

"Maybe that means the track is all open ahead," I told him.

"It probably does at that," he told me but I did not believe his tone. I went and looked at the map again.

"Looks like we did some good turns getting away from that last compound," I told him.

"Yeah, and it actually put us on track for a pretty straight run at the next one," he told me as we slowed. "Looks like we will have to switch the rail up ahead. You're up, it looks like."

I felt us slow and looked out the front window into the rising sun. I could see the rails split just ahead and I moved closer to the front door. As we slowed more I went outside and quickly made it to the ground. I ran in front of the train, like I was getting used to doing, and moved the lever. I watched it slide where it was supposed to and gave George the usual sign. I heard the low rumble and waited, jumping onboard as it passed.

I went back into the cabin and sat at my chair for a while. I went and looked at the maps and tried hard to memorize all I could. It seemed to work well, having a good memory of the area before I went out and walked in it.

I moved back into the burn chamber room and sat looking out over the passing landscape. The sun had made it past the horizon and really started shining brightly under the clouds that hung over us. The glare was unreasonable so I looked out over the not too far off hills. I watched some cattle get up and run as we passed and saw several antelope ignore us. Groves of trees passed us now and then and once I saw a small, long abandoned town zoom by. Looking, I still saw the sun glaring in my eyes, making it impossible to see that way.

George startled me as he appeared out of the glare at the catwalk. He moved past me and hit the lever that sent sand through the exhaust. I apologized for not doing that for him but he told me he needed a reason to stop looking into the sun anyway. I smiled and looked ahead.

To my great amazement I watched us turn a little and saw the tracks ahead of us clearly. We were heading down a small hill which put the sun a little higher in the sky and took away its glare. As the tracks came fully into view I saw what looked like some grain cars just ahead. At first I wondered what I was seeing, then with alarm, I knew.

"George, there's cars on the tracks ahead!" I yelled and jumped to my feet.

He raced to the doorway and swung around it to the catwalk with one movement. I followed him with breakneck speed hitting the cabin door frame hard as I tried to rush through it. I saw George yank hard at the levers inside the cabin, jumping into his seat and pushing on things that I did not know what were for. I yelled into my radio to brace for impact as I felt us slowing only a little with the hill only helping our momentum. I knew a crash was imminent.

I saw four grain cars blocking our way and coming so fast that they too looked to be moving. We seemed to be sledding down the small hill toward them and I remember wondering why I did not feel us slowing more, though George was still moving levers that I did not know the meaning of. I remember wondering if the grain inside the cars was going to look like a snow storm from far off. I remember also yelling into my radio for everyone to brace for impact.

CHAPTER 8

We crashed into the cars and the sound of it was deafening. I had been in a car crash once and the noise did not even compare. I was thrown forward but not as violently as I would have thought. I hit the middle round section that came through the floor in the middle of the cabin and bounced into the front side door, which opened and landed me onto the catwalk. I stayed where I was and let the reality of what had happened settle.

We completely stopped and I saw wheat floating down around the catwalk I was laying on. We were still upright which I knew was a good thing. I felt steam coming around me from below and I was not sure that was a good thing. I sat up slowly to make sure everything moved as it was supposed to. When I felt it did, I jumped to my feet.

I yelled into my radio for everyone to check in as I ran into the cabin. Dust was settling still. The dog was in the middle of the floor looking around dazed. Moving past him, I went over to George who was pulling himself up from the floor in front of the other door.

"You okay?" I asked.

"This is Davina, are you okay?" I heard my radio ask.

"Fine, how about you?" I asked, feeling afraid for her.

"I'm good," she said. "Chris and Laura are okay too."

"I'm good, son," George told me. "Go check on everyone else." He reached for a CB looking mic. "Margie, hon, are you okay?" I heard her say she was and asked him in return.

I rushed out of the cabin and down the catwalk to the ground. I saw Davina jumping to the ground from our boxcar and she gave me a nervous expression. I gave her a smile and she returned it. I then looked and saw Shay getting helped down by Sterling though she did not seem to need it. Jake followed Sterling to the ground. Chris and Laura had followed Davina outside from our boxcar. Lastly, I saw Margie making it out of the caboose. I heard George coming down the ladder behind me. I was so glad no one was seriously hurt.

I looked at the engine beside me and did not see anything different. I was worried as I looked forward. I scanned everything in my view I made it to the front, but I did not see anything damaged. I turned and followed George as he started to the front. It was a slow pace we took.

Steam still poured out from underneath and I was hoping that meant nothing too major, though I know that anything different could potentially be disastrous. Making it to the front of the engine finally, I saw what damage we had incurred.

The front bottom piece on the bottom of the locomotive was pushed in, it having been some piece of metal that stuck out and looked to be the triangular bumper. The two steps that went off the end of the catwalk and ended at the ladder were smashed. The ladders themselves were basically gone. Looking where George was inspecting, I saw that the front bumper had been pushed back and up, wedging its remains against the smaller front wheels. I saw him shaking his head and did not chance a question. As we stood there a pipe ruptured and blew steam all around him. He moved out from among the metal pieces.

I looked at the grain cars and saw there were three of the cars still on the tracks. The front car's wheels were pushed back about half way under itself and turned sideways. The front of the car was smashed back into crinkled metal about a quarter of its length. Grain dust still floated in the air but it was clear the car had been empty. Looking with some worry, I saw that the tracks seemed unharmed. I looked over at George with at least a small piece of relief.

"You okay, George?" I asked him. He seemed pulled back to reality.

"Huh? Yeah, I'm fine," he said. "No one's hurt right?" I told him we were all fine. "It could have been a lot worse really. I think we need to check the line to and from the pressure chamber. This steam has to be coming from somewhere." He looked back at us. "It's fixable." I was glad to hear him so optimistic but I was just hoping it was not something else.

I turned and saw everyone looking around where George moved. As he looked at something we all bent over and looked too. As he looked puzzled, I am sure we did too.

"Should we take a few minutes and sit down?" I asked him.

"No, we need to check right away," he said. "Shut down the burner!"

"Set a perimeter!" I yelled as I turned back toward the rear of the engine.

I ran to shut the burner down. As I ran into the room to do that, I saw smoke billowing out of the burn chamber. Staying low and looking into the chamber I saw the mostly full tray that held the oil in the center of the chamber was empty and that the oil was splattered all over the walls of the chamber. The oil was burning still and causing the smoke. I slammed the chamber door and turned off the air intake levers.

I came back out to the ground. I saw Chris and Laura starting to survey the surrounding area with Jake moving along the grain cars. Davina was heading to the back of the train looking all around as well. I was sure the noise of our crash could have been heard for miles. I could only wonder who might come to have a look at what it was, probably in hopes of scavenging a little.

"Chris, Laura, you guys check the horses and get them ready to move out of here," I told them. "Sterling and Shay take over for them." Looking around, I saw there was a hilltop only about a hundred yards out to the north. "I'd like to have you guys give me a report from that hilltop over there," I said pointing north. They nodded and took off running. "Jake," I told my radio, "hold off on calling home. I don't want NASA knowing our every setback. Let's see how this plays out."

I got an affirmative from him as I watched him move to the other side of the train. Checking my rifle, I moved to look for George. I watched as he disappeared under the engine.

"Davina, can you cover our tails back there?" I asked the radio again.

"I'm already here," she said. "I'll keep us clear."

"What shall I do?" Margie asked. I looked over at her, still standing at the front of the train.

"I was hoping you could just jump in wherever you saw fit," I told her.

"No," she said. "I want to be a part of your team. You are in charge and I need to know what you would have me do."

For some reason, it was weird actually hearing the words that I was in charge. The role just seemed to fall naturally to me without it having to be often spoken. Hearing it now from Margie, it did not seem to fit. Maybe I really was not thinking of her as part of the team yet. I shook my head and figured I had better start getting with it or things would fall apart.

"I need someone up high to keep an eye on us," I told her. "Can you get up on that caboose and call out if you see anyone in trouble or anything else that doesn't belong?"

"Yes sir," she told me and that really felt weird. I watched her jog off.

I looked under the locomotive and finally found George on his back among some of the steam shooting out from under some mechanical parts. He was looking intently at something. He moved around as I watched him look at it from a different angle. Turning around to lay on his back again, he looked up and down the underside of the engine.

"I know it's a stupid annoying question, but how does it look?" I yelled over the steam still hissing out. He yelled something back but I could not hear him.

He moved around some more and I followed him. He was running his gloved hand down a pipe and checked a few fittings. Pulling hard on something else I saw what he was trying to move but could not. I hoped at least that was good news. I saw him coming out and waited for him.

"You were saying?" he asked me.

"Sorry, just wondering how she looked," I told him.

"There's a few problems but we won't know if we have the big problem until the steam runs out," he said, seeming to be matter of fact. Maybe it was my own worry but I thought he seemed to be acting a little calloused about the whole thing. I tried to keep that to myself, however. "It will take a bit before that happens."

"How long?" I wondered to him.

"Maybe fifteen minutes," he said. "We could help it if we need to but I want to see how it bleeds off. It's good if it takes longer. It may mean our pressure chamber is still okay. Might as well check out the track up ahead." He turned and walked off and I followed.

We walked over to the grain cars and I could see the dust had mostly settled. The tear in the metal that held the grain was grim just to look at. It was like a huge wound that took some unexplainable force to cause. The smashed parts of the rest of the car looked just as bad.

"We are in place and everything looks clear," I heard Sterling say.

"Copy that," I said. "We may be here for a little bit. How far can you see?"

"I can see everything for miles from here," he told me. "There's a town southeast of us a few miles."

"Small, farm town thing?" I asked.

"No, looks like some grain silos and the like," he said. "It's really far off though, so I can't really tell."

"Okay, keep us clear," I told him.

"Will do," he said.

George walked passed the first grain car, looking underneath as he went. I too looked there to see how the tracks fared. The wheels of the car being pushed back so far made it a little difficult to see the entire rails and I watched as George went in among the wreck. He pulled his head back out and ignored my questioning glance. Moving around, he looked some more and I went in for my own inspection.

The wheels had in fact turned and broke in half as they got pushed back under the grain car. It lifted the car and wedged the metal that held the wheels into one of the grain release mechanisms. One wheel I saw was bent in a severe angle to the others. Holding my breath, I looked at the tracks. They were in perfect shape, though a few of the railroad ties that held them in place were a bit scarred.

"Looks okay to me," I told him, although I had no idea how we were going to move the car off the track to be able to get by it. I heard George only grunt.

He continued down the tracks, looking then at the other cars. He ducked under the next one and then pulled back and looked to the top of it. Walking over to some levers he pushed them and again grunted. He moved on to the next one, doing the same thing. Finally, he had made it to the last one and walked around it. We saw Jake standing at the back of the car, scanning the area.

"How's everything looking?" I asked him.

"I haven't seen any movement at all," he told me. "Looks like some serious clouds are already moving in, though." He indicated with his head down southwest and I turned and looked. "They are moving fast but don't seem to be holding much moisture. It will be windy today if nothing else." I nodded.

"Okay, thanks for the update," I told him. "Keep on it. You doing okay?"

"Yes sir, I'm fine," he said.

"The radio okay?" I asked.

"Yeah, I broke its fall," he said, rubbing his hip a little with a smile. "I think your warning helped a lot." I smiled and patted him on the shoulder, looking for George.

I did not see him until I moved around to the other side of the cars. I saw him walking back to the front and had to jog a bit to catch up. He was still continuing his investigation as I pulled up beside him.

"Empty," he said and I wondered if I had heard him right.

"Huh?" I asked.

"Empty," he said again, looking at me. The sternness in his face made me stop for a second. "They are all empty," he said again and his face cracked into a broad smile. He saw my confusion, I guess. "You see if these had been full, we would have probably totaled ol' Rusty there and maybe none of us would have survived. We pushed most of our momentum into that first car and it absorbed it well. We moved them all back quite a ways, that's for sure. This could have been a lot worse." I was glad to see him taking it so well. "Let's get back and see if we've bled off enough steam."

I walked back with him but still saw steam coming from under the engine. I heard him again sigh in irritation as he looked to see exactly where it was coming from. He moved around and I was tired of following him and I was sure he was getting a little irritated at having me there.

"Keep me posted George," I told him. I think he acknowledged that I had spoken. I walked back to our boxcar.

I moved out of the way as Laura led Chris's horse down the ramp. The horse looked calm which I took to mean that Laura had done a great job in what she was doing. I saw the corral had been hastily put together down the small slope of the tracks and in a little dry ditch there full of long grass. Two other horses were already in the pen and Chris was standing at one of the panels ready to open it for the incoming horse.

"How are they?" I asked.

"None the worse for wear," Laura told me as she made it to the ground. "All are pretty skittish though."

She led the horse to the corral and let him loose inside as Chris closed the panel behind him. It shook its head and gave a small buck as it ran over to the others. They all then gave a whinny which was taken up by the horses still inside. Laura rushed back up the ramp and walked over to the stalls.

"I'll let you all do what you're doing," I told them. "Looks like you have it under control." I got a nod from Chris as he stood petting the neck of Davina's horse, which was not looking to want to relax. "Do you need any help?" I asked on second thought, though I was sure they did not need me in their way.

"Would you mind getting Rosy?" Chris asked.

"Rosy?" I wondered.

"Yeah, that's what we call their burro," he told me.

"Sure, I'll get it," I said and turned to walk to the other boxcar.

I pulled at the ramp and held the rope that let it down. I let the rope slide through my hand and lowered the ramp slowly to the ground. Securing a few bolts like I had seen George do several times, I walked into the car.

Rosy was standing as far away from the door as the pen would allow. She looked nervously at me and I started talking to her in a calm voice. Her ears went back as though she did not believe what I was saying and I could not blame her. I walked around the pen and she moved out of range. Stepping into the pen, I walked up to her and she turned her back to me, still unsure what was going on. As I petted her rump and moved up beside her, she leaned into me and seemed to need comfort of some other body's contact. I let her feel me close to her and moved up to her neck. I continued talking to her in a soft voice and kept stroking her shaggy coat. Moving my hand in among her ears, she seemed to relax.

"I wish the girls would have responded that way to me in high school," I told her and looked around. "Come on, let's get you outside."

I grabbed the short rope that was at the bottom of the halter that always stayed on the donkey. She raised her head and I easily led her to the gate. Walking her out I felt her still pushing up close to me. I let her and we made it down the ramp. I directed her over to the corral and looked up at Chris.

"We shouldn't put her in with the horses right now," he told me. "They are a little too skittish. Let's stake her close though." He yelled into Laura to bring out a line for the donkey.

Laura appeared at the top of the ramp of our car and held a coiled up rope. She threw it to me and I undid it and attached it to the halter of Rosy. I tied her to one of the panels of the corral and being satisfied I started to walk off. Rosy followed to the end of her rope as I smiled. Moving on I heard her make that loud distinct donkey sound. I moved back close to her and petted her ears again.

"You'll be okay, Rosy," I told her. She rubbed up against me and tried to circle me, snagging me in her rope as she did. "Okay, you silly donkey, I'll rub you a little more but then that's it." I untied myself from her and stroked her again.

I spent some time then and petted her. She had so many places to itch it seemed, that I figured I would never find them all. Her ears were her favorite spot to be touched and I spent some time with them. I am sure I heard a few chuckles from Chris and Laura. I tried to ignore them as best I could and when Rosy seemed to be content with eating some of the tall grass, I took my chance at escape, hoping she would not notice. It was a false hope.

She again followed me to the end of her rope and looked at me with some serious question. I shrugged at her and immediately looked around to see if anyone saw I was trying to communicate with a donkey. Chris and Laura did not do very well at pretending they were not watching. I turned and ignored them all, including the indignant hooved animal.

I went to find Davina at the rear of the train. I found her posted on the other side looking at the rails running behind us. I walked up to her and started to make some conversation.

"We have movement," I heard Sterling say. "East along the tracks, three of them headed your way."

"How far out?" I asked.

"Looks like half a mile, moving slow," he told us. "They came out of the hollow in the hill. Looks like there may be a road running somewhere over there. They might have just got off of it but they are heading down the tracks."

"Watch for anyone circling," I told them. I walked to the other side of the boxcar but saw Chris already moving up to be beside me. "Kind of sitting ducks out here, I guess," I told him.

"There's a small rise a little south down there," he told me. "I think it will hide me well enough."

"Great, get there fast!" I told him. "You and Laura spread out though. No more of that bunching up stuff." I got an alarmed look but a nod followed as he moved out with his rifle in hand and Laura close beside him.

"They are still moving right at you," Sterling said. "I will be in range from up here if they get close enough. They are headed right down the tracks."

"Copy that," I said. "Jake are you seeing them yet?"

"No, I don't see anything," he said.

"Stay in cover," I told him. "I'm headed your way. Everyone else report in."

I got reports from everyone then as I started running toward the grain cars. I still did not hear from Margie so I glanced up atop the caboose as I ran by. I saw her looking hard forward but not seeing what she wanted to find.

"See anything?" I asked. She shook her head.

"Too much steam fills the air," she told me.

"Okay, but I need you to check in with that report," I told her. "Do you have a radio?" She nodded and still looking forward she held it up for me to see.

"I will," she said and put it back where she had it, somewhere under her loose fitting blouse. I shrugged as I ran on.

I made it to the front of the engine and saw George still looking at his pride and joy, feet working hard to push himself farther underneath and pulling his torso up close to see one thing or another. I thought about pulling him clear to tell him what was going on but decided I should let him be. I jumped over the tracks in front of the engine and ran along the grain cars. I stopped just before the end and saw Jake ducked low behind their rear wheel, aiming his rifle toward where the people would be coming from. I crawled under the car and took cover behind the opposite wheel there.

"Talk to me Sterling," I told the radio. "You got the spotter position." I told him that so that everyone would not be checking in with their movement. We had worked that out some time ago.

"They are slowing down a little," he said. "They seem to be checking to see if they can see anything. They're still moving forward. They obviously know we're here. The big steam cloud down there insures that."

"I see them," I heard Margie say. "Three are moving along the tracks."

"I'm in position," I heard Chris say. "I'm at your four o'clock."

"Copy all that," I said.

Just then I saw movement coming over a small hill about a hundred yards down the track. They must have fully seen the train then, as well, because they stopped and started pointing ahead of themselves. I saw they were well armed.

"They stopped," Sterling said. "They look to be deciding what to do. No, they started toward you again."

"Copy that," I told him. "I have them in view. Nobody fire until we have to. Let's see what they want. We won't let them get too close though." I heard everyone but Davina agree. "How we looking out the back?" I asked.

"You are looking good," Sterling said. "I don't see anything moving there."

"Copy," I said. "Davina, how's it looking?"

"Fine, just like Sterling said," she told me.

"Find some cover and watch from there," I told her. "This could be the old decoy move."

"Will do," she said.

I saw the people on the tracks clearly then. It was two men and a woman walking right along the rails. They were not aiming their rifles at anything, in fact they had them slung over their shoulders though, one of the men had his dangling under his right armpit, much like I carried mine. They stopped at about thirty yards out and raised their hands. I was very interested at what this was going to turn out to be.

I stood up then, still aiming my rifle at the three of them. The man saw me and stepped a little in front of the woman. She moved to stand beside him, blocking the other man from view. He too then moved a little to stand beside them. I moved out a little bit toward them but still did not pass the end of the grain car.

"Anybody see anything?" I asked. I got negative reports all around. "Are they in range of everyone?" Again I heard from everyone and was told they would be as good as dead had we wished it. "I'll go see what they want. Everyone stay calm but ready. Hand on top of my head means take them out." I heard everyone say they understood.

"I'm going with you," I heard Jake say and he was up and walking around the grain car before I could tell him anything. I figured it may help if it came down to it.

Jake and I moved slowly up to the three of them, seeing them still in the middle of the tracks. They kept their hands raised a bit and seemed to try to be looking to want to play nice. When we had moved about twenty feet from the grain car the man on their far left put his hands down and the others followed suit. Jake and I pulled up.

"I think that's about close enough," the man yelled. "We're friendly but we ain't stupid."

"What do you want?" I yelled.

"We heard the crash and saw the smoke," he yelled back. "Thought we'd come check it out. Everyone okay?"

"We're fine, thanks," I told him, still watching him close.

"Mind lowering them rifles?" he asked. I lowered mine and let it hang under my arm. I saw him smile. "I like that. It only seems to make sense."

I walked forward then, hoping much but ready for anything. I know the world could not be all bad but I knew I did not yet have evidence of that. Jake walked with me and I am sure he was thinking much the same. Getting to within ten feet we pulled up.

"I appreciate you looking in, but I think we'll be okay," I told the man that I had been talking to.

He was a well-muscled man, and looked like a hard worker. He wore a long sleeved flannel shirt with a buttoned up leather vest. He had a holster which held a 9mm semi auto pistol that looked like it just came out of the box. Looking hard, I saw what looked like a pipe with a shoelace grip and a cap on it strapped to his back. His longish dark hair moved in the wind. He had an AR15 hanging under his armpit.

The woman beside him was a beautiful well-built woman, strong and well ready to prove it, though it looked like she could be nice if she wanted to. She too was armed with a rifle but it was slung over her shoulder. Looking, I saw she had a matching pistol in a holster that she wore low on one hip. Her long, large curled hair played at her shoulders where she had two freshly killed rabbits tied together and slung.

The other man looked like he was curious and wanted to ask me something but was keeping himself from doing so. He wore a wide brimmed hat that needed washing though the rest of him was clean and immaculate. He had on a denim jacket and a small backpack. He wore his gun in a sling that held it on front of his chest. His arms rested on it.

"That's a hell of a setup you have there," the first man said, looking passed me. "I guess I should introduce us. I'm Quade, this here is Teal and that man there is Axel."

THE END, AS IT HAPPENS TO THEM

I introduced Jake and I. I was not sure what to do next as inviting them over did not seem right. They seemed nice enough and genuinely concerned, though I did not wish them to know that we were stranded for the moment.

"Did you guys hit those grain cars?" Axel asked, moving to look around Jake.

"Yeah, but thankfully they were empty," I told him.

"That's an old steam train, huh?" Quade asked. I stayed looking at him. "I saw one of those somewhere I think, maybe a picture, I guess."

"It is steam," I told him. "Chugs right along."

"I have a diesel one myself," he said and watched my reaction. I tried not to give him one, though my interest was immediately peeked. "I guess it's more Lincoln's than mine."

"It's all of ours," Axel said. "They all are and you know it."

"Where would you get diesel?" I asked, trying to act uninterested.

"We settled not far from a couple of oil tankers," Quade told me and I looked sideways at him. "They're mostly empty now though, as we don't drive much. Yeah, we started up a town not far from here a few years back. Everyone's welcome as long as you leave your troubles at the door." I worked hard to control my interest.

"You have a town somewhere out here?" Jake said with some excitement. "How could that be?"

"We keep the peace by force at times," Axel told him. "Most of the time people just get along. Outsiders come and go all the time. They buy, sell or trade. Most people around here have heard about it. We don't want any trouble and don't put up with any." For some reason they all looked at me.

"Sounds like a good idea to me," I told them. "Whereabouts is this town?"

"Head straight down these tracks and the next dirt road you come to will be Road 42," Quade told me. "We are south about four miles. Bring something to trade. You can buy almost anything there, I'm sure." I wondered what he meant exactly but I did not have to stretch my imagination, I was sure.

"Well, thanks again for checking in," I told them. "Maybe we'll head your way before we move on this morning." I hoped they would buy the small lie as I was not sure how long we would be there.

They looked again at our wreck and smiled at me. We all said some pleasantries and they turned to leave. I was glad for that, though I was not yet convinced of the innocent curiosity that brought them there. As I watched them disappear behind the small hill down the tracks, I thought about the kind of town that could survive in the world with the way it had become. It sounded pretty interesting. I asked everyone to check in as I turned and headed back to the train.

CHAPTER 9

I grabbed the radio off my vest and told everybody that Jake and I were clear, though I knew everyone but Davina must have seen that. I asked Sterling if he saw them anymore and he said he did not. I still wanted to stay on alert and told everybody so. Jake and I hurried back toward the train.

"That could have gone worse," he said and I agreed. "They seemed pleasant enough. That guy had his rifle slung under his arm just like you do. That was a little weird."

"Yeah, that kind of freaked me out," I told him. "It didn't seem like they were hiding anything."

"It didn't seem like it," Jake seconded. "I wonder if there really is a town up and going somewhere close."

"I hope we're not here long enough to find out," I told him but was truly not sure about that. "But it would be cool to see it if there is."

We walked back to the train and a small sprinkling of rain started to fall. I looked up, not real thankful but wondering how long it may last. Looking at Jake I saw him shrug and walk back toward the rear of the train.

I had asked Sterling and Shay to stay at the top of the hill for a while. I also asked Chris to stay on our flank and Davina to keep watching our rear. I looked at our surroundings again and did not like what I saw.

The steam had let up a lot and I saw George still wiggling around under the engine. He had two pipe wrenches this time. He had one on a pipe, pulling it and pushing the other on a fitting next to it. Whatever he did was not coming loose until he pulled all of his weight off the ground and pushed against the wheel with his legs. I watched as he eased back and then easily twisted off the pipe. He moved over and with his wrenches, banged on some part, hammering with all his might.

"How're we looking George?" I yelled between banging's'. He looked out at me and shook his head. "What does that mean?"

He slid out from under the train and pulled himself up. He held a pipe and a connector. He pulled two elbows out of the pocket of the dirty set of coveralls he had put on. Rolling them around in his hand he looked up at me. The answer he was giving me did not seem obvious as the fittings looked fine.

"These ones right here are fine," he told me and I furrowed my forehead a bit. "They are the only ones I could save on the pressure line to the slave shaft. I think I have replacements for the ones that I can't." He turned and walked away.

"Does that mean we are okay?" I asked him, feeling about a thousand times better. He nodded his head.

"I think we'll be fine," he said, stopping and turning. "Once I get this put back together, I'll have to check it when it gets up to temperature. It looks fine though, if I have these parts. We will need to figure a way of getting the bumper off of that front wheel. It looks wedged pretty good."

"I'll work on that," I told him.

"I'll bring you my pry bars," he said and moved back toward his boxcar.

I went to see what he was talking about, though I had remembered seeing the bumper pushed pretty well around the wheel. As soon as I got close to the front I could see what a huge task it was going to be to get the bumper out from where it was. I breathed in deep and let out a big sigh.

The bumper and all the brackets, and metal that held it firmly in place, were now several different balls of crushed metal. They were all perfectly wedged in places that would make it impossible to move the train without getting them all the way out. I saw one particularly large ball was pushing hard on one of the cylinders that moved the drive shaft on the two smaller front wheels on that side. Moving to the other side of the engine, I saw things were no better over there.

I yanked at some pieces that looked easy enough to move. I found them well stuck and my hope for them dwindled. As I looked around some more George came around the engine and handed me several long tools and a small sledge hammer.

"Careful there on those shafts," he told me. "Break those and we may be here permanently." I nodded to his back as he walked to the other side of the engine.

"Jake, I need you at the front of the train, now, please," I told my radio. It only took about three seconds for him to be standing beside me.

"What is it?" he asked with earnest. I handed him a long pry bar.

"We have to get the bumper there out from around the front wheels," I told him. He looked at the train, confused. "Pry where you think will help but don't even touch the shafts a little bit or anything else that looks important for that matter."

He acquiesced and moved the bar into one of the crushed pieces. I moved around to the other side and did the same thing. Just guessing where to start, I pried a little at different spots to see if I could find a weakness. Nothing budged and I moved over and took off my jacket.

After about a half hour I was impressed with what I had done. The hammer really was what seemed to be doing the best for me. When I had a big piece moving with several blows I would work the pry bar in and together remove some small bits of the dense mangled ball. As sweat dripped, I went in close and looked at my progress. The wheel edge was mostly clear of one of its obstacles. I decided I would go and give Jake a hand, feeling a little bad for leaving him without a hammer.

As I moved around to his side I saw his arms elbow deep in and around the wheel. A large pile of gnarled metal sat behind him and he presently used the long pry bar and loosened yet another piece. He threw it behind himself and it landed with a clink on the top of the others.

"I think I mostly got it away from the wheel," he told me. "How's your side doing?"

"Oh, just about done myself," I lied and went back to my side. (I am sure you do not like a show off either.)

I worked harder at getting more pieces out and ignored most everything else. I think I did better that second round and I could actually start seeing some good progress. I saw George out the corner of my eye then and watched him walk up into the burn chamber room. I figured round three could wait a bit and followed him inside.

I made it to the room as he was moving the lever on the pump to put more oil into the tray inside the burn chamber. Watching him, he made it look like one fluid motion. He had the fire going in no time and turned to look at me.

"Find all the parts you needed then?" I asked him.

"Yeah they're a few more elbows than there needs to be but she'll work okay," he told me. He seemed to still have a worry aura to him. "We should know in a few minutes if we have any real problems."

"Well, if you don't mind I'll stay with you," I told him. He nodded and started down the ladder to the ground. I followed.

"How far did you all get on getting us loose under there?" he asked as we walked to the front of the engine. He bent over and looked. "Seems like we have a bit more to go, huh?"

"Yeah, this side is pretty smashed up," I told him. "I think it's coming though."

"I'll give you a hand once everything checks out," he promised. "It can't be any fun, I'm sure."

"No, it's a pretty good workout," I admitted.

"How's Jake doing over there?" he asked with a smile. I tried to ignore the innuendo.

He pointed to several things that needed moving that I had not noticed. He did spend some time helping. We would move back some and give it a look and then come and pry some more. There was a time that I was not certain if a few of the smashed pieces would move. With a smile however, George finally moved out and looked. With a smile he handed me the pry bar.

As we started to walk over to the other side of the track, steam started billowing out from under the rear of the locomotive. It started small at first and then it came out in large clouds and seemed to be puffing. I tried to see where it was coming from but it was impossible to do so.

"Let's shut'er down," George said and I ran to the burn chamber and shut the door. Looking out the side of the room, I saw George more disappointed than I ever had before. He shook his head as steam was shooting out the starboard side of the locomotive.

I made it to the ground and walked up to stand beside him. I tried not to show any disappointment and hoped it was working as he turned to look at me. He was nodding and then only shrugged.

"Looks like a big problem," he said and smiled.

"What do you think is doing it?" I asked.

"It has to be the manifold," he told me. "It's bleeding right out of the chamber when it puffs like that. I looked at everything under there. The only thing you can't get a good eye on is the manifold."

"I know you probably don't want to hear it but…" I started.

"No, it's fine," he said. "Is it something I can fix, right? I'll have to get to it first to see. It means taking off a lot of parts but there isn't much choice. I'll get right on it."

"I'm here to help if I can," I told him.

"Okay, let's go look at where my tools are," he told me and headed back to his boxcar. Again, I followed.

He took me over to some of the large toolboxes and started opening drawers. I tried not to look at how disorganized the crash had made the place but watched instead what he was showing me. It looked like my job was going to be getting him the right tool in hand. I was fine with that too.

He loaded up on tools before he left and he asked me to bring several more. I grabbed a bag he pointed at and put them into it. I followed him outside and went with him to the front of the train where we saw the steam had stopped flowing.

"Looks like it's time to get to work," George said and Jake, who was taking a small break, thought he was talking to him.

"Yes sir," he said and jumped up off the rail he was sitting on. I tried not to smile and shook my head at him as we passed.

"Have you ever had to work on this kind of thing before?" I asked George.

"No, not with the pressure chamber," he said. He laid down on the wet tracks and slid underneath where the steam had billowed. "I refitted the burn chamber which was hard enough. I guess these old beasts are easy enough to work on if you can get into them. We'll just have to hope it's nothing major when we see what's going on." I wondered what he meant by major.

The next hour passed with George taking off various parts from under the train. He asked for a few different buckets and I saw him use them for the bolts and screws as well as whatever else would fit in them. I made several trips back to the boxcar and was glad to find everything he asked for. As the drizzling rain started to gain some force he came out holding a square looking piece of metal about twelve by eighteen inches with rows of large short pipes coming out of it.

"Looks like the wreck pushed some of the tubing back and broke these pipe fittings off right here," he said, rubbing some places on the piece of metal with his greasy fingers.

He walked back to his boxcar with the part held tight. It took him some time but he managed with some effort to get it entirely clean. I watched with some boredom as he took extra care to get every single speck of blackness off of it. To my surprise however, when he was done the piece looked brand new.

"This is the starboard pressure manifold," he told me. "There are two on this side. The other one is okay. If we have enough juice, which I'm sure we do, we can use the welder and fix this one. Some extra pieces of metal could be welded here and here and then some new fittings mounted here and here." This did not seem to make him happy.

"So why don't you look more happy?" I asked him.

"I know I don't have the fittings with that thread pattern," he told me.

"I saw a tap and dye set in there," I told him. "Can we cut some pipe and make the right kind?"

"It's a good thought son, but I don't have a set this big," he said, pointing to one of the pipes that was torn off of the manifold.

"Any adapters that would fit onto a different pipe, if it got welded on?" I asked, grasping at straws. He shook his head. "What's the answer then, George?" I started to get a little annoyed.

"I can try and see if I can tee all of the pipes off of the other manifold," he said. "It comes out of the same side so the pressure loss should not be too bad."

With some new purpose we set off to look at what could be done. This time I got under the train with George and saw firsthand what he was dealing with. We followed every pipe and talked over different ideas but after another hour we were standing beside the engine shaking our heads.

"We're going to need some larger pipes than I have, Randy," George said sincerely. "I'm sorry there's no other way."

"Maybe we can get them from that town," Jake said and kind of startled me. I had almost forgotten post-apocalyptic wasteland there for a minute, being so involved in what seemed like a plumbing problem.

"What town?" George asked.

"The one those people were talking about," he said. George looked weird at Jake.

"What people?" he asked.

"That's right, you were working and missed the people that came by," I told him and watched his face gather some fear as he looked around. "They're gone and Sterling and Shay are watching from that hilltop over there. We're fine." I saw him relax a little.

"They were from some town?" he asked.

"Yeah, they said they had a town not too far," Jake put in. "Sounded like some trading went on there. We could go check it out and see if they have something we can use to get that thing you guys have been talking about fixed. Maybe they even have a new one." He must have really been wanting to go check to that town as he seemed to be getting overly excited.

"They aren't going to have one exact but there is definitely different parts we could use," George said.

"I guess that's true," I said as Jake came to stand beside us.

"The only other option is us searching for some other train engines and seeing if we could rob one of them of some parts," George said. I smiled.

"One of the guys said they had some diesel engines," Jake told him. George jerked his head up and looked at Jake. I saw hope on his face again.

"Where is this town?" George asked and we explained where the people told us it was. "Sounds like it may be worth a try. It's either that or we start walking. Ol' Rusty ain't going nowhere until this manifold is fixed."

"I'm so sorry, George," I told him.

"No, it can't be helped sometimes," he said. "Sometimes life just turns the page and we move along with what we get." I always liked his attitude.

"Are we going then?" Jake asked.

"Sounds like we are going to go have a look anyway," I told him. His excitement was obvious. "Let's call everyone in and see how this can best be done."

I keyed my mic, and finding everything clear, I asked everyone to show up in the caboose for a quick meeting. I got the obvious worried response, but everyone started moving in that direction. Jake was the first one inside.

When we had all gathered I leaned against the cabinet by the entrance door. Margie was looking out of the area at the center of the caboose that stuck up about two feet higher than the rest and had windows that let you see all around us. I was glad to have her there keeping an eye on things. Everyone was a little antsy, wanting to know what we were doing still staying here. I too wondered what we were going to do to get out of there.

"So, looks like we need some parts for the train and we can't move unless we get them," I told them. George jumped in with a short explanation.

"So what does that mean?" Sterling asked.

"Those guys that came earlier, they said there was a town close by," I said and got the shocked response I thought I would. "I'm not convinced they were telling the truth so we'd have to check it out pretty good first. The guy said they had train engines there. It's our hope to find something to trade for."

"Why would there be a town out here?" Davina asked and I could not answer that.

"It's a good question," I told her.

"What choice do we have?" Shay asked, coming to the heart of the matter. Everyone went quiet.

"We can ride on," Laura said. "I know you guys said its fifty miles, well a little less now, but that's rideable." I looked at George.

"If that's what we decide then I'm in," he said. "I'd like to spend some time first to see if something could be done to save this train. But if we need to leave her, then let's do that."

"I totally agree on giving it a look first," I said and everyone agreed, except Chris, which was understandable.

"I wasn't saying we run off right away," Laura said defensively. "I'm just throwing out all of our options. I thought that's what we were doing."

"No one's saying you're wrong," I said. "We need to brainstorm here and we need all the information on the table. You are right, we could ride on and make it. But if this place turns into another bust then we may be heading far away. This train is the best way of getting there. I think we have some time to try and get George's train here back on the road."

"I think we should give that town a try," Jake finally put in enthusiastically. "The guy didn't bat an eye when he was talking about it. He told us to bring things to trade. He said it was known around these parts."

"Really?" Chris asked. "What kind of town could live out here? Must be pretty rough. We'll need to be ready for trouble."

"I agree with that," I said. "And not everyone should go." The whole train started thinking what they could say to make themselves a necessary participant.

"Maybe the ladies should stay here," George said. Margie looked at him hard. "Sorry, but that is a precious commodity to some who think of you all as objects."

"I'm going if Chris is," Laura said matter of factly.

"Okay, wait, before this gets out of hand," I said over the small murmuring that was starting. "I know none of us have seen civilization or much else of the world and we'd all love to see it back working again. I'm up at the top of that list. But we have to think of this as something else. A small recon team should go have a look around. We need to stay focused on that."

"They said they had trains, maybe they have one we can take scrap from," George said.

"They really have trains?" Chris asked and the murmurings started again.

"Okay, let's think rationally about this," I cut in. "Chris you should go and hold a position outside of the town if there turns out to be one. Laura, you have to follow orders just like the rest of us and watch out from here. Take a position in the small hills around us and watch over the train. It's a classic trap to get some of us to leave and attack while we're gone. Jake you stay and coordinate coms. Sterling you and I go in as backup while George asks around for what he needs. Everyone else stays here spread out with your heads on a swivel. Agreed?" There were some unhappy faces in the caboose but there were agreements all around. "Let's everyone be ready in ten minutes."

We all left the caboose and made our way to start preparing. I went to our boxcar and rummaged through the heap on the floor for a coat and gloves I knew I had. Finding them I turned and saw Davina standing in the doorway. She moved in and let the flap fall.

"I don't think I like you going off by yourself," she told me.

"It has to happen like this," I said, stopping and looking at her.

"I know, I'm not saying that," she replied. "I just don't like the idea of you far away. I think we made a deal a while ago, remember?" I had not thought of that.

"I'm so sorry, my love," I told her. "You are right, I did say that. I'll tell Jake to go and...."

"No, no no," she told me. "I know I need to let things like this happen. It's just hard. I shouldn't' have reminded you." She moved over to where I was standing.

"No, it's good to have someone keeping me in line," I told her and put my arm around her waist, pulling her close.

"Don't have too much fun," she said in mocked sadness.

"Well you never know what I may find," I told her.

"Yeah, like what?" she asked and I knew I painted myself into a corner.

"Like a bath," I told her, moving away and again looking for my jacket. "I wonder if they have power."

"If you come back smelling all pretty and clean I'll know you've been up to something," she told me and I looked to see if she was serious. She laughed at me and walked over to me again. "Just checkin'," she said, laughing at my confused look.

"You're my everything, love," I told her. "I'll only try the post-apocalyptic brothel for a little while. It'll mean nothing to me." I got severely hit for my attempt at trying to be funny, though she laughed as she hit me.

"Just come back to me in one piece," she told me. I turned and held her close. "Promise?" she whispered in my ear.

"I promise," I told her and kissed her long.

We heard others moving around the car and it brought us back to what we were supposed to be doing. I found my coat easily then for some reason and remembered putting the gloves in the burn chamber room. I checked my clip on my AK47 and found it full. I checked the ones at my belt as well. Going through the typical ritual, I found I was ready.

Running to grab my gloves I hurried and met George at the horse corral. I saw my horse was saddled but I went and checked it anyway, seeing Chris and Laura were there waiting. With a nod Laura headed off up the hill toward where Sterling had watched us earlier. Jake showed up and did a radio check with everyone.

Sterling was next to show up at the corral and as he got there the four of us heading out, jumped on our horses, George with a little help from the corral panels.

We turned with some focus and rode fast down the tracks and set into a smooth canter. The horses seemed to still be a little skittish and I wasn't sure if we should let them run for the first little bit.

The people who visited us were right about the road being just ahead and we made it there with ease. I looked around and saw nothing out of the ordinary. Checking in with Jake we turned onto the road and headed south, hoping much for what we would find ahead.

It did not take long for the horses to warm up to the idea of being ridden. They really seemed to want to move into a fast run and we decided to let them. I was more than happy to get to the place where we were told the town was so that I could stop wondering and hopefully find the parts we needed. After what must have been a couple of miles, I too was warming to the idea of the ride.

As we topped a small hill on the dirt road, I saw structures far off. They were sitting lower than us in the surrounding area. I pulled my horse's reins in and it took a lot more pressure to get him to slow up. Not wanting to be overbearing I gave him a chance to calm a little, knowing he was probably still suffering a little confusion from the crash. With a few pats on his neck and a squeeze from my legs, I felt him respond. He then easily listened to what the reins were telling him I wanted.

"Looks like something over there," I told everyone and we made it into a walk. Looking hard we tried to figure out just what it was.

I knew they had to be some sort of grain storage silos. There were two different sets of them and both stood over a hundred feet tall. There were things called elevators built into them and taller than the silos. Pipes and railings led everywhere along the top of them. We could not yet see where they touched the ground because of the slope of the land. I was, however, not surprised that whoever was there could have seen the smoke from our crash.

"Looks like that's kind of where they said the town was," I said.

"They look a lot like the sugar buildings back at our old town," Sterling said. I agreed with him.

"I guess we walk right in, huh?" George asked.

"I guess," I said as we walked down the road.

We made it down the road a little more and Chris let his horse have its head. We followed and soon were back to running. I saw him pull up sharply and spin. Immediately my rifle was at my shoulder and I was looking around for the threat.

"Movement on the road down there," Chris yelled, pointing ahead of us. "Looks like a...like an old wagon?" He said curiously.

I saw then what he was pointing at and squinted to see it. I pulled out my binoculars and focused them in on the movement. It came in clear but the wagon did not look familiar. I had to smile.

"What is it?" Sterling asked.

"Looks like there's a couple of riders." I told him. "There's a couple of pack horses too. Looks to be like they're driving about eight head of cattle. A big wagon being pulled by a couple of horses is coming straight at us."

"No way!" Chris said. I handed him my binoculars, wondering where his were. "Laura usually carries those," he said when he saw my glance.

"Want to get off the road and hide until they go by?" Sterling asked. Looking around and seeing no cover that would hide us, we all shrugged.

"Looks like we'll have to ride on past them," George put in and started his horse walking. A little nervous, the rest of us did likewise.

CHAPTER 10

I looked down at the dirt road we were on and noticed that it was well traveled. Hoof prints were everywhere as were ruts where wagon wheels often dug down when they passed there in the rain. The hoof prints were of various sizes and obviously from both horse and other animals like cattle and sheep or goats. Sterling saw what I was looking at and nodded.

"Looks like there's a lot of traffic on this road," he said.

"Yeah, I noticed that too," George said, looking down. "Looks like cattle and horses both, sheep and goats some too. I wonder where they're all headed. Looks like they're headed in both directions."

"Yeah, out of town and into it," Chris put in, still watching the approaching caravan.

We kept walking slowly and soon came close enough to be able to make out the faces of the group of travelers. An old man sat on the wagon with a young kid. The wagon was full of wooden crates, closed tight so that I could not tell what was inside. There were actually four horseback riders, all of which were lazily pushing a small herd of twelve cattle in front of them. Two goats seemed to be struggling to keep up. They all looked ready for trouble, including the kid who held a nickel plated revolver hanging between his legs as he leaned forward with his elbows on his knees. As we came close he spit a mouth full of tobacco juice over the side of the wagon, hitting a large rock dead on and splattering the surrounding weeds.

We moved off the road as they got close, trying to give the group the right of way and trying to give ourselves a measure of reaction time should things go wrong. We rode along the fence equally spread out and hands ready to yank our firepower into play should the need arise. I did not like being that close to outsiders, especially with knowing so little of the area. We rode close enough to make out every detail of the potential disaster coming down the road, albeit seemingly innocent.

"Morning to you there," the old man said from the wagon. "Thanks for yielding,"

"Morning," I told him as we started to pass. "That be a town up ahead there?"

"It is," the man told us. "Good place for tradin' or just to rest up a bit if that's what you're after." I saw a warm smile cross his face. "Good day to you now." He turned back to looking at the road.

The horsemen eyed us as we passed, as did the cattle. The goats ignored us however, much too worried about catching up. The hairs on my neck rose as the group kept walking, them now behind us. It was definitely a new feeling.

"That was not fun," I said as we got to the top of the next hill. I turned and saw the wagon disappearing over the hill we had just come over.

"Yeah, that was kind of spooky," Chris added.

"Looks like something we may have to get used to," he said, pointing ahead. Two more riders were on the road ahead about two hundred yards away.

"I'm not liking this much," I told them, though we all kept riding.

The town still looked over two miles away. The details of the towers were coming better into focus but it still looked like a mystery of what was happening there. The rain was not helping that and I figured whatever was going on there we would see soon enough. For the time being I turned my attention to the riders.

They looked like every apocalyptic horsemen riders you would meet on a dirt road that you could imagine. Both had rifles. These two wore cowboy hats and leather chaps. As we got close to each other I saw it was actually a man and a woman. I saw the woman had a long scar down the middle of her face and a bruised left eye and puffy lip as though she had recently gotten into a brawl or worse, put up with an ill-tempered man. The man looked in an ill mood for talking, him too bruised about the face. I agreed with him and looked to ride on.

We passed each other, us on our side of the road and them on theirs. The man's sunglasses did not allow me to look into his eyes but he was watching us. I could not blame him for that as I too kept a sharp eye on every part of them. We passed without incident and again my neck hairs raised.

"Okay, that's just too weird," Chris said and I was glad he said it first. "I'm not sure that's going to get easier either."

"I don't think I'm liking that myself," George put in to my surprise.

"Maybe we'll find civilization up ahead," Sterling said. We all looked at him and he shrugged.

We rode on in silence then and watched two side by side grain elevators draw closer. We saw a road turn off ahead and it looked like one that would lead us right to the structures, which is where we assumed the town was. Making it to the road I pulled up and looked all around, seeing the flat Kansas plains and those structures. I could see trees north of the grain elevators and some of what looked like there may be some houses and other parts of a town mixed in there.

"Doesn't seem like anywhere for you to take up position, Chris," I said. "Looks like you'll just have to come in with us." I saw him smile. "Let's keep everything tight. Let's stay together and if it seems like anything is not right we turn and get out." There were agreements all around.

I called Jake and told him we made it to the outskirts of town and that Chris was coming in with us. I also told him about coming across the people on the road, making sure he knew there were people in the area. As I put the radio back on my vest there was little left to do. We took the dirt road that led to the town. It did not take us long to get close enough to want to pull up and look at the place.

The grain elevators had looked like one long structure from where we were when we first saw them. As we got to the dirt road now that turned us to head straight for the town we could see that there were two different structures roughly the same size about fifty yards apart. They were rectangular in general shape and indeed were over a hundred feet tall. They were over five hundred feet long and about a hundred feet wide. You could see where the grain would be housed in the rounded silos which were lined behind a square front structure that seemed to touch the sky from where we were looking. (Atop that square portion of the elevators we could see a four story structure that was about ten feet on every side shorter than the building on which it sat and had a flat roof and windows on every side. Behind the square, four story structure was another single story structure that was as wide as the square and ran all the way to the far end of the elevators atop the silo part of the building. There looked to be windows every twenty feet or so in this single story structure.) The buildings were a faded white. The four story structure on the elevator on the right had metal stair cases and rails going all around it. The other elevator structure only had a single framed in metal ladder leading to the top. Both of them had railing all the way around them.

The post-apocalypse look of the place did not lose its effect on me. The place was, of course, a faded white as I am sure that enough paint to coat the buildings no longer existed. Haphazard rope bridges, complete with wood planks, connected the buildings at different levels and were spread out all the way to the far end. Sections of the round silo walls had been broken out and windows put in place. They were all over the side of the buildings. Laundry blew in the wind there and showed the place well-lived in.

Between the buildings on the ground we saw what looked to be a wall that protected the space between the elevators. It was made up of railroad grain cars. They all had their wheels covered, well-barricaded with sand bags about four feet high. A four foot high metal railing was on top of the cars and stayed connected on a bridge of some sort that went over top of the hole in the fortification which was basically right in the middle of the wall that connected the buildings. On the bridge painted in yellow was a sign that said, 'Welcome to Brewster'. I saw three sets of train tracks leading right through the hole in the grain car wall. I wondered if there was a gate somewhere that would cover the opening in the middle of the wall as I did not see anything that would act as such.

Outside the tall grain elevators and the wall between them, there was what could only be explained as shacks. They were spread out and seemed to take up a lot of the area on the south side of the southern grain elevator. Some looked to be made of mud and sod. Others were wooden and not very well put together. Still others were made with metal siding and looked more taken care of, though those were far less frequent.

Behind the shacks was a large, tan, metal sided building with wooden corrals surrounding it. Standing a little up in the saddle I could see that the corralled in area was rather large. It covered an area of at least twenty acres. It looked to be divided into a grid with smaller areas corralled, making different sized enclosures. Cattle filled some of the areas and milled about.

Looking to the north of the grain elevators I saw the remains of an old farm town. The remains of several homes which had been burned to the ground were there and a row of different buildings poked in here and there. Lush trees hid most of the rest of what was there but it was obvious that not a lot was going on with the place.

"Looks like we ride up to the entrance," Chris said.

"Should we just walk our horse's right in?" Sterling wondered aloud. I had not noticed that we all had stopped in the middle of the dirt road.

"Can't see much else to do," George put in.

As we spoke someone walked out of the gate area between the two buildings and turned to head for the shacks, paying us no mind. Watching, we saw the person pass by them and go into a door at the building attached to the corrals. Movement at one of the shacks caught my eye then and I saw an old man sitting in a rocking chair on what could have been called a front porch. He watched us with some amusement as he rocked and smoked a cigarette.

"Looks like someone who might know what's going on," I said and started toward the shack.

It was on the southernmost edge of a small cluster of them and not too close to the grain elevators to seem like we were committed yet. The man did not stop rocking as we drew near and his expression did not change. He did put his hand out to calm a very mean looking dog.

"Hello to you there, mister," I told him as we got close enough to talk. "Mind filling me in on what's going on around here?"

"How do you mean?' he asked.

"Just haven't seen anything like this before," I told him. "We don't want to be doing anything wrong or heading into somewhere we're not supposed to be."

"I've seen a lot of people with that same look on their faces as you gents have over there," the man told us. "People are amazed by what they see, that's for sure." He paused to take a long drag on his cigarette. "You'll find the town you're looking for in there, between them buildings there. Just go in at the gate. Everything will be obvious once you get inside. She'll be as friendly to you as you are to her."

"Well, I much appreciate your help," I told him.

"My pleasure," the man said.

We turned and left the man to his pleasant morning. We moved past several shacks and saw for certain they were someone's living quarters. A group of young kids started keeping an eye on us until an older woman yelled at them and they scattered. Riding past them, we made it to the gate of the grain car wall and looked around.

I looked up first and saw the grain elevators towering over where we stopped. I could see better some of the large windows that were built into the side and I was quite impressed with what I saw. I did see a few hides had been hung out to dry and also what looked like some strips of meat. It looked like a good place to do such things.

I turned my attention to what was inside the gate. I looked twice and probably blinked several times. I saw what looked like an old west town pushed up close to both the grain elevators and running their entire length. At the other end of the buildings there was a similar wall connecting them, complete with an opening to come through. I saw now the gate used to plug up the hole was none other than a well-positioned grain car. If the need arose, the car that sat in a ready position off to the side, with railing fabricated for just an event. I saw that cars could easily be pushed into place and secured to make the final piece in a heavy-duty fortification. I nodded at the idea and led my horse under the bridge.

"Hey dad, did you see that sign?" Chris asked and pointed. Looking where he directed I read, 'Kindness will be returned, and so will everything else'. I smiled.

"It's a good motto to live by," I said as I passed it and walked under the bridge.

"Sorry Gents, but there's no horses allowed inside of town," I heard a voice from above me. Turning my horse sideways, I looked up. "I've been begging for a bigger sign for a while now," a man I now saw above me standing on the bridge said, looking at me. "Damn kids were stealing it there for a while. But I guess what else is there to do in an old cow town besides bug the old guys?" He offered a pleasant face and I tried to return it.

"Where would we put our horses then?" I asked him.

"The livery is just on the north side of the building there," he said and pointed to the northern grain elevator. "If it's your first time here, your first day there is free."

"Okay, thanks for letting us know," I told him. He dipped his hat and disappeared from the railing.

We all turned our horses in the direction the man told us and made it soon to the livery. There were many separate corrals and a long barn that ran along the elevator that connected most of them. Dismounting at the large double door of the barn, the rest of the group followed my lead. I tied my reins at the hitching post and walked inside. It felt weird not having spurs that rattled.

"Need something?" I heard from above me again. I hoped that would not happen often as I looked and saw a man leaning over the railing of the hayloft.

"Yeah, I think I need to stable four horses," I told him. "The man at the gate said it was free if we hadn't been here before."

"It sure is," he said, coming along the railing and down the stairs at the other side of the loft. "They need separate bunks?"

"No, you can put them in together," I told them. "And not sure what your policy is but we'd like to leave the saddles on."

"No, no, I understand that," the man said with a grin. "I hear that a lot from first-timers." He turned toward the door. "These them?"

"Yes, they are," I told him. He walked up to our group and genuinely seemed interested in the horses.

"If you'll just tie them to the post outside I'll take care of them," he told us all.

"Can you help us out with a little information, sir?" George asked the man.

"I will if you'll call me Brady," he said. George made introductions all around and the man nodded to each of us. "Now, what can I help you with?"

"We are just here for a part off of a....of a... well, off of a locomotive," George stammered. "Do you have someone around that deals with parts like that or maybe know of some trash heap of old cars or an old train even?" I liked how he did that.

"The person you're going to want to talk to is ol' Lincoln," Brady said. "He's the lead engineer around here."

"You guys have an engineer?" George asked excitedly and then seemed embarrassed.

"Yeah, he can fix you up with whatever you need," Brady said. "But he ain't going to be up this early. He plays poker at the bar at the end of Main."

"Main?" George asked.

"Oh yeah, sorry," Brady said, coming over and petting my horses face. "Main is what we call the area between the elevators. There's a bar at the end of the north side called 'Lucky's'. He's in there every night unless there's a rodeo."

I almost burst out laughing and I was not sure why. It was awesome seeing such a thing as this. It must have been so great living in an area where there was something close to normal. These people had achieved more than I thought could be possible. I felt bad as I stood there in silence.

"Okay then, we shall look for a man named Lincoln," George said and moved to leave.

I followed him out and we moved back toward the gate. I did not see anyone standing on the platform that ran along the top of the wall, though I kept an eye there. We made it there and I looked for the sign that told us no horses were allowed and I finally found it, upside down with a sandbag covering most of it. It reminded me instantly of my childhood.

We walked through the gate and along the rails that went down the center of the town. Shops were labeled with different names and signs that told what was inside. I saw a palm reader's sign was over a building on the south side of the street and a blanket with all of the constellations on it blowing in the wind under the porch there. Beside it was a glass windowed shop that had digging tools and handles. The sign there read something about leather goods. I looked across the street and saw a sign that said tattoos. The sign said 'Self-Inflicted Studios' and

I thought I would want to visit there if I had more time. A decayed molar sign showed the next stop to be a dentist. The crudely painted, decaying tooth was on a piece of old barn wood and nailed across the window there. A bar was next to that shop with a large door that was closed tight. Looking, I saw the name of it was 'The Mill'.

"Brady said it was at the end, right?" Sterling asked.

"Yeah it must be that building down there on the left," I told him.

We walked straight for the building at the end of the street and we passed an area where the buildings stopped for a small space. It looked like an alleyway and it led up to the elevator building. A hole had been made in the side of the elevator and a heavy-duty metal door was made to fit there on large hinges. Looking down a bit more, I saw another such alleyway and several more like it across the street. The place was becoming a wonder, I thought, as we finally climbed the wide steps of the bar we were looking for.

The two doors swung open when George pushed on them. We moved in fast and each covered a section of the place. I took the far right and saw I was seeing a room half full of empty broken tables and chairs and trash thrown everywhere. There were other unbroken tables and chairs to sit at but we figured to wait on that. Turning, I saw the counter of the bar to the far left. No one was there behind it.

"Anyone home?" Sterling said loudly.

"Be right there," I heard in a feminine voice that seemed far off. "That was a rough one last night so...." A woman moved a sheet aside at the end of the counter and stepped into the room. "Oh, newcomers. You're always welcome."

"We're glad about that," Sterling said and went and sat at the bar.

"What can I get for you all?" she asked and came down to stand in front of Sterling. I went and stood beside Sterling.

"Well, what I hear we need really, is to talk to a man named Lincoln," George told her. "I think he is the engineer around here."

"I don't know about that," she answered. "He fixes stuff when it gets broken, sure, but I don't know nothing about him being an engineer."

"Okay, fine," George said. "Would you know how we might find him?"

"I think he's sleeping off a long night," the woman said. "We had a big brawl in here last night if you couldn't tell by all the sloppiness over there. Lincoln didn't start it but he didn't help either. I wasn't here but my sister said it was crazy. I sure didn't want to come to work today to clean up this mess." George was patient and waited for her to finish.

"Can the man be disturbed, please?" he asked her between gritted teeth. I do not remember seeing George so annoyed. "It is pretty important that we speak with him."

"I think we could," she said. "I haven't even checked to see if he...."

We all turned as a man came through the door. He stopped on seeing us and kind of put his hands out to us to show that he was no threat. I remembered the man as Quade, the man that had visited us at the train.

"I see you all made it to town," Quade said.

"Hi Quade," the woman behind the bar said delicately.

"Hey Lacey," Quade said as casually as he could.

"Want something to eat?" she asked him.

"No thanks, Teal already made me breakfast," he told her. She frowned and walked to look closer at Sterling. "Was thinking I may see you all here." He waited then for us to speak.

"Yeah, it seemed like a place we should have a look at," I told him and he turned to look at me.

"How's the wreck?" he asked and watching hard I could not see any coyness in his question.

"It's okay," I told him.

"They're looking for Lincoln," Lacey said, seeming to try to tell on us or something. "They think he's an engineer." I saw Quade nod his head.

"Something broke, did it?" he asked. I waited a second but finally nodded.

"Yeah, a piece on a manifold," I told him. "We can weld it, it's just we need the right fitting."

"I bet that old train has some stuff no one's ever seen before," he said. "Where'd you guys find that thing?"

"George there worked in the mountains before the war," I told him. "He found it in a shed up there gathering dust."

"Wow, that is cool," he said. "I know Lincoln well and I know he's going to want to get a look at it." He looked up at us sharply. "That's only if you guys don't mind him drooling for a while. He loves stuff like that. Classic, just like him."

"Is there a way we can talk to him?" George asked.

"Yeah, he's up on the roof already," Quade told us. "He's trying to get sight of where your wreck happened. I woke him up this morning on the way back. When I told him about you all's old train and that it was running, he had to see it."

"Were you guys really out hunting this morning?" I asked him straight.

"Sorry, but no," he said. "Robert and Asia were on watch on the high tower this morning and they saw the smoke. We rode out quick to see what it was. Sorry if we scared you all. We just try to keep an eye on things that are going on around us. Teal just shot those rabbits she was carrying with a sling shot." I saw him smirk.

"No, that makes sense," I told him.

"I'll take you to see Lincoln if you'll just follow me," Quade told us. "I'm sure he can fix whatever you have."

"I would like that very much," George told him and came up to the man.

"There will be hot lunch today, Quade," Lacey said as we all turned for the door. "I'll save you some beef strips."

"Thanks Lacey," Quade said. "I'll tell Teal to stop by."

"No, that's uh...." she started as we all moved out of the door.

Quade led us almost back to the opening in the wall and turned at an alleyway there. He pulled hard on the metal door at the end and it swung open. We all walked inside and he closed the door behind us. He turned on a flashlight as I turned on mine. He led us to a door at the far end of a hallway. Opening that, we turned and walked down another long hallway. He pulled open a door at the end of that one too and we saw we had made it to a large open room that connected us to some loading docks. Looking outside, I saw we were looking over the livery stable. Quade walked over to a support post nearby.

"Lincoln, this is Quade, over," Quade said into an old phone receiver and waited. "Yeah, the people from that train are here," he said. "They need you to look at a part for them."

"Haven't seen one of those for a while," Sterling said.

"He'll be right here," Quade said as he hung up the receiver. "Seriously, he's going to want to look at your train so prepare your answer now."

"I don't mind, as long as we are on our way out," George said.

"How bad is it?" Quade asked him seriously.

"We can make do," George lied. "I'd rather we didn't have to but if we have to scavenge on down the line then that's okay."

"No, Lincoln can fix whatever you got, surely," he replied flatly.

As they spoke I heard a rumbling sound coming from somewhere close. I looked around and wondered what it could be. It truly sounded like an airplane was flying by overhead.

"It's just our elevator," Quade told us. We all looked at him questioningly. "No, an actual person elevator." He pointed to the far wall as a man stepped out of an elevator door. I'm pretty sure we all nodded.

The man came over to us and looked quite thrilled. He seemed not to know who to start to talk to so he just looked at us all in turn. I made introductions and he held out his hand to me.

"This is the man you'll want to talk to," I told him, pointing to George. "We would much appreciate you looking at this part for us."

"Yeah, no problem, where is it," Lincoln asked, looking at George. George pulled the manifold out of his backpack and handed it to Lincoln's awaiting hands.

"It's the pressure manifold," George told him.

"Wow, you're not going anywhere with this thing looking like this," Lincoln said. I looked over at Quade and he only smiled and shrugged.

"We only need the fittings for these two pipes coming out here," George told him, pointing out the pieces needing fixed.

"Looks like this one is not doing good here," Lincoln told him, pointing somewhere else on the part.

"Yeah, I think I can live with that one."

"I'm sure I have all the pieces to fix them all. If we weld a strip here, here and here we can make this thing even better than new."

"I think I can weld it okay," George said, taking the piece back from Lincoln. "I just need the pieces to do that."

"You have enough power on that rig to use a welder?" Lincoln asked, amazed. "You must have it set up pretty good. If it's okay with you....."

"We're in an awful rush actually," George said.

"Just a quick look?" Lincoln asked. "I'll help you install that piece and only steal glances as I can. I know that couldn't have been easy to get off."

"Let's see about these pieces first," George told him.

"My shop is right this way," Lincoln said and pointed ahead of the way he turned to walk.

We all followed him and saw that he was leading us through the docks. He took a ladder that led to the ground and beside the livery. He headed for a large shack that was built-up against the grain elevators on the outside. Trucks, with hoods up, and tractors littered the area. A door was tucked in amongst some tumbleweeds and a rain barrel. It looked like the house I would imagine for an old engineer.

"These old tractors had some of that big stuff on them," Lincoln said, going in among a row of junk.

He turned over a few piles here and there and asked George to follow closely. He would pick up some piece of metal and hold it close to the manifold and throw it down when it did not match. A couple of times they both looked with some excitement at a certain part, only to throw it down again and move on. I watched, not liking the experience.

"You all in a hurry then?" Quade asked.

"Yeah, looking for someone," I told him.

"I never try to get involved in that," he told me.

"I can't say as I blame you there," I told him. "Looks like you guys have a good thing going here."

"Yeah, it really is nice," he said and seemed to mean it. Seeing two people coming into view behind Quade, I moved out to have a better look. Quade turned to see what I was looking at. "That's my wife Teal you met already on the right and her friend Lynn," he told me. We watched them approach.

His wife looked a little mincing at first, though I am sure I think that of everyone at first. Her movements were that of someone well-trained and physically fit. Her well-slung AR15 said she could handle herself. As she came close she gave me a smile and I saw she was a beautiful woman, yet nothing compared to my Davina.

Lynn had the same look to her as Teal and they could have passed for sisters. Lynn held the handle of her 9mm which she wore low on her hip. She did not seem to be holding the gun to be confrontational, she just seemed to be used to having her hand there. She smiled easily and I was glad.

"I heard you guys crashed your train north of here," Lynn said. "Is everyone okay?"

"Yeah, a little rattled, but fine," I told her. As George and Lincoln continued to look for parts, the rest of the group formed around Quade and Teal.

"We do have a doctor if you need one," Teal said.

"No, really, we are all okay," I told her. "The grain cars we hit were empty. George over there told me if they had been full, then none of us probably would have made it. I do appreciate the offer though."

"Wow, pretty scary stuff," she said.

"What are you guys doing out in these parts?" Lynn asked.

"They are looking for someone," Quade told her.

"Oh, family?" she asked.

"No, a damn freak who took a couple of women," Chris blurted out "I guess you could call him a doctor, though more like a mad scientist."

"Somebody took some of your women?" Quade asked, seeming to be now interested. "You think he came here?"

"Yeah, we trusted him and he grabbed them while we were out.....hunting," I told him, not sure what it could hurt. I figured it might help to have someone else on the lookout for him. It seemed like he did not like the idea of kidnapped women. "It looked like he was headed somewhere out here."

"What does this guy look like?" Quade asked.

I explained all of the features I could think of. I told them of Jadee's daughter and this seemed to anger Quade a lot. I kept going and told them about Olivia, saving the part about her being pregnant until the end. It seemed like Quade was wanting now to get involved.

"Sick pieces of crap," Quade said, anger boiling. "Why are there people like that?"

"I don't think he wants them for pleasure," Chris said again, always not helping to keep our mission to ourselves.

"What does that mean?" Teal asked. They looked at us harder as we remained silent. "You said he was a doctor, kind of. What sort of doctor?"

"He was a research doctor," I told her. "He worked on the virus before the war." I saw Teal look at Lynn.

"Yeah, and?" Lynn asked.

"I'm not sure much else," I lied, not liking the way this was starting to escalate. "He was in charge of basically the whole thing for a while, I guess. It just means we need to get this part and get on our way."

"A scrawny guy you said, with a light complexion," she said. "It couldn't be, not way out here. Where did you guys come from?"

"We're from Colorado," Chris said and I looked at him harshly. He seemed to understand.

She looked at Teal again then back at me. She nodded, seeming to try to doubt some thought she was coming up with. She smiled and then frowned.

"He couldn't be way out here," she said to Teal. Teal nodded.

"It's not him," Teal said.

"It's not who?" I asked.

"A doctor named Roosevelt," Lynn said. "He was a researcher in California. Doctor Kevin Roosevelt was his name."

My heart leaped in my chest. There were not many reasons that this woman could know that. Did it mean we were in imminent danger, I wondered, as I started to move my hand slowly to my rifle. As I felt the trigger with my index finger I looked for an easy way to take the three of them out.

"How the hell could you know that?" I asked her. I saw Quade look up at me as his body tensed and I looked into his eyes. Chris looked at me, then at the women standing in front of us. Sterling faced off with Quade as well.

"Because, I used to work for him!" she said and we all turned to look at her.

CHAPTER 11

My tension in the situation did not wane, knowing that Lynn worked for Kevin. My mind raced for sure, trying to find what this new turn of events could mean. Confusion was mostly all I got.

"Is that the guy who moved you around?" Teal asked. I noticed Quade turn back to look at us.

"Yeah, he was so horrible," Lynn said. "If he has these two women, then that is very bad for them."

"We kind of figured that," Sterling said what I thought.

"No, I mean he has done unspeakable things," Lynn said.

"Lynn, I don't think that is helping them right now!" Teal told her. I noticed that she was taking a more angled stance toward us.

"Is that the guy you're searching for?" Quade asked.

"Yeah, he headed out this way somewhere," I told him.

"I was a researcher in a facility out in California," Lynn said. "Kevin Roosevelt was the scientist in charge. A lot of us left when it started getting bad. I know who he is. I'm so very sorry that he has those women."

"Why don't you take your hands off your rifles and we can look at this rational like," Quade told us. I kind of relaxed with the idea that this lady who worked for Kevin was not looking to sing his praises.

"Success!" I heard George yell from a couple of junk heaps away. "Yes, this will do nicely!" I did not however turn to look at him.

"What makes you think he is headed out this way?" Lynn asked. I saw real concern in her eyes.

"Lucky guess," Sterling said and I watched Quade turn angry with him.

"Not sure I like that tone," Quade told him. I heard George coming up behind us.

"Let's hold on here a minute," I told everyone. "It's a little shocking that the person we are looking for is known by one of you, that's all."

"That doesn't mean anything," Quade said.

"I agree," I said plainly.

"Have you guys seen signs of him heading here?" Teal asked. "Are you following some trail he's leaving?" I was not sure how to explain this next part.

"There's some military group that's looking for him," I said at last and it kind of felt good to have someone else finally know. Quade's attention went straight to me.

"What kind of military group?" he asked with something deep in his voice that was more than wonder.

"The kind that says they know all about him and don't want to let him start up again," I told him. "They showed up just after he left."

"Is that what he's doing?" Lynn asked. "But it's too late to stop it."

Looking, I saw George glancing around and seeing the strained conversation going on. His happiness faded as he tried to decide what to do. He moved up beside me and waited.

"We can only assume," I told Lynn.

"How does this military group know he's coming this way?" Quade asked, looking right at me.

"Something about him sending research equipment out here," Chris said. I thought to have a long conversation with him later.

"What?" Lynn said. "There's nothing like that here."

"No, not here," I told her. "There are facilities around here. They said they have some records of where he sent some equipment before he left California. Sounded like he did that all to the end. They said something about him being in charge there and how he was preparing to move off on his own. They found some areas where he was sending stuff and setting things up. There are a few of those areas out here." It felt like I was playing all of my good cards and showing my hand.

"I don't know of any research facilities around here," Teal told us.

"No, it's farther past here," I told her. "We were headed that way when we got in that wreck."

"Wait, isn't that a research compound out west of here?" Lynn asked and looked at Quade.

"You mean New Haven?" Quade asked with some distain in his voice. My ears perked at the question. "Yeah I think it was some kind of research thing."

"Where are you talking about?" I asked Lynn.

"About thirty miles west of here," Quade said instead. "Northwest really, I guess it is. There is an old government compound that is run by some....shall we say purists. They aren't much into anything besides the true race, if you take my meaning. I don't think the mixed brood over there has found out what that is exactly just yet either. There's some fundamentalism thing going on with them. Not all of them though, I guess."

"I think I get it," I told him, looking at George.

"You think this science guy went there?" Quade asked Lynn.

"No, we've already been there," George said.

"Really, they let you guys in there?" Teal asked.

"Not exactly," I said.

"Yeah, we didn't get a warm welcome," Chris added.

"I'm not surprised about that," Quade told us. "They don't come around here much for major support anymore. I think they are finally on their feet. They still come now and again to trade though. Some of their women come here to get out of there and we help them. They'll follow them, looking here for them. We've had to push some of the more fundamentalist men out of here a couple of times but we let them in when they agree to play nice and are only offering to trade. I think we have an understanding now though. Not sure they are ever going to be easy to deal with if they stay the way they are. We're all hoping they're not going to last as a group for long. But somehow those types seem to hold on forever." I wanted to hear more of that story but figured it would not help.

"We're now headed out east some more," I told them, trying to get back to the subject at hand. "There is another compound they told us about."

"Where is it?" Lynn asked. I did not want to say. "Is it close by?"

"We're not exactly sure," I lied. "We have some coordinates and are just following where they lead us from the map." Quade looked at me and I could tell he did not believe me. I shrugged inside and figured there was no use them knowing where we were headed.

"Maybe we can help," Lynn said and everyone looked at her.

"That's true!" Lincoln said. "The least we can do is make sure this part works. Sounds like you all are in a bit of a bind."

"I appreciate it but we are in quite a rush too," I told them all. "I'm sure you guys can understand that."

"I'll weld that part for you in the time it takes to eat breakfast," Lincoln said. "I wouldn't charge you anything for doing it. Maybe I just get a small look at your locomotive." He smiled some charismatic smile that seemed to change his whole face.

I was liking the idea of getting the part fixed right away. It would help if we started welding it and found we needed something else. It would be nice to be right where there were more parts. I did not want to ride back and forth to this town. I looked at George and gave him a shrug.

"Sounds good to me," he said unenthusiastically.

"Okay then, let's stop all the gobbledygook here and get on seeing what we can do with getting those parts together," Lincoln said.

"Where's your welder?" George asked him.

"Right this way," Lincoln said and held out a hand to lead us back toward the livery.

"You guys hungry?" Teal asked. Everyone looked at me.

"How long you figure this welding to take?" I asked George.

"Should be about an hour at least," he said. "You guys go ahead."

"No we should stay together," I told him, kind of in a low voice but I was sure everyone heard the seriousness of it.

"You all go to the shop then and we'll bring you something," Teal told me and I smiled at her.

"We really appreciate that, ma'am," I told her. She smiled back.

THE END, AS IT HAPPENS TO THEM

"Please don't call me ma'am," she said. "It makes me sound old." I gave her a nod as she and Lynn turned and started back the way they had come.

"There's all we should need right this way," Lincoln said, and pointed to the way the ladies had gone.

We went back inside the grain elevators and walked through some of the docks. Lincoln went to a corner and pulled open a small door which showed a large room inside. Coming to the doorway, I saw just about every kind of metal working machine I could think of. There were four lathes in the middle of the floor and a drill press of every size beyond them. A bench ran along the far left wall and I could see various welding helmets and gloves lying about. Leather aprons hung on nails next to the bench. Tall bottles of different sizes stood in the corner. Wrenches of every kind hung from the wall. An anvil took up some room in another corner. Hammers filled a shelf behind it. What looked like a medieval forge was in the corner to the right.

Sterling went wide-eyed as we entered, as did George. Lincoln watched them, proud of a section that must have been his own. I think we could have easily been captured at that moment.

"I think we should use this welder here," Lincoln said, going over to the bench. George followed and seemed to agree. Sterling was right beside them.

"Want to wait outside?" Quade asked Chris and I, looking incredibly uninterested in the room, as was I. I gave him a smile.

"Sure," I told him. "I should call and let our other people know we are okay."

"You guys keep in touch pretty good?" Quade asked.

"We try," I told him.

"Sounds pretty damn smart. The top of the building is the best place," he told me. "We have a pretty good system up there. Reception is crap down here." I looked at my radio and thought to give it a try.

"Jake, come in Jake," I said.

"This is Jake," I heard it say. Quade shrugged. "Must be pretty good radios."

"You're not coming in very good," I heard my radio say. "There's a lot of static. Say again."

"It has something to do with all this metal and something else," Quade told me. "Axel explained it to me once or twice."

"Come again," I heard my radio.

"Okay, I guess going up wouldn't be too bad. I'll let them know where we're going," I told Quade.

I walked back into the machine shop and saw they were already getting started on grinding something. It was good to see and I hated to interrupt. I did however, and got a response that said they kind of knew what I was saying. I became rude in my interruption then and made sure they heard me. Then did and I walked back out and asked Quade to take Chris and I to the top of the building.

He smiled and walked over to a large open topped cage. He pulled back on a door and the whole thing swung out. He indicated we should get in and we did. He closed the door behind us and, walking over to a couple of buttons on the wall in the cage, he looked up. He pushed one of the buttons and we jerked into an upward motion.

I looked up and saw mostly metal framework and different stories of the building coming at us. I saw the cable system that pulled us up which connected to the cage at the four corners. It grew dark the farther we went and I decided I did not need to see up anymore.

"It's amazing that you all still have power here," I told Quade.

"Yeah, sorry it's a bit of a secret how we keep everything powered," he told me. "We do have a lot of solar power."

"No, I get it," I told him, respecting the fact that he understood keeping things to yourself was sometimes important. "I'm sure it's a pretty tough job keeping this place going and safe."

"No, not really," he told me. "The people around here want a place like this to work. They seem to be okay with whatever rules the town decides and most everyone follows them. There are a few knuckleheads, of course, who think they can take or run things. We've mostly dealt with them though." The elevator stopped and he pushed a different button. We started up again. "Really, they need a place like this," he continued. "Without it, a lot of people around us would probably die. We need the trade too and the safety that that gives us. People don't want others messing with their business, which is what some of it's about. Most of it is the feeling of family. It kind of just all works together somehow."

"How did this place start?" Chris asked. "Did you live around here before?"

"No, we came here about three years ago, basically right after the war. We came on a train from Oregon." He watched me look at him sideways. "There were a lot of people here when we got here and we picked up a few along the way. We just mostly look out for each other and everybody knows it."

We made it to the top of the grain elevator and Quade walked over to the gate. Pushing it open we stepped out into a small room with a large double door on one end. He went to it and pushed it open, allowing light to flood in and a mist from the rain to hit us in the face. Putting on my sunglasses, I stepped outside.

I was amazed at how far you could see. We were looking west as I walked up to the railing that allowed me to see all the way down to the ground. I could see Quade had brought us to the top of the grain elevators but had stopped at the bottom of the four story structure that went up from there. Everything looked to be on a miniature scale from up there.

Walking a little off to myself, I tried my radio again and got a worried Jake in return. I told him what we were doing and that it may be an hour or so before we were ready to head back. He was happy to hear about our manifold being restored.

Davina came on and we talked about the town some. She sounded worried and I told her we would rush back as soon as we could.

As I was talking I was looking around at the taller structure that rose out of the top of the grain elevator. There was a door and several windows on the west side where I stood. A metal enclosed ladder led up the side and led to the roof. About half way up were more windows. I could see on top were antennas of different sizes. Moving some so that I could see farther down the north side, I saw that there was a satellite dish on the east side of it. My interest was well-peeked.

Finishing off with the radio I went over and asked Quade what the tall structure was. He told me it was where their radio was and offered to show Chris and I inside. Chris looked at me with longing eyes and I too shared his want. Thinking about the security of the situation, I did not see what it could hurt us, we already being spread far thinner than I had wanted. I did not figure it would hurt any. I hoped those were not famous last thoughts.

He led us to the door that was back inside the room just off the elevator and pulled it open. We walked through a short hallway to a metal stairwell and started up. The stairs ended at the third story and we made it through yet another door. Walking inside the large area, I saw there were no walls and that the ceiling was actually the roof of the structure two stories overhead. Light poured through the windows all the way to the top.

There was a long, sturdy table set up on the wall closest to the door we came through and to its left. A huge window allowed you to see out west and capture all the glory of the Kansas plains. Several different types of radios were set up there and mostly took up the entire space but for various stations of computers waiting to be used. Some old, long, office cubicle walls sectioned off the area a bit farther into the room. Wires ran all over the walls everywhere. I looked and saw they came in through the windows and down through the roof.

Looking at the rest of the area, I was not so impressed. A wide, metal staircase led to a roof access door on the wall to the right. Two huge, wood burning stoves were up close to the elevator door with large fans aimed at the squared off cubicles. The rest of the area seemed to hold a variety of items that had long been forgotten. Walking over to a window in the wall that allowed me to look east, I pulled up in surprise.

There were two large satellite dishes in the way of getting a clear view of the top of the single story structure that ran all the way to the end of the grain silos and was just about as wide as it. Solar panels crowded just about every inch of the space on top of it. Looking into the background I saw what seemed to be fields of wheat, though not perfectly lined up like the long rows you would think to see when farmers had their powered farm equipment at work.

"Is that wheat?" I asked Quade, who had come up beside me and was looking out as well.

"Yeah, there are some hard workers out there," he said. "Steve and Suzie run that farm over there. I don't know how they do so much of it really. They work it all with the old-time farm equipment. It's awesome to watch a harvest from up here. Actually, it's awesome to watch most anything from up here." He looked at me with a grin.

"I could imagine," I told him.

"Our compound is topped by some fifty foot water tanks and sits in a little hollow where no one can see us from a hill away," I told him with little thought. "Sitting on top of those things is the best place in the world at sunset."

"I know what you mean," he said. "Sounds nice, being hidden away. I could use that sometimes."

"Yeah, it feels good being tucked away," I told him. "I could see how this would be good too, though."

"It really is," Quade said, looking far off. "It's overwhelming to watch the things that go on in the land around here." I nodded understandingly.

"That's a lot of solar panels," Chris broke in. "Is it the same on the other building?" We both leaned in to look over.

"Yeah, it's the perfect spot for them," he said. "They sure make life a bit better around here. It's been pretty cloudy lately though, so the yield isn't as good. They keep up though."

"What's up with those satellite dishes?" I asked, trying not to hint that I was more than just curious.

"Yeah, that was Wanda and Axel's idea," he said. "They keep trying to see if anyone is still out there listening. It keeps them busy through the winter."

Chris looked at me but I ignored him, hoping he would not say anything. It did not feel like we were in danger from these people but I knew with the right information that could all change in an instant. I was not sure what that could be from us, and I felt a little silly thinking like that when these people were being so generous. I tried to clear it from my mind. I saw Quade's forehead furrow and I quickly tried to change the subject.

"You guys do anything with wind power?" I asked. "I've seen a lot of the turbines spread out since we've been in Kansas."

"No, they are all too far off," he said. "It would be nice though, because sometimes the wind just howls around here."

"I bet," Chris put in.

"Actually a couple of the townspeople are looking into some wind powered stuff," Quade told us. "I don't think we can handle those big ones but we have been looking around for the smaller ones. I guess they put the word out for traders too but we haven't seen any up and working yet. Shall we head back down?"

We thanked him for the personal tour and for the chance to call back to base. He smiled and seemed pleased to do it. The ride down was silent and I was glad to be closer to the ground.

I found the three in the welding shop where we left them. George seemed pleased with what they were getting done which in turn elevated my spirits. They said they were almost done when we got there and I was triple glad about that.

"Teal left you all some breakfast over there," Lincoln said and pointed to a close by workstation.

Quade led the way there and we all nodded at what looked like a bowl of oatmeal and some buttered toast. It smelled great as we got closer and I spotted a thermos of coffee and I think I picked up my step. I could smell it was the brewed kind and not the instant that I carried around in little baggies. Quade got there first however, and started pouring it into the three cups set out. I grabbed a bowl of oatmeal and saw honey poured in circles on top. Finding a spoon close at hand I dived in and felt a little bad when I looked up after it was all gone.

"Did you breathe at all," Chris asked with a chuckle that Quade shared.

"Sorry, it was just pretty good," I told them. "I don't think we've had oatmeal for a while." Chris nodded agreement. "That honey was great!"

"Yeah, Dick runs the bees over north of town," Quade told us. "He has a field of hives. It's grown pretty crazy over the years."

"Vince talked to me a few times about hives," I told him. "He started up last year actually. He's wanting to expand."

"Well, if you let them they sure get away from you in a hurry," he said. "You've heard about rabbits multiplying? They don't have anything on honeybees."

"I do think Vince was talking about breaking off and starting another colony," I told him.

"Do you guys farm?" Quade asked.

"Yeah, we've turned our water tanks into a greenhouse," Chris said. I saw Quade's confusion.

"They're only made to look like large water storage tanks," I told him. "They were really the entrance to the compound. The ceilings are semitransparent and they open up for some reason. It works great for growing crops."

"Sounds like it," he said.

"Vince is the man in charge of all of that for us," I told him.

I finished off my two slices of toast and finally started on the cup of coffee. We all walked over to look over the shoulders of the ones working on fixing the manifold, covering our eyes when the times called for it. It started to feel like it was taking a lot longer than I was hoping when George held up the manifold and turned it around in his hands, looking at it from every angle.

"This is better than it was when it was new," he said. "I do think that last little bit did it. Lincoln, I can't thank you enough. You, sir, are a master at your craft."

"No, you did most of the cutting and patching," Lincoln said. "But I am sure that thing will never break again."

"I wish I had time to refit them all like this one," George told him. "When we find a place to settle in for a while, I think I'll do that very thing." He looked around at the rest of us and seemed to understand that we were waiting for him. "Ah yes, back to work. But I think I owe you a look around our beast of a locomotive." I saw Lincoln's eyes light up.

"I'd like that very much," he told George. He looked over at Quade.

"I think it would be fine," Quade said. "Just take someone with you."

"We've had a look around your place," I told him, not really sure why I continued. "If you're wanting to, we won't mind at all having you as some company." I watched as Teal and Lynn walked into the machine shop. Axel, a man that we saw earlier out by our train, followed close behind.

"How was breakfast?" Teal asked.

"It was great!" we all said in unison.

"Looks like they got their part fixed," Quade told them.

"We're going to go help make sure it works," Lincoln said almost childlike. He seemed embarrassed at the response and we all gave him a smile.

"Mind if we tag along?" Teal asked. Quade looked over at her.

"We'd like to talk more about Kevin and those compounds," Lynn said, looking straight at me with a serious look on her face.

"I don't mind you coming but I don't think we can be much more help with that," I told her. I looked over at the new man in the room, who looked friendly and stood next to Lynn.

"This is Axel," Lynn told me. "He's our communications director." He moved forward to shake my hand. I returned it and introduced everyone in the room.

"Lynn filled me in on y'alls situation," he said. "Sounds like Lincoln is getting you fixed up."

"Yeah, I think we are ready here," I told him. "I guess we should get moving that way."

"Agreed," George said.

"I'll get my horse ready," Lincoln said.

"Mind telling Brady we're going, too?" Quade asked.

"Sure thing," Lincoln said and moved off.

"I'll just get my things and be to the stable in a minute," Quade said.

"I'm ready," Lynn said. "I'll walk you guys there."

"Me too," Teal said, as we all started out of the machine shop.

I was not sure how to feel about bringing so many people back with us. It seemed extraordinarily different for us, and I was starting to feel the strain. I figured with any luck we would be back to base and get the part on before I could think much more about it.

We made it to the livery, which was just outside the docks and saw Brady already leading one of our horses to the front. I was glad to see the saddle still on as he tied it to the hitching post and moved off to get the others. He stopped and talked to Teal about them needing their horses and tack and I saw him pick up his step. Lynn moved off into the corrals and started nickering to the horses in a different pen.

It did not take long for everyone to be ready to move out. Quade had come back, well-armed and looking ready to take on whatever trouble might present itself. I made sure to check my saddle before I climbed aboard but with nothing else to do, we turned as one and headed away from the large grain elevators and back toward base.

I let Quade lead the way and saw that he did not take the road. We crossed many tracks that went every which way and I saw George studying them. We walked north and toward what was left of the small town. Rubble was most of what we saw.

"Looks like a disaster area here," I told Quade as we moved through the streets littered with debris.

"Yeah a tornado came through a couple of years ago, right after we got here in fact," he told me. "It was a tiny one and really there wasn't much to the town anyway. It's mostly grown over now and everyone seemed just as happy to take up a home in the elevators."

"That makes sense," Chris said. "You guys get a lot of tornados?"

"No, we are kind of in a bowl here, but it's obvious they can get to us," he said. "I haven't seen one since that day though."

We rode on in silence for a while and I watched as Quade called home on a small radio. I did likewise, letting Jake know we were heading back plus five. That seemed to alarm him and I too was still not too comfortable with it. As my thoughts gathered, we moved past the town. I was glad that we finally moved into a trot which quickly turned into a run.

We moved north until we passed several old farmhouses and a few large barns. Some of the fields there seemed to be worked and were growing a major crop of corn or something else I did not recognize. Before I knew it we had made it to the tracks and Quade turned us west.

We crossed the road that looked familiar and I knew it to be the one we got on to head south toward the town. We crossed it and Quade held up, saying he would prefer to stay beside us. I radioed Jake and told him where we were. We rode over the small rise and saw our train at the bottom.

"That is beautiful," I heard Lincoln say. "I've never seen a train like that."

"It's a Camelback locomotive," George told him.

"And it runs on coal or wood?" Lincoln asked, wonder in his voice.

"I refitted the chamber to burn old motor oil," George said with pride.

"What?" Lincoln asked and I could see that it impressed Quade.

"Yeah, I figure there will be enough of that around for a while," George told them.

"I would figure every town you entered would have enough to keep you going," Lincoln said. "What's the range on it?"

They started talking shop and I mostly ignored the details. I tried to see if I could make out where Laura was watching us, without really turning my head. I did not see her, though I did see Margie atop the caboose. Movement to the left of the boxcars showed me where Davina was. We stayed moving forward and took the curved tracks up to the grain cars.

I stopped us there and dismounted. Lincoln finally stopped his questions and we all walked slowly around the cars and up to the front of the engine. Quade's group looked at it and I moved beside it so that they could see all of the cars behind it, making sure to keep us on the side that would give Laura the shots she would need if the situation called for it. (Not sure why I always think that way.) We all stood there as the visitors took in the scene.

"It is a beautiful set up," Quade said. "It's the perfect vehicle to travel the wastelands. Are those things armored?" He pointed at the boxcars.

"No, not yet," George answered before I could lie.

"Wow, I love the caboose," Teal said. I saw Margie standing on top watching us with her muzzleloader hanging down in her arms. I knew she could fire from there in under a second.

"I should get started with getting this thing reinstalled," George said.

"Of course," Lincoln said. "Just tell me how I can help."

George, Sterling and Lincoln moved toward the side of the engine and I asked the rest if they would like some coffee. They all seemed to like the idea and I asked Margie if she would mind us taking over her caboose with the guests. She smiled and nodded. We all moved inside and I saw that Margie made it there ahead of us. I looked at all of them and watched the amazement on their faces.

"I think it will take only a few minutes to get the water ready," Margie said. She handed me a basket full of biscuits in the meantime.

We all found a seat and I saw Davina coming in the back door of the caboose. She smiled at me and then looked at the visitors. Quade and Axel stood up to be polite and she seemed to appreciate it. Jake made it in behind her and Shay came in next. I waited and seeing no one else coming in, I made introductions all around.

"Thanks for letting us come here," Quade said. "I'm sure it's pretty hard to trust people out here."

"We welcome you," Margie told him.

"That's a nice radio you're carrying there," Axel told Jake. "I bet the range on that thing is awesome. It has a satellite feed too, doesn't it?"

"Yeah, it's in a compartment on the inside," Jake told him. I looked harder, not knowing it had that.

"We are set up pretty good in the tower," Axel said proudly. "We have satellite dishes there and we're looking to see if anything is still up and running. If it's there we'll find it." We tried not to all look around at each other.

"How long will it take to get that piece on?" Quade asked and I told him I had no idea.

We switched to talking about the town, telling the others what we had seen there. We talked a little about the messy bar we had entered and Axel told us about a fight that had broken out there the night before. Quade still seemed a little concerned about a few of the people that had started it. Poker was blamed as was the high-quality alcohol that we were told was a local favorite. Quade did not seem to be a fan. We all had finished a second cup of coffee when we heard the engine burner come to life. (I quickly told a nervous Quade what the explosive sound was.)

We all went outside and looked at the engine. George moved to the other windows from where he usually sat and looked out from above at his pride and joy. A worried smile played at his lips as I am sure one did at mine. I knew the next few minutes would pass slowly.

We all waited there outside the engine, watching George coming down and him and Lincoln crawling all over underneath the engine looking for leaks. Steam seemed to start to come from the regular spots and I saw George starting to relax. I turned my mind to saying goodbye to these newfound friends and thinking about what all needed done before we could move out of there.

All of a sudden steam blew from the other side of the engine. This time the steam did not continue but came out in a huge cloud that billowed skyward and looked like the remains of a large explosion, forming a huge mushroom cloud which you probably could have seen for miles. I heard a grinding sound and jerked my head to look at George. He was running headlong the catwalk that led into the burn chamber. I felt horrible for him and also felt the seriousness now of our situation. I watched as George slowly made his way back down the ladder. I did not however know what to say to him.

"It looks like we ride on from here," he said, looking at me with what I knew had to be a heavy heart. Margie walked over to him and wrapped him in her arms.

"Let us help," Teal said.

"Yes, please, we can help," Lincoln said. "It's got to be something with the pressure chamber. We'll take it to town and weld it up too."

"How could we do that?" Sterling asked. "It would take a line of horses a mile long to pull this sucker."

"We have a train too and it's fueled and ready to do some work," Quade told us and I saw a spark return to George's face.

CHAPTER 12

I was not sure how to respond to that. It made my heart race for sure, but I tried to keep the idea in perspective. Ideas of some well-needed rescue came to mind as I watched George move to stand beside Margie.

"What kind of train?" he asked Quade.

"It's a diesel engine, but Lincoln knows more about it than I do," Quade told him.

"Is it something that can tow us in?" George turned to Lincoln and asked.

"Without the slightest trouble," Lincoln told him.

"I know that a town like that there doesn't run on charity," I said, looking at Quade. "I'm not sure we have a lot to trade that can equal the help that it seems it would take to do what you're talking about."

"We don't mind," Lynn said and Teal echoed it.

"I'm sorry we haven't proven ourselves more friendly," Quade told me.

"It's not that and I'm hoping you're not taking this the wrong way," I told him. "I know your time is worth something. I just want to make sure we can afford to pay you what's fair."

"Lincoln interrupted me earlier when I asked you to let us help," Lynn said, cutting me off. "What I really was asking is if you would let us help you find Kevin."

Everyone stopped moving or doing anything else besides looking straight at her. She stood there without moving, standing behind her question with raised head. I knew I was going to like this town for a long time.

"Why would you want to do that?" Sterling asked as we continued to stare.

"Cause it looks like you need it and that's who we are," she said boldly. Sterling seemed to accept that answer.

"It couldn't hurt, us getting into town anyways," he said and gave Lynn a smile.

I knew Sterling meant it innocently but I looked at Shay, wondering what would be the look on her face. She did not seem to notice or did not want me to know she cared. I am sure of the latter as the proper conclusion.

"Well, we should find out first if it's something we can fix," I told them, looking at George.

"I'm sure it's the chamber itself this time," he told me. "With the way it lost pressure so quickly, it's got to be." He looked at Lincoln to concur which he did with his head down and shaking.

"What good is it going to do to get it into town?" Margie asked. We all turned to her, then to George.

"If it's fixable, I think that is the only place to take it," George said and looked at Lincoln. I did not like asking this next part.

"How long do you think it will take George?" I asked.

"Let's just get a look and find out," he told me.

We all moved around to look at where the steam had escaped from the side of the engine. George was in front and I watched his worried face as he tried to find the new disaster. He pulled up and looked hard between the two rear wheels. His expression was one of calm resilience. I turned to the train as I came to stand beside him. He moved in to get a closer look. Lincoln and Sterling moved in close as well.

Immediately there seemed to me like a large cause for concern. The side of the burn chamber had been blown out for at least four feet. It was a jagged hole that was open and peeled back some. I watched as George went up and put his hand in the hole and spread his fingers wide. They still did not touch any metal.

"Not as bad as I thought," Sterling said and I looked at him to see if he was just trying to make George feel better. George turned and looked at him as he moved in to be able to feel the edges. "We'll need another piece of metal to overlay here and here. Some permanent straps should go over them every sixteen inches or so and bolt in on the bottom and top. It may not look it but it's the best kind of break that could have happened." We all looked at him, then at the hole again. "You see it's basically right down the middle, except for down there where it angles toward the top," he continued, pointing as he went on. "If we put reinforcements here and cut these edges down we should be in good shape. I can do it with what they have back at that town." He looked again at Lincoln.

"You're welcome to use whatever I have," Lincoln said. "If it gets this beauty back on the tracks, I'm glad to be of service."

We all watched George look back at his engine and run his hand along the edges of the break. If it had been a woman I would have said they were having a tender moment. I felt bad for what he must be going through. I knew this was something that we should try to do.

"Okay, let's give it a try," I said. "If you guys would help us we would be forever grateful. We can ride on to the coordinates once we get you out of this traffic jam and check them out. Sterling, you and George stay in town and get this thing ready to move on."

"I'll radio home and let them know to get things started," Quade said. "Eric can get the diesel headed this way." I saw him look questioningly at Lincoln who in turn nodded.

"We'll need to clear this wrecked car out of the way," Lincoln told him.

"Maybe some horse power can get that done," George told him. Quade nodded and turned to call home.

Davina moved up next to me and put her arm on my shoulder. I turned and gave her a smile and she returned it with a beautiful one of her own. She looked more deeply at me then and I could tell she was wondering how I was doing.

"I think this is the right thing to do," I told her. She nodded and just stood there beside me. I was glad for her there.

Quade came back and said that their train would be there soon. We all turned and walked over to the grain cars that stood in front of our train and tried to access the best way of moving them out of our way. They looked pretty serious about staying there.

"Any reason we shouldn't just pull them over the side there and let them roll off," George asked Quade.

"No, I think that's a fine idea," he told him. "Think we can get them to tip?"

"I think with the right amount of leverage, we could do it," George replied, he spirits seeming a bit better. "We may need all the horsepower we can get, though."

"You can use me and my horse however you see fit," Quade told him. The rest of those from town added their agreements to that.

"If you all will help me unhook these others I think this will take no time at all," he said.

We all let George lead us then, him pointing in every direction. Chris and Laura were instructed to get all of the horses down the small slope beside the tracks and Davina and I helped with that. Margie ran for all the rope that we had. I could not see what George and Lincoln were doing up by the coal cars but I assumed they were acting in accordance with whatever comprehensive plan they had come up with. As we awaited further instructions we gathered down the slope from the cars.

"How long do you think it will take to get the other engine here?" I asked Quade.

"It shouldn't take too long to get here," he told me. "We keep them in at small depot inside a building outside of town for cover. I guess it's not so much a depot as it is a thrown together lean-to shed that used to be an old airplane hanger. It took some time but we got it moved. It keeps them covered pretty well. But to your question, it's not so much how long it takes to get here as it is how long Eric will let the engine warm up for. It pisses Lincoln off when he starts it right up and takes off."

As he said that George came down the hill and started talking to us about the plan he had for moving the cars. He told us that we should only have to move the one grain car we smashed. He said that the rest could be transported to a switch track to move them out of the way. He told us we were waiting for the other engine to pull the other cars away from the wrecked one. As he said that we saw the diesel engine pull over the hill just to the east of us. I did not think we had been waiting that long.

"Looks like Lincoln may not be so happy with Eric," Quade told me with a smile.

I was listening to him but was also looking at the engine that had just come over the hill. It was a typical modern day locomotive, orange on the bottom and grey on the top. However, that was all that was normal looking about it. The small railing on the side of the catwalk had been beefed up with metal plating that was about four and a half feet high. Machine gun posts were positioned about every ten feet and set in a place where the metal was positioned to give the shooter better cover. Likewise, the front catwalk of the train was plated and well-armed. A short turret was fashioned to the top of the cabin with what looked like a fifty caliber machine gun. Thick wire mesh covered all of the windows of the cabin. Armor plating also came down almost to the ground coving the wheels and everything over the side, including a thick well-framed box around the gas tank. My heart beat a little faster as I watched it approach.

I heard the brakes being applied as it pulled up close to the grain cars. The rumble that had taken over the ground mostly stopped and I saw the smoke, coming from the top, die down. I watched the train stop and watched a young man come out of a front door that was at the center of the front of the locomotive and make it down the ladder from the front catwalk.

Lincoln had started walking toward the young man as he made it to the ground. Quade told us that it was Eric and he yelled something as he started to move up the hill toward the two of them. I followed and came up to them as Lincoln was saying something about carelessness.

"I told him to hurry," Quade told Lincoln. Eric did not seem to be effected by the tirade from Lincoln. He must have heard it before. "It's my fault."

"Let's just get these things hooked up," Lincoln told Eric. "Inch forward and I'll hook you on. Back up just a little after that."

"Okay, I'll look for your signals," Eric told him and turned on his heels and headed back to the engine.

Lincoln and Eric then seemed to have a language all their own. It was a sign language that was played out with precision as the engine moved forward at different speeds and then inched back at a finger's movement from Lincoln. I watched and tried to learn some of it but soon found little of it made sense to me. As Lincoln clinched his fist, I saw that the cars had been moved back ten feet and the one left was the wrecked one which now needed to be pulled over the side.

George took over then and directed us to bring our horses to about thirty feet away from the train. The slope was not very long and it seemed that one flip of the car would get it all the way down it and well out of the way. It did look a little dangerous if the car was to keep rolling but we were instructed to keep our ropes taut. He told us not to tie the ropes to our saddle horns but only to wrap them around it keeping pressure on the back side so as to be able to let it go if the rope got caught in a tumbling car. It still seemed dangerous but that is what we were about. With all in place we led out our horses and one burro into position.

At George's instruction we all pulled our ropes tight and waited. As he yelled we backed our animals and put pressure to our ropes. I felt the strain of my horse as he leaned into the weight of the car. We were told to keep up if the car started to move and for sure not to let it go back down once we got it going. As I then saw the car start to move I encouraged my horse and soon saw the car teetering on one set of its wheels. We all continued and with some ease backed away with taut ropes as the car flipped over and then once more as it landed on it's top at the bottom of the slope. A loud hurray went up and I could see the gladness on George's face.

We got quickly into action gathering all of the ropes and putting our horses back into the boxcar. Chris and Laura put the corral away as Lincoln figured out how to hook up our engine to the line. I helped where I could and tried not to look too much at the train. It took us little time and we were hooked to the other engine with two grain cars between us.

The all aboard was sounded and we all scrambled to jump on. George went into our engine's cabin and I followed him. He pushed some levers and then gave a hoot on the whistle. He sat in his chair and leaned out the window. I sat across from him and looked out my side as we started to move. I felt Davina's arms around me and I reached up for her hand.

We moved quickly across the first few hills and then noticeably slowed. I saw we had passed the road and had kept going but before we reached the top of the next rise we started turning south. I looked down and saw that we were switching tracks. I looked over past George to see where we were turning but I could not tell. Looking back, I saw that we were pointing now toward the large grain elevators.

"Is that the town?" Davina asked me.

"Yeah, kind of between those two grain elevators there," I told her. "But there is a lot going on around them too."

"I'm excited to see it," she told me. "I know you're probably not too excited about doing this," she said as she started massaging my shoulders. "You doing okay?"

"Yeah, I think these guys have proven a little bit of who they are," I told her. "I don't say we should let our guard down, though. It's interesting seeing a thriving town out here, to say the least. That grain elevator to the north there has a pretty cool radio room. You can't see it but there are a couple of satellite dishes on the side. I guess you should be able to see it from up north here."

"Really?" she asked looking closer out the front window. As she did that we came to a curve and started heading back east again. "Are their communications picking up the same thing we are?" she asked with some concern.

"It looks like they aren't really sure how to use them. I did see they have some big screen TVs hanging up and they look like they're hooked into some computer. They didn't seem to be working, though. Sounds like they are still trying to pick up some reception."

"Well, I'm not looking forward to riding up to those coordinates," she told me and I agreed. "That rain could come back any time." I kicked myself for not even noticing that it had stopped. Looking overhead, I could see the clouds even starting to give way to a partly cloudy sky.

"When did that happen?" I asked in a way that must have seemed funny as I heard Davina chuckle.

"You didn't notice?" she asked. "Well, there's a lot on your plate." I smiled up at her.

"Let's blame Jake," I told her. "He didn't give me the report."

"You can't always blame him, you know," she said as I moved out of the chair and made her sit down. I took my turn now rubbing her shoulders.

"Oh yes I can," I said in the meantime.

"You can try, I guess," she told me softly.

"Looks like the town is getting closer," I told her, changing the subject, still knowing full well that Jake was to blame. "They said a tornado took it out a couple of years ago."

"Oh great, tornado alley," she said.

"I bet it has something to do with the constant changing weather patterns," I told her. "They are in a bowl here."

"It doesn't look like it totally destroyed everything," she said. "I can kind of see how it moved through." We both looked at the damage as we moved along the north side of what was left of the small farm town.

We passed the grain elevators and moved to a set of metal buildings about a half block east of them. I saw other engines there, some fitted out in armored garb like the one pulling us. Some cars of different sorts were there as well, some being fitted with different types of rails and everything post-apocalyptic you could think of. There was a large pile of scrapped train cars and several engines that looked to be cleaned to the bones, all off to the side on various rails. It was kind of cool to see. A long dock with a building attached ran beside a set of engines. As we got close we pulled to a stop.

"Looks like this is our stop," George said, pulling himself back inside. He had a look of excitement on his face.

I got on the radio and told everyone to still be on guard. I was not sure why I did it so matter of factly but I just did not want to get too relaxed in the present surroundings. I heard back from everyone and I looked at George.

"Make sure to stay ready for anything," I told him.

"Understood," he responded. "I don't think I've ever seen anything like this." I agreed with him as did Davina.

We all stepped off the train and moved forward. Lincoln was already there directing what to do with the new grain cars. Eric listened and moved off to get started. I saw him move into the building attached to the docks.

"Looks like once we get these cars out of the way and move ol' Billy there, we can fit you right in," Lincoln told us. "It shouldn't take too long. Eric has gotten pretty good at it."

"Is this where we are going to fix it up at?" George asked, seeming to want to ask more.

"Yeah, this is where we put most of the big stuff together," he replied with a smile, us all looking at the well-armored engines.

"How do you fuel diesel engines?" George asked, fully mystified, like the rest of us.

"Some things we keep to ourselves," Lincoln told him. "Not meaning to be rude, mind you."

"No we understand that," George told him and we all nodded.

We watched Quade, Teal and Lynn coming over to where we were standing. It reminded me that we should be moving on with our mission. Lynn moved right up to us.

"So are you going to let us help?" she asked. I looked around at my entire group standing around.

"What exactly did you have in mind?" I asked her.

"We can take you to the coordinates you said you had," she told us. Quade and Teal looked at me and waited.

"This is not just about finding Kevin," I told her. "There is a lot going on." Her forehead furrowed as did the others.

"What do you mean?" Quade asked, moving forward some.

"Maybe we should sit down and share some coffee," I told them, figuring five minutes should do it. "After we talk a bit, then you can decide if you are still up for helping." This seemed to put worried looks on their faces.

"Okay, let's let Eric and Lincoln move these things around," Quade said. "We can go inside and have a sit-down at Lucky's." He pointed to the east gate that was in the wall between the grain elevators. I saw Teal roll her eyes.

"That sounds good," I told him. "George, why don't you and Sterling stay here and get started on fixing what needs it. George, you know where we'll be." I got a nod from both of them.

The rest of us walked toward the tall towering buildings and I watched my group look at them. I wondered if I looked the same as when I had approached them. Everyone was amazed at their height and the sheer enormities of them. They grew taller as we approached. We slowed more by the gate as the others tried to take the whole scene in.

"You havin' breakfast at da' pub, mister Quade?" I heard from above. Looking up, I saw a large black man standing on the bridge that stood over the doorway. The M16 in his huge hands looked small.

"Yeah, heading that way Fredrick," Quade told him.

"Who you got with you there?" a shorter man standing beside Fredrick asked, looking menacingly at our group.

"Come on Ray, them there's from that train over there," Fredrick told him, pointing to where I looked and saw our train moving. Ray looked at the big black man.

"Well yeah, I know that," Ray said. "I mean what are they doing here?" They both looked down at us.

"We'll see in just a few minutes, I guess," Quade told him. "For now they're getting their train worked on and we're having some coffee."

"Mornin' to ya miss Teal and miss Lynn," Fredrick said as we walked under the bridge and entered the town.

"Mornin' boys," they both said together.

"Tell Lacy hi for me, will ya miss Teal," Fredrick said and I saw Teal shake her head. The men above snickered a little.

"Sure thing, Freddy," Teal said as we walked under the bridge. I heard Ray laughing at the large man.

We walked into the bar that was just inside the gate that we had visited earlier. It was surprisingly cleaned from the mess that it had been when we had first seen the place. A red-haired well-tattooed man was sitting at a table at the far end of the room. A pretty dark-haired lady that reminded me of Marla sat across from him. They looked at us as we came in.

"Morning, Allen," Quade said. "Morning, Jackie."

All the pleasantries were exchanged with the couple and they got back to eating their breakfast. We found a spot in the center of the room that would fit us all, taking up a few tables as we spread out some. I watched the lady we had met earlier come over to us.

"Morning all," she said. "Good morning, Quade," she added sweetly. I saw Teal looking at her with eyes of steel ice.

"Morning, Lacy," Quade told her flatly. "Coffees all around, unless you all are eating something?" He looked at all of us with a glance, but we all declined. "Coffees it is then."

The waitress turned on her heels and went back to the counter. They all looked at us then. I took some time to think about all that I should tell them and maybe some of the things I should leave out. I took a deep breath and almost began. Our coffee came then and gave me a little more time.

Lacy put a tin cup in front of all of us and then sat a large pot of coffee in front of Quade, trying to give him a smile. Teal grabbed the pot, still giving Lacy the evil eye. The young woman was oblivious to her life being in danger.

"You can move on now," Teal told her. Lacy, removed from her trance, turned on her heel, this time a little gruffly, and walked off. Teal poured us all some coffee as Quade tried to hold back a smile.

"So, I guess you all have something we need to talk about," Lynn said as Teal sat back down.

I started with the basics of what we knew about Kevin. As I went into further detail about his experiments and research only Quade seemed to be surprised. Knowing that I could only talk about that for so long I finally came to the part that would mean the most to the people in front of me. I hoped I could make them understand the seriousness of it.

"We had no idea who this guy was," Davina put in when she saw the others looking at us with concern.

They seemed to be wondering what we could come up with next. As she spoke Axel walked into the bar. We all turned to him and he pulled up short.

"Just looking to see where you all went," he said. "You weren't all just talking about me were you?" He saw the serious looks on all our faces and quickly lost his smile.

He made it to the end of the table where the others were sitting and sat in the closest chair. The room stayed quiet then for a full minute as we drank our coffee slowly. Looking up, I saw everyone staring at me.

"Our compound back home is a really old command center for several different launch sites," I started slow. "We have a large control room. One entire wall is dedicated to four large computer screens. Jadee, our computer genius, found out how to use the satellites to look down on us. We can find specific coordinates and zero in right on them."

"What?" Axel asked with more than a little enthusiasm. He had picked a perfect time to walk in. "The satellites are still operational? I knew it. How did she get them to work? I mean are they giving off a signal or something?"

"I'm really sorry," I told them. "Honestly, I have no idea. I think she probably didn't sleep for a week working on getting them going. We still don't know how to use them all."

"Why can't you just look down at the coordinates you are headed for to see if you can find evidence of Kevin being there?" Teal asked.

"First off, because it's been cloudy since we got back home," I told her. I saw Quade's forehead furrow. "And second, Kevin knows we will be able to see him from overhead so he's going to be smart about what he leaves out in the open."

"Yeah, but didn't you say he doesn't think you know where he's going?" Quade asked. "I'm sure he knows you can't look for him with the satellites everywhere."

"Yes, but we plan on looking for him as much as we can," I told them. "And if we do see him, then we are going to need to be wherever he is quickly. It would be nice if we are just down the road. That's kind of why we came out here with very little info about that one compound out west of here. At least we're out here and ready to move whenever we do find him." They seemed to agree with that. "That's not really the part that we wanted to talk to you about."

"I think we are all very interested in what it could be that makes you so concerned," Quade told us. "I'm thinking it has something to do with those military folk you told us about."

"Not long ago we got a message on one of our screens," I told them. "We didn't know who it was from. They told us they were sending the message from an Embassy in Kenya."

"Kenya?" Lynn stated. "What did the message say?"

"It said someone was watching us," I said. "They said we were giving off a signal. We asked them for proof so they gave us their coordinates and lit a fire. Sure enough we watched a blaze start at a town at those coordinates in Kenya."

"So who was watching you?" Teal asked.

"We still don't know if we've found out," I told them. "They also said they sent us some important information to some coordinates south of us. They said it was life-or-death and that if it fell into the wrong hands it would be the end, again."

"So the experiments must have gone on," Lynn said and I could not tell if she was asking. "Kenya was a hotbed of research for a lot of Roosevelt's ideas. They were saying they were studying effects on apes and not humans which we all thought was a little weird given what all else he was doing." I looked at Shay. "I used to receive research papers from that team a lot. It didn't ever seem like anything important."

"They were trying to get us to take that info to Missouri," Shay told them.

"Why Missouri?" Lynn asked.

"They said there was another team there," I told her.

"There were some researchers out that way," Lynn said. "But there were researchers everywhere. I wonder what was so important about those ones."

"How is it that you know this stuff?" Margie asked her.

"I used to work for Kevin Roosevelt," she told everyone and I heard a few shocked replies. "I didn't have much of a choice and when I saw what was going on I tried to escape. Most of us did. We were working at a prison then, with all research patients. I was in charge of a team that went through the data that came in."

"Was that where they were doing all the human experiments and all?" I asked her.

"That was only one of the places," she said with little feeling. "There were literally hundreds."

"Any out here in Kansas?" Chris asked. I jerked my head over to look at her and wished I had thought to ask that.

"No, not that I remember," she replied and it looked like she could tell we all were a little disappointed. "There was nothing that came out of the areas around here. It was mostly California and Minnesota. Most of the rest came from other countries or were encoded I guess, now to think of it. I guess that could mean they came from anywhere. Research was going on at a frantic pace at that time."

"What did you guys do when they told you someone was watching you?" Axel asked, getting us all back to where I was wanting to go.

"We went out and got the information, figuring it would help us figure out who may be watching us," I told him.

"What was it?" Lynn asked. In for a penny, in for a pound I thought, and we were definitely in for a penny.

"It was info about all the research Kevin was doing and all about his secret serum," I told her.

"Was there anything on there so important it had to get somewhere?" Quade asked.

"Not that we saw," I told him. "The only thing life-or-death about it to us was the knowledge that Kevin wasn't who he said he was. He had always seemed to be this little quiet guy."

"Really?" Lynn asked. "I always knew him as this bigger than life monster."

"Yeah, he played us pretty good," I admitted.

"You said you picked the information up," Lynn seemed to be starting a question. "They must have sent it via satellite to have sent it from Kenya."

"Yeah, I guess," I told her, wondering where she was going. "Our old systems couldn't download it right. They sent it to a place that was still powered and able to receive it."

"How did you retrieve it?" she said, cornering me.

"On a pin drive," I told her straight. "The coordinates led us to a missile command center, a rather up-to-date one, and we downloaded it out of the system there."

"You guys went inside a missile command base and took information out of their data center?" Axel asked shocked. "That must have been unreal."

"Yeah, it was a little freaky being inside a Minuteman Capsule," I told him.

"You went inside the capsule?" Axel asked, growing in excitement. "You guys are frickin' awesome."

"I do understand so far, I think," Quade told me, trying to put a stop to where Axel was starting to go. "But what does that have to do with us needing to know something important?"

"When we got back home from that trip, Kevin was gone, with Tara and Olivia," I told him. "When we came upstairs from our search for him, a line of Humvees was sitting on the hillside."

"Wow," Axel said. "Who were they?"

"It gets a little strange here," I told them all. "The leader said he was looking for Kevin but that they had watched him leave ahead of us getting there. He said they were part of NASA."

"No way!" Axel said. I saw Quade start to get a little annoyed.

"We talked to Kevin on his way back, just before he left," I continued. "He mentioned something about a new space station orbiting in the southern hemisphere that they had been building for a long time. He said a lot of stuff and I'm not sure how much of it to believe. The guy that came to our compound said he was part of that group."

"So he admitted there was a station?!" Axel asked boisterously and then seemed to understand Quade's annoyance.

"He said they were looking for other groups like Kevin, and kind of said there was a station," I said. "He told us some coordinates of where Kevin might be headed and so here we are. We've been talking to NASA ever since. They're the ones we got the next coordinates from." Axel almost fell out of his chair, looking at me with his mouth wide open.

"So what are you wanting to tell us?" Quade asked, getting back to the point of our long conversation.

"I want you to understand that when you say you want to help us find Kevin, that it's not just that that you're getting into," I told him. "We still don't know who these NASA people are and if it wasn't for Kevin having our people, I'm pretty sure we wouldn't be out here." I was not sure that was entirely correct. We had gone after the information, after all. "Jadee back home has been in constant communication with a guy from the space station. They are trying to pour through whatever information they have about where Kevin could be."

"Why do they think out here?" Teal asked.

"They said he was sending medical equipment to areas around where he started," I told them. "They said that was out here."

"Really?" Lynn asked. "That's kind of creepy, us settling out here and now finding out that's where this all started."

"Where are the coordinates that they gave you?" Quade asked.

"Some place close by," I told him. "It looked like the place was in a town called Colby."

"We've been there, lots," Quade told us, looking at the others. "There's no research lab there."

"They said he sent the equipment to some Reserve Unit and that from there he could have ordered it sent to a nearby compound without anyone noticing much. We have the coordinates of the Reserve Unit and the compound." I watched Quade's eyes.

"We cleared out the Reserve Unit a long time ago, what was left of it," Teal told us when Quade went quiet. "There was no equipment, especially medical research stuff. He must have sent it to the compound."

"Sorry, but I think we should look closely at the Reserve Unit," I told her. "Maybe there's some paperwork that says something. It's no guarantee that Kevin is headed to it but perhaps we can find where else he may have sent the equipment and it would tell us where our next move is."

"That's a good idea," she said.

"Do you have that pin drive with you?" Lynn asked and stayed looking at me.

I was not sure that we should let them all the way in. We had not known them for too long and it was not that hard to put on a front. But I had to admit to myself that nothing here seemed different from what it was. And what was more, what could they do with the information anyway, I wondered. Knowledge of the past did not seem so top-secret anymore. I truly did not see the harm in it.

I was not sure why I had gone into such a long discussion with them but it did feel good to have someone else care about what was going on. I could not lie and say we had this thing all under control. Here were some people that could be of big help to us, in more ways than one. It felt a little weird talking so openly but I figured I had better get used to it.

"I'll let you copy it onto your computer system," I told them. I felt my entire group's eyes on me. "I really just want you to know what could be in store for you by you becoming part of this. I don't even think we know yet. We aren't going to run and tell these NASA guys that you are in on it with us now, but I'm sure they will find out. We can't help with that."

"I can see that," Lynn said, but not in the insulting way that it could have been taken. "But if Roosevelt, Kevin I mean, is doing more research on this virus, I think we all need to try and stop him."

I wondered what part this woman had seen that made her so serious about the way she seemed to talk about Kevin and things related to the subject. Working for a guy who let the antidote out on the world would have been bad. With what I saw on the pin drive of what Kevin was capable of doing, knowing that he was at it again, must have been pretty scary for Lynn. She stood up and then we all did.

"I wouldn't mind getting a look at that drive," she told me.

"I can follow you to whatever computer you have available," I told her, wondering if I should think defensively. (I think I will always think this way.)

"I'll take them up to the tower," Lynn said.

"I'll go with you," Axel said.

We all left the bar and went to the elevator that took us to the top. I tried to stay alert and tried to give everyone else the sign to do the same; they seemed not to need it. We all piled onto the large elevator and I was surprised when no one said anything. The elevator moved up just fine, though a little slower.

We made it to the room we had been in before with all the computer stuff and the cubicles and the like. A woman was there at the radios, complete with headphones on. She looked at us with some curiosity and stood up when we started walking more into the room. She smiled and nodded at me and I gave her a smile.

"This is Wanda," Axel told us. "She's Comms most of the time here." She waved at us and we all returned it.

Lynn led the way to a certain cubicle that held a desk and two large flat-screen monitors. She sat in the chair there and hit the power button on the tall, hard drive at her feet. She pulled out a keyboard and looked over at me. She held out her hand as the computer screen came on.

I dug into my vest pocket and figured I was all in. These people were now also all in and I was not sure how I felt about that. It did feel good though as I found the pin drive and placed it into her hand when she looked softly at me and thanked me. We all watched as she plugged it into her computer.

Nothing really dramatic happened at first and I was getting used to watching people hit keys on a keyboard. Different things started and she closed out some items she had been doing; I did not catch sight of what they were. With a ding, another small window came on and she opened it. I watched as she copied the contents of the pin drive. She pulled it out then and handed it back to me with a look of gratitude.

"Let's see if we can pull any of it up now," she told me. Again, I watched as keys were hit and different screens did different things. "You said this was a file of Kevin's old research?"

"Yeah, and we watched everything on it," I told her. "There's some pretty bad stuff on there. There were a few new things Shay found but that's it."

"This is a data update, sent to connect with existing research," she told me, seeming to be confused. "This right here," she said, moving the curser around the screen as I nodded. She clicked onto the only item that George could bring up but she moved it quickly into another screen that was new to me. "How long ago did you get this?"

"A few days," I told her.

"This here tells us there are eighteen update files worth of research. It could be other stuff too. There is no way you could have gone through all of this in two days," she said. "You couldn't have even made it through one file." My heart leaped in my chest.

"So what's all there?" I asked her.

"I don't know," she said. "It will take a week to find out even some of it."

"Any idea if any of those lines could be the one that leads us to Kevin?" I asked her. "Right now, that's all that matters."

"I understand that," she said, looking up at me. "Nothing here gives us any directions right off. They are mostly coded file names or numbers."

I wondered what to do. It still did not seem to matter what information was on the pin drive; that would only seem to matter if you were a mad scientist in search of some new breakthrough. It seemed right having someone that would actually be able to tell us what we were seeing. I hated coming to someone and laying this kind of burden at their feet.

"Are you all sure you want to get involved in this?" I asked and looked over at Quade. He looked at Lynn who nodded, as did Teal.

"We'll help, and do whatever we can," he said. "Some maniac holding women against their will has never been something I've been able to ignore."

"Okay then, maybe I should hook you up with Jadee back home," I told Lynn. "Jake there, can give you the frequency." I took in a deep breath and let it out slowly. "We will try our best to keep you off their screens."

CHAPTER 13

"Are you sure we should do that?" Davina asked.

"That does seem kind of chancy," Chris said. "NASA might not want us to get anyone else involved. We want them giving us all the information we can get. That might dry up if we start pulling others in."

"I don't want NASA to know that we are getting help from anyone or that anyone else is involved at all," I told them. "Jake, I want you to have them run all communications with them here, through the armory. Tell Jadee to figure out how possible it is to keep NASA from knowing what we're doing. Maybe that's not even possible at all but if it is let's use it." Everyone nodded to that. "Tell them not to mention anything about the people here having any information or really anything but our different attempts to find Kevin. We need to keep our connections here a secret as long as possible."

"I'll do it," Jake told me. "Anything else?" I looked around.

"Just fill in Jadee about who Lynn here is and tell them what we're doing," I told him. "See if they found the same thing that Lynn did with the extra files but don't mention that until you're routed through the armory. Tell Jadee to keep that to herself if she finds anything. I know we gave NASA the pin drive but for now let's let them find some of this stuff out for themselves. And ask her if she's had any luck working with Mack. If this next site isn't good, I want to know where he thinks to send us and what he's going off of to get us the next set of coordinates."

"Don't you think we should give NASA as much info as we can?" Shay asked. We all looked at her. "Maybe if they can open that file more it will lead them somewhere we aren't seeing. They have all the facts that we don't."

"It's a good point," I told her. "Let's give it a day and see what Lynn comes up with first." We all seemed to settle on that.

Jake moved over to the side of the room and pulled the radio off his shoulder. We all watched him for a minute and then turned to one another. When nothing was spoken we turned to watching Lynn at her computer. That was truly uneventful.

"I say we get started on getting ready to be out of here," I told everyone.

"I'll get started on getting our engine ready," Quade told us and started to move away, seemingly glad to have something to do.

"Are you sure you have the fuel for that?" I asked him.

"We should be able to get by," he told me as he turned and walked to the stairs, disappearing through the door there.

"Are you staying here for this one?" Teal asked Lynn.

"You're right," Lynn said and started to get up.

"No, I really think you should stay here," Teal told her. "I think whatever you find on that drive is going to maybe help. You should put some time into that. Plus, we've been to Colby a hundred times. If he ain't there and the compound's clear, we'll come right back. If he is, then we'll take care of business and be right back too."

"Yeah, I guess it should only take a couple of hours, round trip," Lynn told her, leaning back in her chair. "I wouldn't mind seeing if I can get an idea of what's here." She leaned forward then and put her hands up to the keyboard again.

"I think Axel should stay and get the communications up and going with these guys' home base," Teal continued. I saw Axel shrug.

"That sounds right," he said. "Wanda and I could get whatever done here to make it easier. I'll get the frequency stuff from that other guy and see what I can do to get us up and running. Maybe I'll ask her to work on that while I see what they have with the satellites." He turned to me. "I'll do whatever they need me to do to keep this under wraps. We still want their help for sure. I won't jeopardize that."

"I appreciate that," I told him. "My daughter's name is April and she's the one heading up Coms over there. She's been at it for a while so she should be able to keep up."

"Sounds good," Axel said, walking to the long table that held all of the radio stuff and telling something to Wanda. He looked at the table's entire length and took a deep breath, as did Wanda.

"Home knows what to do," Jake said from behind us. "I've been working already with the radio running through the armory. I figured we may not want them knowing our every move; actually it was April's idea. We should be ready anytime you are."

"I just need that frequency," Axel told him from the table of radio equipment.

I moved away a little, knowing that all that was about to go on was going to be foreign to me. Davina followed and looked at me closely. I gave her my best smile and she outdid me with hers in return.

"You doing okay?" she asked. "That must have been hard for you."

"Yeah, I just figure if they can help, we need it," I told her.

"No, I totally agree," she said. "It's just not normal for us doing this kind of stuff." I definitely agreed with that, but somehow this did not feel all that weird. "Pretty impressive, this town and all."

"Yeah, we were all pretty amazed when we first got here," I told her. We watched Margie, Chris and Laura walk over.

"This place is huge," Laura said looking around. "I've never been inside one of these things. I don't even think I've been beside one. These things are so tall."

"Yeah, me either," I told her. "These things are pretty gigantic. The views are awesome."

"They seem to have good protection here," Margie said. "It looks like everything someone would need is here."

"It's pretty awesome they are wanting to help," Chris said. I nodded.

"I'm just glad George is getting his train fixed," I told Margie. "If we don't get anything else out of this at least that is a good thing." She gave me a smile.

Teal walked with Jake over to us and we became silent. He told us all was ready for Axel to be able to communicate with home. My heart skipped a beat for a second but I tried to tell myself this all would work out. With a reassuring smile from Teal, I seemed to calm a little.

"Right this way," she said, pointing at the way we had come in.

We followed her down and then outside. She led us to where our train was. I looked to see if I could see George but I could not.

"I think we will be ready, in only a few minutes," I told Teal. "We should probably take our horses."

"I think that would be bright," she said. "We too have a boxcar set up kind of like yours. I'll make sure Eric knows to come pick your car up and add it to ours." She turned and moved away.

"I'll go see how George is doing," I told everyone. "Let's unhook our boxcar and just take the horses." Everyone seemed to think that best too. I looked to Margie to make sure and she nodded.

"I'll go with you and see how it's going," Shay said dryly. She must be wanting to see Sterling I knew. Margie wanted to come as well so we all three set off.

As we moved up from the boxcars and caboose I could see that the locomotive was not at the front. Looking around, I could not see it anywhere. I walked over to the docks and looked there but again could not see it. Walking inside a long building I saw a man sitting by a small fireplace built into the wall. It reminded me that it was a little cold outside. Looking over at Shay and Margie, we all shrugged.

"I'm looking for the old steam engine we brought here?" I asked the man sitting there.

"It's around back," he said, not looking up at me but moving his head to the left a little.

"Thanks," I told him and looked in that direction.

The building was old but well-maintained. You could easily tell that it had always been a workshop as the work-stations were well thought out with even a forge in the corner; I was a little surprised to see it glowing. I passed through a metal shop of hand tools as I made it to the back door.

"I bet Neil would love this place," I told Shay.

"It all looks pretty organized," she said. "Looks like you could make about anything metal in here." I agreed with her and looked around a bit more.

"George will have a hard time leaving this place," Margie put in. I smiled at her.

Going outside I pulled my coat a little tighter and resented the man who reminded me that it was, in fact, getting closer to winter. I immediately saw our train but pulled back at the site. Lincoln was hanging precariously from the upper section of the burn chamber as Sterling was grinding something. George too, was working over a ways from them, smashing something with a large hammer. What really struck me, however, was the gigantic hole that was now in the side of the locomotive, much bigger now than it had been before. Walking closer, Lincoln saw me and looked up.

"It looks like we are getting somewhere," he told me. "It's not as bad as it looks." I must have had a concerned look on my face.

"This is going to turn out perfect," George put in from where he was.

"I believe you," I told them. "It's just it looks pretty bad from here." I saw Sterling turn and seeing Shay he put the grinder down.

"How'd it go with everything in there?" he ask, moving his head to indicate the town. "They still interested in helping us out?"

"Yeah, they say they want to take us to the next compound," Shay told him.

"That's awesome!" he told her and looked at me. "I think their engines are pretty well-fortified," he said with a smile.

"I think I would agree with that," I told him.

"I'm talking to George about maybe fitting ours out a little," Sterling said, looking over at George.

"It won't take much," Lincoln said.

"I think it's a great idea," George said. "I'm just wanting to get this ready first."

"I concur there," I said. "Looks like you all are doing a big job here."

"We are just cutting out the bad stuff," George said, pointing to various areas. "There was a lot of it."

Margie and I walked with him back to the side of the burn chamber and he tried to start explaining what really happened. (Shay went over to the building, talking to Sterling about something.) He ran his hand along some pipes, saying they led to certain things and telling me how the pressure had built up inside the weakened chamber. He pushed several times on different parts for emphasis, all of which meant nothing to me. I listened intently, however, pretending to understand it all.

"Once we overlay this hole here, it will be as good as new," he told me. "If we have time we are planning on welding metal straps on these places. It will be indestructible."

"It sounds great!" I told him. "I'm so glad it's fixable, George."

"You say the word, if we don't have time for this, and we are out of here," he told me with a way too serious look on his face. I appreciated the thought.

"No, we have some time," I told him. "Quade and his group are taking us to Colby and the other compound. We shouldn't need even that many people to go.

You stay here and get this done. We should be back by the end of the day, hopefully with the girls."

"I hope that's true," George told me, again turning serious. "Smash that guy in the head once for me."

"Without even a thought," I told him. "Do you think you will be done here by the time we get back?"

"Yeah, we are almost ready now to start welding on the new piece," he told me. "We still have to cut the piece and we haven't found it yet, but we will." He looked seriously at me. "We will be done with this piece by the end of the day."

"I think that sounds great!" I told him. I did not want to mention my worry about that not being the end of the problems with how we had seen it break a few times so far. "Are you going to need anything from us?"

"I can't think of anything," he told me.

"Okay, well keep the radio handy and still watch your back," I told him a bit under my breath, though with the noise Lincoln was making with the grinder, it was totally unnecessary.

"I will," he said with a smile. "I think these guys might be some of the good ones." I smiled at him and hoped so.

I walked over to where Sterling and Shay were still talking, leaving Margie to say her goodbyes. I watched them look at each other and it was nice to see the look of affection on both of their faces. I knew it was only a matter of time before they acknowledged it and it seemed like that time was coming soon. I started to hope that Shay would give in just to see their happiness bloom.

"I think we should let you get back to it," I told Sterling. "Looks like you will have a pretty long day ahead."

"Yeah, I agree," he said. "But wow, I'm going to enjoy it! I haven't used tools like these in forever." He looked up then, feeling guilty for having said so much. "If you need me to come though…"

"No, no, we will be fine," I told him. "We are surely taking too many." He smiled at that.

"Good luck," he said and looked tenderly at Shay. It made her smile.

"We'll see you by the end of the day," she told him.

"I'll be waiting," he said.

"Stay close to that radio too," I told him. "And keep a sharp eye out. This place seems friendly enough but you never know."

"I will," he said to me with a serious nod. "I have my radio right here." He patted a pocket of his coat.

I turned and started walking away and Shay was a little slower in doing so. Margie saw us start to leave and came up behind us. We went back through the building and saw the same guy sitting at the fireplace. As we passed he threw in another log. That seemed like a great way to spend my waning years.

We made it out front and saw that our boxcar was being pulled away from the others. My group stood around watching and we joined them. It only took a minute for us to start walking behind the moving car.

"How are Sterling and George doing?" Davina asked me, coming to walk beside me.

"Looks like they are hard at work," I told her, sorry to say now that I was thinking of other things.

"Is it able to be fixed?" she asked.

"Huh?" I asked her, wondering what she was talking about.

"Are they going to be able to fix the crack?" she asked.

"Oh, sorry," I told her. "Yeah, George said they should be done by the time we get back."

"Thinking about Colby?" she asked, but I am sure she already knew the answer.

"Yes, I am," I told her plainly. "Sorry, it's just the way I'm wired."

"I know," she said. "There's no need to apologize."

"Yes, there is," I told her. "You mean more to me than all of this. I should listen when you speak. It's the voice that keeps me going." That got a beautiful smile from her.

We walked behind our boxcar in silence together then. I wondered where they were taking it but knew I was just along for the ride on this kind of stuff. They pulled it past one switch track and started it back along another as we all got out of the way. We stood there as the massive locomotive, we had seen earlier moved our boxcar into another one and rammed it home.

"I can't wait to see inside the cabin of that thing," Chris said, reminding me of when he was a young kid. Laura too was excited and said as much.

Looking around, I saw that we were beside the train junkyard that had the building next to it where our engine was getting worked on. There were different cars on several different tracks. A few more engines were a couple of rows down. A line of coal cars started farther past them and led back into the city. As I continued to look, I saw Brady bringing a horse toward us from the stable. Teal followed him.

It seemed to start the parade of horses and people coming toward us. I turned back to see Eric coming out of the cabin of the engine and he waved back behind the train that was now formed of the engine, our boxcar and now one more. With a sign and a thumbs-up he turned and saw us watching him.

"She's ready when you are," he told us and headed back inside the cab.

We started toward our boxcar. Davina and I stopped and waited as we got to the front of the engine. I was wanting to see who all was coming with us. Just then I saw Quade come out of one of the many doors that had been built into the grain elevators.

He looked truly ready for action, complete with his AR15 that dangled from under his right arm, like mine. (That kind of weirded me out for some reason.) His long trench coat hid much of what he carried, though he had a long pipe strapped to his back; I was sure there was a story behind that. He had on a stocking hat that he pulled low over his forehead and moved his head slightly against the small wind that had started. The wraparound sunglasses finished the look and made him seem mean without him having to try.

I turned to look and see who else was headed for the train. I saw the large black man and the shorter man, Fredrick and Ray by name of course, that I had seen on the bridge earlier, each leading a horse in our direction. Brady had made it to the train and was heading for the boxcar behind ours with the horse he led. Teal came and stood beside me, waiting for Quade to get to us.

"Looks like it will be a good day," Teal told us.

"I think so too," Davina told her. "The wind will kill any noise we make." Teal looked at her and smiled.

"That's exactly what I meant," she said. "You must have done this kind of stuff a time or two." They shared a smile.

Quade made it to us and we all watched Fredrick and Ray pass by with their horses. They were going on about something and only Davina and I seemed to notice them. Quade looked at Teal and she nodded.

"Are we all ready?" she asked him.

"Yeah, I told Steve what was going on and he said he would bring in Berk with him to watch over the town while we're gone," he told her. "Robert and Asia are up on the tower watching everything."

"Something to worry about?" I asked, getting a little concerned with what sounded like trouble.

"Last night, remember, there was that brawl at Lucky's?" Quade told us. "Some of the rougher characters from New Haven, that's the place out west from here, got a little drunk and started pushing some drifters around. They got more than they bargained for. One of the New Haven guys got stabbed to death. We broke it up before it kept going but those New Haven guys aren't the letting things rest type. We just need to make sure they don't come back to town in force and try anything."

"That actually sounds pretty serious," I told him. "Are you sure you don't need to stay here and take care of that? We can ride the small distance to the compound and check it out ourselves."

"No, Lynn sounds pretty intent on helping with this and I have to agree," he said. "If we can get you there quick enough to get those girls before anything happens to them, then I think it's something we should do. We have enough people here to take care of things while we're gone. Really, it's just a precaution."

"Okay," I told him, it seeming a little abrupt for the seriousness of what the conversation had been. "When we get back, we will do whatever we can to help, if you need it, I mean."

"Anything can help and I appreciate it," Quade told us. "Hopefully we won't need it."

We turned then and saw Brady coming down the side of the train. On seeing Quade, his face turned and he looked down at his feet. He continued to walk toward us, however.

"Your horse is tied in good, miss Teal," he said, looking at her.

"Thanks Brady," she told him and walked past him. Quade smiled and did the same.

"There's plenty of food in the car if you need some," Brady told me.

I thanked him for the thought. He looked back at Quade and Teal, who had made it to the ladder of the engine and were starting to climb aboard. He turned and walked back toward the stables. Davina and I turned and started toward our boxcar.

"Do you think he gave your horse some grain this time too, miss Teal?" I heard Quade asking Teal in a playful way as he walked behind her on the catwalk toward the cabin.

"Still not funny," Teal said with an embarrassed smile as she saw us watching her. She made it to the cabin door as we walked by below.

"You all should ride up here with us," Quade told us over the rail. "You all are in charge on this, not us."

"I'll ride with you all up there, but I don't think it's fair for us to be in charge," I told him. "How about you showing us the best way of getting there and we'll do all the dangerous stuff when we get there?"

"No deal," he replied shortly. "How about we just work together and see how it goes?"

"I will take that," I told him. "Let me check on what we look like back in our car and then we'll be ready to go."

"I'll get us situated up here," Quade said and followed Teal into the cab of the engine.

"I think I'm starting to like these people," Davina told me as we moved back to our car. (It felt kind of different not passing the caboose as we walked passed the engine.)

"I'm trying to stay on the fence a while longer," I told her. "Not sure how long I can stay there though." I gave her a smile and she returned it.

We made it to our boxcar and went inside. I looked and saw the horses doing well. Someone had fed them, I saw, and looking I saw Laura brushing one of them. Chris was there too, moving some barrels around.

"They gave us some grain," he told me. "It was just in here when we got here."

"I would guess they have enough of it around here," I told him. "Still we should thank them."

"I will," he told me. "We heading out?"

"Yeah, are we ready in here?" I asked him.

"I'm just reorganizing this area to put it in with the feed better," he said. He pushed the barrel he was dealing with under the tack that hung from the wall and secured it with a bungee cord. "We are now."

"Okay, let's have a small meeting," I said loud enough for everyone to hear. They all moved closer and by the area outside of the walled in spaces. "I think we are going to try and stop outside of Colby and ride in so if we can get the horses ready for that."

"How long do you think it will take to get there?" Jake asked.

"I'm not sure with this new engine," I told everyone. "I assume even faster than our train." I looked at Margie and she smiled. "These people said they have been there before, a lot. Sounds like it's pretty straight forward but let's be ready for anything. They are wanting to get involved which is a help for sure but it could be a bit of a hindrance since we don't know how they work. I think we should be the ones to move in first with them as back up. They've been there a lot before though, so they should ride up front on the way in. We need to keep this low-key though so we should keep the lead on everything. Seems like they are okay with that. Let's just make sure to do it our way."

"Yeah, they could be the Rambo type and move in and scare Kevin off," Chris said.

"Do we think he could have made it there yet?" Shay asked.

"I still would say no, but he could have," I said.

"He could have found another way to travel besides our wagon," Laura put in. Everyone nodded to that.

"Either way, we are looking to move in slow and with as much stealth as we can," I told them. "I'm going to have them park this thing well outside of town. We'll move on the Reserve Station and clear it. I'd like to have a long look around there. I think you are going to be in charge of most of that part, Shay." She looked harder at me.

"Of what part?" she asked.

"We are looking for anything with medical supplies and the like," I told her. "Let's see if they have anything about what's shipped in and out of there. Hopefully, they have a log for the last few years before everything fell apart. I know it's a long shot but we can hope. I think that is first priority." She nodded. "Jake, I need you keeping us connected. Tell home what we're doing and how."

"I have been telling them everything," he said.

"Okay, but whatever we find, let's kind of keep it to ourselves until we've had time to go over what it could mean," I told him. He nodded. "What's the weather looking like?"

"Clouds are moving in from the northwest but they are in long streaks," he told me. "The wind is going to be around, probably for the day. It's going to get colder.

There is some movement from the southwest, I can see, so we may have a few nice days coming up if they bring some warm air with them. Still partly cloudy for a while, at least for the next few days. Not exactly sure about warm or cold."

"Is Jadee able to see us here?" I wondered aloud.

"She said she saw this town and the grain elevators for a while this morning," Jake said. "April....I mean. She said it looked weird from overhead, seeing the farmland being worked around here. The satellite went out of range before they could see much. They were able to focus on Colby a little and she said it looked quiet."

"Stay on that and get us a better look over Colby and the compound we are headed for," I told him. He nodded. "Let's be ready when we get there to get right on it. Ask Neil what kind of compound we are looking at entering and get as much out of him as you can about it. I need a better report by the time we get there. We all know what our jobs are so let's get this over with." I got affirmatives all around.

Davina and I walked back out of the boxcar and made the short trip to the engine. Climbing the ladder it almost felt like betrayal as I walked down the catwalk and opened the door of the cabin. Stepping in, I saw a whole new world of train technology.

There were lighted screens overhead and next to the chair at the side of the cabin where George was usually sitting in our train. There were still the levers and a few pedals but the pushbuttons took over most everywhere. A staircase with four or so steps ran down the center of the train and led to a door. (That part looked familiar from the other train engine we had seen not long before.) A table was set in the back of the cabin, with a swivel chair bolted into the floor in front of it. A large radio hung on the back wall and a set of headphones hung on a peg close by. I had thought I saw a turret coming out of the cabin of the train from outside but I did not see where it was from inside. Quade stood up from the chair at the opposite window on the left side of the cabin.

"We ready then?" he asked.

"We are," I told him and looked out the front windows. They took up the whole top half of the front of the cabin. "Nice view."

"Thanks," Eric said. "You would think the wire mesh outside cuts down on visibility, but it doesn't at all. It seems to work more like tinting." I looked and agreed.

Eric turned back and busied himself with pushing buttons and looking through sheets of a tablet. It seemed like he was going through some checklist and I started to watch. With a few turns and another switch flipped he put the tablet away. Reaching up, he pulled on a rope that hung above his head. An air horn blew outside and he gave it three more short pulls.

Teal came up from the stairwell and gave us a smile. She moved over to Quade who moved so she could sit down. He indicated a bench seat that ran along the wall beside where he was standing. It went from the back of the window and ran over to where the door led outside to that side's rear catwalk. Davina and I sat there.

"A little different than ours but not by much," I said to whoever was listening.

"Yeah, I haven't gotten a chance to look inside yours, but I sure would like to," Quade said, holding onto a handle overhead. Looking, I saw one above myself and standing up, I watched us pull out.

"I thought I had seen a gun turret coming out of the cab here," I told Quade.

"No, it's just behind the cab," he said. "You get to it from the catwalk on this side. There's a ladder that leads up to it. One of Lincoln's cool designs. He said it would have taken up too much of the cab if he would have put it in here. I'll show you sometime if we get the chance."

"I'd definitely like to see that," I told him.

We towered over everything around us as we moved passed the junk yard and eased onto different rails. I saw two different people running to different switch tracks ahead of us and I was happy I for once was not given that duty. We made it past several small buildings as an irrigation ditch drew closer. Eric moved a lever and I felt us rumble and pick up speed.

"I hope Lincoln didn't hear that" Teal said and winked at him.

"He'll find something I did wrong anyways," Eric said with a frown and then smiled. "I might as well have some fun."

"Lincoln thinks he owns this thing?" I asked.

"Oh yeah, he's sure he does," Quade told me. "I just hope we don't get a scratch on it somehow. I'm pretty sure he does an inspection every time we go somewhere without him."

"He does," Eric said. "Last time we went south, I didn't hear the end of it for a week. I know I didn't do anything to it but he said it sounded different. He's still trying to overhaul it and blaming me."

"Looks like all's clear," Axel's voice said from the radio at Quade's shoulder. "Asia said she can see some horses on the rail a ways ahead, but that's all."

"I'll keep an eye out," Eric said. Quade reported back and thanked him for the information.

Quade turned and looked out the window on his side of the cabin. He waved vigorously and Teal turned and did likewise. I looked to see what they were waving at but I could not see anyone. I saw Eric looking as well.

"Steve and Berk are heading into town to watch over things for the rest of the day," Quade told him.

"Are we worried about New Haven?" he asked.

"Maybe," Quade said and looked back out the window. "It will be fine, I'm sure." I was not sure how to read the man yet but he did seem confident in what he was saying. He turned to me. "Are your people back home able to see what's going on around here?"

"They are," I told him. "They looked at Colby this morning and said it all seemed calm. There was no report of anyone there. Sounded like the satellite wasn't in range for too long though and it's still a little cloudy." I figured after I said it that he was probably talking more about what was going on around his town.

"That's just the way we want it," he said and turned back to looking out the side window.

"Are you really expecting trouble from that New Haven place?" I asked him. "I know you probably always have to be ready, but is it a serious concern?"

"One of the drifters that started the whole thing is still in town," he told me. "The New Haven boys really were asking for it from what I heard. The drifters seemed like nice enough people. I guess some people just shouldn't be messed with. The guy in town isn't the one that did the killing but he was involved. Some of those New Haven guys are always trouble.

"We know a couple of our town's people like the New Haven crowd. The shops there make some of their living off of them, so I can't say as I blame them. Really, I guess, they aren't in town much." He turned and sat on the bench beside Davina. "A few of them are nice guys though. I guess truly most of them are. They come and go and we have a fair trade between us but only about once a month or so nowadays. Sometimes, we won't see any of them for two or three months. They like some of the beef and buffalo we get and a few of them like the brothel. But it's the more fundamental purists that screw it up for the rest of them sometimes. Hopefully this will blow over but we won't be sure for a few days. I think the guy who died was named Roger. Mean bastard, and got what he deserved. We're hoping New Haven thinks the same way."

"Sounds like it could turn into something serious," I told him.

Quade turned and looked out the window and I tried to see where he was looking. I saw a small old farmhouse with a few sheds surrounded mostly by trees. Quade waved at someone I did not see.

"John Moss's place," he told me. "He raises chickens mostly and stays to himself out here. He's meaner than them damn fighting roosters he raises too, if he has to be, though you'd never know it to meet him."

"It's amazing to me to see people living so out in the open like that" I told him.

"Yeah, I don't know how they do it sometimes either," he said. "There is a lot of good around these parts."

"I'm sure that has a lot to do with that town you have going there," I told him.

"Yeah, people want to live out their lives in peace, given the chance," he said. "New Haven will just have to come in line with that if they want to keep dealing with us."

"It's probably the more fundamental ones that are the dangerous kind!" Davina said.

"They create some dangerous ones," he told me. "That religious stuff is hard to get away from. We left some of that behind us in Oregon. We brought some spiritualists with us and they set up shop in town. There's still the roots of the religion we brought along here. But it is about peace and the like. The fundamental purist crap will never work together with that."

"I did see some palm reading shops in town," I told him.

"Yeah, that's the sort that we brought here," Quade said. "Some go a little deeper but it's all about unity for them. I don't much get involved with it, though I appreciate its worth."

We stayed quiet then and I heard the train switch onto a few different tracks, us still heading east and the town already far behind us. It did not take long until we slowed and I saw the track ahead divide, one heading off north. I figured that was the one we should take.

"Is there more than one way into Colby?" I asked Eric and longed for George's map.

"No, there's just the one," Eric said. "That one heading north there is it."

"I was hoping we could stop a bit before we get there and ride in on horseback," I said, hoping I was not stepping on any toes. "Is there a place out of sight to hole up before we get there?" Quade stood up and looked over at Eric.

"Let's stop at Henry's pond," he told him. Eric nodded. "I agree it's a good idea. If we're looking for someone we shouldn't just barrel on in. We've been there a lot though. There's a few townsfolk there but mostly it's a ghost town."

"That might be best, actually," I told him. "I was hoping not a lot of people would see what we're doing."

"I think that sounds right," he said. He sat down again beside Davina.

"I'm not sure it could mean much to you, but maybe we should talk about what happened with us when we got to New Haven," I told Quade. He looked hard at me for a second but then shrugged.

"I think I can figure it out, but maybe it would be good to hear everything," he told me. "Did you have a bad run-in?"

"We didn't even see anyone there," I told him. Teal turned to listen. "We climbed the fence and went into the hanger." I paused a little, seeing how it all went down in my mind. "They shot Roman, a friend of ours, killing him right as we stood inside the door. We all made it out in a rush, shooting as we went."

"Did you guys take any of them out?" Quade asked. I shrugged.

"I don't think I got any of them," I said. "I started firing and whoever I saw ducked for cover. As we made it out of there I saw the whole place abuzz though. They were all running for the hanger we were in."

"Wow, never thought anyone could get inside their place," he said. "Sorry about your friend but I don't think it should mean anything to us out here. Thanks for bringing it up, though."

"Did they follow you guys out of their compound?" Teal asked. Quade looked over at us with a wrinkled forehead.

"We had made it to the farmhouse we had stashed our horses at down from there," I told them. "We high-tailed it to our train and raced off down the tracks. We didn't see anyone the whole way. We took a bunch of switch tracks after that and didn't see anyone last night." That seemed to satisfy them. I wondered about it and the mission ahead as we turned north and Eric hit the throttle, quickening our race to Colby.

CHAPTER 14

The wind started to blow wildly outside, gusting in fits of seriousness. I liked the gently blowing grass that covered the hills but this stuff I hated. It was the kind of wind that would blow away anything not attached and most things that were.

We traveled for a good half an hour and finally started to slow. I saw a tall grove of trees over the next hill and it seemed the closer we got to it the slower we moved. As we finally topped the hill, I saw the large pond that came right up to the trunks of the trees. As we drew beside the waving branches, we came to a complete stop. It scared off several ducks that were swimming about in the dirty water.

"Colby is still a bit east of here and about a degree north," Eric told us.

"How far east?" I asked him as I checked my pockets again, feeling all things familiar there.

"It's about two miles," he said. "It's all under cover from the hills to this point. No one could have seen us coming in. It will be an easy ride in from here."

"I'll lead the way, if that's okay with you," Quade told me. "I know the easiest way there."

"I would much appreciate that," I told him. "Something with a back door approach kind of thing would be nice."

"That's right up my alley," he said. "Teal, mind telling Ray and Fredrick to keep an eye on things here? We shouldn't be long."

"I'll tell them and meet you at the horses," Teal said and walked out of the cabin through the stairwell in the middle front of the cabin.

"I'll meet you on the ground ready with ours," I told Quade as we turned to head toward the door of the cabin.

"Up for coming with?" I heard Quade ask Eric.

"I wouldn't miss it," he said.

"Take Ray's horse," Quade told him.

"I had Brady load mine. I can't stand Ray's ugly horse. I think it's spoiled on all that grain he feeds it."

"Okay sure. Let's move out of here though," Quade told him. "I'd like to be back to town before dark today."

"How far away are those other coordinates?" Quade asked.

"I think it showed the compound a bit northwest of Colby," I told him. "I think it was twenty-three miles out."

"Okay that should be doable," Quade said.

"I guess we haven't been much north of Colby," Eric said. "Never had a need to go that way. It's always been kind of like our border."

We all made it to the ground and split off to our respective boxcars. I saw Laura leading my horse out of its section and I took it from her. All the horses were saddled which I was glad for, though I, of course, checked over mine. Everyone waited as Laura and Chris brought them their horses. Leading them to the ground we climbed aboard.

Our horses were excited to see the new faces of the other group's animals. A couple whinnied back and forth. My horse tried to turn to get a better look. I let him do what made him feel comfortable. With the newness soon over, I looked at the small hills to the east.

We walked to the front of the train and I saw the two men standing at the gun posts that were built there on each side. They were looking all around. On seeing us approach they put on a smile.

"You just heading into Colby, mister Quade?" Fredric asked.

"Yeah, fellas, we shouldn't be long," he told them. "Just checking out the Reserve for some paper trail."

"We'll keep her safe till you all get back," he told Quade. "Same code?"

"Yeah, let's leave it the same," he told them. "Keep a sharp eye out."

"Yes sir," Ray said matter of factly.

Quade turned his horse east and got it moving into a trot. We all followed easily and quickly topped the first hill. We ran down it and made some good time to the top of the next few. After about a mile and a half we slowed to a walk and cut a more northeasterly approach to the town we could not yet see.

"I'm interested about the code thing you were talking about as we left," I asked Quade as I rode up beside him.

"Code thing?" he asked, not knowing what I meant. "Oh yeah, that's a military kind of thing. If you see someone you might know or are moving in friendly territory, it's good to have a way of telling if what's around the next corner is on your side. We set up some calls and specific answers."

"Yeah, we do the same thing," I told him. "It's worked well for us. Things like that have helped us come a long way as a team out here."

"This kind of stuff will do that," he said. "We came out here from Oregon and started out as mostly separate groups. I can't much remember who was from where anymore. We're all family now." I knew what he meant.

"That's a long way to travel in this world," I told him.

"Yeah, we hit a few bumps along the way for sure," he said.

"We sure did," Eric put in. "I was military and stayed on a base. I jumped aboard in Nevada when these guys visited but I think that is where the fun started."

"Something like that," Quade told him, and it seemed there was a lot going unsaid from the man.

We topped the next hill and a large town laid out in front of us about a mile away. There was a huge barn on a hill by itself. A grocery store had been well-burned and only some of the bricks from it still stood. Small businesses lined the wide paved road that led from the interstate and finally it led to some homes.

"The Reserve Building is right there next to that little stadium," Quade said. He pointed to what looked like a small fairgrounds area with a set of covered bleachers and lots of small buildings. A fenced in dirt track was in front of the seated area. "It's that small bricked building with the big fence around it."

"Okay, I see what you are talking about," I told him. "Let's find a place to tie up our horses and move in."

We looked and found some trees off to our left. There was an area around the base covered with small bushes and shrubs. It was back down the hill a bit so it would be a perfect spot to keep them out of the view of the town. We turned and walked the small distance to them. Dismounting, we all tied up our horses there.

Quade led us to the top of the hill again and looked over the area. We all watched for movement and waited. A full five minutes passed without anyone saying anything and us seeing no movement below. I saw Quade start looking over the fairgrounds area with some earnest.

"What are you thinking?" I asked in a low voice, though with the wind whipping at everything, I'm not sure why I bothered.

"I say we go in on the other side of that far building there," he said, pointing.

The fairgrounds area was small but well-spread out. You could call the building he was talking about a barn but just barely. Another building was up close to it and seemed to be great cover to be able to get us to the small stadium seats. From there it would be all open to the fence surrounding the Reserve Building and I could see it truly was the best way.

"I think that looks fine," I told him. "Anyway, you'll let us go in and you cover us from here?"

"Now that wouldn't be any fun at all," he told me and moved back down the hill we were at.

We followed him for a ways and finally, after looking a few times to see how close we were getting, he pulled up. We gathered close and my entire group rechecked their rifles and side arms. Quade and his group followed suit. With a thumbs-up he gave me a shrug.

"Looks like little else left but to do it," he said. "I'll make it to the barn first. Everyone follow one at a time when I get there. I'll move out as soon as the first one gets to me." My group all looked at me and smiled. "I guess you all have done this a time or two also."

"No problem," I told him. "It's good to keep it straight. If you hole up somewhere out there give me a sign and I'll leapfrog past you or flank." Quade nodded approval and went over the hill, crouching low.

I watched and when he made it to the barn I signaled for someone else to go. Margie jumped up and moved over the hill. Eric stood expectantly and when Margie made it I nodded to him. I wanted to be next.

"Chris, you bring up the rear," I said. "Stay at that stadium and Laura, you spread out from there. I'll keep you posted on what we find in there and how we're doing on getting out. Not sure how long it will take so just sit tight and watch."

"I'll keep our asses covered," he told me.

"Shay, you're with me," I said. "Let's move out now."

Her and I moved over the hill together and quickly made it to the barn. It was a simple cover move I could easily tell, and we moved on as soon as we got there. We all worked together to get to the Reserve building, the fence long since being pushed down in several places. We ran inside, all the doors and windows being open to the elements.

"I wish everything was that easy," Eric said from behind the counter just inside the door.

I nodded but Shay did not take the time. She ran to where Eric was and started looking around. I followed closely and looked where she did not. Right away I could see our task was going to be hard.

The area we entered was large and a well-opened space. We all looked around at the long counter and most of us ran behind it. Shay was pulling out everything left in the drawers that had not been thrown all over the floor. I saw someone must have been through the place several times.

"I'm not seeing anything in here," Davina told me. "I'll try one of the offices."

"Wait, let's clear this place before we spread out," I told her and it made everyone stop what they were doing.

I gave signals as to who was to go where. Quade and Eric just faded to the back as we moved forward and to the hall that led to three offices and a backdoor at the end of it. Jake turned into the first office and I followed him. When we found no one we moved back out and watched Shay and Margie move into the one across the hall. Quade and Eric took the final one and they moved back into the hallway with nothing to report. In under a minute we stood in the hallway and all shrugged.

"Let's divide and take an office," I told everyone. "Take any paperwork you can find. If it looks official we need to look it over."

"I'll look some more at the front counter," Davina told me.

"I'll do that with you," I told her and followed her.

I called Chris and told him it looked like a mess in there. I was not sure how long it would take but I told him I would keep him updated. When he said all still looked well outside, I turned to the job at hand.

We made it back out to the front entranceway and systematically started to go through everything. We found things that did not even belong in the place, like trash and what looked like the remains of a lion's pride killing. We still moved everything, checking every scrap of paper on the floor and anywhere else we looked. The truth of the situation was, there just was not that much of it.

"I think I have something here," I heard from the hallway. It was Eric's voice. "Yeah here are some papers about supply lists." I was already partway down the hallway and heard him talking from the far office.

"Anything about medical supplies being shipped in or out?" I asked him.

"Anything with orders from California too," Teal added from behind me as I entered the office.

"No, just everyday stuff so far," Eric told us. "Looks like a transfer of vehicles here a couple of times. Here's one that is for the quartermaster sending in supplies for a cement pad somewhere. Nothing on medical stuff."

"How much of it is there?" I asked him and came around behind him.

"Half a drawer looks like," he told me. "It's spilled all over the floor here." He pointed into the corner he was working at.

"I don't see any more paperwork stuff in here," Quade said. "The filing cabinets look like they got stolen or something."

"Yeah there's nothing in that office either," Jake told me. "Even the desk got taken."

"Looks like there's some more supply list stuff here," Eric put in again. "Still nothing important, though."

"Can you gather it all up and we'll look at it on the train?" I asked him.

"Yeah, but I'll need a little help carrying it all," he said. "Mind if I stuff some in those packs of yours?"

"Not at all," I told him.

We all moved in turn and grabbed as much as we thought would fit into our small backpacks. I wanted to sit and go over every detail of each piece but I knew the better idea would be to do that on the way. Pulling off my backpack, I filled it so it bulged and moved over to the door.

"Looks like we move on to the compound, huh?" Quade asked softly.

"Yeah, I think we should hurry out of here and see what we find there," I told him.

"Maybe there's something in there that will help," he said, looking at me with a sideways glance.

"I hope so," I told him, trying to thank him with my smirk.

"Let's get out of here then," Quade said and looked at me.

I nodded and we moved toward the back door. I called Chris and told him we were heading out. He said everything looked quiet and I passed on the report. Looking both ways, Quade again took the lead and ran for the closest building, which this time was a brick outbuilding that was inside the fenced in area. I made it there and he left just ahead of me. Looking inside the building through the smashed in door, I saw only blown in dirt and broken down shelves. It symbolized the trek so far to Colby and I fought to keep my disappointment in check. I ran on to where I saw Quade had made it to the stadium.

We leaped frogged from cover to cover and made it back to the horses without incident. My horse was glad to see me and turned into me as I stepped beside him. When I saw we were all in the saddle, I turned and put my horse into a fast trot. Quade strode up beside me and we rode on in silence. No one said anything as we put away our horses.

"Jake, I'd like you to ride up in the cabin with me for a while," I said. "I'd like to talk to Jadee for a few minutes."

Without a word, Jake followed me to the cabin as did Davina. I felt the train start and watched everyone silently take their seats. As the motion of the train took hold I went and sat down at the radio table at the rear of the cabin.

"I'll take that radio if you don't mind," I told Jake and he handed it over. "Show me the frequency you've been using."

"I've had to use the satellite feed through this channel here," he said and pointed to some buttons. "It works the phone receiver there on the side."

"When I'm done here, I want you to show me everything there is to know about using this thing," I told him. "This time I mean it."

"Yes, sir," he told me and found a seat on the bench.

I called home and got April, of course. We talked a little about how things were going, mostly though, about how she could see the town we were in. She reported they could not see much of where we were headed next, however. I asked her then to put Jadee on.

"Sure, dad, I'll go get her," April told me and I heard the squelch sound as she turned off her mic.

I waited and felt the train moving ahead slowly. Eric asked for the exact coordinates of where we were going and I gave them to him. I was surprised when he brought out a map that looked a lot like George's. I watched as he flipped through the pages and then finding the right one, ran his finger around the map. He switched between two different maps and I could not see for sure all he was doing. I tried not to be too nosy about what he was doing to get us there.

"George has one of those maps," I told Eric.

"These Freight Interchange Maps are awesome," he told me. "They can get us anywhere there's a rail, which is just about everywhere. This other map is more about latitude, longitude stuff. It's an old weather station map. Never really used it much. Glad to have a chance to."

"This is Jadee, come in," I heard the radio say.

"Yeah I'm here," I told her.

"Sorry it took so long," she said. "Mack and I were finishing up a file. You know some of the stuff we are looking at is microdot stuff."

"I guess I'm not exactly sure what that means," I told her.

"It's information reduced down to pinhead size," she said. "It's some of the original stuff brought out of China. I guess the Chinese at NASA didn't even know what they had. They were pretty spread out."

"Anything we can use to find Kevin?" I asked her abruptly and immediately felt bad.

"Nothing solid, but it seems like it's all pointing somewhere," she said. "Sorry I can't be more help."

"No, it's not you," I told her. "We just made it to the coordinates of the Reserve and the place was a mess."

"Wait!" I heard Davina say with some excitement. "This one has Kevin's name on it!" I saw she was going through some of the papers we had gotten. "It says something was received. Some code for what it was."

I turned and looked at her hard. She had brought a handful over to me and pointed to Kevin's name. She pulled it back and flipped over to the next page.

"I'm sorry to hear that," I heard Jadee saying. "Are you guys headed for the compound now then?"

"It looks like Davina found some paperwork with Kevin's name on it!" I told her.

"Really, so he did send stuff there," Jadee said. "What does it say he shipped?"

"It doesn't say," I told her.

"Here's another one for a bunch of chemicals," Davina said. I watched Jake pull some of the papers out of his backpack and started going through them.

"Looks like the first one is coded and now some more for chemical stuff," I told Jadee.

"It sounds like they were right," Jadee said and I could hear some relief in her voice.

"We are headed to the compound now Jadee," I told her, finally able to share some good news. "If he's there then we'll get him. It does sound like NASA knew what they were talking about."

"I've had Neil looking for you guys since you've been gone," she told me. "He found Colby but we still can't see the compound."

"Okay, no problem," I told her. "We'll take it slow and move in carefully. I'm not sure if he could have made it there yet but if not we'll lay in wait." Jadee did not answer. "Jadee, you still there?"

"Yeah, I'm here," I heard her say a little choked up.

"We'll find him Jadee," I told her. "Let's not think of this just yet as anything but another place to clear out. We'll go in and get this done. Meanwhile Jadee, I need you to stay on task. Let's look through the facts of whatever all this is and find where to go next."

"You're right, I know," she said and I heard her sniffle. "I'll just act like she isn't there and keep searching."

"I'll keep you posted every step of the way," I told her.

"Thank you," she said. "Thank you all for being out there and for doing so much."

"This is what we do for family," I told her. "We're actually kind of getting good at it." I was trying to lighten her mood.

"I bet," she said.

"How's things going with Mack?" I asked her. Davina held up another piece of paper when I looked her way.

"It's good," she said. "He's been sending me everything they can find on all the research. I can say I never want to see this stuff again."

"Yeah, I saw my share for sure," I told her.

"There's another person, Filipino woman named Jessica that's been helping too," she said. "She seems to know everything there is about all that we're looking at. She was a doctor for NASA from the beginning in some way."

"Is there a way that you can look through some information without them knowing what you're looking at?" I asked her.

"Why, what's going on?" she asked. "We have the armory up and running but we've just been using it for talking to you guys."

"We found something more on the pin drive."

"What was it?"

"We're not sure yet. One of the women in the town we came to was a nurse that worked under Kevin. She downloaded the pin drive and right away found out how to get somewhere to things we haven't seen."

"Oh, I think NASA found some stuff too," Jadee said in a low voice. "We've been pouring over a lot of that too." I felt a little silly now bringing it up in such a way.

"Okay, well that's good then," I told her. "Is there anything on it that seems to help?"

"No, not yet. I'm learning a lot about all of the stuff that no longer matters and it's kind of grossing me out."

"I can understand that."

"I won't stop until they're found though," she promised.

"I know you won't, Jadee," I told her. "And we'll do everything out here that we can."

"I know," she said. "But please be careful. Jake said you got shot already."

"No, just a graze, really," I told her. I reached down and felt my leg and it was only a little sore.

"Sorry about Roman."

"Thanks. He was a good one," I said. "This will be over soon, I hope, for all of us."

"I hope so too," she said.

"Okay, well I'm going to start looking over some of these papers we found," I said.

"I guess I have my own work to do too," she replied. "Take care."

"You too, over and out," I said and getting up, I handed the radio back to Jake. "Did we find anything good from those papers so far?"

"I don't have Kevin on any of mine," Jake told me. "It's all acquisition stuff but nothing with Kevin on it."

"How about yours?" I asked Davina.

"More of the same," she said. "There is a ton of encoded ones. Numbers are on everything. The only ones not encoded are the ones for chemicals."

"What kind of codes?" Quade asked.

"I mean numbers, really," Davina said. "They have line items but there are numbers under descriptions. The quantities are plain but then more numbers after that."

"Does it say where they are coming from?" Teal asked, coming over.

"No, it says where they are going to which is that Reserve Base," she said. "I mean there's a Colby address on the 'ship to' line. It says sent from here but then more numbers."

"I think that sounds like something NASA could be good for," I told them. "I think the first thing should be checking that Colby address. Jake, you send whatever she tells you and feed it right to Mack. See if the numbers all over that thing mean anything."

I got a nod from him as he got up and sat at the table, putting the radio in front of him. Davina came over and sat on the bench as close to him as it would let her. Jake started the call and Davina started writing things down and circling others. Teal sat beside her and Davina handed her half of the stack of papers.

"How long before we get close?" I turned and asked Eric.

"Twenty minutes or so," he said. "There isn't really a great place to stop any closer so it might be a longer ride on horseback."

"No problem," I told him. "Are you pretty firm on that twenty?"

"I think so," he said. "There's one switch track that could slow us down but not by much."

"Okay, thanks Eric, I'll have my people ready by then," I told him with a smile.

I went out onto the catwalk that led to the rear of the engine. I noticed the wind still blew the tall grass but not as much as it had been before. Looking up, I saw the clouds breaking up and that pleased me immensely. Some old oil rigs, long-stopped and whose bases were extensively grown over dotted the far-off-slopes. I saw large wind turbines, some still moving with their massive blades cranking out energy to I wondered where, if anywhere. A field of what once was packed with rows of corn zoomed by, now only littered here or there with a stalk or two.

As we winded around a slow moving curve I saw a herd of cattle so large it took up most of the sides of the hills we were going to cut through up ahead. They were still about a quarter mile off but I felt us slow immediately. I was pretty sure what this meant for our twenty minute time window as I walked back into the cabin.

Quade and Eric were looking intently out the front of the cabin. The area where the cattle herd started drew near and as they did I could see them covering the hills around there. I saw just about every type of cow I could remember.

"This counts in the twenty minutes, right?" I asked Eric and he looked back to make sure I was joking.

"Sorry, I should have said switch tracks or cows," he said with a smile.

"I've never seen that many," I told him.

"They sometimes gather in herds like this and the rails are the easiest way for them to travel," Quade told me. "Roads and interstates are another good way for them, too. They're no fences and the areas beside the tracks are pretty wide and full of grass. It happens a lot like this a lot more on the highways and big roads. But yeah, I don't think I've seen a herd like this either lately."

"Just like before people came here the buffalo used to roam the land," Eric said.

I heard Jake reading numbers off at the table, sending them to Jadee back home. Teal and Davina were sorting them into piles and there were several stacked all over the table. It was good to see. I just hoped something would come of it as I looked back outside and wondered at our new problem.

"Can we push through?" I asked.

"Yeah, we just have to go slow about it," Eric said. "If you are in need of beef now's the time to get it." I could easily see that.

Quade headed down the stairs in the middle front of the cabin and I followed him. He opened the door and we both entered a small dark room. There was a door ahead of the one we went through and when he opened it light flooded in and I could see the small area we were passing through. It looked much like the same area in the other diesel engine we had looked through, complete with a set of lockers. This one was a bit better equipped however, with a row of M16s affixed in a bracket that was secured to the wall. Cabinets were everywhere and I could only imagine what was in them. I followed Quade outside.

"You want us to blow a hole for us to fit through, mister Quade," Fredrick asked. We both walked to the front rail and watched as the cattle drew closer.

"Man, you can't shoot no hole as big as a train through that many cows," Ray said.

"Maybe you can't," Fredrick said. "I could blow a hole through anything with this."

"Anything?" Ray asked, looking over at the large black man standing behind the gun post that was made into the catwalk.

"Anything," Fredrick said, looking back and shaking his body as he said it slowly.

"How about an antelope?" Ray asked, looking back out front. "You shoot a hole through an antelope Fredrick?"

"You talking about that one I shot that you said I didn't?" Fredrick asked, still looking at Ray.

"You didn't shoot no antelope," Ray said. "You missed two of them standing right in front of us."

"You know that's a damn lie," Fredrick said. "There was one antelope and I shot him. I can't help if he runs away."

"You shot him with that gun there and you're saying he can still run away?" Ray asked pointing at the gun mounted to the railing. I saw the cattle drawing ever closer.

"Yeah, I did," he said. "I shot right through him and he didn't even know it."

"Man, I ain't never heard nothing like that," Ray told him.

"How about you shootin'," Fredrick asked him. "Member that time you shot the tracks and we had to stop and fix it? Member that?"

"You know this side misfires sometimes," Ray said in his own defense.

"Misfires?" Fredrick told him. "Misfires? That thing ain't never misfired on me. And I sure as hell ain't never shot no tracks."

"Yeah you ain't never shot no antelope either," Ray shot back. "If we see someone you better pull out your side arm or something because you sure ain't going to get them with that thing."

"What'd you say?" Fredrick asked him. "You sayin' you better at shootin' stuff with these here than I am? Man, when we get back we gonna see. I mean it Ray. We gonna see what..."

"Hold up there, gentleman," Quade said. "Let's see if these here cows will know how to move for us."

I saw the ones closest to where we were coming to, move off the tracks and bunch up as best as they could as we got close enough to being able to reach down and touch them. They must not have been feeding as they were already well-bunched and looked to be on the move. Pushing the cattle off to the side made a chain reaction that we saw ripple through the herd. It was easy to see however, that there was not going to be enough room for them to move entirely out of our way.

"I don't think we are going to make it through with them in front of us," Quade said. I felt the train still moving forward but at a snail's pace.

"Looks like they are moving back south the way we came," I said. "Any way to get them moving faster?"

"Anything we do could turn them around and get them stalled or heading in the wrong direction," Quade told me. "If they stop here we might just be stuck. If they turn back, we'll have to move at a cow's pace behind them. We have to inch forward and just wait them out." I tried to look past them to the tracks ahead but they covered them for miles.

"How long could that take?" I asked, not sure I was ready for the answer.

"We'll make it through this in no time, you'll see," Quade said with a smile and went back inside. I was not sure if that was a worried look on his face.

The smell that was already hitting my nostrils was not much to my liking. The animals looked fat from grazing and their rumps looked like they would make perfect steaks. (I secretly wished Marla had the problem of getting rid of too much beef like these.) I saw a large bull get stubborn and stand his ground. We inched forward still and with our large plow, pushed him out of the way. I watched as others held their heads high and moved slowly past us.

Twenty minutes passed and we had only made it about a hundred yards. I could, however, see the end of the herd on the hill about a mile ahead finally, though it did not thin out in the least around us. Several times we started them moving in the wrong direction but only for as long as it took them to figure out that the herd was moving in the other direction. It took us another twenty minutes for them to thin out enough for us to pick up any kind of speed. It was soon a memory though, to me, a bizarre one.

We picked up speed quickly. I watched the clouds roll in from the south as I sat on the back end of the catwalk, feet hanging over. I looked hard for the Rocky Mountain range, I missed seeing it off in the distance. I tried not to think much about the compound which lay ahead or all that it could mean. It worked a little.

I was lost in thoughts on how everything was coming together and did not hear Davina sitting down beside me. I felt her hand on my shoulder and it caused me to jump a little. I felt silly and told her so.

"We are all a little jumpy I think," she told me.

"Hear anything back from home?" I asked her.

"No, but I think we got it all sent in," she said. "There wasn't really that much when it all boiled down. I guess it only takes one trail to lead us to the right place though."

"That's very true," I told her.

We looked out over the landscape and if anything it got flatter. Some of the hills started losing their grass and were replaced with hardy shrubs. Sharp ended long-leafed yuccas now played a part and all the trees disappeared. I wondered what part of Kansas had a desert because I thought we had found it.

"Doesn't look too inviting out there," Davina said. We both heard the cabin door open and Quade stepped out.

"Looks like five minutes," he said and we both gave him a nod.

"I was hoping we were going to drive through this part," I told Davina. I radioed everyone to start getting ready.

"I think it will be a little weird," she said as we both stood. "I hope there aren't any rattlesnakes. Is that a plateau over there?" She pointed northwest of us.

I looked far off into the horizon there and saw what she was talking about. It was barely visible but the long, flat-topped formation was coming better into view. I saw it ran off toward the west.

"I wonder if that's where the coordinates are," I wondered to Davina.

"Let's go see," she suggested.

We walked into the cabin and saw Jake still on the radio. Quade was looking over Eric's map and I went over to see if I could join in. I kicked myself for not asking George if I could bring his.

"Hey, it looks like the coordinates are right here," Quade said, pointing to the map.

"And we are stopping just ahead somewhere?" I asked.

"Yeah, somewhere right in here," Quade said and pointed again. The map did not give any indication of what was there.

"Must be pretty flat there," I said. "There's no topography lines anywhere close to there."

"Yeah, it looks that way," Eric put in. "It's far enough out though, not to let us get seen."

"That's great," I told him. "What's up with those plateaus up north there?"

"We've never been up this way," Eric said. "They are new to me."

"We'll have to come up this way and do some exploring sometime," Quade replied.

"Looks like we are headed straight north," I said. "I guess we'll miss them."

"Yeah, it looks that way," Eric agreed. "Any idea what kind of base we are headed for?"

"No, our home base hasn't been able to see it because of the clouds," I told him. "NASA just gives it a number."

"It's truly weird to be working with NASA and visiting these sites," Eric told me.

"You said you were military?" I asked. "What branch?"

"Air Force, sure enough," he said with a little pride.

"Hey Jake, is Neil able to see that compound yet, at least enough to tell us what kind it is?" I asked, looking over at him. Jake asked home and looked at me and shook his head.

"Wow, that is amazing you can still use the satellites to look around," Eric said. "Must be pretty cool."

"It's weird when you see an area from overhead and then have to walk around in it," I told him.

"I know," he said. "I did a lot of that stuff in the military."

"What kind of stuff did you do for the Air Force?" I asked him.

"I started out wanting to fly jets but ended up flying cargo instead," he said, moving levers and hitting a couple of switches. "I guess my eyesight wasn't what it should have been. The cargo stuff didn't really do it for me so I went back to school and got real familiar with every aircraft that I could. It turned out I liked working for NORAD better."

"You worked for NORAD?" I asked him. "That must have been different."

"You never told me you worked for NORAD," Quade said.

"I didn't get very far," he admitted. "I got all of the studying done I needed to advance, just in time for the war to break out. I never really got to use much of anything I learned. They assigned me to some remote base in the middle of nowhere. It was a step-up for me though, and I enjoyed it while I was there." He paused and stood up, looking hard out the front window. "Looks like we found our place to hide. Not much else around. It's pretty flat everywhere else."

I looked outside and saw we were headed northeast around a long curve. The flatland outside had gathered more vegetation and a few trees could be seen nearby. Grass returned in patches and I thought I could see evidence of a stream out the right side close by. Looking, I could see the plateaus far west of where we were.

"The coordinates are about five miles north of here," Eric said, pointing out the front.

"Okay, we'll be ready in five," I told them and I saw Jake already packing up.

We left the cabin and did that activity that we did so many times already that soon saw us all in the saddle atop our stomping horses. Fredrick and Ray were asked again to stay aboard and watch things around the train. I saw Quade calling home and I asked Jake to do the same. It took us no time to be trotting down the side of the tracks headed for yet another compound.

CHAPTER 15

We set a good pace and the horses seemed to like it. We did switch between a walk and a run a few times, the horses taking advantage of the walks to taste the local vegetation. It did feel good to be back in the saddle but I was not sure if that was just because I wanted this thing to be over.

The wind died down significantly as we rode the gentle hills that were starting to return to the landscape. (I was happy for that as I did not want to just walk right up to a compound that could see us coming from miles away.) Looking around, I did not see much in the way of interesting things to explore. We did move away from the tracks and I was surprised that there were no fences at all, as far as I could see. The clouds were still the long streaked kind that Jake said meant some high winds would probably continue. Still trying to find something to look at, I did see some vultures circling overhead and had to smile.

We slowed our horses and they all walked for a good ways. I looked at my GPS and it said we were still three miles out. I tried to see where we were going but I did not see anything ahead but the slow rise of some long hills. I was glad when the tall grass started filling in everywhere. I tried to line us up with the coordinates and rode on for a couple of miles.

We topped a hill we had been seeing in the horizon for some time and we finally saw our first fence. It was the four-strand barbed wire kind and ran east and west and as far as we could see. It was out right in front of us and just down the hill a bit. Looking over to the next hill about a mile away, I saw some rounded tops of some structures past it, but we could tell they were still over a few more hills.

"I say we make it to that fence line there and sit and look at whatever's over the hill there for a while," I told everyone.

"I agree," Quade said. "Maybe we get there and decide, but I don't want to just walk up on the place. How far off are we." He pointed to my GPS.

"Looks like about a mile yet," I told him.

"That small rise there should be a good observation point then," he said.

We cut the fence in front of us and I saw Quade mark it with some white strips. I thought that a smart way to give us a clue where to head for if we needed out of there in a hurry or just to simply give us an idea where to ride to when we were done here. I started liking even more the way this man's mind worked.

We walked most of the way to the next fence and dismounted a little down from the top of the hill, if you could call it that. I looked at Eric and I could see he was excited about getting a look at where we were headed. We all staked our horses and turned to walk to the top of the hill where a tall chain-linked fence now sat in front of us.

"Any idea what those rounded things were?" I asked Eric.

"Yeah, they had to be radar system structures," he said. "Not sure why there were so many of them, though. I saw four."

"That's how many I counted too," I told him. With that we got to the fence and I pulled out my binoculars.

Far off in the distance, probably about a quarter mile away, was another hill which hid some of what was behind it but not all. We could see the tops of buildings and the round structures came fully into view. The compound was set up, well-fenced on two separated forty acre sites, the second forty acre site being cut in half by some shipping containers.

The first forty acre site, which held the four round structures, was on the left. There were actually three, smaller round structures and one big one off the left of the others which sat in a line with a cement road that went to each one. A large square antenna that looked like the kind that would rotate was between and back a little from the two round structures on the right. The large round structure on the far left was up close and I could not tell from there but it looked to be attached to a long building between itself and the other round structures. The building was at least thirty by a hundred feet long. Another building was closer to us than the round structure and sat across a large paved area. This building was twice as big as the other one. Another smaller building sat about fifty feet to the right of the later building. Paved roads led out of a tall fence around the site and through a gate that led to the other forty acre site.

The other two, half sites were well-fenced and looked a lot more simple. The top section of the site held an L-shaped building on the left of two other smaller rectangular shaped ones, all of which looked to be some buildings for important official business. Paved walkways and roads moved throughout that site. The other section had three, smaller rectangular buildings off to the side of two, long short, separate but identical looking metal railing frame work structure. The buildings there were smaller and sterile looking.

I am pretty sure we all looked the buildings over but that is not what held our attention, at least not mine. Mixed in everywhere around the military structures, but well spread out, was a homemade village of sorts. There were small houses built everywhere inside the fenced area. Some of the buildings could not be called anything close to well-built but there were some that looked to be of solid construction. Some of the places were lean-to sheds built off of the military structure. A short row of old metal sided mobile homes were set up close to the L-shaped building in the site on the right. The entire northern half of the section that was cut in half on the right was taken up by a corral area for horses and cattle (Sheep and goats, I could see, mixed in there.) I could see no real design to the layout of what the builders did but it did look like the place was well-occupied. By the spread out nature of the homes it was by no means up to capacity.

Another interesting thing was the sheer volume of semi-trucks and box shipping containers that sectioned off the areas. It turned some of the areas around the radar structures into a maze of some kind. Some of the containers were stacked two high and they looked to be well-lived in, complete with decks and all. Obviously some of the semi-trailers were used for homes but some looked to be used for shops, some even being labeled with a name; for instance a couple of the semis were attached together and had a sign nailed to one side that looked like it read 'Ronny's'. There were several more like it.

I looked on from there and saw what looked like a deep, wide ditch surrounding the place outside the fence. Long poles with sharp points came out of the ground everywhere between the fence around the compound and the ditch. A well-made watch tower was about every two hundred yards around the compound, looking over the ditch and just inside the fence.

I looked first to see if I could see anyone walking about down there and I found the place alive with activity. We could still not see the entire place as we were still a hill away, but the small amounts of smoke coming from some of the structures and seeing several spots of movement answered the question as to its occupation.

"That's an old NIKE site," Eric said. "It was an air missile, defense system." We all looked at him and then back to the compound.

As we watched we could see more movement and was shocked to see a large military truck moving into view from behind one of the round structures in the left site. Two more smaller vehicles moved into view and headed for a section in the far side of the fence that had a makeshift gate in it. A set of tall shipping containers made up the sides of the gate with a semi-truck and trailer working as the gate and opening mechanism. As we watched, the vehicles moved through the opened gate.

"Well, they obviously have fuel," Quade said aloud. "And they could obviously run us down if they found us here and wanted to."

"I'm sure they wouldn't take kindly to us spying on them," I told him. "You said this is a NIKE site. What are those round structures there?" We all looked at Eric.

"Those are different types of radar," he said. The large one on the left there is High-Power Acquisition Radar. They called it HIPAR for short. It would locate hostile targets like incoming missiles or bombers. The other smaller ones were radar used for guiding our outgoing missiles once launched. The first smaller one on the left is the Target-Tracking one, then the Target-Ranging one and finally the Missile-Tracking one. That building in front of the HIPAR structure is a power-generator building."

"What's that big antenna looking thing that looks like it can rotate there between those two round radar things?" I sounded silly asking such an uneducated question.

"That's for Low-Power Acquisition Radar or LOPAR," he told me. "You see that a lot on ships. The real interesting part is those long, metal rails. Those are actually missile launch rails and racks. Back when this place was active there would have been a line of missiles on them and a magazine below each set of rails. That metal door in the ground in front of them is actually an opening that allows the missiles to be elevated up from below and attached to the launch rack. The buildings in that area are for putting more missiles together and maintenance."

"What's that other section below it for?" Quade asked.

"Those are barracks and administration," he said. "The one in the middle is the mess hall."

"Are there any underground areas to the place?" I asked him

"Just the ones for the magazine of missiles and some administration stuff," he told us. "This was an above ground site. I see a lot of antennae that don't really belong here, though. It looks like a lot of HAM radio stuff. They can probably communicate pretty well for a long ways."

"We haven't seen many working vehicles around the wasteland," Quade said. "They must have a refinery somewhere close."

"I think what I saw moving down there was all diesel," Eric said. "That doesn't take much to refine. It could be built pretty easily, even right off of an oil pump and there are still enough of those around."

"Yeah, I guess I'm surprised we don't see more of it," Quade said.

"I guess not a lot of people know how to do it," I put in. They both nodded.

"Well what do you think?" Quade asked me.

"There is something a little strange," Eric said and we all looked at him. He did not go on but just looked at the compound and the surrounding area.

"What is it Eric?" Quade asked, a little annoyed.

"Oh, well usually these sites were put up close to something," he said. "I mean put up close to something strategic-like."

"Strategic, like what?" I asked him.

"Like a command center or something," he said. "Sometimes they would be up closer to large populations or something they would need well-guarded. New York had something like forty of them back when things were serious. Los Angeles had twenty or so. But out here in the middle of nowhere, why have a missile defense system set up?"

I looked all around us. I did not see anything besides a sparse landscape with a few cattle roaming about. There was not a sign of anything manmade except what was in front of us.

"Maybe you should ask NASA what else is out here," Quade told me and I agreed.

"Jake, I need Mack on the line now please," I told Jake who was sitting beside me listening to all we were talking about.

I watched him make the call and looked around some more. I tried to decide if it was worth a closer look or if we would just be asking for trouble. I did not think of Kevin as the sort that would come to a place like this, one so fully occupied. Questions began to form as Jake handed me the headset.

"Come in," I said as I put the head set on and adjusted the mouthpiece.

"Hey, it's Jadee," I heard. "What did you find?"

"A big spread-out compound," I told her. "It's some missile defense thing."

"Does it look like we are getting somewhere?" she asked, not hearing any excitement in my voice.

"I'm sorry Jadee, but no," I told her. "This place is occupied by some group. Nothing military looking. But it's definitely taken over by a group of some sort over there."

"Kevin wouldn't go there would he?" she asked, hope draining from her voice.

"I don't think so," I told her. "Are those numbers off of the paperwork coming up with anything?"

"Not yet," she said.

"Could you talk to Neil and see what he has to say about NIKE sites?"

"NIKE sites, like the shoes?"

"Yeah, one of the guys here knows what this site is. But he is saying they are mostly only here to support something else. So I'm really calling to talk to Mack. I want to know what else is around here that is worth protecting. It seems like that's the place we should be. Maybe it's an underground command center like ours there."

"Okay I'll get him on the com," she told me.

I waited and looked around some more. Still nothing looked at all interesting. The vultures still circled which I knew would not be good for us staying there for much longer. The sun was breaking through a lot more and I saw the clouds Jake had said were coming up from the south pushing in a little more.

"This is Mack, is this Randy?" I heard through the headphones. It surprised me as I thought I was going to have to relay messages.

"Yeah Mack, we are here at the coordinates and it's an old NIKE site," I told him.

"Really, that's an old missile defense compound," he said. "It didn't come up as an old code like that."

"You didn't know this before?" I asked him with a lot of anger starting to well up.

"No, we just looked for the closest militarily operated compound to that Reserve site," he told me. "There's nothing else within seventy miles of there."

"Weren't these sites set up to defend something important?" I asked him plainly.

"Yeah, wow, those old NIKE sites were for homeland defense," he said. "They were designed to destroy incoming threats to the US."

"So what is this one protecting?" I asked him. I did not hear a reply and I waited a full ten second before asking the question again.

"Hold on, I'm checking," he said with some concern in his voice. I waited. "Nothing is coming up as an asset in that area which constitutes that level of protection. Their range is about five hundred miles. I can look over the area and some of the old government information to see what else they may have out there."

"I thought we already did that," I told him, no longer able to hold my anger.

"Yes sir, we have," he told me. "I've found nothing else anywhere close by. But a NIKE site does indicate something there. I will have to look further but it will take some time."

"How much time?" I asked him.

"I can't answer that," he said. "I'm not even sure if there's anything to look over. We can only go off of what's filed. I know for sure....." I saw Quade jump up and turn. It caused me to look where he faced.

I pulled the headphones off and looked harder. I heard the sound of a motor of some sort but just barely and without any idea of where it was coming from. I could tell, however, that it was getting closer. I handed the radio back to Jake.

"Tell them we are moving out quickly and we'll talk later," I told him. "And make sure he knows we expect him to have something for us. We're not interested in any more of his theories and wild-goose chases." Jake took the radio with a nod.

The noise of the motors got closer and sounded to be coming from the west. I motioned for everyone to get ready but there was no need as everyone was on full alert, guns in hand. I gave the sign to move out and we headed for our horses which were just down the hill about fifty feet away.

"Look there," I heard Margie say as she pointed west.

It was easy to see what she was pointing at as three dirt bikes with riders came into view around the curved side of the small hill we were on. They were about a hundred yards away and were inside the fence with us. Their bikes were aiming right at us, though they had pulled up and were looking in our direction. I watched as one seemed to be bringing something to his mouth.

"Looks like they are radioing for backup," Quade said before I could. "Let's double time it to the horses."

We set out at a run and each of us made it to our own horse. Jumping into the saddle, I spun around to get a good look at the three bikers watching us. They did not get any closer but just sat there looking.

"If we set out at a run they will overtake us in no time," I said to whoever was listening. "It looks like they could get back-up easy enough."

Quade looked around then, as did I, looking for any solution. It was obvious we could easily be outflanked here and this could all be over in under a minute's time. We both tried to come up with something else but it did not take long to see there was nothing much to do.

"I say we walk out of here and see if they are inclined to follow," Quade said. "If they don't want to let us go it will be evident soon enough. Maybe we can make that hill and put up some defense there." We all agreed and turned to walk back where we had cut through the fence.

"I hate dirt bikes," I said aloud and most of my group agreed.

I watched the dirt bikes, waiting any second for a line of them to appear. None did as we got to the bottom of the hill and started up. We made it to the fence then and still they did not move. As we passed through I allowed myself a tiny bit of hope. It was short-lived, however.

The hills around us started to echo with the sound of motors. I could tell they were a different kind. I could also tell that they were coming on fast in a few different directions. My heart raced as we started down the slope that would bring us out of sight of the bikes and the compound. As we left their sight, we all kicked our horses into a full run and headed along the hill in a westerly direction. It seemed like that was the line that would give us the most cover, though it would not last long.

The hill we were on curved a little in our favor and started back southwest. We went all the way to the bottom as we rode along it and started up the other side. The motors continued to get closer and we ran still as fast as we could. I could see soon we would have to top the hill as the small hollow we were in was quickly running out. We raced on, however, all abreast basically, trying to run from the trouble that was coming.

The top of the hill, up from the tiny bowl we had made it in, was just ahead. It felt to me like we would be popping our heads up and the idea made the hairs at the back of my neck stand on end. As we topped the hill I looked back and saw that we were being pursued, both by the small group of bikes and three vehicles, two of which were old VW bugs all quite apocalyptic-looking. The other vehicle was an old Ford Econoline van, light brown and with a metal framed bumper that took up most of the front of the grill. Some rough looking people were hanging out the windows of all of them.

Our pursuers had lost track of us and were heading in the way they thought we had gone once over the hill. On seeing us top the hill then they turned and started for us. They were about a half mile off then and of course coming on fast. We raced down the small slope we were at that was not steep enough to hide us anymore.

"Look there!" I heard Eric yell and I looked where he had pointed. He turned before any of us and we all followed.

I moved my horse's line slightly so that I could move out from behind Eric and see where we were headed. I saw thicker shrubs in the area and hoped he was not suggesting we try and use them for cover in the up-and-coming gun fight. As I continued to look, however, I saw what looked like a small creek bed. It was not deep but it had a slope on both sides and would offer more cover than the open flatland all around. It was fifty yards ahead and we raced there as the sound behind us grew louder.

Shay was the first one to be inside the creek bed and Margie was right behind her. I saw them pull up sharp and jump down as I heard the first of the shots from behind us. As I heard a bullet wiz by my ear and figured it had to be less than two inches, the rest of us made it inside the sandy bottomed creek bed.

It may sound here like we had made it to safety, that was not exactly the case. The creek bed I am talking about was about three feet deep and about ten feet wide with two foot steep sides only here and there as it curved a little in its southeastern direction. Blowing dirt and sand had obviously filled it up over the last few decades or whatever, when it had failed to flow for who knows how long. The place we came into it at had gentle sloping sides and offered little protection.

As we made it to the floor of the bed we all jumped down and turned to our pursuers, most of us keeping behind our horses for cover. I saw three of the vehicles and two of the dirt bikes coming on strong, all of them kicking up dust behind themselves about a hundred yards away. We were taking fire but no one had been hit as far as I knew. As one, we returned firing.

We could see one of the VW bugs heading straight for us along side of the van. The dirt bikes had spread out and were going to try to wrap around what was left of us from the left side; all three of them moved that way. I did not see the other VW anywhere and I started trying to find it as the battle got underway.

My horse bucked violently in front of me and moved to my right. I did not see what had happened to him as I turned to look where I was still firing, having taken my eyes off for only a second. He took off forward but seemed to be tripped up by something. He reared up a little and made it about two steps before he fell, his front legs trying desperately to find a way to keep himself up. He landed hard on his side. I could do nothing for him but send a quick thought of gratitude his way for taking the bullets meant for me.

I did not have time to think where everyone was. I knew everyone was fighting for their lives and that they would set some sort of frontline. The firing we were doing told me we were in this to win it.

The vehicles were only about fifty yards away but coming on fast. None of the vehicles had a windshield and I saw the passenger firing from the van get hit. He moved out of the seat violently. With the sheer volume of bullets coming at them the van turned to our right, seeming to be wanting no more of us. I saw the one VW was full of people, hanging out the side and still firing at us.

I saw movement at my right side and I turned to it quickly, me standing fully out in the open now without a horse to hide behind. I watched as Margie moved out from behind her horse, still looking at the approaching vehicle. She took two steps and moving her rifle to her shoulder she drew a site on the VW. It seemed to happen in slow motion and as her back foot planted and her front foot landed she fired, a cloud billowing out in front of her. I saw her lower the butt of the rifle to the ground and start the fluid process of reloading.

I looked at where she shot and saw the VW veer off and turn slightly. A rain of bullets was still coming from us and I saw it now concentrated on the side of the VW whose driver was now dead. Soon all of the people hanging out of the windows there were done in, just like the driver. We watched as the Van drove farther away in the opposite direction.

The fight was not over, I knew, as I still heard the motors of the dirt bikes. The sound of them filled the air and I wondered where the other VW was. Looking around quickly, I was surprised I could not see it.

I looked to the left, where the bikers were headed in on us and saw Chris taking aim and firing at something. Laura too was taking aim but she was not firing. I saw her moving her rifle slowly and then firing. She looked over her scope with some satisfaction. I watched as Chris looked at her with a smile. I heard but did not see the other bike gun its engine. In only a few seconds we could tell it was moving away.

"Where's that other Bug at?" Quade asked, looking around as we all were.

"I don't hear it," I told him.

"Looks like that Van is still headed out," Chris yelled from his spot on a small bend in the creek bed.

"Great shot on that driver, Margie," I told her. "Everyone okay?" I asked. I got affirmatives all around.

"Let's keep a sharp eye out for that other car," Quade said, still nervously scanning all around.

I moved the small ways up out of the gentle slope of the creek bed and looking over the shrubs and waving brush, I looked all around. I still saw the van moving off to the east, dust flying behind it. I wondered why it did not go back to the compound but did not have much time for the thought. I was more interested in finding the other VW. Presently, I saw a dust cloud moving south of us and circling to catch up with the van. Looking quickly, I saw another dust cloud, which was the other dirt bike moving straight west, again not going back to the compound.

"I think I see that other VW trying to catch up with that van," I said. I felt Davina move up next to me and looking, she gave me a relieved smile which I am pretty sure I returned. I saw Teal and then Quade move over next to us from where they were looking around, us now all out of the creek bed.

"That idea of us coming to this little gully saved us," Quade told Eric. "Great thinking." We all echoed that.

"Yeah, looks like they are turning tail," Teal said.

"Looks like they got your horse," Margie said with some concern. I did not want to think about that yet as I nodded my head to her.

"Let's have a look at the VW," I told everyone. "We should be getting out of here so everyone grab your horses. Maybe I'll take the VW back."

I walked on as everyone grabbed their horses and together we walked over to the VW. It was a gory scene to say the least. I already knew, it but I saw again that Margie was an excellent shot as the driver's head was mostly gone. The rest of the car was full of gore.

"What the hell is that?" I heard Chris say from beside me. "No way, that's a Mauser SP66 sniper rifle! Wow, they could have just sniped us from three hundred yards out with that thing. And MP 40s, you have to be kidding me! Those are some oldies." He reached in and took the sniper rifle out through the back window. "I wonder which one was the sniper." He looked around inside as he set the rifle down. I heard him sound some satisfaction. "There you are. I'll take that off your hands since you won't be needing it anymore, you piece of crap." I did not see what he took as I was again watching the area around us.

"Looks like it's time to move out," Quade said as he got on his horse. "That compound there must have heard most of that firing and will be sending reinforcements for sure."

"I'm sure that's true," I said, looking again at the gore inside the car. "I think I'll take one of the bikes." I saw Chris holding up two other rifles out of the car.

"MP 40s," he said with a smile. "They take 9mm rounds. They are an old design, but effective."

"Time to mount up and be on our way," I told him.

He nodded and handed one of the guns to Laura, who as always was standing beside him. They both went quickly to their nearby horses. They hurriedly tied their finds behind their saddles once they had climbed aboard.

"I'll head over to one of those bikes," I told Davina who was next to her horse by then.

"Climb on," she told me. I ran and jumped into her saddle and pulled her on behind me.

"Laura, where did those bikes fall?" I asked.

"I'll show you," she said and took off at a fast trot. I did not see everyone mount up but as one we moved out.

Laura took us about fifty yards to the right and started looking around. Shrubs filled that area a bit and we could not see all that was around. I grew a little nervous and shouldered my AK.

"Be careful," I warned. "They could be alive still."

"No, they couldn't," Chris said. "Laura has gotten pretty good. She took them both out before I could."

"Wow, nice," I heard Davina say from behind me.

"Here," Laura said from a few yards away.

We all moved over to her and I jumped down off the horse. The dirt bike was lying with its handle bars turned sideways and the throttle side bent at an odd angle. I hurried to the bike and pulled it out of the dust. I looked for a second for what rock must have smashed the front in such a way. Finding no simple explanation for it, but seeing the bike was obviously not rideable, I let it drop.

"Here's the rider," Quade said from a short distance away. "Yeah, he's dead as hell alright. Damn, that was a good shot for a moving target." Laura smiled but moved off to find the other bike.

"The other one was over here," she said.

That one we found easily and I walked over to where everyone was gathering. That bike was obviously well intact which I was well-pleased about. I lifted it out of a thorny shrub. Pushing it back and forth I got it into neutral. Jumping on, I gave it a kick but nothing happened. After a few more kicks I started remembering all of the back trails I used to take with my family and friends and why it was always good to maintain your bikes.

"Another MP 40," I heard Chris yell and I saw him jump off his horse.

"Yep, that guy had it too," Quade said from where Chris was bending over. "Remind me not to piss you off, ma'am." Again Laura smiled.

"Look!" I heard Margie say in some alarm.

"Crap," Davina said. "Leave that thing and let's get out of here." Just then the bike roared to life.

"Move out!" I said, and looked at Margie to get an indication of where she was looking. She was looking toward the compound. "Let's make it back to the creek. It's the best cover we have!"

Everyone nodded and, turning their horses, ran toward the creek bed that had saved our lives thus far. I spun the bike around and headed toward the dust cloud that was coming from the compound. I stopped at a cluster of shrubs nearby.

I saw four, late model trucks following in a line and heading down a road that ran along a fence that was on the west side of the compound. I was sure they could fully see us as the land there was flat and every move we made created a small cloud of dust. I saw they were racing in our direction.

I did not like the look of these vehicles as they fully came into view around the fence. Two of the trucks had mounted guns that allowed someone standing in the bed to use them to cover anything in front of the vehicles. The other two trucks had large plows on the front and several soldiers in the back. My heart pounded in my chest as I thought about the next part of our fight. I turned and started to race to where the VW that we had taken out sat. I figured it may add to some of what we had for cover and would allow us to spread out a bit. I saw Davina waiting a few feet away for me to get to her before she would move. With a glance of pure love she looked at me and we both headed for the best cover we had.

CHAPTER 16

We rode first quickly to the spot we had defended thus far. I saw everyone looking for a better sloped spot to take a stand behind. Few looked promising and my heart started to sink.

"Let's put Chris and Laura together in the little curve right there," I said to everyone, pointing to a spot about twenty feet away. "The rest of us should spread out over there on that hill up from the creek bed on the left. Jake, back up Quade and Teal. It looks like we can fire on them from the shrubs and fall back to the creek if things go badly. I'll head over to that car and give us some depth."

"Want me to call home?" Jake asked.

"Yeah, you better," I told them. "Just tell them some vehicles are approaching for now. Be ready, if we are biting the bullet out here, to tell them what's going on. I don't want them wondering forever." He nodded his head in understanding and moved off to find some cover.

"I think that sounds pretty good," Quade said as the sound of the vehicles could be heard drawing ever closer.

"I'll try to draw them to me," I told everyone and felt Davina looking at me. "I should be able to outrun them on this thing. If I am, I'll meet you back at the train. No one fire unless we have to. Maybe they'll go for the bait and leave you all here with a backdoor." Looking, I could not see the vehicles but we all heard them.

"There's no way they didn't see us," Quade said. "They know we're in here."

"Then I'll circle out to draw some of their fire away and you all start flanking and take the shots that will get us out of this," I told them. Quade and the rest shrugged, knowing it was about all we had.

Davina and I made it with no trouble to the VW. We looked to see where the vehicles from the compound would come in on us at. A high spot in the nearby hill, if we are calling long gentle slopes hills, looked obvious as it would allow them to come in over top of us. We would be sitting ducks for sure no matter what we did.

I saw Eric riding quickly over to us. He jumped down off his horse and ran around to where we stood looking at the approaching doom. I saw he carried the sniper rifle Chris had found.

"Looks a little flat out here," Eric said with a smile. I appreciated his attempt to lighten the mood.

"Ever use one of those things?" I asked him.

"Not like this one, but I had some practice shooting at long-range now and then," he told me. "Never was really ever any good with these scopes things though." Davina and I both jerked our heads to look at him. He wore a large smile and I had to return it.

"Well, let's hope they all hold their heads up high and just look for us for a while," Davina said.

I saw the truck's dust cloud before I saw them coming into view about two hundred yards away. They seemed to know where we were as they headed straight for us. I guessed the VW was drawing them as were the horses standing behind it. I felt Davina's hand find mine.

"You know you're not 'drawing their fire', right?" she asked me.

"It may help if I circle far out," I told her. "I can keep myself from giving them an easy target and maybe give you guys some easy targets in return." The vehicles made it to a hundred and fifty yards out.

"We are not arguing about this," she told me. "You're not riding that thing out of here to give them anything to aim at."

"I'll ride it," Eric said from where he was looking through the window of the VW. "I used to race dirt bikes when I was a kid. My dad and I would travel around to the dirt tracks every weekend and spend all day at the races."

Davina looked at me and looked to be wondering what I would say. I shook my head to her and I saw her jaw start to set. She started to form some words but then did not say anything. She instead nodded her head at me. I looked and saw the vehicles coming on still at a hundred yards.

"I can't let you do that Eric," I told him. He shrugged and stuck his head back into the VW.

"I know there has to be some more bullets for this thing in here somewhere," he said, now hurriedly moving things around inside the blood filled car.

"Don't go," Davina told me and threw her arms around me.

"We are not here to harm you," I heard a mic yell loudly from the area that the vehicles were coming from. The voice had a deep oriental accent. "We will not harm you."

I saw the vehicles then, as plain as day. They had stopped at just under a hundred yards. The men in the backs of the trucks with the mounted machine guns were aiming them in our direction and I saw soldiers jumping out of the backs of the others and disappearing into the grass and shrubs all around where they stopped. I saw Eric continue to look through the car for some more ammo.

"What did he say?" Eric asked, looking at the vehicles through the car. "Not here for us?"

"Is anyone down there wounded?" the same voice of the microphone asked. "We have medical help."

Before I could do anything, I saw Quade and Teal show themselves and raise their hands. They started to walk up the small hill but stopped after a few feet. I raised my AK47 and aimed at the mounted gun that turned to them.

"Eric, aim at the gun on the left truck," I told him. "Honey, you take out the one on the right. You move to the back of the car and take aim from there."

I knew that was the best place to be as the engine was back there and it may block the rounds that may any second be coming our way. One of the larger guns was aiming right at us and I knew in under a second it could send rounds both through the car and us without even a question of whether or not we were all completely dead. I smiled at my wife.

"We are not here to harm you," the voice said again. "We will help you."

"Maybe we shouldn't go off on that motorcycle after all," Eric told me as he pulled his head back out of the car. I saw he had found some ammo.

"Why?" I asked him.

"Sounds like whoever attacked us was not from wherever these new guys are," he said. "If you go out on that thing, they may just think some of those guys are left."

"Good point," I told him. I heard Quade yelling something.

"We will not approach unless we see all of your hands," the voice said. "You all, over by the vehicle, you also must come out and raise your hands. We will not harm you."

"Are we believing that?" Davina asked the obvious question.

"Well, quite frankly, I don't see what choice we have," I said. "They could take us out with those guns and we wouldn't even get one of them." Davina looked at me and I tried a smile. "Chris, can they see you and Laura?" I asked my radio.

"No, I don't think so," I heard back from him.

"Stay down and cover us," I told him.

"They are sending men everywhere to flank," he told me.

"I saw," I told him. "Let's see how this plays out. Stay down and let's see if they mean what they say."

"Copy," he said.

I put the kick stand out for the bike and made sure it was in neutral. I swung my leg over and got off, leaning the bike over. The kickstand pushed into the soft dirt and fell over before I could catch it. I had to shrug as I turned to look back at the guns facing us. I stepped out from around the VW and raised my hands.

"We will not harm you," I heard again. "Everyone come out with your hands high. We are not your enemy."

"They sure look like our enemy," Eric said as he too moved out from around the vehicle beside me. We stood there in front of the VW, hoping not to feel the violent impact of bullets ripping apart our chests.

"Not much else to do," I heard Davina say as she too moved out from around the car and stood beside it with her hands up. This was not how I had envisioned our end.

I saw Shay stand up then, and sling her rifle behind her shoulder, raising her hands as well. I waited to see Margie but she did not stand. (I hoped that meant she could not be seen by them.)

"Everyone, please come out in the open with your hands high," we all heard. "We will not harm you."

I moved forward then and told Eric to stay there. I walked with my hands up but elbows bent; it gave me a little bit of comfort, thinking I could get to my rifle a split second earlier. I heard Davina fall in beside me and we came up beside Quade together. Several men looking like jump-suited soldiers stood up and kept a bead on us as we went.

"What are we thinking now?" Quade asked as we pulled up next to him. "Not sure I want to be a prisoner here in some wasteland hotel."

"I think I would agree with that," I told him. "I'll walk up a little closer and see what they say"

"Like hell we let you take that on," Teal said. "You ain't got to do that."

"What, I'll be the only one to make it," I told her with a smile. "Those big guns can't swivel as good on a moving target up close." I saw her smile nervously back and then look back up the slope.

I started walking up to the vehicles and saw the soldiers still keeping their long rifles aimed at us. A couple more of the soldiers came into view and I saw how outflanked and outgunned we really were, if I had not noticed before. As Davina and I came to within a hundred feet of the vehicle, a soldier moved in front of us to stop our progress.

"You will not be harmed," the mic said again and I silently wished the man would shut up.

"So, what do you want?" I asked as politely as I could, trying to keep from the sarcasm I really wanted to say.

"We are here to help only," I heard.

Looking, I saw the man speaking. He was inside one of the vehicles with the plow on the front. I saw him holding a CB mic to his mouth. He was looking at us. I turned and started walking toward him.

The soldier who blocked our way actually fell in beside us and seemed to be escorting us to that vehicle, still keeping his rifle aimed at my chest. Another soldier came up on our other side and did the same. I was amazed that we were led to walk right up to the front of the plow.

"We will not harm you," I heard the mic say again.

"Yeah, we heard that part," I told the man with the mic. He opened the door and stepped out.

He was a tall, oriental man with a thick mohawk running down the center of his head. He had a thin moustache and several nose rings. He was dressed in a jump-suit like the rest and kept his hand on a silver revolver on his hip. He attempted a smile but it came off as rather menacing.

"We do not want to hurt you," he told me as he came around the door.

"Then why are you here?" I asked him.

"We knew they were out here today, those scavengers," he told me, pointing in the direction the van had gone. "We were going to come out here, when we saw the vultures, and run them off but you seemed to have done that for us. We heard your gun battle. We are sending people after them but they will not catch them. They know these areas better than we do. They always escape."

"Who are they?" I asked.

"We call them Raiders," he said. "They are constantly trying to descend on the people trying to make it to our city here." He pointed to the slope that kind of hid the compound.

"Raiders?" I asked and he nodded his head.

"We cannot keep them from doing so, though we try often," he said. "They come from the plateaus over there." Again he pointed but this time northwest.

"So now what?" I asked him.

"Is anyone hurt down there?" he asked.

"Just my horse," I told him.

"Please come to our town and enjoy your stay then," he said and started to turn back to the truck.

"Just like that?" I asked him.

"All are welcome to trade and pleasure themselves at Missile Town," the man said. "I will buy you a drink myself for what you've done here."

"How about giving me a horse?" I asked him.

"I have none to give," he told me. "But you can trade for them in town."

"Interested in trading for that bike I saw you on, mister?" someone asked from my right. I looked and saw it was one of the men from behind the mounted guns. "I'll give you a good deal."

"I think I would be interested, yes," I told him.

"I know Kyle will give you a pretty penny for that car over there too," he told me.

"Okay, I'll trade for all of it," I told him.

"Names Carl," he told me. "Come find me when you get to town and I'll give you a fair deal. Kyle will too."

"I will if I can find you," I told him.

"I'll keep an eye out," he assured me.

"What's your name?" I asked the oriental man standing behind the truck door.

"I am Thomas," he said. "You will be treated with care at Missile Town."

I nodded at that and knew that care meant different things to different people; I could only imagine what it had come to mean out here. Thomas nodded back and got into the truck, closing the door. The soldiers backed away from us and got into the bed of the truck. I saw Thomas give a hand signal and all of the trucks backed up as one. In another few seconds we were watching them heading back to the compound.

"Well, that could have gone much worse," I told Davina. She nodded and spun on her heels and walked back down the slope to return to the others.

We walked back and joined the others that were all standing in a small circle then. I saw Eric had joined them and I heard Jake reassuring home that we were okay. Quade too was at his radio telling someone of our situation.

"So, that seemed to go okay," Teal said.

"What did that guy say?" Quade asked.

"He said those guys that attacked us, they're called Raiders," I told the group. "They are scavengers, it sounds like, waiting outside this town to pick off what they can. Sounds like the town tries to keep them from getting too much."

"Yeah, I bet word of that going on here keeps people from coming here," Quade said.

"Sounds like they want to trade for that car and the bike," Davina said.

"Really?" Chris asked. "What would they trade?"

"I'm not sure," I told him. "I'm not really sure what currency they use out here. Maybe a bunch of food or something."

"There's a lot of stuff to trade really," Quade told me. "They could have their own currency, a kind of buy anything in town kind of thing. Who knows, it could be a lot more."

"We aren't thinking of going in there are we?" Laura asked. "It's pretty obvious Kevin isn't here."

"Yeah, I agree with that," Chris said. "If things get hairy like this again, we might not be so lucky."

"I think I would like to have a look if everyone here is up for it," Quade said. Teal nodded. "I've heard of another trading town up this way but I thought it was a lot farther away by what everyone I've talked to says. I'd like to see what it's all about down there. Those guys coming out here shows a little bit of what kind of town it is."

"I think we have some time," I told everyone. "You guys okay with that?" I asked Laura and Chris.

"I'm up for it," Laura said. "I guess I just want to make sure we know what we're getting into."

"Agreed," I said. "We definitely go in on full alert."

"We should stay together and leave at the first sign of even a hint of trouble," Quade said. "It's easy to find down there, I'm sure."

"Okay, whether or not we have traded for anything or not, if it doesn't feel good, we cut out of there," I said.

"What are you going to do for a horse?" Margie asked. We all turned and looked at my horse, bloodied and fully expired.

"Maybe that's the first thing we trade for," Chris said. I agreed.

I walked over to my horse and looked down at it. I was pretty saddened seeing him lying there. He had been a great horse and we had become friends.

"We'll find you a good one," Davina told me.

"Yeah, he'll be hard to replace," I told her. "Could someone help me get my saddle off please?"

I unbuckled the saddle's strap and pushed it off the horse as much as I could. Chris and Laura helped push on the carcass, but it would not budge. Chris then started trying to dig some of the softer dirt out from under the saddle. I saw Davina go get on her horse.

A couple of our other horses had moved off a bit and were pretending to feed, but nervously. Quade and Teal were out in the field approaching them slowly, trying to recapture them. I saw Eric over pulling bodies out of the VW as Jake was talking on the radio.

Davina threw me a rope and nodded her head to me. I smiled at her and tied it to my saddle horn. She wrapped her end around her own saddle horn and inched her horse forward. The saddle easily slid out.

I picked up the saddle and took it over to the car. I did not envy Eric the gruesome job he was finishing up and when I got there I saw nothing but blood throughout the inside. A few spots looked worse than others.

"I think I'll put my saddle in the trunk," I told Eric who simply smiled.

I went over to the front of the car and pulled open the compartment there. I was not surprised to see little there besides a spare tire. I put my saddle inside and saw that it was not going to close all the way. With a little piece of rope I cut out of what I had, I secured the lid down and turned to Eric.

"I'll drive this thing into town," he told me before I could say anything. "I'll have Quade pull my horse behind him."

"You sure you're okay with that?" I asked him.

"Yeah, you're riding that bike, right?" he asked.

"No, why don't you let me drive this thing and you take the bike," I told him.

"No, I'm fine here," he said and got into the driver's seat.

I heard the car startup which stopped my worrying about that. I asked him how much fuel he had and he told me it read half a tank. Walking around, I went to the dirt bike and picked it up off the ground. It surprisingly started after just a few kicks and wiping some grass and debris off of the clutch cable I looked around at the group. It seemed we had all survived and were now ready to move ahead. I let out the clutch and moved out in front.

I thought to lead us the way we had seen the trucks coming at us from the town. We quickly found a dirt road and looked where it led. Seeing that it led in the direction it should we started down it and moved to the slope that slightly hid the compound.

With a full invite to the compound I felt better about moving mostly out in the open. We all still kept a sharp eye out and I was ready at any second to be sprung upon by some evildoers. We did however, continue down the well-worn road and crossed a cattle guard that was the break in the fence there.

I saw the compound come fully into view on my right. It looked a lot bigger from so close and I could see a lot more people milling about. Semi-trailers mostly lined the back fence standing about fifty feet back and pushed up close together with a railing attaching them along the top and making a perfect spot for someone to walk along the whole row of them and keep an eye on what was going on in that area outside the tall six, foot chain-link fence that surrounded the place. I could still see the cement buildings that were the original part of the compound standing only a little shorter than the semi-trailers. The trailers gave way as we went along the fence and were replaced with tall shipping containers of various sizes. Again, they were put close together and a heavy-duty railing was attached to the top. A line of them ran all the way to the corner and blocked from view what was behind them.

I did see every hundred yards or so atop the trailers and containers something that looked like a small shack built. They had several layers of metal siding attached and different-shaped vinyl windows facing toward the fence. A door was on both sides so that if they were open one could continue to walk along the top without having to find a way around them. As I watched one such shack toward the corner, I saw a rather ugly-looking woman stand up and start staring harshly at us. I figure all such towns needed one of her.

We rounded the corner and saw the gate a few hundred yards ahead. Outside the gate was a shanty town full of old looking campers and what looked like quickly put together shacks. A few dogs ran about, half-starved and curious as to whether we would be of any help to them. Looking at everything I could, I turned to the gate and moved on.

I circled out a little so as not to drive through the poor village of campers and shacks. I saw the gate was open and to my great surprise I saw quite a few people walking in and out. Most of the movement was done on horseback, I saw but there were a couple of wagons. The two I saw seeming to be leaving together were carrying something under large tarps. They did all look heavily armed. We moved through the large open chain-link gateway and immediately saw a stable to our left. Stopping just inside the gate but moving over to the left so as not to block it, I continued my scan of the town.

There was a wide street that went straight for quite a ways and ended at one of the tall cement buildings. The street was lined with shops that were made out front or half inside of the shipping containers we saw from outside. A few long campers were in line with the containers and also seemed to be making some type of shop out of themselves. I could see through a few breaks in their continuity what looked like alleyways. There looked to be several streets that made up the city or whatever this thing was.

"We stabling our horses?" Chris asked from beside me.

"Yeah, let's see how much that will cost us," I told him. "Want to find that out for me?"

"Sure, I'll be right back," he told me. He and Laura left, riding toward the stable.

"Looks like my kind of town," Quade said on the other side of me. "Straight to the point kind of thing."

"I would say that too," I told him. "I thought they would be around but I guess I never really imagined these kind of places existed."

"Really, me either," he told me. "I thought we were pretty unique."

"This place looks crowded," Teal said. I saw her and Davina riding beside each other.

"Looks hungry too," Davina said. I saw her looking at a group of small kids poking their heads out to see who the new people in town were.

"Yeah, those ones probably eat better than us," I told her and got a smile from her which I tried to return. I knew how tenderhearted she was toward children.

"I called home and gave them an update before we made it in the gate," Jake told me.

"Awesome job," I told him. I looked overhead and saw the clouds breaking up and mostly going away. "Can they see us?"

"They are looking and should be able to in a few minutes," he told me. "Jadee is wondering why we are moving in on this place here. I think I worried her with telling her about the vehicles earlier."

"Did you tell her we are in and out of here in a hurry?" I asked him.

"I did, and it helped a little," he said.

"Okay, great," I told him. I saw Chris and Laura walking back over to us without their horses.

"Looks like everything works here on these special stamped quarters," Chris said.

Laura threw me one. I looked at it and saw the letter M stamped with a T stamped over it on the face of George Washington. Flipping it over again I saw nothing unfamiliar on the back.

"I got four of them and they said we could keep all of our horses here for the day," Chris said. "I traded them for one of those MP 40s I got from that VW. I kept all of the bullets though."

"We'll have to figure out what the value of one of those quarters is here," Quade said. "Mind if I see it." I threw it to him. "Oh yeah, I've seen these before. People bring them to our town to try and trade with them. We never accept them, but now I know where they're from."

"What are we going to do with this thing?" Eric asked.

"One of the guys on those trucks earlier said he'd trade for it," I told him. "He said he'd keep an eye out for us. Maybe we can park it over by the stables until we find him."

"Want me to move it over there?" he asked.

"Yeah, we better not stay here in the middle of the street," I told him.

We all moved over to the large stable which was really a long shack with a bunch of different corrals attached to it. I saw lines of different saddles and tack on saddle horses hanging on the wall when I looked behind what could have been called a counter. Numbers labeled their spots and different colored tags hung from strings down the row of them.

"You wanting to park that thing here too?" I heard a gruff voice ask. I looked up to see a short portly man scowling at me.

"I was thinking about it," I told him. "That VW too, if that's possible."

"It costs you a quarter and we don't guarantee against no theft," he said.

"Okay, I think we can do that," I told him. I watched Chris throw him a quarter.

"Park them at the end of the corrals down the way," the man said, leaning out and pointing back toward the gate. "Nobody ought to mess with them. I just have to tell you that in case they do."

"I understand," I told him. "We shouldn't be long."

"That's what they all say," the man said. I meant to prove him wrong. "You want grain for all the horses?"

"If we can afford it," I told him.

"How much you got?" he asked with a smile.

"On second thought, we'll just let them be for now," I told him.

"Here's your ticket then," he said.

He handed me a square, wood piece with a set of numbers on one side. He reached up and pulled on a rope that hung from the ceiling and I heard a small bell ring. Two teenage boys came into view, looking for what work needed done. Putting the wooden piece in my pocket I turned back to the car and dirt bike.

"Maybe we should park them down there out of the way until that Carl guys finds us," I told Eric. "Looks like we have the spot for the day."

"Can do," he said and got inside the car.

I parked the bike as close to the fence as I could where we were instructed to put it. I had Eric pull up next to it and mostly wedge it in place. I saw him try to roll up his window and then smile at himself.

"Those must be long gone," he said as he got out. He pushed down the knob for the lock, out of spite, just before he closed the door.

"You take the keys?" I asked him. He dangled them and then put them in his pocket.

The others made it to us by then and we, as one, looked over the town. I wanted to wait for Carl or maybe Kyle for a little while, hoping to be rid of our burden and maybe secure a horse before anything else was accomplished. No one seemed to mind and it gave us a better chance to see what was on Main Street.

I was again surprised at seeing all of the people in the town. Most seemed to be going about with a purpose, like the ones I saw carrying water to and fro. Others were standing around watching much like we were, though they mostly seemed to be having drinks in hand. A few were making nuisance of themselves by trying to sell one thing or another. I did see a few men and women in jump-suits. Loads of long corn stalks were brought in and unloaded out of wagons at a nearby dock; there was a continuous flow of them. I watched the wind blow down Main Street and swing all of the hanging merchandise and dust as it passed.

"I say we have a look around," Chris said after we stood there for at least ten minutes. Laura seemed to agree.

"I think it's been long enough," Quade said, looking at the watch on his wrist. "Did you tell that Carl guy you'd wait for him?"

"No," I told him.

"Did you commit to sell just to him?" he asked.

"No, I sure didn't," I said. "I guess we can try and find someone else to deal with."

"Yeah, I don't like standing here like this," Teal said. "Lynn would have gone crazy by now."

"Yeah, let's see if we can find somewhere to get a horse," Quade said. "Probably a good place to start is this stable."

We all agreed and moved off to go back to the counter of the stable. When we got there no one was in sight. I saw our gear hung nicely with only one wooden token dangling from them. I guess the colors must be for the different care to be taken with the animals. Looking harder, I saw down the long building and could make out a few different doors. The smell of leather and hay hit me hard in the face as one of the doors opened and the man we had dealt with earlier came into view. Seeing me, he walked up to the counter.

"Done already?" he asked with what could be called a smile. "Still cost the same."

"No, I was just wondering if you sold horses here," I told him.

"I get some every now and then," he said. He stood there looking at me.

"Well, would one of those times be now?" I replied with some annoyance.

"I could look around and see what I've got, yes," he said. "What would you be paying for a good horse?"

"What is one worth?" I asked him.

"It depends on the animal," he said with a smile. I could tell I was not going to like dealing with this guy.

"The best horse you have," I told him.

"That could be a lot," he said. "Horses do go for a lot around here, I can't do anything about that." I felt myself being led astray.

"Maybe we'll shop around for a bit," I told him. Davina, beside me, grunted agreement loudly.

"Not sure who else has any," he said.

"Good ol' Sampson, you trying to fleece our new guests," I heard from behind me. I turned and saw Carl standing close by.

"No, Carl, as a matter of fact, I was about to send these guys your way," the man behind the counter said.

"Yeah, I bet you were," Carl said. He turned to me. "Still interested in trading for that bike?"

"Yeah, I am," I told him. "Obviously, we are not too familiar with how things around here work."

"I'll fill you in," Carl said. "I told Kyle about the car. He said he'd give you whatever was fair and said I could make the deal for him. I'll be honest and tell you that car is worth a lot. I'm not as happy about telling you, so is that motorcycle."

"Whatever works," I told him. "I'm just needing a good horse to get me through the plains."

"Where you all headed?" he asked.

"Missouri, I guess," I told him without skipping a beat. "Heard some good things about the place."

"Really, I've never heard much about it," he said. "Sounded like a ghost town, what I heard. But you know how rumors go around here. We got a saying out here, 'believe nothing of what you hear and half of what you see'."

"Sounds pretty damn smart. But you think you will be able to help me with a good horse?" I asked, trying to change the subject.

"Sure thing and then some," he told me with a smile. "Those rides there are worth more dough than a horse."

"What's so special about them?" Quade asked.

"The Raiders suck, but they sure know a lot about mechanics. They change the engine in them to be able to run on straight ethanol, you know the stuff you can get out of corn. They seem to have all of the right parts."

"Yeah, I know about ethanol," I told him.

"Sorry, must people don't know squat about this postwar stuff," he told me.

"I see all the corn coming in," I told him. "Must be pretty prevalent around here."

"Yeah, it's our main labor around here," he said. "Keeps us busy and keeps the lights on, literally. Say, you all want a beer before we start wheelin' and dealin'? There's a place just up the street and Thomas said he was buying the first round. They'll believe me if I tell them that. It too is corn beer and pretty damn good."

I looked around and got a shrug from most. Others did not seem to care and offered a frown. I turned and nodded to Carl and with a smile, he led us down the main street.

"The first thing you learn here is there's nothing free here, unless you know the right people," Carl said and turned with a broad grin. "Now, you all killed some Raiders so you'll be welcome by everyone around."

"Sounds like they are a pain in the ass," Teal told him. I saw movement coming toward us at my right side and turned that way quickly, shouldering my AK47.

"Wow, easy mister! I was just trying to get a closer look at your squaw there," a rough-looking man said. "Interested in selling her?"

"She look like our slave, asshole?" I asked him.

"Could be, I figure," he said. I looked at him intently and he backed away and leaned up against a nearby burning trashcan.

"Sorry about that, but there are all kinds here," Carl told Margie as we moved on. "Don't take no offense. There are some that buy and sell in such ways. It ain't allowed here leastways but, no one really holds the laws too strict-like."

"There should not be people that do such things," Margie said. She seemed to be somewhere else.

We wound our way down a few streets. The place he was taking us did not seem to be just down the street after all. We did, however, get a good view of what made up the town.

There were several rows of large metal boxes, mostly what looked to have once been the same kind of containers as were along Main Street. They did not look much like them now, however. They were sloppily painted all sort of different ways and cut into odd shapes to accommodate the different-sized spaces they were fitting into. Some of them had small wooden porches and even a small fence along it which seemed to want to help the building appear to have some room in front of it. Clothes hung on lines and people stood about watching as we passed.

All the space was not taken up by the metal containers I saw. The space between the metal boxes, which were now dwellings and small shops, were mostly uncovered. Several of the open areas had tents of all kinds. Other areas were well-covered with thick sheets of plastic or canvas and were mostly dwellings that looked to be trying to keep themselves out of the elements. We were definitely not in the best part of town.

"It's just up ahead," Carl told us. "Curly's looked a little full so I figured we'd be more comfortable over here. Harvest time is always crazy around here."

"Harvest time already?" Quade asked.

"Sure, we try to get a little jump on it," Carl said as we made another turn. "We waited too long really. The Raiders must have been busy elsewhere this year as they didn't take much."

"They always taking your crop?" Quade asked.

"Some of it at least every year," he said. "We can handle that as there is not really that many of them and they only take small portions. It's getting pretty old though."

"I bet," Quade said.

I was paying too close attention to the slums we were walking in and did not see when we walked right inside one of the shipping containers. We had come through the open double doors of the container and straight on through. We were led inside an area that I could see was made out of the block like shipping containers. Two set up long ways and joined end to end made up a wall and there were all four walls present. Other shipping containers were stacked above us to make a second level. The double doors on the containers that made up the wall to our left were open and some business girls leaned on the frames and looked our way. Carl waved several away that started toward us.

"We'll get better service here anyways," Carl told us. "And the place with the real good horses is just over there." he pointed in some random direction.

"I think I've seen all I care to," Quade told me. "We can get your horse and be on our way."

"Well then let's have a drink and get to business," Carl said as he stood beside some tables and motioned with his hand to move us all closer.

As we moved farther inside, I saw the place was only about half full. There were tables evenly spaced throughout the middle of the floor with booths lining the walls to our right and left except where the double doors of the containers were open. A long bar, who's stools were about half filled, was at the far end of the structure. Lights were hanging from two different places above and were shining their light all around. It was surprisingly bright in the place. A sign reading 'Lisa's Place' hung low behind the bar.

"Hey, Carl, who you got there with you?" a woman asked from the bar.

"Hey, Lisa, these here just took out a group of Raiders," he told the woman. "Thomas offered them a drink on him."

"Well, okay then, they are sure welcome around here," Lisa said.

Looking around the bar, I saw we interrupted a poker game. Five men were sitting at a table and were all turned our way. Several of the men and women at the bar turned and looked but with a shrug turned back to their conversation or whatever they were drinking. A few more of the tables were filled and I saw the remains of some plates of food. It reminded me that I was hungry.

"Take whatever spot you want and I'll be right over there," Lisa told us.

Carl led us to a section that was mostly untaken but up close to the poker game. I heard some grumbling from that table as the dealing got back underway. We all found a spot as Carl moved us to several chairs. At last he sat down just as Lisa made it to the table.

"So, what will you all have?" she asked from behind a tablet of paper.

"You all should try our tall glass of our corn beer," Carl told us. "We make it a couple of streets over in one of the old Missile buildings."

"Boy, I'd love to see that," Eric said.

"If you all have the time, I'd take you over there," Carl said. "It's mostly for the tanner and for brewing beer. It doesn't look much like it used to."

"So, beers all around then?" Lisa asked. Everyone kind of nodded and I too was not sure about a warm beer in the middle of the afternoon. She turned on her heels with a warm smile to Carl.

"Kyle might make it if we are here long enough," Carl told us.

"I wouldn't mind getting down to business," I told him. "I think we have a long ways to go before dark."

"Okay then, so all's you are needing is a horse, you said?" Carl stated. "I would have to be honest with you again and say that that car is worth a lot more than that."

"How much more," Davina asked.

"I guess we could say you could buy about five horses and a wagon for that car and bike," he said. I liked this man's honesty.

"How about some medicine then?" Shay asked out of nowhere.

"I'm not sure about that," he told her. "We kind of have a doctor but he's more of a veterinarian, people say. Thankfully, I haven't had need of him yet."

"Does he give out medications?" Shay asked him softly.

"I've never heard of that from him," Carl said. Just then Lisa came to the table with two other women carrying all of our beers.

"Does the doctor here give out medication?" I asked Lisa.

"Doogie?" Lisa asked with a smile. "You don't want what he's given out. I haven't ever heard of him curing anyone. He gave Linda over there herpes a year back. He ain't even allowed in here no more."

"Maybe we should pass on that then," Shay said and reached for her beer. We all followed suit.

I swigged a bit down and put the beer back on the table. It was warm, like I figured it would be, but the taste was something I had not expected. It was a bit sweet but tasted like warm cream of wheat. A bit of maple syrup and it could have been breakfast time, minus the warm feeling that followed, of course.

"Very good beer," I told Carl as I took another long drink.

"I think I'll call home and let them know what we are doing," Jake said from across the table, having downed his beer. "How much longer do you figure we'll be here?"

"Minutes, if I can help it," I told him. "Chris, you and Laura go with him. Just right outside is far enough."

"Understood," Jake said and Chris and Laura got up to accompany him.

"So where are these horses?" I asked Carl. "I think if we can get one of them and maybe some gear we will be on our way."

"Okay then, they are a couple of streets over and back by the fence," Carl told us. "I am sorry to have brought you all this way just to bring you so far again just a little over from where you came in."

"No problem," I told him.

"Might I at least get you all something to eat?" he asked. "I will pay for that and then take you to find your choice of Kyle's herd. They are fine animals."

"I think we can make that happen," Quade said, more to me than to Carl. "We are in a rush but we can make time to have a bite. We should keep up our strength." Shay seconded that. I wondered what Quade was playing at.

Carl smiled and got up to tell Lisa that we would be eating also. I saw Jake and the others coming back over to us, Jake eyeballing the poker game at the other nearby table. He came up to the table and gave a report that was much like all the rest. Carl came back and told us the food was ordered and would be out shortly.

"Mind if I get in a game?" Jake asked me and lifted his head over toward the poker table. He took off the radio and set it close to me.

"Looks like the game is full," I told him.

"We have room for one more I think," one of the men at the table said.

"We better sit this one out," I told Jake and he reached down and picked the radio back up with a nod.

"Yes sir," he said and went and found a seat that put him within earshot of the game.

We waited for the food to arrive and grew bored of the conversation Quade and Carl began having about how crops did in that area and other such subjects that would only be of interest to someone living close in the state. I turned my attention back to the beer I had not yet finished. Davina played with my feet under the table and I returned her kindness.

I saw Thomas come through the front door of the bar and everything stopped. Carl stood up and waved him over. As he came over to sit down things got back to normal.

"How do you like us so far?" Thomas asked us.

"I like the beer," I told him and everyone joined me on that.

"Lisa has her own recipe," he told us. "Mostly the bars here make vodka out of our corn supply."

"Well, she is doing a fine job," Quade told him.

"I'm glad you have had the experience," he told us. "Where are you all headed?"

It sounded like a pointed question, meant to lead us somewhere.

"Out east," I lied, kinda.

"What is wanting you there?" he asked.

"We have heard good things about it," I told him.

"Yeah, and a few of us have family there," Quade added and I silently thanked him.

"You all handled yourselves well today," he told us.

"We appreciate you all coming out to try and help," I told him.

"We do that all the time," Carl told us. "Although, we haven't had to do that for a few weeks. A couple turned up dead about five days ago but that was something else, we think."

"What do you mean?" Davina asked.

"They were the rich type," Thomas told her, looking harshly at Carl for airing the town's dirty laundry. "They flaunted it all around and then rode out of town as though the world was still a nice place." We all nodded.

I heard something from the table where the poker was going on. I changed my attention to listening to what was going on there and saw Jake do the same thing. The noise was starting to affect our conversation.

"Just buy him a beer and call it even," one man was saying.

"I lost a hell of a lot more on that hand than a damn beer," someone else said.

"Maybe you should learn to play your hand right," another man told him.

"I won't be taught by someone like you," he replied. I was sorry for the nearness now of our table.

"I'll buy you all a beer," yet another man said. "Let's get this game going and screw them damn blinds."

The game went on and one of the men called a woman from the bar over. He ordered some beers for the rest and she went to retrieve them. Before she could leave the table, however one of the men grabbed her.

"How much for you for the night?" he asked her. I turned to see what was happening.

"That ain't my trade, damn you," she told him and punched him in the mouth, making him let her go. The man next to him quickly stood and knocked the woman out cold with a well-placed fist to the jaw. Three of the four men still sitting at the table started laughing.

"We don't take no lip from no damn likes of whores," the man said.

"I ain't sure I see what's so funny," Jake said, standing up.

"What'd you say, greenhorn?" the man that threw the punch said.

"Greenhorn?" Jake asked. "What kind of stupid-ass cowboy movie did you get that out of?"

The man Jake asked the question to jumped away from his chair and rushed Jake. Jake saw what he was going to do long before he got close and easily moved out of the way throwing a punch into the man's stomach as he got close. I heard the only man at the table that had not laughed, curse. I saw then the whole table of them get up to take on Jake. I then stood up. Chris was already up as was Quade. Eric was right beside him.

"If you want it we can all get down," a man from the other table asked.

"It's not really up to me," I told him. "But if a man of you moves then you'll force our hand." The man said some pretty weird combination of curse words and spit in my direction. I thought I had figured out his answer.

I moved around the seats that were at our table and tried to get closer to the man. I looked at Jake as I did and saw him moving in on the man that charged him and who was coming in for another try. With one straight punch he sent the guy to the floor. Chris stepped in to take the other guy who moved in to help defend the guy now on all fours.

I moved in quickly on the man that had talked so tough from the other side of the table. He was moving back, hoping to find some place to launch an attack. He moved toward his colleagues some but they were previously engaged. I saw fear fill his face but I was still pissed off about my horse.

I sent a double jab to his face which brought some pain to his expression. He pulled his hands up to a fighting position but he was ill-suited for what was coming. I threw a straight right and broke his nose. I followed that up with a solid liver shot that dropped him at my feet. I kicked him a couple of more times in the liver just to make sure he understood what I was talking about. I did not expect much from him for the next several hours but I stomped on the back of his head just to make sure.

Turning, I saw Chris had finished off one of the men and Jake was onto his second. Another of the men stood off, not wanting to take part in the bloody fight that his group had started. Jake was about to take on the man that had grabbed the woman. I saw Quade ready to back him up if he should need it.

Jake moved out of the way of a quick jab but took a straight right to the forehead. He tried his own combination but the man was obviously trained as he slipped past them all. I began to get concerned but just then Jake tried again and hit the man with a jab and then another. It pissed the guy off and caused him to come in swinging. I was proud of Jake when he defended the wild punches and countered with an uppercut that rocked the man. At that, the guy faked another wild volley of punches but instead grabbed Jake and tripped him to the ground. Jake tried to roll as he landed but the guy was in tight. He lifted up and hit Jake hard on the temple and then again. Jake tried to block the next one but the man changed angles and hit him hard again. Having enough of that, Jake grabbed the man's hair and pulled him in close. I watched Jake and the man wrestle for a position that would allow one to punch the other. I saw Jake jerk his hips to the side and the man lost containment of him. Jake started to get away but then screamed in pain. He screamed again, but I could not see why.

I was about ready to move in as Jake finally broke free and rolled away from the man. I saw blood coming from Jake's chest and arm, dripping heavily onto the floor. The man rolled around to face him, getting his feet under himself. He stood up slowly and I saw the knife in his right hand. I shouldered my AK47.

"No, wait," Jake said on seeing me. "If this coward is that sort then so be it."

Jake pulled a pearl-handled switchblade out of his pocket, the same one I had watched him cut up his dinner with. He held it up as the blade moved into its locked position and started toward the man. I saw the man smile and move toward Jake. There was a blur of movement as I saw Jake block a swinging blow from the knife the man held. Jake sent his knife straight into the man's throat and I watched as it disappeared there. Jake did not stop there but pulled back and stabbed a second time, again the blade disappearing into the man's throat. The man started to fall back and Jake slashed the man across the face and a gigantic wound opened there. As he hit the floor, grabbing at his throat and trying to stop the blood that was squirting out in two streams, Jake looked at the other man standing close by.

"It was a legitimate kill," the man said. "You had every right to do what you did."

I watched the other men from the table, now holding their wounds, form into a tighter group, all but one of them now beaten and dying on the floor. They looked at us with some hatred, although the one that had not gotten involved looked a little scared. The woman that had been knocked to the floor was also standing but with the help of Lisa. She looked at Jake with adoring eyes.

"Sam ain't going to like this," one of the men said to Thomas who stood against a post nearby.

"Then have him come talk to me," Thomas told him.

"I tell him what happened," the man promised. "But he still ain't going to like it."

"That's fine with me," Thomas said. "You all aren't welcome to this establishment any more either. Spread the word to your boys."

The men grabbed the man that was barely bleeding anymore and hauled him out of the door. A red trail on the floor followed them out but thinned as they went. It seemed that man would never harm a woman again. Looking, I saw several such streaks on the floor.

"I think we may want to get our horse and be on our way," I told Carl.

"Can't say as I blame you," he replied and turned to Lisa. "Sorry, darling but we won't have time for dinner."

"Thank you for what you did, young man," Lisa said, looking at Jake. "They've been harassing my girls for some time now." She said this looking straight at Thomas.

"I will keep someone posted here for a while," Thomas told her. "I will put the word out that anyone causing trouble here will be dealt with."

Lisa turned with the young woman in her arms and mostly carrying her to the bar, but not before the woman could give Jake another fond look. I saw Jake smile and nod his head a little, trying to reassure her that things were going to be okay. When she had moved out of sight he reached down and grabbed the radio, shouldering it and adjusting its weight. I did not remember him setting it down.

"I should look at those wounds," Shay told him.

"They're nothing," he told her.

"I'll be the judge of that," she told him, coming over and trying to see where he was bleeding from. "Take off your coat and this vest."

"What for?" he asked. The look he got from her answered his question.

We all stood around then as Shay examined the knife wounds Jake had taken. The one on his arm seemed more serious. It was a stab wound and I could not see how deep it went. It bled a lot still and Shay worked there first, probing it much to Jake's discomfort. The other wound I could see was a long slash along his collar bone. It did not look too bad.

"I really should sew this up," Shay said, looking at me. "It will literally take two minutes."

"Do whatever you need to," I told her. "Is he too far gone? Maybe we should just leave him here." It got a small chuckle from most but I guess it was the wrong time for jokes. "You did great, Jake."

"Yeah, I got a little concerned when he had you on the floor there, but you pulled it out good," Chris told him.

I moved over to talk to Thomas as the conversation there continued. He was talking to Carl about something and turned as I got closer. They both tried a smile as I came up to them.

"I hope we didn't cause too much trouble," I told them.

"What, this?" Carl asked. "No, unfortunately this is a constant occurrence in this town."

"Not much we can do about people getting rowdy," Thomas said. "Not sure I care to either. I am no governor."

"Don't you run this place?" Quade asked from beside me.

"No one really runs this place," Carl said.

"No, there is a council that decides large issues but mostly people just live here free to do as they please," Thomas said. "The council only makes it so no one takes over here."

"So they're in charge of the guards and all," Quade asked.

"Exactly," Thomas said. "They make sure all is fair here, and deal with things that come up." I was pretty sure I did not want to know what those things were.

"We are all done here," Shay said and I turned to see Jake getting dressed.

"I'll carry that radio for a while, Jake," I told him.

"No, I got it," he said and hefted it to his shoulder.

"No, you should let someone else carry it, at least for the rest of the day," Shay told him. "I don't want you to pull open those stitches." He frowned when I came and took it from him.

"You're still in charge of it," I told him. "I'll just keep it until you are doctor approved to carry it." I got a rather rude look for my remark, both from Jake and Shay. I turned quickly away.

"I will take you to choose a horse now," Carl told us.

We followed him out of the bar and Thomas followed. We twisted and turned often so much so that I began to think we were going in circles. We passed a well-spread out area that turned out to be a school and playground of the apocalyptic type. Everyone one of us stood amazed as we watched the kids there playing at something. We were in a bit of a hurry though, so we quickly moved on.

We made it finally to a large junkyard looking area and Carl pulled up, seemingly to say we made it. I did not see anything resembling a horse and told him so. He smiled and waited for a moment. When I started to get nervous he waved at something and moved us on.

"Sorry, but when we move down here we are watched," he told us. "We have to be waved through different sections." I looked around and did not see where he was talking about but decided to take his word for it.

We finally got to a corral of horses. A breed of large cattle was also corralled next to them and I heard Eric admiring what he saw there. I could soon see it was worth the walk through town as I looked at the horses.

"Kyle said you could have your pick," Carl told me. "They're all ridable and pretty good-spirited. Kyle should have been here cause I don't know which ones he wanted you to look at."

"Are they used to rifle fire?" Laura asked.

"Most of them are," Carl said.

"What are those pens over there," Margie asked.

"I think Kyle was hoping you wouldn't look over there," Carl told us. "Those are the stallions. There are quite a few nice ones. Kyle trades and breeds well. This is his passion more than anything else. He's headed in from the field if you all could wait about an hour or so. He's trying to trade-off his guard duty so he can be here."

"Sorry, but we really have to get moving," Quade said as I started to.

We walked over to get a closer look at the animals Carl had pointed out. I did not see right away the horse I wanted, though there were quite a few nice ones. The corrals there were smaller and it took a while to get around some of them. Still I searched however, nothing quite hitting me right.

"Do you feel drawn somewhere?" Margie asked.

"I'm not seeing the right one yet, I guess," I told her.

"Listen to your spirit," she told me. "The horse you lost is leading you to where you should go. He will tell you if you will listen."

It took a while longer and several more horses almost seemed to fit the mark. Still, something was not right with the ones I had seen. Finally, I made it to the final pen and still none felt like a right fit. I will admit it was a weird feeling as we were surrounded by beautiful horses.

"I do not see the one for me yet," I said and looked at my group who were getting a little annoyed.

"I think there is another pen over by the breeders," Thomas said.

"Yeah, just one over there," Carl said. "I think it looks just like all of these."

"I think I would like to see it," I told him.

Carl jumped down off of the fence of the corral and looked to be pretty unhappy about leading us through the different corrals. We went by a bunch of corrals full of mares and a few filled with young colts. Finally, we made another turn and I heard a deep snort followed by a whinny. I looked around and saw a large animal in the corral just ahead.

I came up to the corral and climbed to the top. Seeing a beautiful stallion, I moved over and jumped inside. The horse looked at me sideways and with wonder about this new animal put in with him. He seemed, however, responsive to my approach and turned to have a full look at me. He sniffed a little harshly and moved away some, then turned again. I stopped and let him get used to me and then moved in on him again. He allowed me to come up to him then, snorting a little as I got close.

He was a tall, very dark brown horse who looked black from far off. His long tail touched the ground and flowed behind him as he moved. His back was straight and wide. I petted his long dark mane and he seemed to enjoy it. I felt a little guilty taking on a new horse, my other one not yet passing from memory.

"This is a good horse," Margie said from the top of the corral. "A gentle spirit but strong. His eyes look at you. He wants to know if he can trust you." I gave him a smile and petted down the front of his face.

"I'll take him," I told Carl.

"If you do you better be fast about it," he told me. "He probably didn't mean this one when he said your choice. That's why he's way out back here. He was saving him for something special. He's going to kick my ass for sure if you take this one. How about you take two instead of that one. Maybe you can take a stallion and a mare. I'm sure he would prefer that." I saw a worried look come over him as I felt the horse push up against my arm as I scratched beside his ears.

"No, I think I'd like this one," I told him. "And we will leave now, straight out the gate."

"Well let's go," Carl said. "I guess that's what he gets for not being here. I'm telling him you let him take that one." He was looking at Thomas.

"I will keep him busy for the next few days," Thomas said with a smile to me.

"Just keep him away from me for a while," Carl said and went and opened the gate. "Damn it, he's going to be pissed."

I led the horse out by the halter and followed Carl to the entrance of the town. Eric gave him the keys to the car as we all got our horses and I retrieved my saddle and tack. They fit fine on my new horse and almost cinched down exactly the same. I watched as the horse stomped, ready to be taken out for a ride. I hoped it would be the start of a long relationship as I climbed aboard and walked slowly out the gate, the others close behind.

CHAPTER 17

I was glad to be heading back to the train and us only a little worse for wear. The hope of finding Kevin would have to be extended to some other place. I knew the day's end, which was coming on soon, could have been far worse.

My new horse rode easily and responded well to all of my commands. He trotted with head held high and seemed to actually enjoy the time spent now in some form of freedom. As we moved into a run I could see what he was born for.

We made it back to the train, with Quade calling well ahead to see how things went there and to let Fredrick and Ray know we were heading in. The sight of our ride, still far off, had been a pleasant one as we moved back into a walk. I was, however, much relieved when I walked up the ramp with my horse and smiled as Laura took him from me.

"I'll brush him down and put him away," she promised. "He looked like he did well."

"Yeah, I think he is going to be a great horse," I told her, petting him as he moved off.

Quade had told us we would be ready in only a few minutes to move out. He said we would be heading backward to a switch track and heading in a different way before we could turn around. I listened, but knew he had things in that regard under control, so I left him to it, asking only that he call if he needed any help. When he assured me that he would, I went back and started a fire in our drum, hoping for some coffee.

I felt us moving before the water boiled and I sat down in the doorway, overlooking the landscape. It was things I had already seen that went by, but I took some time to have a closer look. I saw a hawk trying to escape a pair of birds that were dive-bombing him for having gotten too close to something that belonged to them. Rabbits were everywhere and darted from spot to spot as we passed. Antelope filled the hills as did various breeds of cattle. I wonder what the next step in evolution would be for the wild cow. When I heard my water boiling, I made my coffee and sat back down to work on some of this manuscript.

Time passed and I got lost in my thoughts that I was putting on paper. When I next looked up, I saw we were headed south and moving in a forward direction. I noticed also my coffee cup was empty. I looked around and still saw Laura brushing the horses and Chris fixing some leather pieces near her. The smell of saddle soap filled the boxcar. I heard Jake talking to April on the radio and did not even get mad.

I stood and saw someone had moved the water pot off of the fire. The water had mostly gone out of it so I decided against more coffee. I did not remember enough of the scenery outside to be able to tell if we were getting close to Quade's town. Sitting back down in the doorway, I continued to write.

It did not take as long as I thought to get back to the grain elevators that signaled the end of our trip. I must again have gotten lost in thought as I remember it taking longer to get to those places we visited. It was a happy sight to see however, and as we stopped I helped with the ramp and walked to the ground.

I pushed away the thoughts that ran along the vein of failure for the small trip. I knew we were no closer to finding Olivia and Tara and my heart was heavy at the idea of them still with Kevin, but I knew I would be no good to them if I allowed myself to become negative. I held my head up and decided to see how our own train was doing.

"I need to check on some things, but I'll be around if you need anything," Quade told me as he walked back to our boxcar. "Eric will get you back attached with your caboose there."

"That sounds great," I told him. "Thanks Quade to you and everyone else for taking us there and getting involved in all this. It shows a lot of the kind of people this town is."

"Not a problem," he said, stopping at hearing the compliment. "We needed an adventure around here anyways."

"Please keep us advised with what is next," Teal said from beside Quade.

"Yeah, I will," I told her. "And you guys do the same. If there's trouble brewing here we will do what we can to help, if you want our help."

"I think that would be nice," Quade said. "I'll keep you in the loop."

"And I'll make sure our next piece of information is a little bit better thought out," I told them.

"No worries," Teal said. "Whatever's next is fine."

"Make yourselves at home," Quade told me. "I'll probably be up in the tower there, but tell someone you're looking for us and I'll get the word."

"I will and I'll call home and find out what's our next move," I told them.

"I'll check in and then come find you," Teal told Davina. "Maybe we should have a drink and go over that paperwork with a fine-tooth comb."

"I think that sounds great," Davina said and I could tell she was pleased.

Teal and Quade both nodded pleasantly and moved off toward the stable. I saw Chris and Laura were on the ground and looking around. Margie and Shay headed off in the direction of where our engine was getting worked on earlier. I thought to head in that direction but saw Eric heading our way.

"I'll get you hooked back up again," he told us, pointing to our boxcar. "Should only take a few minutes. You all should come check out our small town if you need anything. There's lots of stuff for wastelanders, if you're in the market for stuff."

"I might just do that," I told him. "I'd like to see how our engine repairs are coming."

"I heard they are coming along pretty good," he said. "I called home on the way back and asked."

"I wouldn't mind checking out some of the town, if that's okay with you," Chris said, looking at me.

"No, you guys go ahead," I told them. "Check in a lot, though."

"We will," he told me.

"If you'll wait until I'm done here, I'll show you around," Eric told him.

"Sure, that would be great," he said.

"I'll be checking out the engine and then probably going up in the tower there to figure out our next move," I told Chris.

"Oh, want some help?" he asked, feeling bad about his excitement.

"No, it's kind of a one-man job thing," I told him. "You go ahead."

With a smile Chris and Laura followed Eric back toward the front of the train. I was wondering why Jake had not come out yet and walked back up the ramp to find him. I yelled for him a couple of times and finally he came out from among the hanging walls. He looked tired.

"Talking with home?" I asked him.

"Yeah, everything there is good," he told me. "Dan is still staying on there and sounds like Vince is bugging everyone with his security measures. Jessie is getting better."

"Can they see this place yet?" I asked.

"Oh yeah, they did see it and they were pretty amazed," he told me. "They also saw that other compound we just left. It sounds like it was in the middle of nowhere. They were pretty amazed by that too. They said they're going to have to start looking around more carefully."

"Well, Chris and Laura are headed over to look through the town if you want to go with them," I told him.

"No, I think I'm going to go talk with that lady Lynn that we let copy the info from the pin drive," he said. "Sounds like Jadee and her have been talking pretty much nonstop about it."

"I think I'll be coming with you," I told him. "Sound like they are coming up with anything?" We turned and started toward the tower.

"Sounds like they are talking about a lot of serious stuff is all I could gather," Jake told me as we walked.

"What do you want to do honey?" I asked Davina.

"I think I'll head upstairs and see what we have going on too," she replied.

"Teal seems nice," I told Davina as we went.

"Yeah, I think so too," she said. "Pretty awesome they are helping us out. They all seem pretty tough."

"I agree with that," Jake said. I smiled to myself and tried not to wonder how much more trouble we would get them into.

We made it to the elevator and headed up to the tower we had visited earlier. We got inside and pushed several things but nothing happened. We closed the door tighter but still nothing happened; slamming the door did not help either. We started to step out when we saw Brady coming up.

"I thought I heard someone in here," he told us. "Trying to head up?"

"Yeah, we are checking in up there and seeing what the scoop is," I told him.

"I see," he said. "You have to turn the power on over here," he told us and walked around the corner. I followed and watched him flip a switch. "Should be ready to go now. It's the second red button from the top."

"Thanks," I told him. "This could take some getting used to." I was sure this is how visitors felt when they entered our home.

"No problem," he said. "If you ever have a problem, just think Brady and come find me. Chances are I'll know what you're talking about. I'm always here around the stable."

"Much appreciated," I told him and he continued on his way.

We all got in then and still had to push a couple of different buttons to get the elevator to start up. It was a weird feeling being lifted in such a way, as I had not been in one for some time. I was glad when we reached the top and Jake pulled open the door.

"That will take some getting used to," Davina said.

"I think it moves faster than a normal elevator," Jake said as we stepped out.

We made our way into the large room we had been in earlier. I saw Axel and Quade standing in front of a large Kansas map on a roll-around chalkboard. They turned as we came in.

"Hey guys," Axel said. "Quade's just telling me about what you all found up north. We had no idea." He seemed a little excited.

"Yeah, and they seemed friendly enough," I told him.

"I think that plateau country should be circled as hostile," Quade said and they went back to looking at the map.

"Hey, we're over here," Teal told Davina with a smile from one of the cubicles.

"You go ahead," I told her. "I want to have a look at this map." She smiled happily and kissed my cheek. She went over to Teal and disappeared among the squares there. Jake walked over with me to the map.

The map, which was laid out and plastered somehow to the chalkboard, was a much larger state of Kansas map than I had ever seen. When I mentioned that, Axel told me they had gotten it from a courthouse in a town east of them. I saw lines going all over the place, some following roads but others moving straight across the plains. Areas were colored in and some seemed to be done with great care. I saw most of the activity with the map was south of the town we were in and mostly west of it.

"Looks a little complicated," Jake said what I was thinking.

"Yeah, we've spent some time on it," Quade said. "We try to keep up with what's going on around us. Really, it's quite surprising to find someone so close. The world we have seen really isn't that full anymore."

"Coming from Oregon, you didn't find much?" I asked him.

"There were pockets here and there," he said and I got the sense that he could have said more.

"I'm very interested in what all of this stuff on the map means but I'll hold my questions until later," I told them. "Are you looking over that place we were just at?"

"We are," Alex said. "We are wondering just how far in these plateaus are populated."

"I think they told us there were not a lot of them," I said.

"Yeah, they did say that, I remember," Jake said. Axel looked at Quade.

"I guess we just mark it as unknown," Axel told him and Quade nodded.

They were concentrating on the area we had just left and the two of them were talking in some jargon that meant nothing to me. I saw them draw lines, then draw code signs along them. As it grew beyond me and I thought I had my fill of the map, I turned and headed over to where Davina had disappeared, Jake following close behind.

I moved around a couple of cubicles, thinking I remembered where we had left Lynn working. I found her and the others not where I would have thought, but upon finding them I saw it was in fact the place Lynn had been before. They all looked up as we came into view.

"Finding anything that's likely to help?" I asked Lynn hopefully.

"There is a ton of stuff on this," she said. "There is a lot of stuff confirming the old research but I can't quite see anything that will help us know where they expected Kevin to be. I have been able to figure out that whoever sent this was in fact from Kenya."

"How's Jadee doing with it?" I asked. (I did not think to ask her how she knew that.)

"She's doing good," she told me with a smile. "We've been figuring out what to feed NASA although they have all this info too. We're thinking they don't think we can open it."

"Are they holding stuff back?" Jake asked.

"Not that we can tell and we haven't found anything worth yelling about," she said and then shrugged. "A lot of what I've gotten through is all medical stuff. Maybe some of that paperwork you guys found will have something on it that will help." I saw Davina and Teal were laying it all out on a nearby table.

"Yeah, we're looking for file names or anything else like that," Davina told me. "There has to be something here."

"Okay, that sounds good," I told her. "How can we help?"

"No, we got this," she said.

"I think Axel had some questions about hooking into your satellite system," Lynn said. "We didn't want to do anything until you all got back but I think he found a way of marrying the two systems."

"Does NASA know about you helping us out?" I asked.

"As far as we can tell, no," Lynn said as she grabbed a cup from the table and found it empty. "We are running everything on some HAM system, I guess. You will have to talk to Axel about that."

"Maybe I'll see if we can pull them away from that map," I told her.

"Good luck," Teal said.

"Yeah, once they get started on that there's little chance at getting a word in," Lynn added.

"You good here for a while?" I asked Davina.

"Yeah, I think I'll help out and see where these papers lead," she told me. "I'm right here if you need me."

"I always need you," I told her and got a wink.

Jake and I moved back out into the open area and walked back over to where Quade and Axel were up close to the map. They had made a little progress on some lines but they were still talking in a different language. Quade started using a red highlighter on the area that we saw the plateaus in.

"I hear you may be able to hack into our satellite feed," I told Axel. That brought him around sharp. "What does that intel?"

"Really, I just need the frequency and some positioning stuff and we should be able to link up on our own here," he told me.

"Is that going to make you guys stand out like a light bulb to whoever might be monitoring such things?" I asked him.

"I think it will," he said. "There's no hiding yourself once you're on a network like that. I have been close for a long time and I've gotten in on some satellite feeds but they all are nothing. I mean, I can't even see the weather or anything like you guys can."

"I don't even think we know all that our systems can do," I told him.

"I wonder if you guys are dealing with military reticulation," he said, looking at me as though I had a clue.

"I used to barely be able to find the internet in the old days," I told him. "I don't even know what reticulation means."

"No problem," he said, smiling. "I'm just wondering what kind of network you all are on. If the civil system is still up then I think I would have found it by now. It must be some military thing."

"Didn't all of the civil band stuff get pirated a long time ago?" Quade asked.

"Yeah, I think it did," Jake told him.

"No, you guys are talking radio stuff," Axel said. "I'm talking about satellite systems and networks. Those were all private, I mean the ones I'm interested in."

"I wish I could help you with that," I told him. "I'll ask Jadee and see what she says. I don't mind giving you whatever you need to get wired in here but I better talk to the group about it."

"That's fair enough," he said. "They said the same thing. I'm glad to finally find a group that understands that."

"I would really like to talk to you about what it could all mean if you do get hooked in," I told him. "I guess we did that a little already, though."

"I think that's something we are going to have to talk to ourselves about also. I guess we aren't sure yet how it could help or possibly hurt," Quade said.

"Sounds like a long discussion," I told him. "Let me know what you come up with and I'll talk to my group."

"Will do," he told me. "They finding anything out in there?" he pointed to the cubicles.

"It sounds like days' worth of putting stuff together," I told him.

"Maybe we should set you all up in a few rooms until we get it figured out," Quade told me, turning to me with a serious look on his face. I thought about it for a minute.

"No, I appreciate it but we should be fine in our boxcar," I told him. "I think I'll check in at home and also see how our repair job is coming on the engine."

"Yeah, I think I'd like to see that too," Quade said. "Maybe I'll see you down there." I nodded. "You all are welcome here. If there is anything we can do, let us know. I know I keep saying that but I mean it."

"Well, thanks," I told him. "How's the trouble you were having panning out?"

"Oh, still a bit up in the air," he said as he rubbed his head. "The guy that stabbed the man left town while we were gone. I hope if anyone comes asking about him then that information will turn any trouble away from town at least. It should work out fine now."

"We'll keep an eye out, though I don't know if that will help much," I told him.

"Everything will help," Axel said from beside Quade.

"Dinner's in an hour or so at Lucky's," Quade told us. "There's a room in the back. Just say you're with us and they'll show you where we are."

I told him we'd try to be there and gave them both a smile. Jake and I walked outside and looked over the plains for a while. It was a beautiful view with the sun heading down in the late afternoon. It seemed the clouds were looking to become taller and more tumultuous before dark. We walked along the rail to the end of the square structure we had come out of and looked down the long way that led over the rounded grain storage areas. We quickly ran into a guard on duty.

"I think I saw you before," I told the man.

"Yeah, names Robert," he said. "That up there is Asia."

He pointed to all of the enclosed metal ladder structures that ran to the top of the square structure. I saw a woman wave from overhead and felt a little irritated at being watched over, though I did understand it. I nodded approval and waved back.

"I like the view from your post up here," I told Robert.

"Sure can't beat that," he said with a pleasant expression. "When the clouds roll in like that over there and the lightning starts, there is nothing more relaxing. The warm breeze that comes first should be here within the hour."

"Yeah, definitely some rain coming in tonight," Jake said.

"It may shift north some but we should get a little," Robert agreed. "Wanda is thinking rain tonight but I think Axel is right he says cooler with morning fog. We always have a friendly bet. Guard duty isn't going to be fun if it's the cold stuff. Thankfully, I'll be off by the time it gets here. I heard you guys found another compound. How was it?"

"It was an old missile defense compound I guess," I told him. "They seemed nice enough."

"We don't find things like that around here anymore," he told me. "Maybe it will be good to have someone else to trade with."

"They looked to have fuel of some kind," I told him.

"I hope we can get along," he said, seeming to be wondering. I understood what he meant.

"I like the view out east too," I told him, looking over the side and out over the silos to the plains that way.

I saw the fields better from over close to the rails and saw several fields swaying in the gentle breeze. I wondered at all of the work it would take to do such a large area, especially with old-time farming techniques. I could see the train tracks closer to the grain elevator a lot better from there and saw the junk yard and buildings beside where our engine was getting worked on. (I could see the top of our engine just past a building there.) I saw the lines of train cars. I looked over the blown-away town again and still did not see much.

"Didn't look to be a very big town," Jake said from the railing beside me.

"No, there was not much to it," Robert said. "It wasn't much of a tornado that took it out."

"What's down that way?" I asked Robert, pointing along the rail to where the grain silos were.

"Sorry, but I can't let you walk all the way around. Axel would kill me if one of his wires over there got disconnected."

"No trouble," I told him. "I understand security issues. What's over that way?"

"I think he said a bunch of the stuff is for some radar he's been trying to test for," Robert said. "I don't know how he figures out what cables goes to what. He's always up here trying out new ways to run something."

"What are all those windows along that long, flat roofed area?" I asked him, pointing passed several large antennas and a satellite dish.

"Those are windows and vents for circulation for the rooms we've made down below here where the grain used to be stored," he told me.

"It's pretty amazing you've made housing out of those," I told him.

"Yeah, it works pretty well too," he told me. "It was easy, really. The only real hard part was the stairs and the like."

"Well, I'm fully impressed," I told him.

"If you really want to see, I can take you around this other way," he told me.

"No, I was just out here to get away for a minute or two," I told him.

"I can understand that," he said. "I'll leave you to it." He walked to the bottom of the ladder and climbed up to where Asia was.

I turned to Jake and saw he was looking out west. I looked there too and watched the clouds tumbling and churning. Some long streaks were coming up from the south but it did not seem to effect the thunderstorm headed our way. It was quite a scene, seeing the sun poke through and brightening different areas of the formation before the clouds moved and created a whole new scene.

"Looks like this one is going to hit pretty good," I told him as we stood against the railing.

"I think so too," he said. "Sorry, I thought maybe that stuff from the south would push harder."

"No problem," I told him. "It's always been an impossible job. Just a rough idea helps sometimes."

We stayed silent then and watched for a while. People came and went below us and the horses in the stable stood bored. I watched some geese flying high overhead and it made me think of home.

I wondered if the winter would hit as hard this year as it seemed to be pushing for; usually it was still hot at this time of year but we had already gotten our first snow. I thought about Vince harvesting some of the outdoor crops we had tried to make work and I was interested in how much we would get. We had already missed out on enough hunting trips, so I knew our winter was going to be a bit lean, although meat was not too hard to come by. (Just a quick note; I no longer consider goose as edible meat if you haven't noticed.) I often looked forward to our times underground that winter afforded. I was not even proportionally through my large library yet and there was nothing better than getting lost in a book as time slowly moved by. But even more pleasing was the time spent down there with family. I tried here not to think of what that would feel like if Olivia and Tara were not there.

"I think I'll call home and check in for us," I told Jake. "Why don't you get cleaned up and I'll meet you down at the train in a little bit."

"Okay," he said and pulled off the radio. "I hope we are good to go with George's train by now."

"I'm interested to know, but I want to give myself a little time to think about something else just in case," I told him.

"I know what you mean," he said.

"I thought Shay told you not to be carrying this thing for a while," I told him as he handed me the radio.

"It feels okay," he told me. "He hit some meat but really not bad."

"You feeling okay then?" I asked him.

"Yeah, I am. Any idea where we're headed next?" he asked, trying to change the subject.

"No, I have no clue," I told him flatly and did not like the sound of those words. "I'm going to push to find out though. Looks like Missouri, but don't quote me for sure."

"It sounded like these guys made their way through a couple of compounds too," Jake told me. "I wonder how they found them."

"Eric showed them how to find them, right?" I asked, starting to wonder if he could be of use.

"He was Air Force, I think," he replied.

"Find him if you can when you get down there and just ask him about it," I told him. "I'll find you in a bit if I can and see what you come up with."

"Okay, I'll do that first," he said and moved off.

I keyed the radio and tried not to get my hopes up. Finding the next potential site to look at was of course top priority but not if Kevin was not there. I wanted to get to the right one and I figured that meant several things had to come together, including perchance the information on that pin drive.

"This is April," I heard the radio say perfectly clear. "Is that you dad?"

"Yeah, it's me," I said. "How's it going?"

"It's going good for me," she said. "Jadee is still at it. She only ate a little lunch but I've been trying to keep after her. I think I'm just getting in her way."

"You're doing great, I'm sure," I told her.

"Neil is trying to help figure some of the stuff out that they're working on," she said. "I guess there were a lot of missile sites in northeastern Colorado and all around there."

"Are they thinking we came too far?" I asked with a little annoyance.

"I'm sorry, but I'm not sure," she said. "It looks like they are not ruling anything out. Dan went home for the night but said he'd be back in the morning."

"Yeah, I bet he's missing hearing his sheep," I told her.

"Yeah, he's probably building us a pen somewhere outside," she said and laughed. "He's been doing something a lot with Vince and Mary."

"I'm sure whatever it is, it will be great," I told her. "It's awesome for him to be over there. It makes me feel more comfortable out here."

"I bet," she said.

"You guys getting that storm yet?" she asked.

"No, but it looks like it's coming soon," I told her. "Looks like a slow mover. Geese still flying out there?"

"Yeah, I went outside for breakfast and they flew over every five minutes," she told me. "The flock staying around the pond is pretty big this year."

"Well, let's hope they move on before Marla sees them."

"That's my hope."

"You holding up okay?"

"Yeah, I'm doing okay," she said. I could hear a little sadness in her voice. "Missing Tara a little but I'm trying not to think about it."

"I'm sure that's a lot harder than it sounds," I told her.

"We were together all the time. I was teaching her everything in here, but I think she was just more into hanging out with me."

"I think I saw that too."

"Looks like Jadee is coming up here. She may be wanting to talk to Lynn. Yeah, she's wanting to."

"Put her on with me for a minute, will ya?" I told her.

"Will do," she said. "Talk to ya later. Love you, Dad."

"Hey April, it will turn out okay," I told her.

"I know," she said. "I just got to get out of my own head for a while. See ya."

"Love you, kiddo," I told her.

"I know you do," she said. I could not tell if she was crying but it sounded like she may have been.

"This is Jadee," I heard. "I've heard a little about that compound. How was it?"

"Nothing that will help us find Kevin," I told her, changing gears quickly. "I'm sure you heard about the paperwork we found at the Reserve Building?"

"I did," she said. "We've been getting some reports on what they've been finding out about them. Nothing real helpful so far."

"We'll stumble across something," I told her. "Are the space creatures helping out at all?"

"They're trying," she told me. "We've started over several times and we are working a few different angles. Seems like there may not be a way of telling."

"Don't lose heart, Jadee," I told her. "This has to all make sense somehow."

"I'm not losing heart," she said. "I'm too busy to do that."

"Is there anything you can tell me that I can go on?" I asked.

"I found out Kevin not only sent equipment, he also sent arms to these different places," Jadee said. "The military kept closer tabs on what they did with their weapons so we are concentrating on that a little more. We found a place in

Nebraska that he sent a lot of stuff to but when we looked up the coordinates the whole place was bombed out. NASA found out that it is one of the places Kevin looked at before he left here."

"How did they find that?"

"They know what satellite he was hooked into and they got some coordinates from it."

"Were there more than just the one set of coordinates he looked at?"

"There was. It looks like he was trying to find some places in Missouri. All of them were cleared out a while ago by McQueen. He was also looking at where you guys were when you picked up the information that Kenya sent."

"So, Missouri is clear as in Kevin wasn't there?" I asked her. "Just because it was cleared back then doesn't mean anything now."

"Sounded like that place got crossed off a long time ago," Jadee told me. "He could be heading there now though, especially if he thinks its crossed off our list."

"How is any of that making sense?" I wonder, more than asked. "I wasn't sure whether or not to talk to NASA about Missouri. I guess it doesn't matter. I was thinking that was our next move."

"We aren't sure," she said a little disgusted. "I'm really sorry Randy, but they are saying there are tons of sites around this area."

"Then we won't rest until we've gone through them all," I told her matter-of-factly. "I'd just like a little bit of research on them before we go in."

"Yeah, sorry about that too," she said. "It's good to hear that at least that one was friendly."

"True," I replied. "We're trying to stay out of trouble out here as best we can. Anything else going on that we can think through? How's it going with Lynn?"

"It's going really well with those guys there," she said. "I'm having Lynn go over some of the research stuff that isn't making a lot of sense to me. Mack isn't aware of Lynn. I've been telling him Shay has been going over it."

"That's a good idea," I told her. "I was wondering about giving these guys our satellite hookup info."

"Yeah, Axel asked me about that," she said.

"Is there a way they will find them here if they do?" I asked.

"It sounds like with what he's been trying already with the weather satellites and trying to break into some of the systems he has, they already know they are there."

"Any thoughts on that?" I asked her.

"It doesn't seem like it would be a problem for them if we are trusting NASA," she said. "I think if they start snooping around with this research stuff it will put them on a different kind of watch list."

"Are we trusting NASA yet?" I asked her flatly.

"Mack seems to be cooperating with everything he says. He doesn't seem to be holding anything back, as if we would know if they were."

"That's true. Is he giving us anything new that's of use?"

"He sent me the coordinates for everywhere Kevin was looking; he seemed to know where they were. They didn't help though, so, no, not really."

"Let's stay on the fence for a little bit about trusting them, I would say," I told her. "It's not like there's a lot they don't know about us but let's not give them anything they don't have to know. I'd like these people here to stay out of their radar."

"I understand that," she said. "Are you wanting to give them the satellite info? I can start working on what channels and all to give them."

"Let me run it by Neil really quick and I'll have him let you know," I told her. "Any way these guys here can find our compound if we give it to them?"

"I don't know," she said. "If they have certain equipment they surely can. But really, anyone can with the right scanners, I guess, obviously. Do you not trust those guys there?"

"It's not that," I told her. "It's just my weird sense of caution creeping in. I think I would trust these people pretty much with anything. They've stayed in the fight when they didn't have to. I just hope we don't have to keep bringing it on them."

"That makes sense," she said. "It doesn't seem like there's a lot we can do with people looking at us from overhead. I do think it's a safe idea to keep that kind of info to ourselves if we can, though. But to your question, no, the satellite info is not a sure way of finding us here."

"Okay, I'll keep that in mind too and talk to everyone here," I told her.

"You want to talk to Neil?" she asked.

"Yeah, that would be great," I told her. "And Jadee…"

"Yes?" she asked when I did not finish.

"Take a break every few hours," I told her. "It doesn't sound like it but it may give you the fresh look now and then that we need to keep when we're looking at this thing."

"I understand," she said. I wondered if she would do it, however.

"Hey buddy, how's life out there?" I heard Neil ask.

"It's going good," I told him. "Seems like we made it pretty far from home."

"Kansas, huh?" he asked, but already knew. "Pretty flat, it looked like from in here."

"Have you been able to see the grain elevators we are at?"

"Yeah, they look pretty interesting. How tall are they?"

"About a hundred and twenty feet or so, I guess."

"Wow, you could probably see the whole state from up there."

"Yeah, probably on a clear day I could. Looks like rain pressing down on us here. Big storm moving slowly."

"Yeah, we saw something like that."

"I wanted to talk to you a little about the satellites if you know much about the subject."

"What you got going on?" he asked curiously.

"I just needed to know about these guys hooking into what we are hooked up to," I told him. "Axel here is not sure if we are into the military ones or whatever. I'm not sure either are you?"

"Yeah, it's both, really," he told me. "Back in the day, the military used subcontracting on a lot of their projects. It was kind of scary how much was actually not done from inside. But you could say for all intents and purposes that all of it was military. I'm sure that doesn't help, does it?"

"No, I guess I don't know the right question to ask," I told him, a little frustrated. "I'm trying to figure out if giving these people here our satellite hookup info will draw them into what we have going on. I'm thinking of keeping them from a bad connection kind of thing."

"I know you have a hard time with that, buddy," he said. "The real answer I think is that we don't really have a monopoly on these systems. I heard the guy there has been searching for a while to try and break into anything he can. He'll eventually find everything we have to offer him. It would be nice to tell them what we have found with these guys so that they can steer clear of that. What is he trying to find?"

"He hasn't really said for certain," I said. "I think he likes the idea of looking overhead globally. Sounded like he was really interested in the ability to see the up-and-coming weather. I guess everyone wants to be able to look around the planet and see what it looks like nowadays."

"That's probably true," he said.

"Well, thanks for the short talk," I told him. "I miss being able to come downstairs and talk to the crazy guy in the basement." I heard him laugh.

"Yeah, I think you're just out roaming around so you don't have to lose at chess again," he told me.

We talked then for a while. I could tell he was needing it and probably, so was I. He told me how everyone was doing and it felt good to hear that things there seemed to be going well. I told him a little of our adventure with the town and some of the bar fight, making him promise to keep the Jake getting stabbed thing to himself. He kept asking how I was doing and I hoped that did not mean I was sounding in any way depressed or the like. We did laugh a bit and I think I was feeling better than I had in a while.

"We'll see you soon, buddy," he said. "Please take care out there."

"I will," I told him. "Tell April I'll talk to her later. I'm headed to see if our train is fixed."

"I'll tell her," he said. "See ya."

I put the radio on my back and made it back inside. I went and saw Davina who seemed to be doing well in the company of the other women; they stopped talking when I made it into the cubicle which made me wonder a bit. She said she was doing okay and wanted to stay there to help. As I left, I heard a small snickering and tried not to wonder further.

I went over to Axel, who was leaning back in his chair with two sets of headphones on, one speaker from each on different ears. I tried to make some noise as I came up beside him, but I was not sure he heard me. As I got close however, he moved his feet off the desk and turned to me.

"How's things at home?" he asked, moving one of the headphones speakers off his ear. I heard some jazz music coming from it.

"Sounding like everyone there is okay, besides going crazy trying to come up with some answers," I told him.

"I bet," he said. "Anything more I can do to help?"

"Not for the time being, I guess," I told him with a shrug. "I think it's fine to give you guys whatever info you need on the satellite systems we have. I just wanted to check in with everyone and see what they thought. It shouldn't be a problem. I guess we are just concerned that you will be getting into something that could bring you all some trouble."

"I think I understand that," he told me seriously. "We will have to decide what we want to do with the information. I would love to see the planet. I hope it's not as scorched as the TV and radio were leading us to believe in the end."

"I haven't had much time to find out myself," I told him.

"We've been east of here a few times. Most of it is pretty bad."

"I thought the major portion of the war didn't get this far."

"I mean, when we've been way far east, like Missouri. We rode out there a time or two when we first got here, kind of an exploring kind of thing. There was really no point in going any farther, though. That was a few years ago."

"Looks like you've been busy here, getting this place up and going."

"It's been some work, for sure," he said, looking around. "I guess it doesn't look like it does it? Still a little ways to go."

"That will probably always be the case," I told him.

"You got an underground place where you are, right?"

"Yeah, and it's pretty huge," I told him. "Too big for us, really. But I can't think of anywhere else as home." He smiled at that.

"We are pretty fortunate. I see people traveling through here all the time that are looking for such. They don't know it but that's what they're looking for."

"Is there a lot of people out here then?"

"No, I say all the time but I guess I mean mostly the same nomads traveling around. I do see new people often but not in hordes."

"Well, I can say I never thought to run into a place like this, or to meet people like you guys out here. I figured the whole world had turned to something else."

"I'm not sure most of it hasn't," he said. "But I think I know what you're trying to say. I'm glad we met you all as well." He smiled broadly.

"I'll catch you later and let you know about the satellites," I told him. He gave me a thumbs-up and, turning back to the radios, he pulled his headphones back on.

I made it with some trouble back downstairs and outside. I found my way to the train junkyard and the buildings there. I moved around and did not talk to the people I saw, though they gave me a few look overs. Going through the building that brought me before to our train, much because I did not know a quicker way, I looked for the old man stoking the fire. Not seeing him, I moved through and went out the same door as before.

I saw our engine immediately and was floored with what I beheld. I looked first for the long crack on the pressure chamber but saw the overlaid metal there, along with the reinforcement straps, complete with an added cross support. Looking on, I saw metal plating had been added to the side of the cabin, complete with straps. A gun was mounted on the catwalk railing and aimed down in a locked position. I saw sparks flying from the front of the engine and went to have a look there.

When I got close, I saw Margie and George standing close and watching Sterling using a grinder as sparks flew toward the sky. Shay was watching closely at what he was doing. Looking at the train, I saw a large piece of metal that looked like a gigantic snowplow being attached to the front of our locomotive. It was almost touching the track on the right side up, close to the front, and the right side was supported about seven feet high. The whole front of the wedge, however, angled down close to the track about ten feet away from the front of the engine and rode about four inches above it. Moving a little closer, I saw Lincoln with a grinder as well, him on the other side of the engine.

"How's she looking?" George asked over the sound of the grinding.

"Looking beefy," I told him. "I'm liking it. What's going on here?"

"When they get done, it will fit into the framing of the engine," he told me and thought that was enough.

"What is it for?" I asked.

"It's a wedge," he told me as though I had missed the obvious. "If we ever have something on the tracks in front of us again then this wedge will roll it over and push it out of our way if we run into it."

"Now that is a great idea," I told him.

"It should be done in about half an hour," he told me. "Did we find where we need to go next?" I shook my head. "We'll find them." He came in close and put a hand on my shoulder and I gave him a look of gratitude for his trouble.

"I think dinner is in about the same time," I told him. "Let's have a small meeting in the boxcar with everyone just before that."

"I'll let Sterling know," he told me. "We'll be there in half an hour whether or not this thing is done. There shouldn't be any reason why it won't be though."

"I'll see you then," I told him and moved off to our boxcar.

Sitting down and looking outside at the grain elevators that towered overhead I let my mind wonder. I called everyone and told them to meet in half an hour, getting replies from everyone not at the front of the train. I started some more water and again sat down to wait for some fresh coffee. We had not found what we had come out in the plains for, but as I sat down again, I was pretty sure we had found something worthwhile.

CHAPTER 18

I did not empty more than half of my coffee cup before we were all together in our boxcar. It seemed like we had not been apart like we had been lately, for a long while. We had been so close and had gone through a lot before we got to that town. I was glad to see everyone's face.

"I'm sorry it took so long to take care of the engine," George started. "I really think what we've done is going to make all the difference."

"No problem at all George," I told him. "It may save us someday and that's all that counts. And we have no pressing place to be."

"Margie tells me you ran into a little bit of trouble up at that compound," George said, looking at me for more information. I saw Sterling jerk his head around to look at Shay.

"It was nothing we couldn't handle," she told George.

"What kind of trouble?" Sterling asked me accusingly. "Anyone get hurt?"

"No, we all made it out okay," I said.

"Jake started a bar fight," Chris put in and Sterling turned to Jake.

"I'm okay," Jake told him.

"He was defending a woman," Laura said, slapping Chris's arm.

"We all made it back fine," I told Sterling. "The real point is we didn't find Kevin. We did find some papers at the Reserves with his name on it though. They've been looking over them, but nothing yet."

"So, we are on the right track then?" Sterling offered.

"We aren't sure," I told him. "It sounds like they found out that Kevin was also sending guns all over as well. They are looking into where that leads us now."

"Are they saying what's next at all?" George asked.

"No, but everybody is looking at all the data we have so far," I said to a growing murmur.

"The paperwork we got is not real straightforward," Davina added. "We are coordinating with NASA about where it could lead."

"Jadee told me Kevin used our computer system to look at the compound we just left on his way out," I put in.

"Was he checking on his shipment do you think?" Chris asked. "Maybe he was checking to see if the coast was clear."

"I figure that's the only thing it could be," I told him. "It's all just little pieces of information that don't add up when looked at separately."

"So what are we doing now?" Margie asked.

"I'm not interested in us going into another compound unless there's some good information to lead us in there," I said. Everyone agreed. "The only problem is we don't have enough info to go anywhere and Jadee is saying NASA is telling her that there are compounds spread throughout this whole area. We are going to have to clear them out if we don't come up with something."

"I talked to Eric and he is willing to help us spot some of the compounds, if it will help us," Jake said. "He said they are set out a little bit on a grid."

"Yeah, Neil told us something like that the last time," Davina said. "Something about ten in a group and five groups per sector."

"How many sectors are around here?" Laura asked.

"Jadee didn't say they were close by," I told her. "She was talking about eastern Colorado and that general area."

"Should we go there?" George asked.

"I'd like to see if Lynn can help with what she's looking at before we go," Davina said.

"Is she getting anywhere with it," Shay asked.

"She opened it up farther than we could," Davina said. "She is looking over the medical facility stuff."

"I wonder if I could help," Shay asked. "Not saying I could do it better, but just that two sets of eyes are better than one."

"I think she's more looking at the facilities and the like," Davina told her. "She started trying to see where they are and is starting to focus on which facility did what. I guess she worked for some of them. Maybe we should ask her if she needs a hand. They all seem to encourage the help."

"We can talk to them about it over dinner," I told them. "One of the major reasons I want to talk before then is that they are asking us to give them some of our information on how we are able to connect to the active satellite systems."

"Why do they want that?" Sterling asked suspiciously.

"Axel is pretty curious and has been trying for some time to get his to lineup," I told them. "I think it's one more step forward for him and these people here. But it's also one more step we let them in. I was just checking to see how everyone felt about it."

"A step forward for what?" Margie asked.

"I'm not sure what exactly they are wanting," I said, feeling like I was speaking for the town. "I know I'd like to have our ability to look around, if I didn't have it. Axel has been trying to find a better way of being able to communicate. He's wondering if the internet was still around somewhere."

"I thought that went out a long time ago?" Laura asked.

"Yeah, it did," Shay said. "It lasted for a while but crashed right after the war, I think."

"That would be cool if it just went underground," Chris said.

"It sounds like they could work better to help us with this if they had all of what we have," Davina said.

"That's one of the negatives to me," I told her. "I don't want these people getting themselves associated with us in NASA's eyes. We don't know all of what they are yet. I don't want to spread that around."

"Haven't they been talking with home?" Laura asked.

"Yeah, but through the armory and HAM radio stuff," Davina said.

"Isn't that enough for them to be found out?" George asked.

"It may be already, you're right," I told him. "I talked to Neil and he said Axel is on his way to finding the signals anyway so giving them to him wouldn't really matter. Maybe this way we can give them a condition along with the info."

"Do you think they will follow it, though?" Laura asked.

"If they don't, then whatever happens to them is their own doing," I told her. "This way we also give back to someone that's helped us a lot."

"I wouldn't disagree with giving them the information," Sterling said. "I think these guys are pretty stand-up people. I just don't want them having to deal with what we're going through with Humvees showing up at their door."

"Is it going to close down NASA's help to us if we bring someone else in?" Chris asked.

"We could keep them from getting too close to our systems by telling them that," Davina said. "Maybe we tell them we're afraid NASA will close down their link to us if they see someone else involved."

"We'll put it that way," I said. "Is everyone okay then with us giving them what they are asking for?" I asked. "I'm saying it like it's some big thing but I'm not sure we're really giving them that much."

"I guess we haven't heard exactly what they are wanting," Sterling said. "Do they want codes and all?"

"It sounds like they are just asking where they can tie into live satellites," I told him.

"I don't think they are asking to be part of our system," Davina added. I heard everyone saying they thought it was okay.

"Are you saying then that we stay here until we have word from home or whoever else figures out where we're supposed to be?" Chris asked.

"I think there isn't really any place else better to be," Davina said. "I think these people want to help as much as they can. Lynn wants Kevin pretty badly. She knows what a monster he is. Sounds like Teal knows as well. I think Lynn may be able to help us a lot more than anything else."

"We'll all keep working every angle we come up with until we have a place to go," I told everyone. "When we find our next step, let's be ready to give a hundred percent."

"What do we do in the meantime?" George asked.

"Do you have anything else you'd like to get done on the engine?" I asked him.

"No, I think we've used enough of these people's help," he said. "All the improvements are fantastic."

"I'm not sure what we do while we're here then. We'll have to play it by ear," I told everyone. "There is one other thing." I saw I got everyone's attention. "There was some disturbance that happened just before we got here. Sounded like it was the guys from the compound we lost Roman at. I know that's pretty far away but I guess they come here now and then to trade for stuff they can't get. Quade said sometimes they don't let stuff go so easily."

"Are they coming back here?" Margie asked softly.

"Well, it was enough to worry Quade some and that concerns me," I said as plainly as I could. "So, I think we should stay together a bit or at least hang in small groups. Let's stay on the alert and call in at the first sign of trouble. Let's just call in often, just to check in. I know we are going to want to look around. I do too, but let everyone know where you are at all times. Firearms stay close and with a round in the chamber."

"What should we do if there is trouble?" Chris asked, his tactical mind stepping in. "I'm more for the 'shoot first and ask questions later' approach. What if these people won't take the shot that puts us on the offensive before someone gets hurt?"

"I see what you mean," I told him. "They may not want us starting something they are trying to talk their way out of. Well, they have to live here and we don't, so if they aren't making the first move and you see what's coming duck your head. But let's be ready to take it to them if we have to keep ourselves safe. We'll deal with whatever that means when the dust settles. I don't see these guys as the 'waiting to see what happens' type, though. Let's just hope that no more trouble is coming our way."

"Do you think they would know us?" Margie asked.

"I have been thinking about that," I told her. "They could have seen a couple faces in that hanger. We'll have to play that one by ear as well. I'll ask Quade to let me know if he sees any of them in town. If he does then a few of us should lay low while they're here."

The meeting broke up then and everyone seemed on board with what we talked about. Sterling and George wanted to clean up before dinner and I told them I would meet them there. They moved outside and Shay and Margie joined them. The rest of us headed for dinner.

We walked through the area behind the stable because we did not know any other way. We went around front to where the grain cars made an entranceway and went through the opened middle under the small bridge there. The difference we saw in the small town inside was quite different.

People walked about coming in and out of the shops. Lights were on in the windows and we were all surprised to be seeing neon lights. Ropes were pulled tight out front of the shop doors and all kinds of different things were hanging from them. It truly looked like a different town. Hearing some caterwauling to our left, just as we walked through, I looked that way.

"That's right honey, you look over here," some scantily dressed woman said from the porch of the first shop. "Do you like what you see?"

I saw several such women, dressed in hardly anything at all. A couple of men had already been taken in by their advances and were there being fondled and rubbed on, smiles from ear to ear. As the woman that spoke did so again, she moved in some erratic way. I could not tell which one of us she was talking to.

"Why don't you shut up, bitch!" Laura said and I was fully taken aback. I had never heard her curse.

"Why, think your man might be tempted?" the woman asked. "Which one is he, the handsome one there beside you?" Laura turned toward her and started to walk that way.

"Laura!" I yelled. "Not what we're supposed to be doing here." I saw Chris grab her by the arm and lead her on down the street. I think he had a large smile, though I tried to hide mine.

A large bar was next to the cathouse and looked to be doing well, complete with a few old-timers sitting on the porch and smoking their pipes. (I did see a few more ladies of the night but we did not hear anything from them.) The tattoo shop was open next to the dentist's office and I saw the man from the bar, from earlier, sitting on his porch on a swing next to the woman he had eaten breakfast with. (Allen and Jackie, I remembered their names to be.) I saw someone getting worked on through the window by some other tattoo artist as Allen sat and drank some beverage with his feet up. He nodded and gave me a wave which I returned.

We walked on and as we made our way through the small crowd, I saw an ornately-dressed woman standing in our way. Trying to move to be able to avoid her, I saw she moved to be in our way again. She did not look armed so I was not too worried, although I looked around to see if maybe someone was with her. I did not see anyone as we drew near.

"May I give you a reading, sir?" she asked.

"No, get away from me please," I told her curtly.

"A simple look at your palm then, perchance?" she persisted.

"Meaning what exactly?" I asked her gruffly.

"Some would call it your fortune," she said and pointed to the shop that had the tapestries of different zodiac signs on them.

"Oh, I see," I told her, and relaxed significantly. "No, thank you. Maybe some other time," I lied.

"Why lie?" she told me. "You are a Taurus no doubt." She said it with an ease that bugged me.

"Good guess," I told her.

"And this is your son," she told me, pointing at Chris. "And a grandchild in a belly there." She pointed to Laura.

Chris and Laura jerked their heads around and looked at the woman. I saw Laura look down and put her hand on her stomach. I kind of remembered her doing that a couple of times before that, just then. The woman smiled with utter pleasantness at the two and then looked back at me.

"Your journey is long and you have not found whom you seek," she told me. My interest was immediately peaked.

"What do you know of our journey?" I asked her with total seriousness.

"I see it in my spirit, as my entire kind do," she said. "It has been hard on you, this journey to be free and alone."

"Wow, I wonder how she knew you were born in April?" Chris asked a little weirdly.

"Let's get to dinner," Davina said, pushing on me. I think she saw how I was being affected by the woman.

We moved on and I turned to look at the woman. She made some sign and looked to the heavens. She raised both her arms then and brought them down to point at me. I turned and moved along with the others.

"Don't let it bug you," Davina said.

"That was really weird and kind of cool at the same time," Chris said. "If you want I can send Laura back to punch her in the face." We all laughed as Laura made a sneer at Chris. He went and put his arm around her.

We made it at last to Lucky's where we were supposed to have dinner. The place was somewhat full with just enough room to move through the crowd to the bar. Most everyone wore a gentle face and a smile and got out of our way as we passed. Getting up to the bar, I saw Jessica and she saw me.

She pointed to a doorway at the back of the room and nodded. I tried to thank her but not sure if it worked. We all turned that way and had to introduce ourselves to many as we walked through the bar. We were welcomed over and over again before we made it to the relatively quiet of the small curtained off room in the back.

Quade stood on seeing us enter, as did Teal. I saw Axel and Lynn there sitting across from the other two and on seeing them stand they too stood and turned. Eric too was there and stood up on our arrival. Pleasant looks and nods were exchanged and welcomes had. Quade motioned toward several chairs at the table and we all came and sat down.

"Sorry about the crowds out there," he told me. "I should have planned for dinner a little later. Everyone is getting off work from the fields and is looking to spend some of their earnings. We all are used to it. I bet it can be a little claustrophobic if you aren't."

"No problem," Davina said before I could.

"This is the best place in our small town for dinner," Teal said. "They serve a couple of different dishes and have the best wine."

"I think I could eat half a cow," Chris said and Laura seconded that.

"Just tell her beef, pig or goose," Eric told him. "Any of it will fill you up."

"The town outside looks a bit different now with everyone walking around out there," I said. "Reminds me of an old west town."

"I think that too," Teal said.

"Yeah, we even have the saloon to show it," Axel said, looking at Quade who smiled. "Quade, there, isn't convinced we look much like the old west."

"Oh, I wasn't meaning that as a bad thing," I told Quade. "I think it feels nice, seeing something like this up and going."

"No worries," Quade said. "These guys here just give me a hard time, telling me I'm the old west Sheriff and all."

"It doesn't help play down that image when you shoot someone in a draw in the middle of town," Eric said and I could see Quade felt a little uncomfortable about the subject.

"Really, you did that?" Chris asked.

"Had to be done," he said softly. I could see Eric felt bad about bringing it up, although he had said it in a hero worship type of way.

"I do think the prostitutes at the end of the street may not be helping your cause in that regard, either," I told Quade with a smile.

"Yeah, I'll give you that one," he said with a smirk. "I think the town is about half way split about them being here."

"Well, I think one of them almost died just a minute ago, huh, Laura?" I asked. It was her turn to feel uncomfortable.

"Don't worry sweetheart, several of them have almost died a few times," Teal told her and I saw Laura smile to her.

"Are the rest coming?" Quade asked.

He should have waited only a few more seconds as I saw George push the curtain aside and enter the room. Margie, Shay and Sterling followed close behind him. As we all stood, I saw Lincoln come in sideways, talking to someone out in the bar. We waited until they all found a chair and sat down as one.

"I'll go see what's going on with our drinks," Teal said and got back up.

"I am loving this town," George said. "It looks nothing like it did before. It reminds me of an old western town." Everyone previously in the room smiled and looked at Quade.

"You must hear that a lot," I told him.

"Yeah, all the time," he told me.

Teal came back inside and sat down beside Quade. We kind of looked at each other then and were not sure what to say. Thoughts rolled around in my head and I tried not to think of the woman we ran into on the way in. I was glad when a man came in to take our order.

"What would everyone like to drink?" he asked.

We all ordered and the waiter left. I looked forward to trying some of the local wine. I was interested in what all they grew around there, but I tried not to seem so. I did not want to seem nosy about what kept them going.

"It's interesting that you have so many people in this town," George said. "I would not think that an area could sustain so many."

"A lot of the people out there work in the fields a few times a week," Quade told him. "Some run cattle up and down to some of the areas in Oklahoma. There is a large gathering way down south there, just north of the Texas line. We have a name for ourselves as sellers of good beef and pork. We fatten them up on grain and slaughter them here if they want us to. Some just stay and try to make a living however they can. There is work here all the time, though winter is a little slow. It's starting to get into harvest time though, so we get pretty busy with that."

"It is great to see," George said.

"Most everyone in the bar seemed pretty friendly," Davina said.

"We get along pretty well out here," Axel put in.

"You ladies should try the clothes shops before you leave," Teal said. "Some of the local clothes are great!"

"I saw some shops across the way," Davina told her.

"I can take you there after dinner, if you like," Teal told her.

"I don't really have anything to trade with," Davina said.

"Maybe we can figure a way to work that out," Teal said smiling.

"How's your train doing?" Quade asked George as the drinks came in and were passed out, then reshuffled to their right places.

"The train is one hundred percent fixed and ready to go," George said. "I cannot thank you all enough."

"Did you test it, George?" I asked, having forgotten to check earlier.

"I did and it holds even better than before," he said with some pride.

"I love that locomotive," Lincoln said. "George there said he'd help figure out a way to make one of our old piles of junk work in the same way."

"Yeah they have an old Baldwin steam engine," George told everyone with some enthusiasm. "It's a huge sucker. It will take some work but it's totally doable."

"You said there is a conversion rate on the burn inline pressure system?" Lincoln asked.

"Yes, but it has a lot to do with volume in the chamber," George replied and seemed happy with Lincoln's interest. They carried on with their own conversation as Quade turned to me.

"So, we are having a hunt in the morning if you're interested," Quade told me. "There are some large bulls making a nuisance of themselves down a little southeast of here. Sounded like they were some pretty wild longhorns from Texas. One guy said they were mixed in with some buffalo."

"Really?" Chris asked. "How does that work?"

"There are quite a few longhorns that move up this way," Axel told him. "Mostly just the mean fighting ones stick around in the same area. They like to claim territory and try to defend it. Every now and then we have to go get them moving or take them for meat."

"That sounds cool but sorry, I was more referring to the buffalo," Chris told him.

"Yeah they move along with some of the herds of cattle now," Quade told him. "There are a few herds of them that are mostly buffalo, although they don't seem to get much bigger. Most of the herds are turning into the two, bred together. They don't breed with longhorn, I mean. They mostly breed with the Angus they run with most of the time. They call the mixture Beefalo. But every now and then they break off and we find some lone herd of bulls of all types. The cattle are pretty much taking over the plains."

"Are there a lot of them?" Davina asked.

"They're getting bigger," Axel told her.

"How many buffalo herds are there?" Margie asked.

"I saw one about two weeks ago, moving south," Quade told her. "It was mostly buffalo. They were pretty far out east, though. They are a little skittish and move off when we approach. They don't keep well in pens either so we mostly pass them by when we see them. Traders bring in hides sometimes but not very often. Billy, out in the slaughterhouse, likes to deal with those and they get a little expensive so most people just deal with cowhide."

"We should do the hunt tomorrow," Davina said

"How far off are they?" I asked Quade.

"They've been moving around in a little valley about an hour south of us, bugging every herd moving through," Quade said. "They may have moved a bit more south but there are some canyons down there they've been hanging out in, so I doubt it. I think there will be enough for us all to get a share," Quade said.

"I would be interested in one of those longhorns," Sterling said. "How many are there?"

"I heard about six of them," Quade said, looking at Eric.

"Yeah, that's what I heard," he replied. "You all would be helping us out if we could use you for your firepower."

I appreciated the thought that it took these people, who were able to take care of themselves, to ask us for our help, trying to give us a sense of giving back. It was even generous, I knew, as these people would be giving of their natural resources which was surely things they could use to profit from. I looked at Quade with a smile.

"I think we would much like to help," I told him. "But, I think if it's okay with George, we would like to take our train, just to see how it does." We all looked at George who was still talking to Lincoln. "What do you say, George?" I asked loudly.

"Huh?" he said, looking over at us.

"We were thinking of going on a hunt tomorrow and was wondering if you'd want to drive us there," I asked him.

"Yeah, that would be a great test," he said. "How far we going?"

"An hour or so south," Quade told him.

"I think that is a great idea," he said. "It will give us a chance to get out of our own heads for a while. Thank you for the idea."

"I too, thank you," I told Quade.

"No trouble," he replied. "It helps us all the way around then."

"You too must go, Lincoln," George told him. "It will give you a firsthand look at how things work."

"I wouldn't miss it for the world," Lincoln told him. They then seemed to start up again where they left off.

Our food came then and our drinks were all refilled. We talked a little through dinner but about nothing of consequence. They found out that Chris was our shooting champion back home and thought they had someone that could take him. Lynn talked to Margie quite a bit about her Indian heritage. Margie seemed to like talking to her about it.

"Make her tell you how she met George for me, will you?" I asked Lynn and saw Margie smirk a little.

"Really, she won't tell, huh?" Lynn said looking at Margie. "I'm sure there is some story in there. Let me see, I bet it's something sexy, right." Margie smiled broadly and shrugged. "Interesting."

I let the two talk on. I wondered about Oregon and tried to get Quade to talk a little about where he came from but I did not get much. Teal let it slip that he had once been a Navy SEAL but he still did not have much to say. We did find other things to talk about and it felt good to have dinner with them. It felt more like a Thanksgiving dinner than anything else. I was a little disappointed when all of our plates were cleared away and it seemed to signal that our time was over.

"So, I guess we should talk a little about the satellites stuff," I said and drew the attention of most of the table.

"What did you all decide?" Axel asked, overly interested.

"I think we will give you whatever we can that will help," I told him.

"That is awesome!" he said. "I have been searching for a long time. I can't believe I can finally get hooked up. Is the internet still hanging on somewhere?"

"I'm sorry, but I am the exact wrong person to talk to about that," I told him.

"I can help a little but Jadee is the one to talk to," Davina told him. "We can work on it tomorrow after the hunt."

"I'll be waiting," he said.

"We'll talk to Jadee then about what you need," Davina told him. I saw Lynn excited for him as well.

"We just want you to know how serious it is, what you're opening up," I told him. "I'm sure you know more about it than I do, but we just aren't sure about what we are dealing with. I wouldn't want to give that to someone else." I saw Quade look with some seriousness at him.

"I won't hook us into you at all," Axel said. "The systems should be free-running to whoever can grab them. I'll be careful with what I hook into."

"And really, maybe there's nothing to worry about," I told him. "I just want you to know what we are dealing with."

"I think we understand," Axel told me.

"Axel is the smartest guy I know," Quade told me. "He's been searching for a while. I know this is a dream come true for him. He'll do fine. Just keep me posted."

"I will," Axel told him.

Axel stood up and excused himself and Lynn did the same, the both of them leaving together. Davina started carrying on a conversation with Teal and Eric seemed to be content talking with Chris, Laura and Jake. Shay excused herself, saying she was not feeling well. Sterling elected to walk her back to the boxcar, though I had my suspicions he was hoping for some time alone with her. I told them to be careful and keep in contact which they agreed to do. I turned back to Quade.

"Those two seem to be hiding something," he told me with a smile.

"Yeah, I think I would agree with that," I told him. "They keep pretending they don't care about each other."

"I don't think they are pretending to each other," he said with a smile.

"Oh, you think they are…?" I asked. It seemed so obvious when he said it. "Yeah, I guess me watching them for any signs of one giving in to the other would make them turn it into a secret. I have a bet going back home as to which one will give into the other."

"Well, I'm pretty sure it's beyond that," he said. I nodded and grinned inwardly. "You kind of looked distracted all night. Mind if I ask about it?" I was not aware that I had been. Wondering about it, I figured I may know why I could be seeming so.

"I ran into one of those fortune tellers on the way here," I told him. "She said some stuff."

"Yeah, I had that happen to me once," he said. "Did she say anything interesting?"

"She knew my Zodiac sign," I told him.

"Yeah, I wonder how they know that," he said. "Anything else?"

"She knew we were on a mission," I told him. He seemed more interested in that.

"I have heard of detectives solving crimes with using psychics," he said.

"Think she could help?" I asked him.

"I got a reading once before," he said slowly, taking a drink and setting it down before he continued. "She told me stuff that did come to pass for sure and I know for a fact that she could see the future. But the things she told me were not the kinds of things that helped me figure out the present, at the time."

"Did you go to one of the ones here?" I asked him.

"No, it was actually in Oregon where I met a lot of the people that are here in this town now," he told me. "She did a card reading the first time I met her. She was the woman trying to get a lot of these people away from a pretty bad cult out there."

"What did she tell you?"

"Things about me leading her people and having a fulfilling life. It was more than that really, and I am glad that she did it for me. I just mean, it didn't seem to help much at the time."

"So you think I shouldn't go over there then?"

"No, I'm not saying that. Pauline is a very powerful psychic. I just mean, don't make it mean something more than a broad stroke of your life if you do."

"I don't think I want to," I told him. "I guess it's just on my mind, someone telling you things they shouldn't know about you."

"Yeah, I remember not being too happy about it at the time either," he told me with a smile.

We talked on then and I looked around as we did. Everyone seemed to be enjoying themselves and it was good to see. Davina saw me looking and gave me one of her powerfully attractive looks. I tried not to think about it but then it was all I could think about. We talked on and time seemed to fly by. Looking at my watch, I saw it was already nine o'clock.

"I think I better get things set up here for the evening," Quade said at last. "I've much enjoyed your company and look forward to the hunt in the morning."

Everyone agreed with that and stood up to be about the evening. Davina led me outside and I saw it was a late fall evening and bit chilly. The rest followed us out and we all looked around at the nightlife of the town.

People still meandered around but mostly they were at the bars or hanging off the front porches of the buildings along the street. They all seemed to laugh easily and to be having a good time. I definitely heard music coming from somewhere.

"Harvey's got his jukebox on a little early tonight," Teal said to Quade.

"Yeah, he must figure it's going to be a late one tonight," Quade told him.

Lincoln excused himself, saying he was going to see that things were ready for the following day. Eric said he was on duty with something about climbing to his station. The rest of us stood there looking around.

"You are welcome to stay at The Bungalows over there," Teal said. "They call them that but they are just like little rooms made for people to sleep in while they're here. And I do mean little."

"Thanks, but I think we are good in our boxcar," I told her. "I think we have taken far too much advantage of you guys already."

"We are going to start to take that as an insult soon," Quade said seriously. "If you change your mind just tell them we sent you over."

"I'll have to work on my manners," I told him. "We do appreciate all you guys are doing, though." With a grin the two of them moved off.

"They seem like a nice sort," Margie said.

"I think so too," Davina told her.

"I like this town," Chris said.

"Seems like it has a life all its own," Jake said.

"Anyone up for visiting the bar over there?" I asked. They all looked at me sideways. "What?"

"I guess we're all used to you being…I don't know…a little strict," Chris said.

"You're right, we should get back and set a watch," I said playfully.

"That's the man I know and love," Laura said with a sneer.

"And it's the one keeping us safe," Davina said, taking my hand. "We should give it a while before we get too relaxed. We have a long road ahead of us." I appreciated her stepping up beside me.

"True, we have a long day ahead of us tomorrow," George said. "I'll go make sure things are ready with the engine. We'll be ready to move out anytime."

"I will come and help," Margie told him and they exchanged a meaningful glance. The two of them moved off.

"Chris, you and Laura up for taking a watch?" I asked.

"No problem," he said. "I'll set up in the car and see how we're doing. I'll give you a report." Laura moved along with him as he headed off.

"Mind if I help out up in their tower?" Jake asked.

"I would rather you not be alone," I told him.

"I'll go with him," Eric said from somewhere close. I had thought he left for a watch.

"I'll check in often," he promised. "I would like to stay on here instead of hunting tomorrow." I nodded in approval.

"I need you to tell Jadee to go ahead with giving the satellite info," I told him. He nodded and following Eric, walked over to a doorway close by.

"Looks like it's just the two of us," Davina said. "I wouldn't mind checking out one of those bungalows Quade mentioned."

"I think I would like that very much," I told her.

We went to the long building that looked like an old bunkhouse. Walking inside, we saw a counter and an old man sitting behind it. He smiled as we entered and stood up.

"Ah, need a place for the evening?" he asked.

"Yeah, Quade said to tell you he sent us over," I told him.

"Okay, I'll get you the key," he said, walking over to a row of pegs holding keys. "This one on the end down there is the biggest. Check out is at eleven."

"I hope we will still be here that long," Davina told him, giving me a wink.

We walked down the long hallway, past several rooms, some with closed doors, others empty with doors open. We found our room and walking in, I closed the door. There was a bed in the corner and a small end table with a metal lantern on it. I went over to the table and searched a pocket of my vest for a lighter. Fumbling a little with the lantern but finally getting it lit, I saw a Gideon's Bible laying flat on the table and smiled.

Looking at Davina, I saw her already undressed. I followed where her thoughts led and watched as her beautiful naked form moved slowly to help me finish removing some stubborn gear. We took pleasure in each other for a long while, taking our time exploring all the things that came to mind. In the end, we held each other tight and I listened as she slowly drifted off to sleep.

I lay there then, hearing her breathing become deep and rhythmic. I slowed my heart rate and tried to meditate, trying to keep my mind from drifting to anything too close to the mission we were on. It worked a little and I felt refreshed in no time.

I sat up and got my clothes back on. I was not sure what I was going to do besides sit there. I thought of waking Davina and seeing if she would like to move into the boxcar for the evening or if maybe she would have some other ideas. Hearing her sleeping so soundly, I thought against it.

I left the room, locking the door behind me. I stood in the dark hallway and let my eyes adjust to the light. I walked then past all of the doors and moved out onto the porch of the small hotel. I checked in as I looked around and got slow responses from everyone. Putting the radio back into its place at my shoulder, I saw that the nightlife in the town had just begun.

I am not exactly sure at this point what I was thinking but for some reason I turned and walked to the front of the building that had all of the celestial stuff hanging in the window. I saw that a neon light was still on that told me I was welcome. I walked to the door and, pushing it open, went inside.

I saw a counter on the far wall first as the smell of incense hit my nose. I tried to see if I could recognize the scent but I drew a blank. The woman I had seen in the street earlier came through a doorway behind the counter, pushing the beads hanging there to the side.

"Right this way," she said.

I moved past her through the doorway as she held the beads to the side. I saw tapestries of all kinds hanging from the hallway I entered, though the one with a scene of a Roman Calvary man fighting a serpent held my attention the longest. I stopped in front of it and let the woman pass me.

"Are you Pauline?" I asked her.

"That is the name given to me in this plain," she told me. I quickly wondered why I had come.

"Just a little curious, I guess, about what you said earlier," I told her, trying to explain to myself more I think.

"We all have questions," she said. "Only some are brave enough to ask them."

I had not been much into this kind of stuff, the whole palm reading stuff, I mean. It seemed a bit weird, even when my mother had tried to talk about it to me, as there was a time she was into it a little. The facts never seemed to be plain, I figured, and money was always at the root somewhere.

"I don't know what you charge," I told the woman. "I don't know what I have to trade."

"No, not for this," she told me. "We often wait to find people such as you. We call you searchers, the ones that don't even know the power they possess."

"What kind of power do I have?" I asked. I was sure I was hating coming through the door.

"When you are ready, maybe it will be revealed," she said.

She led me a bit farther down the hall and I could see we were headed for the last room. I followed her through the door there and let her close it behind me. She moved past me and pushed aside the curtains that hung from the ceiling. I followed her and watched as the entrance disappeared as the curtains rested back together.

"Please sit down," I heard her say.

I was still looking around as she said it, concentrating and trying to see everything. There were twelve curtains in fact, one for each of the zodiac symbols, hanging from the ceiling around a table in the center of the room. A chair was on each side of the table. I saw the woman sit down in the one farthest from me. I took the other one.

"Might I see your hand?" she asked. I offered her my left as I continued to look at the rest of the curtains. "An artist with a deep meaningful life I see."

"It's a bit rough at the moment," I told her.

"But you are making the bonds of some meaningfulness here, are you not?" she asked. "This line in the center of your palm runs long and is broken several times. That has significant meaning for you."

"I really only want to know about what you can tell me about our mission," I told her, drawing my hand back.

I saw her slowly reach below the table and bring out a tall deck of cards. She shuffled them with care and started to breathe deeply. I wondered at her eyes that seemed to look past me. I really started to wonder what I was doing there as she set the cards in the middle of the table.

"Cut them wherever you would like," she told me.

"I do not want to be rude," I told her gently and almost in a whisper for some reason. "I just want to know what you can tell me about what I'm looking for. Can you just tell me things plainly?"

"I had sensed you were not ready, but I had hoped to overcome that," she told me.

She put the cards back under the table and pulled out a leather pouch with fur pushing out the top. She put the pouch into her palm and squeezed it several times, moving the objects inside around as she did so. Untying the draw-string she pushed open the pouch with her pinky and thumb. Turning it over I saw several various objects fall into her hand. Putting the pouch to the side, I saw several more lumps were still inside it. I wondered at that.

"What do you wish to ask me?" she said in a monotone voice. "It may be only three questions or less."

I tried to think of a good question to test her with but did not come up with anything right off. I thought to try some trickery, probably more to convince myself this was a waste of time than to be rude, but I then thought better of it. I was not sure what I wanted to accomplish by being there but I did not like the idea of insulting someone's beliefs.

"Why are we not finding Kevin?" I asked her then plainly.

I watched as she lifted the items in her hand to her forehead and, closing her eyes and putting her elbows on the table she let them all fall. They landed all over and as she opened her eyes to see what they told her, I looked at the objects. I saw a tiny wishbone right off and wondered what that would tell someone. A domino with one dot on half the side and a blank on the other half was among them. Several other bones of different sizes were there as well. Two, dark six-sided dice were there, which I saw laying with the added total of eight on them, close to her right elbow. A clear crystal had rolled almost all the way to me.

"You are not looking in the right place," she told me.

"That's very funny," I told her and started to get up.

"The bones are not acting as you think they are," she said. I waited. "They do not reply with sarcasm. They mean only to answer your question with some form of reality. There is more to the answer they give, but you are not ready for it."

"Why am I not ready?" I asked. "I've told you plainly what I want to know and have asked a simple question."

"But you do not think that answers are here, do you?" she asked. "I can see you want to listen but you are conflicted."

"I think that is probably a truth in everyone, isn't it?" I asked her, feeling weird for staying in my chair. "Couldn't they be telling me anything that would mean something different for whoever you're talking to?"

"They will not lie," she told me. "It is up to you to figure out what they are saying to you, as no one else but you can know your truth. We all have our own truth. It is in response to all that you ask with that truth in mind that they fall as they do, not just the exact question your mouth forms for them. It is the true answer to the real question in your heart that they respond to. The questions that lie in your being are how they answer, more like the intent of the question. Evildoers are here frequently, most comfortable with the answers, for they know what they are and they are comfortable with the answer which they get. People like you, with morals, have a harder time. That is often why we are not ready for the answers we receive here. We are not ready to ask the question. Sometimes we spend our whole lives getting to the questions. And often we want a complex answer that will prove something to us. Often the true answers are soft and simple. Do you wish another question?"

I thought about what else I could get from such an activity. I could see how Quade was right. It would not hurt to ask another question, but I figured I should not expect to get a real helpful answer. I smiled at her and thought to myself a little more.

"That is good," she said. "Search for the real questions inside. Don't ask what your surrounds ask of you. Ask with who you are, with the real questions you have." That was not helping.

"Will we find them in enough time?" I asked her. She again dropped her objects.

"The question is very broad and I will answer it as they simply read," she told me. "I see a split and forces divided. Two are found and two are lost. The road ahead goes in many directions but leads to where you are searching."

"I guess I don't know how to take that," I told her plainly. "It could mean so many things. Can't you just say go here and find them? Seriously?"

"That is not how life works, Randy," she told me. "You cannot just get what you want, when you want it."

"I was hoping to never hear those words again in my life," I told her. I started to think if I had given her my name earlier when I walked in.

"Heard them before have you?" she asked.

"I have but it's never been something I've thought fit for the way I look at things."

"Sometimes, this journey leads us far off into the long circle that shows us who we are and what things we need to see, before bringing us to where we want to go, and then only when we are ready," she said, sounding like she was almost singing. "In the end we will go where we need to go and it will be where we want to go.

Often beings on this journey will leave the circle before they find these things and never find their way back. A life of frustration and many other things is the result of such behavior in us."

"I'm sorry ma'am, but I am truly ready to find Kevin," I yelled, I think.

"Perhaps," she told me.

"What else could there be then?" I asked softer.

"You are a strong man I see," she said, "but sometimes that is not required." She moved around the objects on the table. "I see you using your wisdom. Sometimes that gets in our way." I was sure none of this was making sense.

I thought of what I could ask that would slice past all of this madness that I was going through. Thinking hard, I wondered what question would get me to the right answer and head me in the right direction. All I really wanted was the truth of where Olivia and Tara were. But it seemed the simple questions received the confusing answers. My conversation with Quade came to mind again.

"Why have we come to this place?" I asked her flatly. I saw her smile.

"At last, a question worthy of the power of the bones," she said and gathered up the objects.

She mumbled to herself as she held them to her forehead. Her arms shook and she nodded her head a little. She let the objects tumble in her hands for a few moments and then with a shrill cry she let them all fall and looked at them with some enthusiasm. She looked up at me then with some concern.

"You have been brought here to find what you really search for," she told me. "Not many find it in this journey."

"What do I really search for?" I asked her, and tried to keep some sarcasm out of it.

"I cannot, nor should I ever attempt to, answer that for anyone," she told me. "You must find that as your circle reveals it to you." I watched as she gathered up the objects and carefully put them back into the pouch they came from.

"Is that all then?" I asked her.

"Yes, for now," she said. "I do hope you will come back from time to time and talk with me about how your journey is going," she told me with a charming smile. "I long to hear such tales. When your circle brings you to me again, I hope you will be ready for the answers from the cards."

"I am not sure that will be possible," I told her honestly. "We are sure to find our next place and move on from here. I do appreciate what you tried to do."

"Well then, if I see you again it will be destiny, right?" she said. I smiled at that attempt at getting a confession from me.

"I know you try to help and for that I will simply thank you," I told her.

She showed me to the front door and I walked out onto the porch. Not much had changed outside though a little bit more of the bars had spilled over into the street. A few fifty gallon drums had been lit on fire and raged toward the sky. I felt like a drink but fought the urge and headed back to Davina instead. Finding her laying there, I snuggled up close to her.

"Where have you been?" she asked. "I rolled over and you weren't there."

"I had to get some fresh air," I told her.

"We should go," she told me. "I would feel better sleeping in the boxcar."

"Really?" I asked her.

"Yeah, it felt a little weird waking up here," she said.

"Okay, I'm up for going back," I told her.

I relit the lantern and watched with much pleasure as she got up and dressed slowly. She played with my urges and I thought about taking her again. I was fully disappointed when I saw the last of her nakedness covered as she zipped up her pants.

"Wow, I thought for sure I would have been attacked somewhere during that," she told me.

"Yeah, I'm a little off tonight," I told her.

"Well maybe when we get back to the car," she said and finished tying everything on.

I blew out the lantern and Davina opened the door. We walked out of the room and immediately heard someone else was in the hallway. We heard a soft whisper and both of us kept extremely quiet. My eyes adjusted to the darkness and I could not believe what they looked upon.

I saw Shay first, looking up at the tall male figure that held her close, him looking down at her. Her back was against the wall and he was leaning against her, his arms holding her tightly. They kissed deep and long as we watched and I am sure my mouth was wide open. Some light from the hallway windows shined on the figure kissing Shay and of course, it was Sterling. He told her he loved her and she gave his words back to him. I am sure here I smiled, but kept myself from ruining the moment for them with what I was desperately wanting to do. They kissed again, even more passionately than before. When they had finished, they closed a door that was opened behind them, I now figured out they had come from one of the rooms down the hallway from where we had been. They moved off toward the front door together, walking hand in hand.

CHAPTER 19

"I'm very proud of you," Davina told me.

"For what?" I asked her.

"Because I know you," she said. "I think I know what you really wanted to do."

"Yeah, that would have been a little fun," I told her quietly. I was sure I had watched the two walk outside, but I wanted to be sure.

"I agree, but I think what we saw was pretty cool," she said.

"I think I will go along with that and say, no doubt," I told her. "Any way, I can get you to tell Dan that Sterling forced the kiss on her?"

"No, but I think they did a little more than kissing," she said, moving her head toward the door they had closed behind them.

"Please, I would rather not think about that," I told her and she smiled.

We made it slowly back to the boxcar, taking the very scenic route that took us a bit down the tracks and then back again. It was a calming walk and by the time I got to the boxcar, I was feeling pretty good. Seeing Chris in the doorway, I told him I would take over watch for a while.

Davina sat up with me and we talked about the things we both enjoyed. We both wondered how the people back home were doing and thought about the harvest Vince and Mary were surely dealing with. We talked about the cold that was in the air and how we each hoped for a mild winter. We even talked a little about the people we had met in this town. We stayed there for some time and finally, I saw her eyes getting heavy.

"You should go to bed," I told her. "I'll watch for a little more and come to bed in a while."

"You mean in the morning?" she asked knowingly.

"I'll go see how George is doing and call in on Jake after a while," I told her.

"Okay, but I'll need you again before morning," she told me as she looked me up and down.

"Don't do that to me before a watch," I told her with a smile. "I won't be able to concentrate." She smiled and kissed me long and moved off to bed.

I sat down then on the lip of the door way and looked out over the place we were staying. I much appreciated this town, in more ways than liking the help they were giving us. I knew there must have been some struggle to keep the stuff safe around there, being so open like they were; it would have driven me up the wall I was sure. I also liked the way they got involved with whatever seemed to trouble those in need; it was not many that would give of themselves. Yes, I am sure, I liked much of the place.

I watched well into the night and figured on checking in on George. I closed the door with the ramp still down and headed to the engine. I called Jake as I got to the catwalk and asked him to come take over the watch, which he quickly replied to. I moved inside the cabin.

"I'm liking how it's looking outside," I told George, as I closed the door behind me. "Think we're up for a big trip in the morning?"

"Oh yes," he told me. "I am excited more about that than the hunt tomorrow." Looking, I saw Margie sitting in the chair opposite of George, at the window. "I think Margie there is pretty excited about the buffalo."

"I did want to ask you about that," I told her.

"I do look forward," she said with a smile. "It will be an honor to hunt a buffalo."

"Have you ever hunted one before?" I asked.

"Yes, several times when I was young," she said. "I still have their bones in my heart and their hides to wear against my skin." I smiled at her and she looked at me quizzically.

"I was just thinking about how that must have been for you," I told her. "That and I like the way you talk about stuff like that."

"I will hope for the skull of one animal if I take it with my bow," she told me seriously.

"I will see how to make that happen," I told her.

"And you?" she asked.

"I think, I would like the hide of one," I told her. "I can think of a million uses for it, including some nice leather gloves for winter."

"Yes, those are nice," she said.

"I don't think I've ever eaten buffalo," I told her.

"Oh, she cooks it so well," George told me. "There used to be a dealer up at Cripple Creek that we used to get some good chunks from. Her slow roasted shoulder is the best."

"Well, I'll have to see about that for myself," I said and gave Margie a smile.

"Quade came by earlier and asked if we would be up for leaving around six," George said. "I told him we would be ready, but if that isn't okay then I can let him know."

"No, that should be fine," I said.

"We will be ready up here," he told me with some pride.

"Okay then, I'll leave you to it," I said and turned to move outside.

"You don't have to go," he told me with a little concern.

"No, I should see what Jake is coming up with," I told him. "He's coming down to take over watch. I'll catch up with you guys tomorrow." They seemed pleased at that.

I walked out of the cabin and felt the chill take over everything exposed. The temperature was dropping and I did not much like that. I wondered if we were in for a fresh storm as I made it back to the boxcar.

I met Jake on the ground and saw he was talking on the radio as always. On seeing me, he got off and put the mic back away. He pulled the door open just before I got there.

"Looks like they are making some progress already with the satellites," he told me.

"Is there anything to be concerned about do you see?" I asked.

"Like what?" he wondered.

"Like they are hooking into the right things and all," I told him.

"Yeah, that Axel guy seems to know his stuff," he said. "I think he feels a little embarrassed that he couldn't figure it out by himself."

"Neil told me he was probably pretty close already," I told him.

"It really does seem to be going well, though," Jake said as we put on some water.

"Do you need to be back up there?" I asked him. "I could take watch for a little longer and then it's Sterling who's up."

"No, I think I wasn't helping at all up there," Jake said with a little disappointment. "I'm liking their weather stuff, though. It's a lot more advanced than what we are ever going to be able to get, I think. His radar system will be top shelf."

"Sounded like they took a lot of time with it," I walking back to the doorway. "Looks like some more weather turning our way."

"Yeah, I felt the cold," he said. "It could have gone either way."

"I'm not blaming you at all. Weather has always been just a best guess kind of thing. How's the wounds doing?"

"They're fine. They were just flesh wounds."

"That was pretty great how you stood up for that lady."

"Men should treat them all with the respect they deserve," he said, looking outside. "I saw you take that one guy down pretty easily. I love that three punch combo."

"You do some boxing ever?" I asked, looking over at him.

"I was golden gloves when I was in college," he said. "I have never found anything else that could keep me in as good of shape."

"Yeah, you either stay in shape or get pretty tore up in that sport," I said, and he nodded in agreement. "Maybe when we get back we can do a bit of sparring."

"I would like that," he told me. "I saw your heavy bag hung up. It looked a little beat up."

"I try," I told him with a smile and he returned it. "I'll take a bit of this coffee to bed. Call Sterling in an hour or two. You need to get some rest on those wounds whether they're just fleshy or not. And since you are not going on the hunt in the morning, be careful."

"Yes sir," he said as I poured two cups of coffee and handed him one.

I went and sat in the area that was sectioned off for Davina and I. I heard her sleeping soundly and it made me yawn. I took my boots and socks off and sipped at my coffee. I hung up my coat on the hooks Chris and Laura had installed for us. My gun, I hung underneath it. My vest, I sat on the floor up against the wall and vowed to find a better place for it sometime soon. I went then and laid next to my wife. My mind wondered a little for sure.

I woke the next morning to my wife's beautiful face over me. She smiled and kissed my forehead and checks. I tried my own smile, but was not sure what I actually accomplished. I got more kisses for my effort.

I saw a cup of steaming something on the table nearby and went over to it. I saw through the pulled back hanging curtains that it was still dark outside. Looking, I saw that it was an oil lamp that gently lit our room.

"You must have been beat," Davina told me.

"Yeah, I guess it was a long day yesterday," I told her. "I hope for not too many more of those."

"This hunt should be a good distraction," she told me. "Think you are going to feel bad for going?"

"Why is that?" I asked her.

"I know how you get sometimes, is all," she said as she too found her cup. "You think you are doing something wrong if you are not on task all the time." I had to agree.

"No, I think this is going to be okay," I told her. "There is nothing we can do without knowing where to go. Jadee, I'm sure is working none stop on that."

"Want me to stay here and help?"

"No way! I need you beside me."

"Okay, just checking. I think it would be cool to hunt buffalo."

"I heard those longhorns can get pretty mean too." I said as I pulled my socks on.

"I wonder how Margie will be, hunting buffalo."

"I wish I had a camera. I would love to capture that and do a good drawing of it."

"I bet that would be cool. We better take everything from whatever we kill," she said.

"Yeah, that's true," I said, pulling on my shoes and going to the coat hooks to finish up.

"We should be heading out in a few," she told me. "I wanted to let you sleep as long as I could."

"Well, I appreciate that, but I didn't get to take care of you this morning."

"You did that well enough last night," she smiled and gave me a long kiss.

We walked out and saw Shay and Sterling on guard duty. They were both standing by the door and looking outside, both with cups of coffee. I smelt some meat cooking and saw something being cooked on the grill.

"You guys look great after last night," I said loudly at their backs. They both jumped around and looked at me with some exasperation at their secret already being out. "It's amazing what good a little sleep will do for us all. You feeling any better Shay?" I yawned and moved over to the fire, ignoring the look I knew would be coming from my wife.

"Yeah, I think I was just a little sick of the smoke," she told me and walked off into the curtained areas.

"All was calm out for the last few hours," Sterling told me. "Seems like the cold is causing a little fog to roll in."

"Anything that's going to mess up us heading out?" I asked.

"No, it's not that thick yet," he said.

"We all ready to move out?" I heard from the door. We turned to see Quade and Teal.

"I think we are," I told him and invited them in.

"Wow, I like what you all have done here," he told us. "Those horses always seem to take up so much room."

"I think so too," Teal said, walking over to the side where we had the horses. "I love how you all are set up here. It looks like you could add several more without too much trouble."

"We could take yours in here if you want," Chris told her.

"I wasn't hinting at that, but I think it sounds like a good idea," she told him. "What do you think Quade?"

"Yeah, it beats us bringing another car just for that," he told her. "That only means if you guys don't mind."

"I guess we haven't proven ourselves the friendly kind just yet, huh Chris?" I said, looking at Quade with a smile. He returned it and nodded his head.

"Understood," he said. "I think we'll have about five more. Is that going to make it a little too tight?"

"No, not at all," Laura said. "We will have to tie some up along the rail there, but that should work out just fine."

"Okay, I'll call Eric and have him tell Brady," he said. "It will help Lincoln from having to hook us up."

"We're ready to leave whenever you guys are," I told them. "I'll let George know to get us heating up."

"The horses will be here before you can get up there to tell him," Quade told me.

I went up to the front and saw that Lincoln was already in the cabin talking to George. They were talking shop again and I had to interrupt in order to tell George we were ready for him to start heating us up. I told him I would get us lit and signal him when we were all loaded up.

"I will be ready as soon as you say," George told me.

"And do you know where we are going?" I asked Lincoln.

"I know the spot we are headed for, but Eric, I think, knows the places down there where the cattle have been hanging out better than I do," he told me.

"I think Margie is cooking up some breakfast," George told me. "Should be ready soon."

"How long before we get to this place where the cattle are?" I asked Lincoln.

"Maybe an hour," he said. "We are riding in from the tracks from there of course."

"How far are we riding?" I asked.

"Sorry there sir, but you'll have to ask Eric that one," Lincoln told me.

I left them talking again, picking back up as though I had not been there. I made it to the ground and caught Eric heading in my direction. I saw him wanting to walk by with a wave, but stopped him.

"Yeah, what can I do for you?" he asked.

"I was wondering how far out those cattle might be," I told him.

"Oh, maybe an hour's drive south of here and who knows how far off the tracks," he said. He must have seen my face full of displeasure at the last part of his reply. "They shouldn't be more than a few miles off of the tracks. They usually stay in a few different hollows. We'll find them right off."

"Okay, thanks for the time," I told him and moved off toward our car.

Passing the caboose, I saw Margie through one of the windows working inside. I decided to pay her a visit and walked up the ladder that led inside. Knocking, I pushed open the door.

"Something smells good in here," I told her.

"Mind if we join you?" I heard from behind me and saw Teal. "Quade's been wanting to have another look in here since you got here. We tried not to be too nosey the first time." I looked at Margie.

"Please have them come inside," she told me.

I waved them in and moved out of their way as they got to the platform I was standing on. I saw them looking around and smiled. I heard someone else climbing the ladder beside me and looking, I saw Davina moved up. I took her hand and helped her the rest of the way.

We moved inside and sat at the table by the door. I longed for some coffee and looked to see a kettle on the stove. Margie was holding a basket of rolls as she waited for Quade and Teal to finish being amazed.

"Begging your pardon Quade, but could you pass those rolls Margie there is holding?" I said. "They are losing flavor with every bit of steam that rises up."

"Wow, yeah, I wouldn't mind at all, if I get one," he said, taking the basket from her.

They came and sat down with us and sat the basket down in front of us. We each grabbed one as Margie brought over the kettle of coffee. She laid out four cups and poured us all some. She refused any help and turned back to her stove.

Margie talked as she continued to cook and I could tell Quade and Teal very much admired the caboose. They talked a lot about the Indian artifacts and were surprised to hear that they were all things she had handmade. Teal jumped at the chance to see some of the dresses that Margie promised to show her later and I saw Quade was more interested in the hides of foxes and elk that he saw everywhere.

I heard the radio telling me everything was ready and heard Quade's echoing the same. I signaled George and relayed the message there. After a few toots of the horn and a few minutes passed, we started moving. I paid no attention to where or how, glad it was one thing, I did not have to think about.

Margie brought us breakfast after we got out of town. It was a perfect beginning to the trip as the plains started rolling by and the clouds were turning brighter, sharing there colors with us. The food kept coming and we all felt like royalty and told her so. Within ten minutes, I was so stuffed with eggs and bacon that I did not feel like even hunting. I saw the rest agreed with me.

We talked a little, but just mostly watched the view moving by outside. The hills were higher here and the glens more deep. Trees started to bunch up, but where still few in the somewhat relative plains outside. Grass was the ruler of the landscape and small streams cut the fields into large thousand acre sections.

"It seems to go on forever," Teal said. "It's so beautiful."

"I just imagine walking out there in the grass and all those flowers," Davina told her. "I could do that all day."

"I definitely could spend a day walking beside a few of those streams," I said.

Margie went outside with some food and a kettle and I knew she would be bringing it to George and whoever else was up front some breakfast. I again, offered my help or tried to, but she kept on. I knew she liked what she was doing and I knew I would only slow her down.

We traveled on and the landscape continued that way for another twenty minutes. It broke up then, becoming fuller of trees and wide shrubs. I saw the rolling hills turn to rougher tall curves in the landscape that actually seemed to turn a little rocky. We passed a small town and did not slow down. As we got a few miles past it and neared an old farm house with a large barn we began to slow. I wondered if we had reached the spot.

"We usually stop in areas like this to put the train in some sort of cover," Quade said, probably seeing me begin to look around at what we were getting ourselves into.

"Sounds like a good idea," I told him.

We all got up and made it outside. I saw already that the ramp to our car was coming down. George was leaning over the railing on the catwalk of the engine. We all seemed to make it to the ground together.

"We should be on them in no time just a few miles east of here," Eric said, pointing east and to the other side of the train. "They may be closer, but I doubt it. They are staying in a small ravine."

"Are they moving much?" Lincoln asked and we all looked at Eric.

"They followed a herd down south for about a mile, pestering it the whole way before it let up," he said. "That's what Frank told me. They probably had enough play time and headed back to their favorite drinking hole. I think we'll find them in the ravine."

"It's a couple miles out?" I asked him.

"Yeah, basically due east of here," he told me. "There's nothing between us and them either. I hear they're pretty damn mean too, so keep your heads on a swivel. Frank lost two good pack horses to one of them bulls. He said he'd pay whoever shot it for one of his horns."

"Why doesn't he just shot it?" Davina asked. "Seems like that would run the rest off."

"Sounds like he had gotten a few," Eric said. "They are smart though, keeping out of range when they see riders with herds. They pretty much stay where they know the terrain and can get into some creek bed and sneak away. They mostly come in at night to cause trouble and steal heifers. They trample the calves too and gore the young males."

"Are you talking about the buffalo?" I asked him.

"No they mostly just run with the longhorns and push them around a bit when they have too," Eric said. "The buffalo don't much like anything to do with humans. It's the longhorns that are the pain in the neck."

"How many do you think there are?" Quade asked.

"No one has been able to tell," he said. "At best count there are about ten buffalo. I've heard tell of about six longhorns."

"Okay, looks like we know what we're up against," Quade said. "I for one am kind of excited to get on with this."

"Just be a little weary," Eric said. "I'm not meaning to tell anyone here what to do, but be careful about running in on them. It may take a couple of shots to take one of them down. And if they're cornered they only know to turn and fight."

We all listened intently and nodded when we were supposed to. It sounded a little more serious than I thought it would be and I started thinking in terms of us all getting out of there alive. I did not want to be last thought of as the man that got killed by a Texas longhorn and then trampled by buffalo.

We gathered our things, including our horses and moved around the train. I saw a small pond with a few feet of deep mud all the way around it, just down the slope and up in front of us some. The area east where we were headed was a bit more turbulent than the far off landscape. I could see many higher hills there. The chill still hung heavy in the air and I tied my coat a little tighter as I waited for the signal to move out. I looked at all of my team and we seemed ready.

"You sure we'll be okay leaving the train here?" I asked Quade.

"The very few people around here know who the trains belong to," he said. "They leave them alone and watch out for them when they're around. There's not many around these parts."

I believed him and his nonchalant attitude about my question convinced me. I saw George had listened intently to his answer as well and when I looked at him he nodded and gave me a shrug. I returned it.

We headed off east and moved into the small valley that was beside the tracks. A small stream ran along the bottom and we stayed with it. Our horses drank from it as we moved slowly. Dust filled the air in the rear were I stayed. I started early on watching our backs with some care.

We moved in and out of the small turns that came and went, sometimes coming over a hill only to ride to the bottom of the next one. The stream moved off and we caught it again somewhere down the line, though I am not sure it was the same one. I lost all sense of where we were, though I could still ride straight west and find our train.

I saw Eric stop up ahead and look over his rifle carefully. I pretended to check mine even though, I knew from my close relationship with it that it would be ready in any instant. My head continued to move in a circle as I nervously watched every dip in the hills that surrounded us. We bunched around Eric and looked at him for further instructions.

"They should be in a long hollow at the end of the next hill," he said in a voice just above a whisper. "It rounds around into a canyon that has steep sides with little off shoots that go nowhere. They should not be able to get out of them and they know it. They can however, escape out the other side of the small canyon. There is only one way in there so they should see us coming. There are a lot of possible spots for them to be hanging out in, like the little off shoots that don't lead anywhere. They could be hanging out anywhere in there."

"What is the most likely?" I asked him.

"I've only been out here a few times with the smaller cattle drives," he told me. "It was last winter and none of the longhorns were up here. The landscape changes a lot around here from year to year, especially these ravines. I just know there is a big bend in the creek up around the next curve. We are probably about a quarter mile from it. It's the biggest part of this area we're at and it will give them the best view of the rest of the canyon and a short distance to their escape out the other end."

"So let's spread out," I told him. "We can put some snipers on the hills up there." I pointed to the top of the hill we were at the bottom of. "Maybe we should have a couple of us circle around and box them in from the other side of the canyon."

"There's nothing but flatland on that side," he said. "They can see you coming for miles from that end if they aren't in the canyon. They'll disappear and we won't see them for days."

"So maybe we should have a couple of us ready to herd them back into the canyon if they see us and keep them out of the plains," Quade said.

"We should ride into the canyon slowly, but without hesitation, keeping bent over so that we do not alarm them," Margie said. "Maybe, they will be curious enough to wait for us to get close enough to herd them or cut off their escape. If they are very skittish like you say, we are likely to only get a couple anyways before they split up and find a way of escape. We should be ready to circle at that point and cut them off before they can get too far. Maybe, they will see us moving to cut them off and gather together for protection. If they do they will be desperate and ready to fight. They may charge the first thing they see."

"Put the snipers up here then?" I asked.

"We should keep them with us until we see which way they'll turn," she said.

"You really have someone that's pretty good with a rifle then?" Quade asked.

"I think so," I told him.

"We'll have to make a wager when we get back home," he said. "I think I've seen the best there is." I heard Chris snort. Quade smiled.

"Chris, Laura, feel like taking up a position when the order is given?" I asked.

"Will do," they both said.

"If we make it into the canyon without being seen, you two should stay put up top to circle around to cut off their escape," Margie told them. "When you hear firing move quickly to the end of the canyon. Do not get in their way if they are in full flight. Stop them before they see the plains or don't bother. You must ride quickly to get ahead of them."

"Where is the end of the canyon?" Chris asked. "I don't even see it yet."

"I should be about a hundred yards long and due east of us here," Eric said. "It does turn a little southeast I guess at the end. And watch your step because there are a lot of small drop-offs around that don't give you a heads up first. If you ride basically straight east from here you should find the end of the canyon I'm sure."

"Watch your background," I told everyone. "We are going to be giving chance most likely and coming over hills that you may not have seen us coming from."

"We won't take the shot unless it's clean," Laura said. Everyone seconded that.

"Okay, I think we can only ride in on them from here," Eric told us. "If we spread out and get into the hills there's no doubt they will see us coming and just use one of their easy escape route."

"Okay, then when we have an idea where they are, I'll give the signal and we'll spread out from there," Quade said.

"Only if we're close enough by then," Margie said. She seemed intent on not scaring them away. "Everyone has to ride low, close to your horse's neck. And don't sit up when they start to move. They will do that only to get a better look at you. They may stop at that point and see what we are going to do. If they are a different sort they will just start out at a full run. This is the best way first. Spread out only when the firing starts. We do not want to look like a bigger herd than they are."

"Okay, we'll wait for the signal from you to spread out," Quade said. "But if we see them on the run then it's every man for himself." I liked the way this man thought, I remember thinking.

Eric turned his horse around and let Margie lead us down along a stream we had found again. We all tried to stay in the looser part of the dirt and not to splash in the water. I looked around, still seeing Margie doing the same, though she switched from that to looking at the many tracks all over the ground there.

"See anything interesting," I whispered to her as I rode up close. She shook her head, but pointed to a jumble of tracks close by.

"They come here often," she said, "Longhorns, but no buffalo." I nodded understanding.

We followed the stream and it led us around a slow curve that ended at a gulley with eight feet tall steep sides. It was not obvious whether or not our horses could make it down without tripping. I saw we would have to walk along the top of it to be able to move forward any more. I also saw a trail that the animals had worn along the top of the gulley. Sterling rode up close to me.

Margie put her hand up and lowered it, herself lowering her torso and hugging the neck of her horse. We all did likewise and I quickly saw the it was impossible to see the surrounding hills. I did not like the idea of riding in on hostile territory with a quarter of the view. We did however ride on.

I did not see the line of us, who followed who, but I did see Davina behind Sterling. She was hanging over on the opposite side and I could not see her face. I wondered if she wore a smile like I did. Looking back ahead, I saw the trail we were on was leading us to where the sides of the gulley became less steep. I saw the trail lead us over the side of it.

Margie disappeared over the side and I followed close behind. I saw the gulley immediately become deeper and more wide spread. A long meadow of low shrubs and trampled flowers was to our right, away from the bend in the creek bed that formed the area. The side of the gulley beyond the meadow turned up sharply and cut off any thought of escape from that point on. Sand well mixed in with piles of crap was along the wall that started to rise at our left as we descended. The wall curved in front of us and entered a tall sided canyon. I noticed the soft sound of a small stream and saw one moving close to the long meadow. Margie headed for the canyon. I was hoping that Chris and Laura were still at the top and ready to circle around.

We came easily to the curve in the wall and was able to see the whole of the tall sided canyon. Eric was right about all of the small offshoots that dotted the space. Some looked quite deep and to be an easy escape route. I hoped he was right that they led nowhere. The canyon however, was only part of the scene.

Six humungous longhorn bulls stood looking at us from about fifty yards away. Ten buffalo stood close to them well spread out, also looking intently at the animals now entering their domain. A small herd of about twenty female cattle was close to the longhorns eating some of the nearby grass that grew along the higher areas of the canyon floor. The longhorns and buffalo seemed on the alert, probably having already heard us approaching a while before. I hoped they would stay there a bit longer, though I did see that we could already start picking them off easily.

Margie stopped and turned away from the animals a little, not wanting to ride straight at them. Two of the longhorns moved toward the far end of the canyon, ready it seemed to be done looking at us. It triggered something in about half of the buffalo and they too moved along the wall they were at, moving slowly but steadily. Margie stopped and we all followed suit. I heard her give off a loud snort of some kind, followed by a long billowing sound. All the animals turned and looked our way as Margie started moving again, still at an angle to them, however, getting steadily closer.

One of the longhorns was well convinced of our innocence at being there and moved forward to put these new animals in their place beneath him. He snorted gruffly and Margie returned it, bringing the longhorn at us a little quicker. Margie quickened her pace and angled more toward the side of the canyon that had a small rise. I followed close and looking back, I saw that we were starting to get spread out. It seemed like the best way of being able to shoot them all.

Looking back, I saw the tall longhorn begin to think about a full on charge. He shook his head violently and his huge horns added to the intimidating effect of his quick movement forward. I saw the others watching this alpha male, wondering what he would find. Margie gave another grunt and that brought the longhorn to a full run, straight at her.

She slung herself off the side of the saddle in a way that made her horse turn and move away from her. I saw her muzzle loader come over the other side of her horse and as her rear foot hit the soft sand she flipped the gun around and brought it to her shoulder. As the butt of the gun touched her shoulder and I saw her pull it there tight, her front foot hit the ground and a cloud of smoke escaped from the front of the barrel. It seemed like she did it all in one move and it looked like a beautiful dance move.

Looking then at the charging longhorn, I saw Margie had hit it just below the middle of the horns. It jerked its head up, not knowing what the new sensation in its brain was. It threw its head sideways and the mighty horns pulled its body with them. I heard another shot from her muzzleloader and saw the longhorn jerk its face again and it fall in a lump to the ground.

I looked where the rest of the animals had been and saw them in full flight toward the end of the canyon. Shots started ringing out and I saw several animals turn and two of the buffalo fell. A longhorn turned toward us. It fell as it completed half a circle. It was only a few seconds until the canyon was fully vacated.

Margie had found her horse and started toward the end of the canyon. I followed close behind her and rounded the curve that made up the tall wall that hid the plains beyond. As we got close to the end, I saw two more buffalo had fallen and one more of the longhorns. Margie ran on as did I and quickly saw another longhorn standing defiantly in our way, waiting perhaps for one of his brotherhood.

I shouldered my AK47 as my horse moved on below me and we moved to within twenty feet. Margie simply maneuvered quickly around the tall beast, but I had not yet taken any bounty so I took aim and fired. I watched as spots of blood appeared down the entire length of the longhorn. I did not affect him like I had hoped it would, as he turned and looked at me with some hatred in his eyes.

I pulled up and circled hard to flank him. He saw what I was doing and moved forward to cut me off. My horse jumped quickly to avoid being gored and I thankfully felt the movement quickly enough to be able to hold tight. As we moved I let go of the saddle horn and again pulled the trigger, aiming for the heart of the bull. I watched as he tried to jump away from the pain, but the bullets robbed his muscles of the pump that sent them blood. The longhorn fell over as it pushed away from me, hitting the wall with its high up horns and then moved no more. Looking around, I saw others riding up to me.

"I think Margie followed the buffalo out that way," Davina yelled to me, pointing to the end of the canyon.

We turned our horses and ran out of the canyon. I saw a dust cloud not too far away and figured that was the way we should take. We past Chris and Laura at the end of the canyon's mouth standing next to a downed buffalo. I saw them say something, but ran to their horses when we did not stop. I kicked my horse into a full run and quickly saw that there was no need.

Margie was about a hundred yards out circling some dark mass on the ground. I saw her hands held high and a bow in one of them. I saw the cloud of dust continuing off in the distance and knew there would be more buffalo for another day. I slowed as we rode up close to the ancient scene of an Indian beside a kill. I was glad that Margie had gotten one for herself and listened as her chant grew and fell in tempo and volume.

"I didn't hit a damn thing," George said as we gathered a little away from Margie.

"That was awesome, the way she pulled in the bull like that and then shot him died on the run," Eric said. "The way she flew off her horse was crazy. That was some matrix moves kind of thing."

"She was using a muzzleloader too," Quade said. "That was even cooler."

"You should see her squirrel hunting with it," I told him and he looked at me to see if I was serious. I nodded.

"That would be interesting," he said.

"Two of them longhorns ran up behind us and got out of the canyon," Chris told us. "They headed up that way, northeast."

"I don't think there's any catching them," Laura said. "They were moving pretty fast."

"I think the big bull that lady there got was the one that's been causing all the trouble around here," Eric said. "Maybe the others will move on now and join some herd."

"I like that spot for hunting, though," Quade said. "And I like that idea of riding in low."

Margie stopped her chant as she came around one more time to the front of the buffalo. We all watched as she got off of her horse and looked down at the fallen animal. She waved us down and we all moved over a bit closer and got off of our horses. I could smell the buffalo and the sage grass that it had lived in and eaten daily. A musky smell radiated from it and that mixed with the dust made for an interesting aroma.

"Join in the feast of honor," Margie said and went to the face of the buffalo.

I could not tell what she was doing put I saw she had pulled out a long knife. She was sawing away as I came around to the front where she was. As I did so she stood up and lifted the tongue of the buffalo high in the air, and startled me with a loud yell. She quickly brought the tongue to her mouth and took a bite out of it. I was more than a little put off as she turned and handed the tongue to me.

I took it from her hands, wanting to honor the beliefs she held. I was not sure how far I was willing to go down that road as I saw a large glob of foamy saliva fall off of the big chunk of meat. Watching her face, I then tried to forget what I was doing and put the side of the tongue to my mouth. I took a large bite and am sure that here I cannot explain the taste that exploded into my senses.

I say senses because there was a lot more than just flavor that happened at that moment. The smell was one of the first things that hit me. Buffalo for sure have no sense of oral hygiene and it was translated into a scent that I once remembered kind of experiencing when I found and removed a weeks old bag of potatoes from where they had fallen behind our pull out trash can on rollers. I tried to stay away from the feel of the foamy saliva filled parts of the tongue as it entered my mouth, but it was basically covered so I could not. I let the saliva slide down my throat without trying to stop it and will not talk about its flavor as I may throw up now at its remembrance. I will talk about the feel of the actual tongue instead.

I made the mistake of biting a little too high on the tongue and got more of the rough top of it than expected. The sandpaper texture of it immediately scraped my upper lip raw and did the same to the top of my mouth. I did not want the thing in my mouth any longer than necessary so I bit hard of course. It was tough meat and I felt something like threads being cut through as my teeth came together. I ripped hard and it felt like I tore dental floss through all of my front teeth. I chewed the bite like a huge wad of bubble gum and hoped it would go down easy. I did try this whole time to keep the face of a solid warrior.

The flavor of blood filled my mouth as I chewed. Some other flavor mixed with it and I will say it continued to get worse. I chomped harder then, trying to keep that somewhat pleasant look on my face. I switched to biting off little chunks of the wad and swallowing them as I could. It must have taken a full minute to get it down. I am quite sure the meaning for such a ritual is all spiritual as the physical act holds nothing pleasing.

I passed the chunk of meat on at some point that I do not remember and as I finished swallowing the last of my share, I saw it continue to the end of the line, everyone having taken a bite. I was now able to watch with some sympathy as they finished off theirs. Margie took another bite and seemed to relish it as the others choked down the morsel.

She gave another yell as blood trickled down our faces. It was some awesome sight seeing this Indian woman standing over a kill and chanting to the sky. I tried my own yell and am sure, I came far short of an accurate response. We all did it then and came up with what sounded like some quality Indian hunting cry. Margie smiled at our effort.

We spent some time then and butchered the animals. George agreed to help Margie and she said with his help they would do fine. The rest of us went back and butchered the animals we had taken. The chill of the day quickly went away as sweat poured from our efforts. I was happy when the huge hide came off in one gigantic piece from the longhorn I had shot. (I did however see that one side of it was filled with holes.)

"What are you going to do with that?" Davina asked as we held up the hide.

"Not sure, but it looks pretty cool," I told her. "Maybe it will be our new bedspread back home." I saw her frown.

Looking up, I saw Eric returning from a quick run over to Margie. He smiled broadly as he told me she said he could have the longhorn she had shot. I nodded and watched him move off.

Noon pressed in and we were still not done with the butchery. Several times I saw movement out of the corner of my eye and finally caught sight of a couple of dogs. I worried a bit about Margie and George out by themselves, but was well-convinced of their safety when I rode out and saw a couple of dog carcasses laying around with arrows in them.

"We are almost done here," she told me.

"Sorry we will probably not be able to take every drop of what we killed," I told Margie.

"What we leave behind will feed the buzzard and the vulture," she said. "The coyote will eat his fill and thank us for our generosity." I smiled and rode slowly back to continue harvesting all we could.

We made several trips, a bit haphazardly at first, to the train to bring the meat there. Eric managed, with some exhaustion, to get the skull of the longhorn Margie gave him. We worked together to get that aboard. I lost count of how many bags of meat we actually piled high in our boxcar.

"Looks like plenty of meat to go around for a while," I told Quade on our way back from the train to pick up yet some more meat.

"Yeah, and that buffalo meat will sell good back at home," he told me. "Not sure about the longhorn stuff. It seems a little tough. If it gets slow cooked though, it should be fine. We can just have a good harvest time cook out."

"That sounds like a good time," I told him.

"It's a little early, but maybe it'll help everyone get more into the spirit of it, if they have a full belly," he said. "We can jerk some for winter of course. That longhorn meat will be perfect for that."

"Looks like you guys always have enough meat, with that slaughter house," I told him.

"Yeah, we are planning on beefing them up a little more before we slaughter them too. Harvest time brings in a lot of extra grain and that helps bulk up the meat. Works out pretty good. But all that meat doesn't last all winter most of the time. It's amazing how fast it goes. We make it just fine, though."

"Well, I'm sure you guys are welcome to all of this meat," I told him. "I'm sure Margie will have taken plenty for us from her buffalo."

"No, we'll trade it back at town and get you some credit everywhere," he told me with a smile. "One hand washes the other."

"I think I'll just be glad to get it all loaded," I told him. He wiped the back of his hand across his forehead and nodded his head.

It was early afternoon before we all walked back to the train, the final load of meat on our horses. We unloaded it and put our horses away. I elected to wash off in the small pond by the tracks and everyone followed me to the water, thinking it sounded like a good idea. The mud felt so good on my quickly bared feet. Putting all of my gear to the side, I saw others doing likewise. I tried to keep a broad smile from forming on my lips.

I did not care who came in first, I just wanted the closest person to me. I figured it would start the chain reaction I was wanting. I thought twice when I saw Teal walking close beside me into the water. With a shrug I reached down and gathered the largest double handful of mud that I could get. She did not suspect a thing.

I let her pass me by, her now ahead of me in ankle deep water, the rest just then starting to come down the bank. I lifted the mud high and threw it, watching it splatter all over Teal's back and head. Several large clumps fell into the water with a splash.

"Oh, sorry," I told her as she turned. Quade exploded in laughter.

I worried for a minute when Teal's expression looked dark and did not change. I moved back a little and kind of moved my head side to side in wonder. I watched as a slow smile moved across her lips. She plunged her hands into the water and came up with two fists full of mud. Throwing them with some force, I let one hit me in the face, but did not see where the other one went. It was all that was required.

The free for all mud fight turned into teams that switched often. Once, we all went after George and fully turned him brown. The ladies turned on us men and with some ruthlessness, drove us to a spot where there was hardly any mud. We pretended to give up and tackled them into the water. It was a great time and we all continued to laugh about it long after we had cleaned ourselves up and boarded the train. George started us on the circle it would take to get us home.

CHAPTER 20

We were mostly quiet on the way back, but I could see everyone was in high spirits. I sat up front with George. Quade and Teal were up there as was Davina. Margie wanted to get a jump on stretching her buffalo hide so we did not see her; I had seen her go into her boxcar. Sterling and Shay elected to stay in our car and Chris and Laura wanted to see how Margie did some curing.

I sat at the desk at the rear of the cabin and let Quade and Teal have the window. Davina sat next to me and looked tired. I let my mind relax and enjoyed the wind-down time that the short trip was providing.

I talked a little bit to George about the performance of the engine and got only satisfaction from him. Lincoln talked a little to him as well, but found he enjoyed the view from the catwalk out front, far too much to be stuck inside. I much enjoyed the air that blew through the cabin and dried all of my soaked clothes.

It did not seem to take as long to get back as it took us to get there, although we had taken a different route. I saw Teal fall asleep in Quade's arms and smiled at having made friends so easily with them both. I was almost disappointed as I saw the town draw near from far ahead. The comfort of the slow ride made for a relaxing end of the afternoon.

"I will have Brady bring the wagon around," Quade told me when we pulled into the depot that had long ago been made into a junkyard. "He'll bring Sam and some others with him and they'll take all the meat you don't mind trading."

"I'll leave that to you," I told him. "Would you mind talking to Margie about what we want to keep? It's beyond me what she may need back there."

"Yeah, I'll do that," he said.

"I could help unload it and all and bring Margie around," I told him.

"No, I'm sure, you are wanting to check in and see if any progress has been made, right?" he asked. I nodded. "We need to know what's going on. You go check in real quick and give us an update. I'll take care of this. I'm assuming you are wanting to keep that hide you shot up?" He asked that with a broad smile.

"Yeah, it will make a great summer coat," I told him. He chuckled.

"You move on and I'll take care of this," he told me. "It has been a great day. Thank you for helping us out."

"Thanks for giving us something to take our mind off of our troubles," I told him.

We shook hands and parted ways as we made it to the ground. Davina followed me to the elevators. We made our way with ease up to the communication tower and found Lynn working at the computers, face close up to the screen. I made some noise as we came closer and watched Axel come out of the cubicle from beside her.

"How was the hunt?" he asked us.

"It was good," I told him. "We got some buffalo and a few longhorns."

"I bet Sam will buy them all from you," he said. "Anyone get hurt?"

"No, it all went well," Davina told him.

"Where's Jake?" I asked.

"He's running some of the lines outside," he said. "I think we are close on the weather satellites."

"Oh yes, how is all of that working for you?" I asked him.

"It's like night and day the difference in our systems," he said and I could see his enthusiasm. "I'm sure you are interested in finding out if there is anything new, right?"

"Yeah, sorry," I told him. "Is there anything that can help?"

"Lynn seemed to be getting through some of it," he said, turning around and walking us into the cubicles.

"Hey Lynn," I said as we got closer. "How's it going?"

"It's going slow and long unfortunately," she said. "I wish I had something to report, but it's just more of the same." I do not think I hid my frustration well.

"It's not you for sure," I told her. "It's the process that is getting to me."

"I totally understand," Lynn said.

"We did find where he sent some of his firearms," Axel told us. "Most of it was in some of the army bases in Wyoming. We actually visited most of them on the way out here. They were all mostly burned out even by the time we made it through. None of them had medical equipment sent to them, though. We've cross-referenced them all."

"I think Kevin talked once about The Monk spending some time in Wyoming," I told him.

"Yeah, we actually spent some time there too," Lynn said. "We were cleaning out another compound that we had found. We had a line of train cars behind us by then. The compound we came to was so full that we stored a lot of what we had in a train yard while we emptied out the compound. We obviously stayed too long as we had to fight just to keep about half what we already had. I think we just found out that it was Kevin's group."

"How do you know that?" I asked.

"NASA had kept tabs on them," Axel said. "I should say they found Kevin and then kept tabs on him."

"How did they do that?" Davina asked.

"Sounds like they had some idea already that he was around there," Lynn told her. "Jadee said Mack told her they found out about some fighting Steve was doing close to that area. It was right around the time we were there that they said Kevin and Steve were there. It had to be them."

"What?" I asked as did Davina. "You guys were the ones they got all of their military equipment from?"

"Not willingly, mind you," Axel said with a little embarrassment. "We fought them pretty hard for a while, but in the end it just wasn't worth losing anyone else over. They did not give us a stand up fight. They fought like cowards, picking off one here and there. We left and figured we did not need any more military equipment. We were happy with what we already had. That's when we set out to go far from any more compounds and found our way out here. I think we all kind of liked it out here in the middle of nowhere."

"Took a little longer than I thought," Jake said from behind me. I turned to look at him. "I was just outside tracing some lines. We don't seem to be getting some of the readings we should." He looked over at Axel. "It's not the lines."

"Okay, thanks for doing that," Axel told him. He walked out of the cubicles and headed for his line of radios.

"Any news from home?" I asked Jake.

"They found some areas where Kevin sent some firearms," he said.

"Yeah, they told me," I told him with a little annoyance. "Sounded like nothing that would help, though, right?"

"Something like that," he said, also disappointed.

"I'm sure you all are doing what you can," Davina said.

"I just wish it would be a little more helpful," Lynn told us.

"Mind going over with me what you've come up with so far?" I asked her.

"Not at all," she replied. "You might want to take a chair."

"I'm going to keep on with what Axel and I were doing," Jake told me.

"Okay, I'm not trying to interrupt," I told him. He walked over to where Axel was working.

I grabbed another chair, as the one already there I gave to Davina. I moved up close to her and told Lynn I was ready to hear all. She smiled with a shrug and started clicking buttons on the keyboard.

She brought us through some of the medical stuff that she had been looking at. We leafed through some of the paperwork we had gotten a few times, none of which pointed us in any direction. Some of it did look to match up with what Kevin was using on the screen. Lynn explained several times some of the more gruesome scenes and it all led to more of the same. When I looked down at my watch, I saw two hours had passed and we truly had nothing to show for it.

"I'm sorry you are stuck going over all of this stuff," I told Lynn, when she had showed us all she thought worthy.

"No problem," she said. "I lived it for a while."

"What was the stuff with Kevin before all of the experimenting was going on?" Shay asked from behind us and startled me. "It looked like it was college stuff. He looked too young to be a teacher."

"It was them scouting him," Lynn said, turning her chair a bit to look at her. "There are a ton of those kinds of videos. He was a lunatic right from the beginning. One of those videos of him in college was where he got reprimanded for killing a pair of Colobus monkeys with some poison. The Animal Rights Activists heard about it from some other student."

"Did he get kicked out?" Sterling asked. I wondered how many people had made it into the room while I was distracted.

"I don't know, but I guess, his experiments there were groundbreaking at the time," Lynn said flatly, seemingly trying not to give Kevin any praise. "They don't usually give students the kind of leeway they seemed to give him. It was almost like he was the teacher, but he was obviously the student. He was working on something to do with diabetes. Looks like right after that they recruited him for some position at the Disease Control. His early years there are a bit hazy."

"What school did he graduate from?" Shay asked.

"I'm not sure," Lynn said. I saw her typing something and Kevin's profile pulled up, complete with a picture of his younger self. He wore a stupid sarcastic grin. "Looks like he graduated from Kansas University."

"Where's that at?" Quade asked.

"Looks like it's saying Lawrence, Kansas," Shay said.

"Axel, we need an atlas," Quade yelled. We all waited as Axel went to a row of books and finding the atlas, brought it over.

"Finding something important?" he asked as he handed it to Quade.

"Maybe a lead," Teal told him.

Quade opened the atlas and flipped to Kansas. He searched with his finger first and then went to the alphabetical list of cities and their grid location. He found it easily then and pointed it out on the map to us. We all saw it was far east Kansas.

"I guess I'm a little confused, though," Shay said. "Those first few screens you showed were of Kevin doing studies and some of his findings were something to do with liver disease. Then the later ones were dealing with diabetic research. Those are two totally different things entirely. And they are not doing diabetic research on monkeys. They don't have the same responses to the disease, so they don't work as test subjects for it. They would work for liver disease tests, though."

"What does that all mean?" I asked Shay.

"I'm not sure," she said honestly. "I was just noting the differences in the studies." I saw Lynn typing away at the keyboard.

"Maybe it was different school subjects for the class he was in over the years he was there," Teal told her.

"Maybe," Shay said. "Usually they don't change the studies like that, though. Diabetes is a subject all by itself."

"Looks like that college is about four hundred miles away," Quade said and looked up from the map. I am sure, the looks he got were not pleasant. "I'm sorry, but I think that's the low estimate."

"Is there anything in his military stuff about Kevin doing business with his old college?" I asked.

"I haven't come across anything," Lynn said. "Sounds like a good question for NASA."

"Jake!" I yelled. He turned around from the radio he was working on and put down the mic from his ear. "I need you to send a message home. I need it to get right to NASA and I need an answer right away."

He hurried over to where we were all standing and we explained what exactly we needed to know. He turned with a nod and went over to the row of radios. I watched with some wonder and Axel came over to stand beside me.

"We have it hooked up to the safe line with your compound," he told me. "Pretty cool you guys can alienate your two systems like that."

"Yeah, I wish I could figure out what it all meant," I told him. "I'm a few decades behind when it comes to that stuff."

"I know the feeling," Quade said.

"Mind if I throw something out real quick?" Sterling asked. We all looked blankly at him. "I went to three different colleges. I transferred all of my credits around a bunch of times. I even changed degrees a couple of times. Most of them transferred over." We all looked at him blankly. "The point is, I moved around. Maybe Kevin did too."

"Maybe that Animal Rights thing was more serious than just them getting sued," Shay said. "Maybe, he had to leave whatever college that happened at and transferred to KU where he started working on liver disease and later graduated."

"That could explain the difference in research subjects," Sterling put in.

"We'll need his college records," Lynn said. I hurried over and told Jake.

"Have them send it to Jadee when they find them. Then have Jadee send them here." He nodded and I figured he had probably already figured that out, having been working there all day.

"Well, it's something to go on," Quade said as I came back over to the cubicles.

"The message we saw on our screens back home said that they wanted us to take this information to Missouri," Davina said. "Looks like it's pointing a little closer in that direction."

"You think he could be heading back to his old university?" Quade asked, but seemed to be giving it some thought.

"He would have all of the equipment for research that he would need," Shay said.

"A lot of the universities worked from their own power," Teal said and we all wondered more. "Add some gas to the generators and they could be up and going." It seemed a likely place to do whatever evil Kevin had planned.

"We should get a look at the college from overhead," Sterling said. "It may be destroyed by now. I heard a lot of the fighting was taking place in those areas."

"I'll tell Jake," Davina said and went over to talk to him.

"Think you are wanting to take the long trip out there?" Quade asked as I moved a little outside of the cubicles.

"It seems far away for Kevin to go," I told him. "I guess not if he changed up and has some means of transportation."

"There isn't a lot out there to choose from," Quade said.

"That's true," I said. "It's a long way to go on horseback, though. How far east of here have you been?"

"We haven't been very far," he said. "We have most of what we need close by. When we first got here we used to make larger circling patterns just to see what was out here. I think we took a trip to far east Kansas once, come to think about it. It was pretty bad most of the way there and back. We felt pretty fortunate when we came back. There isn't much of anything within fifty miles of here, though I guess someone missed that town north of us. That's why we decided to stay. We haven't had any reason to go beyond that anymore."

"Makes sense," I told him. "I guess we should start thinking about a long trip." I thought about that and started to worry.

"What is it?" Quade asked.

"George said we were not doing well on oil," I told him. "We'll find a place between here and there to stop and get some."

"Don't bother with that," he told me. "We have plenty of oil."

"Really?" I asked him.

"We have a few pumps working," he said. "We keep that to ourselves. It's some of how we run this joint. They really aren't close by, but close enough."

"I'm sure that will make George's day," I said. "We can find some way of paying you for that."

"Someday we'll be friends and you'll stop saying stuff like that," he said.

"I still won't use you to further our goals," I told him.

"I was starting to think of us as in this together."

"I'd still like to keep you guys from having to deal with it or wasting all your supplies on it."

"It's a little late for all that," he said, nodding over to Lynn. "Once she found out what it was all about, we were in it for the long haul."

"Okay, let's just figure out what it would take to get us there," I told him. "We'll get a view from overhead and that will tell us a lot, I'm hoping."

"Okay deal," he said. "Meanwhile, you fill up on oil. You'll need it either way."

"Let's just talk to George," I told him. "We'll see what exactly we need for such a long trip."

"I'm feeling like a fifth wheel over there," Sterling said as he came up to us.

"We're heading out to talk to George," I said. "I think we need to see what it will take to make the long trip. I'd like to know that we're ready for that."

"I think that's a good idea," he said. I saw Davina walking back over to us.

"He is talking to Jadee now," she told us.

"Good," I said. "Maybe something will come of it. We are going to go talk to George about getting ready for a long trip."

"Are we thinking of going that far?" Davina asked. "Kevin would have a hard time getting across a whole state, I think."

"I just want to see where we're at for now," I told her.

"That sounds good," she said, and smiled at me. "I'll stay up here and see what I can do to help. I'll keep you posted on anything new."

We got in the elevators and made it to the ground. I was finding my way around a little easier and walked out by the stables. I saw our horses in one of the corrals and was thankful everything was getting taken care of. Quade led us to where the train had been moved, as it was no longer next to the depot. I found George with his oil gun in amongst the wheels of his engine.

"Looks like we may have a lead," I told him. I saw his forehead raise high.

"Something serious?" he asked.

"It's not really clear just yet," I told him. "We are still looking into it, but maybe."

"Well, we're ready to go any time," he said.

"How we doing on oil?" I asked him. I saw his forehead furrow.

"Not really the greatest," he admitted. "That hunting trip took a bit."

"We have barrels of it you can use," Quade told him.

"You mean the stuff from the field pumps?" George asked him. "Sorry, Lincoln talked a little too much. Please don't hold it against him. He's rather proud of what you all have here."

"No problem," Quade said, but I could see him a bit annoyed. "We do have the pumps going a lot of the time. We have storage tanks."

"Sorry sir, but that's a little too crude for our uses," George told him. "It has to be a little bit refined."

"We have a little of that too, though not as much," he said. "No matter, we can part with it."

"I did not know about a refinery," George told him.

"Well, at least Lincoln can keep his mouth shut a little bit," Quade said.

"I mean, it stands to reason that you would have to have one to be able to run the generators you have here," George told him. I saw Quade's face turn to a scowl. It seemed it was not such a well-kept secret. "It must take you a long time to refine enough just to keep yourselves going."

"We keep up," Quade said shortly.

"But, I mean to say, if you give us what you have in the quantities it takes to fill us up you will expend all that you have and probably not fill us up anyway."

"I am not sure about the logistics of it all," Quade admitted. "We can check with Lincoln on that. I'm sure we have enough to spare." He gave George a smile. "I'll need to be talking to him anyway," he said a little lower.

We spent some time looking for Lincoln and I saw the sun was setting on the plains. It was a beautiful, slow end to the day as we moved around finding the places he had just left. I saw more of the place then than I had seen since I had been there and was well-impressed. In the end, we found him in the slaughterhouse.

"We've been searching for you for a while now," Quade told him angrily.

"I've been settling in on what we need for the harvest feast," he told Quade defensively. "I gave Eric my radio."

"Yeah, we found him first," Quade said and then I saw him consciously try to calm himself. "We just have some questions about our reserves."

"Oh, okay," Lincoln said with some private understanding. He turned to the man behind the counter. "You can have half of what the take was, but you provide six steers and ten pounds of Rocky Mountain Oster's, deal?"

"I think we can do that," the man said and reached out his hand.

Lincoln followed us out and we walked back toward the grain elevators. It was mostly dark by then and I myself was starting to get burned-out on how long it was taking to even see if we could be ready soon. I walked on beside George and Sterling, however, waiting for the answers.

"So what about the reserves?" Lincoln asked.

"George here needs to fill up before we head out," Quade started.

"You guys leaving?" Lincoln inquired.

"Looks like we have a lead," I told him.

"Where you headed?" he asked.

"Almost to Missouri," I told him. I felt George look at me hard.

"That's pretty far," Lincoln said.

"So how much fuel can we part with?" Quade asked.

"Even if we gave them most of what was in the refinery, I don't think it would fill up half of their tanker. Plus, with the feast coming up tomorrow night we couldn't keep the lights on."

"We can worry about that later," Quade told him.

"No, we won't run you out completely like that," I told Quade.

"There is an alternative," Quade said, looking straight at me.

"We only take one kind of fuel, son," George told him. "It's not fair for us to run you out like that."

"Then I guess we can give you a ride," he said. "We have plenty of diesels. Hell, we take the sludge off the top of what comes out of the ground and we have diesel."

I looked at Sterling for some reason and he only shrugged. George did the same thing. Olivia's face flashed into my mind somehow and then I thought of the baby she carried. My long-dead friend's face looked at me with the same questions.

"When would we be able to leave?" I asked him.

"Now you're talking!" Quade almost yelled. "Lincoln, line up the cars and get our horses ready. Hook on to their car and tell me when we're set to go."

"I'll do it right now," Lincoln said.

"And Lincoln, give them some fuel from our reserve," Quade told him. "It would be nice for them to have some range on their rig, just to be ready." He nodded and hurried off.

"Thanks, Quade. What about your big harvest feast?" I asked him.

"Oh, it was just a last minute thing anyway," he said. "Someone else will step up and run it. We just did it now because you all are here and we all seemed to need it. It will still go on. We'll have another one in a few weeks. Let's see how they are doing upstairs."

I agreed to that and we started off. George wanted to help with getting the train ready and turned the other way. I knew a lot was about to happen and started going over things in my head as we got in the elevator and headed up.

"Do you really think it's a wasteland close to Missouri?" Sterling asked Quade.

"I heard the rough part of the fighting came out that far at least," he said from the control buttons. "I think Kansas City is a pretty populated area. Huge cities, I figure, mean a lot of trouble and lots of wasteland. I'm sure the war touched them somehow. I remember when we got out that way a lot of the bigger cities were just torn down. I'm surprised we went as far as we did."

"Hopefully our view from overhead will show us something definite," I said as we made it to the top.

"Yeah, that's pretty cool that you can do that," Quade said and pulled open the door.

We walked over to the table Axel and Jake were at. I heard Jake telling his radio mic something about sending more information. Axel was at his side and was writing something on a tablet. Jake looked at it and nodded. They continued in this fashion as we stood there.

Figuring they were taking care of something important, I went to the cubicles and found Davina sitting with Shay and Teal as Lynn worked away at the keyboard. Davina smiled to me and I returned it. It seemed we were interrupting some story Shay was telling. It trailed off as we stood there.

"How we doing outside?" Teal asked as Shay quieted.

"Lincoln is getting us all lined up," Quade said. "We should be ready in not too long."

"Are you guys thinking still of going?" Lynn asked.

"I would like to have a report of what everything looks like from overhead, but I think, the chances are we will be heading in that direction," I told her. "Did NASA have Kevin's college records?"

"It sounds like we should be getting them soon," Davina said. "Jake was working on that first. Jadee was kind of wondering what we wanted those for. I didn't want to get her hopes up so I told him to tell her it was just a follow-up kind of thing."

"That sounds good," I told her. "How long until we get a look at Kansas City?"

"Sounds like they looked in that direction a few minutes ago," she told me.

"Maybe I should just go talk to Jake," I told her with a smile.

I headed to the radios and saw Jake and Axel talking. They stopped as I came up to them and Jake looked at me, seeming to be ready to give a report. I hoped I was ready to hear it.

"I sent in for the college records and it sounds like they sent them," Jake started. He looked at some notes on a tablet. "Jadee sent them to the armory computers and she is waiting for them to format to be able to send here." As I listened, a large screen came on overhead.

"Hold on!" Axel yelled. My heart throbbed in my chest. "This could be what we have been waiting for." He ran to a keyboard and typed away.

"What is it?" I asked Jake.

"He is trying to get a screen up so we can see them at home," he said. "It will be a lot better to communicate with them."

"I agree, but is our system up for doing that?" I asked.

"Jadee is working through some laptops and doing some other stuff," he told me. "Sorry, I'm not sure what all she's doing. Sounds like she was close. Looks like she did it."

The screen flickered between static and fully blue with the words 'NO SIGNAL' in the middle. I heard someone, which kind of sounded like Jadee, trying to talk, but there was a lot of interference. Axel pulled wires from some of his equipment and shoved other ones in their place.

"Copy, over, over?" I heard Jadee's voice loud and clear.

"This is Axel, over," Axel said, pushing a button and speaking into a small mic that sat on the table. "We hear you loud and clear. We just don't have a picture, over."

"Copy, copy, copy?" Jadee asked again. Jake told her over the radio what Axel had.

Axel looked around more and started following wires. He got under the desk and hurriedly shined a small flashlight around. I saw him changing a few wires and pushing others to the side. Satisfied, he came back and tried his mic again.

"She's trying to change channels over on her end," Jake said.

"No, have her try again," Axel told her. Jake did as instructed.

I stood and watched some more and hoped much. I saw some frustration and thought better of offering any of my input, quite sure of that, though it looked like I could help, I knew I could not. In the end, Jadee's face was on the large screen and her voice came through clearly.

I could see she was sitting at one of the computers in the armory. The room was lit up behind her and I saw April sitting at another desk, working at a keyboard, headphones over her ears. Jadee was moving her camera. She looked exhausted.

"Glad to finally meet you, ma'am," Axel told the screen.

"Sorry, but I can't really see your face," Jadee said. I watched him move a large camera around. "Wow, that's a lot better. I can see your whole room." She smiled on the large screen overhead. "It's good to finally meet you too. Your area is huge. I was thinking it was a lot smaller, sorry."

"No problem," Axel told her. "We have a lot more space up here than we know what to do with."

Everyone from the cubicles had come over and were looking at the screen on the wall. We stood around behind Axel. Introductions were made and everyone seemed to be happy with our progress thus far. I smiled at seeing home again.

"Not meaning to get back to business, but I think, I got that information on Kevin's college stuff sent your way," Jadee said. "Mack has been being pretty helpful."

"I don't see it yet," Lynn said, standing at one of the laptops on the table.

"Can you open it, Jadee?" I asked.

"Yeah, I have it on this other screen here," she said and looked away from the camera. "What is this for?"

"We need to see if Kevin had any credits transferred to where he graduated," I told her.

"I can look," she said. "What year would he have transferred them?" I looked around.

"It was probably within his first couple of years," Sterling told her. "Definitely before his last few, but really we're not sure."

"What does this have to do with?" she asked, looking back and forth between screens. "Oh here's something. Yeah, looks like he transferred credits from a couple of different places. He started out with a couple of years at Fort Hayes. He only did about half a semester at a college called Emporia. They all got transferred over to the state college. Looks like he graduated with honors, the piece of crap."

"Anyone know where those colleges are?" Quade asked.

"Here's a letter from Emporia College," Jadee said. "Looks like he got reprimanded for something. The letterhead says it's in the city Emporia." I saw Axel get out his atlas and thumb through it.

"Looks like it's out east as well," he said as I came over to look. "It's right here." I saw it was basically just as far into east Kansas.

"Can you look up anything about his credits from the Fort Hayes one?" I asked her.

"Sure, let me look," she said. "I wonder if there is anything that can help us with some of those manuscripts."

"We'll have to go through all of that too," Lynn said.

"I wonder if Fort Hayes College is in the city of Hayes," Quade said.

"Why, where's that at?" I asked and we all looked at him.

"Hayes is about a hundred and fifty miles east of here," he said.

"I'm not finding anything here that's giving me an address on that one," Jadee said.

"Anyone here a native?" I asked Quade.

"Yeah, lots," he said. "I'll tell Eric to ask a few of them." He walked away a little and got on his radio.

"Anything coming through yet?" Jadee asked.

"Oh yeah, sorry," Lynn said. "Just like before. Looks like our hook up is in good shape."

"Glad to finally talk to you all face-to-face," Jadee told her.

"Same here, darlin'," Lynn told her. "I'll look over everything here and see what it looks like. I'll jump on this and talk to you soon, now that we can do that a little easier."

"I appreciate all you guys are doing," she said.

"I know," Lynn told her and walked back to her cubicle.

"Anything on looking over Kansas City?" I asked Jadee.

"Yeah, we did see a lot of it," she said. "It's a little hazy, but it looks pretty destroyed. NASA is looking over it too. Sorry, I've been trying to keep them from knowing everything we are doing, but there's no hiding what we're looking at with our satellites. Mack did ask a lot of questions about this college stuff. I think he is satisfied now that we are looking into every avenue."

"Are they coming up with anything?" I asked.

"He did say that McQueen got what he was wanting wherever they had sent him," she said. "He didn't give me any details, but it sounded like they got a few of the scientists they were looking for. I got the feeling they were actually saving the scientist from some group that had taken them."

"Nothing about a clue for us in all of that?" I asked.

"No, just one more group of monsters scraped off the street," she said in some disgust.

"Well, maybe they'll get something from them," I told her. "Sounded like they were working with Kevin pretty closely. Maybe they contacted him and NASA can find out."

"I think they were working parallel with Kevin. Mack said something about McQueen saving the planet one more time. He said that group had worked on the virus just like Kevin had. It seemed kind of vague as to whether or not they were partners."

"Did he say where they were headed next?"

"No, but I will try to see," she said.

"Not sure I would be interested in working alongside those guys," I told her. "But, if they can help, I'd take it."

"I wouldn't mind getting my hands on Kevin before they do," Jadee said, looking straight at the camera.

"I know the feeling, Jadee. I hope we can give you that chance soon. Looks like we'll have to have you all look over this Emporia college area too," I told her.

"I will have a look," she said. "We haven't had much luck with getting those screens channeling down here to the armory. Neil has been helping with that. I'll get him word." Quade walked up behind me.

"It looks like that college is in Hayes," he told me.

"I need him to look over the town of Hayes first," I told Jadee. "That will be first priority."

"I'll do that," she said and tapped April on the shoulder.

I heard her telling her something and April ran off. She must not have known the screens were on I figured. I knew they were all working so hard.

"You should get some rest," I told her.

"I don't feel tired," she said. "I'd just lay there and toss and turn anyway and I hate that."

"I want you to try tonight, for a little while anyway," I told her. "You are no good to anyone strung-out. Let April take over for a while down there."

"She's just as strung-out as I am," she said. "But, I will try."

"I'll wait for a report from Neil and April then," I told her. "You are on bed status for the next several hours." I saw her frown. "Seriously, Jadee!"

"Understood," she said.

I walked over to the large map that Axel had on the rolling panel. I looked east for the town of Hayes and found it easily. I saw Quade walking over and looking with me.

"I wish I had George's map," I told him. "It shows where all the railroad tracks are in the area."

"Oh, we have some of those," he said and walked over to the line of books. Pulling one out, he came back and handed me something that looked like George's. "We have a couple of them. They've saved us a time or two."

"I don't think you could travel the rails without one," I told him as I flipped to Kansas.

I looked closely between the two maps and followed the three different sets of tracks that ran around the area. I held it out so Quade and Sterling could look and they too looked closely. Seeing several large clips at the top of the large Kansas map, I put the freight map there and we all got a pretty good view.

"Looks like this set here is out," Quade said. He pointed to a set that turned north before Hayes. "I guess maybe we should get a little more familiar with how the tracks run in this state."

"Looks like a lot of them drop out of Nebraska," Sterling told him. "They sure head south a lot too."

"I've noticed that just around here," Quade said.

"I think this line here runs pretty straight east," I said. "We can jump on this line here and circle out north if we run into trouble."

"I like the way you think," Quade said. "I think it sounds like a great idea, but we should let Lincoln in on it."

"Yeah, I agree," I told him. "We usually let George pick all of the routes."

"Think you want to leave tonight?" Quade asked.

"I think I wouldn't mind getting a look at the city from overhead first," I told him. "I think I've had enough of the walking into the unknown thing. It may need that in the end, but I'd like to give us a chance."

"Then we move in the morning?" Sterling asked.

"I think I wouldn't mind leaving early like two or so," I said. "We would be able to be right outside of town right before sun-up. We could have home look it over at daybreak and then move in if all looks good or weigh our options then."

"I like that," Quade said.

"I think we better decide now how we are going to run this," I said and turned to Quade. "I don't want to be stepping on any toes when we get out there."

"I understand us needing to have only one chief," Quade said. "I am not going in order to be in charge. We'll follow you guys. I will tell you, though, if it looks like we're pushing too hard, I'm going to pull my team back."

"I would expect no less," I said. "And I'm not looking to send in a bunch of scouts to test the waters. We go in together and spread out. We look and see what we can find. And I'm not one to push bad positions."

"Then we're in," Quade said and put out his hand. I shook it with as much appreciation as I could.

"I know you don't have to do this and you'll be putting yourselves in harm's way," I told him. "I thank you for that."

"Me too," Sterling said, shaking his hand.

"Let's just hope we find what we're looking for there in Hayes," Quade replied and walked back over to the radios.

"I should go talk to George," I told Sterling.

"Okay, I'll spend a little more time up here and see what they find," he said. He followed Quade over to the radio.

I found Davina and told her what we were going to be doing. She thought it sounded best and said she would tell the others in the room. I kissed her and went to find George.

CHAPTER 21

George was helping Lincoln with some hoses and things which they were connecting to our oil tanker car. It looked like the lines came out of nowhere and none of it was clear to me what was going on with the system. Lincoln informed me that they liked it that way.

They started moving a lot of different train cars around and it looked like a big job. They made various lines and I watched with awe as several men worked together to get things the way they wanted them. I jumped in and helped out for about an hour and found the hard work went rather quickly.

When we had finished, I talked to George about our plan and he said it sounded solid. He said we would be ready in no time and I asked him about looking at the freight map. He assured me that he would head upstairs and have a look at everything. Feeling my duties there were complete, I made my way to where George pointed me to our boxcar.

I took some time and started a fire in the barrel. I saw we needed some wood and made a mental note to find some at our next stop. I found some old jerky in my footlocker that I had put there for just such an occasion. Seeing Quade step onto our ramp, I dug further and found a small bottle of some alcohol that George had given me. Grabbing an extra cup from the group, I walked over to Quade in the doorway.

"Not meaning to intrude," he said, looking at what I carried. "You might need that. NASA just contacted us directly."

"What?" I asked as my heart pounded. "Do they know you're helping us?"

"It's pretty obvious they do," he told me. "Your wife is trying to talk to them as if you just found this place. I think we all see they aren't really buying it. She's up there now."

I set the cup and bottle down and ran out of the boxcar. Quade followed close. I made it to the elevator and he pushed the buttons. It felt slow going up and I cursed it several times.

"I'm really sorry about this," I told Quade.

"It can't be helped," he said and I could see he too was a little nervous. "It might not mean anything bad."

The door opened and I rushed over to the line of radios. I saw Axel talking to Mack on one of the screens. Davina turned on seeing me and mouthed an apology.

"There's nothing you could have done," I told her. "They were probably on to us from the beginning." I walked over to Axel and looked at Mack. "Looks like you found us out here in the middle of nowhere."

"We understand you're trying to keep this between yourselves," Mack said. "Sorry, but this is too big. We need to use everything we can to find Kevin. He's the last of them. We need to talk to you directly, if we can, and pass information to you without all of the middleman stuff."

"We're just passing through here and glad to find these people had some radio equipment," I told him.

"Yeah, I heard," Mack said. "Sounds like you're headed for Hayes."

"Have you seen anything there that looks promising?" I asked him.

"Not sure why he would head to his old college. I guess it's something to look into. I hear the real destination is the Kansas City area."

"Yeah, but I want to stop along the way at Hayes just in case," I told him.

"No, I think it's worth a stop off too," Mack said defensively.

"I also don't want to walk in without seeing what's going on around there," I told him. "We haven't had the best of luck with that so far."

"I know it's rough on you guys down there on the ground. I'll send you some radar photos of what we have."

"Are they recent?" Quade asked.

"After the war we used some NovaTech satellite systems to map the Earth," he said, looking off to the side and doing what looked like some typing. "We wanted to see how the war had affected everything down there. We did several Strip Map acquisitions over a year's time and overlaid the different passes onto a formation map. It told us if there were any major differences going on anywhere."

"What did you find?" I asked him with some force.

"Not much, I'm afraid," he said, looking over at the camera for a moment then turning back. "Do you have another screen with a separate video feed?"

"We have about eight different feeds," Axel told him.

"Could you power one of them up?" Mack asked him. "I'll send you the live link on it and you can see where it's going. You won't be able to change its course, which sucks, but it will show you whatever it's seeing. Also, you can change to looking at where it's been. That should really show you what you want to see. You can scroll down through the passes and see the changes over the last ten or so passes. Sometimes they're recent passes, but sometimes they are a week or a lot more."

"You mean you had this tech up and going before you sent us into those compounds?" I asked him. "You didn't even warn us that they were occupied."

"Quite frankly sir, we weren't sure what to share with you," Mack said, looking flatly at the screen. "This TerraMap-X research is not one hundred percent ground accurate. The slices tell us there was some activity with objects being in different places in different slices. We didn't know what everything there was. You'll see when you look at it. We don't have all of the high tech stuff we used to which would have shown us a person smiling up at us. Systems fail all the time and we can't get it back. Objects smaller than ten feet don't show up as anything, but shades of gray on these types of systems. If you're pissed off at us, so be it. We need to move forward is all I can say." I tried not to let my anger boil as I knew we still needed these NASA people.

"Why can we see so clear then and you guys can't?" I asked him flatly.

"We can see just like you guys can," Mack said. "It is impressive what you guys have done with the tech you have, that's for sure. But we are using that same tech too. Jadee is using satellite images which only give you a good picture of the ground on a clear day. What I'm sending you is radar from a satellite system which penetrates the clouds and reads waves as they bounce off of the ground. It's not a guaranteed way of seeing what's waiting for you, but it helps."

"The power is on," Axel told him and we all looked at another of the large television screens turn blue.

"You'll need a whole separate system to operate this," Mack told him.

"It's separate," Axel told him.

"Sending link," Mack said, typing away at some unseen keyboard off to the side. "You should be receiving it now."

"Nothing yet," Axel told him as we watched the screen for any change. "Is it going to have to download?"

"No, it should just stream," Mack said. The screen popped to life.

"We are getting something," Axel told him.

I watched Axel move a mouse around the table and find different things to click on. He pulled up a list of numbers and went over some of them with Mack. He listened to how to put in coordinates and learned how to move around the map once it was pulled up.

"That should get you a look over wherever you're going," Mack said. "I'll still keep an eye out up here and we'll do our own analysis. They probably already have a report on Hayes."

"Have you found anything that will send us somewhere more promising?" I asked him. "It's a long way to go."

"I'm sorry, but no," he said. "The trip to Kansas City sounds about the best so far. Please believe me when I say that we are looking over everything."

"I do believe you," I told him, but was not sure if I meant it.

"Look over the Strip Map and get back to me," he said. "I'll do the same. I want everyone down there to hear this. We want to work together on this. I'm sorry that you lost a man. I'll do everything I can to prevent that in the future. I will send you everything we have that you think will help, just as we have been. You just ask and I'll send it." His picture on the laptop went out.

"Well, that was exciting," Shay said after a few moments of everyone gathering their thoughts.

"Not sure I like them having our address," Teal said. "I guess it was bound to happen, though."

"Anything on the radar stuff he sent?" Quade asked and we all looked at Axel.

"I will pull up some longitude and latitude figures and see where we are." he said. "I'm not the greatest on that stuff. It will take no time to get used to, though."

We all waited for him to get up to speed on the technology and it reminded me of sitting and watching Jadee when the computer systems were new to her. A few times we looked at different areas that weren't what we needed, but in only a few minutes we were looking at Hayes.

"This looks like the activity for the last few months," Axel said. "Looks like they are keeping those satellites working around the clock."

"No wonder they found us," I said.

"Looks like they probably already knew we were here too," Quade said.

"I wonder if they have a map of settlements," Davina stated. We all looked at her and she shrugged.

We turned our attention back to the map and saw a multicolored view of a city. Grays and blacks were overlaid with a variety of colors. I looked and counted nine different colors.

"Yellow is the most recent pass in the slices," Axel told us. "Then continues on down the color chart."

"Can you delete the last one so we can see the changes?" Sterling asked.

"Yeah, I'll move it up and down and we will see what's been going on there," Axel said.

With the yellow on the picture we could see a basic town that had several neighborhoods and department stores along with other unidentifiable structures. Trees, we all guessed, were the gray areas that fogged some of the areas around buildings and filled in streets. We easily made out vehicles, though we none could tell which types exactly. The college was found by Shay and we all saw it was a relatively large campus.

"There's no telling which part of that is the medical facility," Shay said.

"And I don't think Kevin is going to do much moving stuff around outside once he gets there, either," Sterling said.

"I'm not too concerned about finding Kevin in these pictures," I told him. "I just want to see if there's a lot of activity. Sorry Sterling, I know what you're saying."

"I understand," Sterling said. "It would probably be more likely that he's there if there's nothing being moved around. It will mean it's safe for him."

"Exactly!" I told him.

"Let's pull away the yellow slice," Axel said and hit the keyboard.

We watched the yellow layer disappear and everyone looked for changes. There were no obvious changes, though we looked hard to find them. The vehicles along the streets remained where they had been. There was no change in the structures that we could tell.

Axel removed another layer and we could see some squares were moved from where they were before. We immediately called them vehicles, but Quade pointed out that they could be wagons. The two new squares we saw were undeterminable. I quickly saw what Mack had been talking about.

Axel removed more colors and we could see some of the destruction of the building that had befallen the town. It was interesting, watching the history of the aftermath of such a city at the end of the war. It seems this one fared well; though it was obvious some of the structures had been fought over and collapsed or burned. Three of the large neighborhoods no longer existed in the later colors, wiped clean and grown over in shades as time passed. It was interesting seeing what happened to this town during and just after the war as the first colors showed all was well and then whole neighborhoods disappeared. We saw no real signs of life as Axel drew back to the yellow color.

"Looks to me like some fighting might have passed through, but no one seems to be fully occupying the place," Sterling said.

"I agree," I said. "I'm not sure we are getting the full picture, but it looks that way from this."

"I don't think this is showing us much, but it is good to see where we are headed," Quade said.

"It does help with a planned strategy on how to best enter the town," Teal said.

"That's for sure," I said. "And I agree that we shouldn't go in expecting no one to be there. Maybe Mack was right on saying they couldn't really tell. I think I'll still be safe and not trust him, but there's something to what he's saying."

"Feel like going over the other towns we're headed to?" Quade asked Axel.

"Sure, I'll pull them up." he said.

"I think I've had enough for one day," Davina said. "I'll head down and figure out the watch for tonight." She kissed me on the cheek and headed tiredly to the door.

"I'm with her," Teal and Shay said. They too left the room with her.

"I don't think I'd want to look all over the globe with this thing," Quade said. "Looks like it would be a little depressing." We all agreed.

I do not remember what we looked at first and now it is all pretty much a blur. I know we did take our time and became very familiar with the two other cities. I can still see in my mind the devastation that Kansas City took; bomb craters everywhere throughout the city. We almost ruled out going there as the place was so devastated. We memorized it anyway and still put it down as our destination.

I saw Quade look down at his watch and yawn. He told us it was already one-thirty and said he needed to make sure things were ready for our trip. I agreed with him and got up to leave. Axel promised to stay on it and to keep us posted on our trip. He seemed to want to be going with us, but he had not given an indication that he was. Quade, Sterling and I made it slowly to the elevator. Quade went his way and told us he would see us in half an hour. Making it to our boxcar, I saw everyone getting things ready. I was not looking forward to leaving that place.

We were ready to move out just after two o'clock. I felt the cold air hitting me in the face as I stood out on the front catwalk of Lincoln's engine. Eric had not been allowed to drive this time for some reason and I had not seen him anywhere when we left. We were bringing along just our boxcar and I saw they were bringing along two of theirs. I had made sure we were all ready and on board before giving the green light to leave. Looking around, I could not see much of anything past the tracks that the train's headlight illuminated. We quickly picked up speed.

I heard some small boisterous discussion and saw the front door of the engine was opened. I went there and looked inside of the room that was below and to the front of the cabin. I saw Fredrick and Ray there playing dominos on a small card table in the middle of the room. A lantern swung overhead as the two looked over their hands. I smelled a small bit of sweat smoke from Fredrick's cigar escape past me through the door.

"Morning sir," Fredrick said as I came inside and pushed the door mostly closed again. "We ready for anything that comes along in front of us. You just say the word."

"No, this looks like a great way to start the morning," I told him.

"Coffee be ready in a minute," he said. "We stashed a kettle and a burner up here a while back so we has some on these long journeys." He pointed behind Ray to where a small one-place burner was plugged in to a wall socket.

"Lincoln will tan us if he knew we had it," Ray said. "He doesn't like anyone using up power without his saying so."

"I like it when Eric drives us places," Fredrick put in. "He ain't so noisy about stuff."

"Lincoln always gets us where were going though, that's for sure," Ray said in Lincoln's defense. "I like Eric too, but Lincoln, ain't so bad."

"Yeah, that's cause he's nice to you," Fredrick told him. "I think he just don't like no black people."

"You're crazy," Ray said. "You just mad because there ain't too many of you left."

"That's right, I's rare in this cowboy plains country," Fredrick said. "Now you go down to Alabama and all, and yo white ass will be working in some black man's house washin' dishes."

"I don't wash no dishes," Ray told him slamming the double five dominos down on the table. "Ten for the good guy." He wrote the score down on a piece of paper attached to a clipboard.

"You do dishes and be callin' some large African 'master' if we was in my neck of da woods," Fredrick told him and slammed down the blank five domino. "Ten for yo master." Ray wrote down the score with a frown and looked back at his hand of dominoes.

"Well boys, I think I better get top side and see what's going on up there," I told them.

"You come on down if you need to get away from all the noise up there," Fredrick told me. "Coffee's always hot."

"I appreciate that," I said and walked out the door and up the stairs to the middle of the cabin with a smile.

I saw Jake still moving things around on the table at the back. A huge radio hung above the table and wires seemed to go everywhere around it. The chair bolted to the floor in front of it was the perfect spot for Jake, I thought, and I gave him a thumbs-up as he turned to look at me.

"What kind of weather are we looking forward to today?" I asked him.

"Clouds are moving out," he told me, holding one of the ear pieces to his headphones off of one ear. "Not much happening with movement from far off, Jadee said. Looks like it could heat up a bit around noon."

"Okay, how's this looking?" I asked and pointed to the radio.

"I think I have everything I need right here," he said, pulling some wire out of a port. "I just need a little practice on what station reads what. I'll get it figured out before we need them."

"Good job," I told him. "Sounds like you're keeping up pretty good."

"I'll make you proud someday," he said with a smile.

"Sorry if I haven't said it already," I told him. "I am very proud of what you've been doing with all of this. You're keeping us on target and we couldn't do this without you." He looked at me seriously and with something else. I patted him on the shoulder and turned to see what else the cabin was doing.

"I spent some time on that map of Axel's and found a pretty good route," George told me. "We'll be heading into the town from the west side. The college is on the southwest side and it looks like we can circle outside of town and get to it easily on horseback. We will have to travel a bit more this time on horseback as I have us stopping a little before we get there."

"Just the way I like it. Sounds like we are settling into a style," I told him. "Did you see the radar NASA sent us?"

"Yeah, I looked at some of it," he said. "I couldn't make much out of it."

"I kind of felt the same way," I told him.

"Not much left of Kansas City," Quade said from the window.

"I saw that," George told him. "Not sure I'd want to see much more of the world with that thing if it all looks like that."

"With the way I heard it going, I'm pretty sure it does," Quade said.

"How long before we get to where we're stopping?" I asked Lincoln who was sitting where I was used to seeing George.

"Three hours at the most," he said. "I think we are up to speed now, but we may have to slow down around some of the small towns ahead." I nodded.

"Pretty weird not seeing you at the helm," I told George.

"It's nice actually, kicking back as someone else takes on that responsibility," he said. I started to say something. "I know you've offered. It's just on our train it seems that's my duty. Here, it's just nice to watch." I think I understood that.

We all sat in silence then and I thought over what lay ahead. We had planned to visit three cities, all of which were a mystery. I knew we would do well moving through them and finding Kevin if he was there. I tried to hope we would find him at the first stop, but I knew that was not very likely.

"Did you get everything going for the feast tonight?" Davina asked Teal.

"Yeah, I think it's going to be a good one," she said. "I saw Doug and Sara already out getting the coals in the pit for the pig. They always start early like this. The meat turns out so good. They have a special sauce they put in it. They won't tell anyone."

"Sounds awesome," Davina said.

"You all will have to come to our next one," she said. "There is so much meat and vegetables and everything else you can think of. Steve's wife, Suzie makes some great pies. Lucky's provides the beer. Everyone waits for this time of year around here." It sounded like a large family and it was amazing to watch her talk about it as we traveled on.

I listened to Jake figuring out the radio and felt the soft air flow that entered and then left the cabin through the opened windows. The swaying of the train was hypnotic and my wife's hand in mine was a comfort. I heard George go outside and knew he was going there to smoke his pipe. (I kind of missed its smell circling around the cabin.) I heard the two downstairs playing dominos and carrying on in the usual way. I was shaken a bit when I woke up and found the train slowing. I had not slept so much in months.

"I think we are here," Davina told me. I looked over and saw Teal also gently waking Quade. I did not feel so bad.

"How far out are we from the city?" I asked.

"Four miles," George told me.

"I radioed Chris and Laura," Davina told me. "The horses should be ready."

"Okay, sounds like we should be moving out," I said, as the train stopped.

Ducking down a little, I looked out the front window at the eastern horizon. A small glow was there that said the light of day was not far off. Reds and a beautiful green played with the clouds there and I felt lifted for some reason.

We silently made our way to the ground. I saw the ramps for the boxcars were already lowered. I hurried to ours and found Margie had made a small breakfast of eggs. She invited everyone to join in and we all did. I went for the coffee first and then took one of the plates from the nearby table.

Looking outside, I saw we had parked beside the interstate where a tall hill blocked our view south. North spread out flatly before me as I gazed there and looked for anything moving. Cattle filled the hills there. A few morning birds got back to singing as the beast pulling into their territory showed itself to be harmless. The clouds grew brighter and I hurriedly finished my plate. With many thanks, the others did as well and quickly found their way to their horses.

I led mine to the ground and gave him several long strokes under his mane. He leaned into me a little and I continued for a bit. I checked my saddle and then looked at what I carried. I looked at the rifle in the scabbard on my horse's neck and found it ready to go. Checking the AK47 under my arm, I found it ready as well. With little else to do, I climbed into the saddle.

"Do you have Jadee online?" I asked Jake.

"I have for a while now," he told me. "Looks like five minutes and she'll be in range. Looks like she'll be able to stay with us for a while on this one."

"That will be nice," I told him. "Let's head up to the top of the hill there and see what we can see of the city from there."

We rode up the small hill and left the train behind. We could not see much in the growing light and I was torn as to whether or not to be happy about that. I did not see lights or plumes of smoke which helped me a little in my hope at finding the place desolate. I was not sure, however, if a camp of well-armed men were just over the next rise. I pulled out my binoculars and had another look.

I could only see the tops of far-off buildings. Tall trees did not help my survey and I put the eyepiece away with a little disappointment. Looking around, I saw everyone watching me.

"Can't see a thing, really," I told them. "The city's too far-off from here."

"Should we walk in a little and see?" George asked.

"I think we are far enough out not to be seen," I told him. "We should be able to ride in a little. I think that road there at the bottom of the hill looks like a good way to follow." Everyone looked at the road that went straight south.

"Fredrick and Ray, I need you guys to hold a position here," Quade said. "Spread out a little on that hill over there and use the train as a fallback. Keep an eye on everything around here. We should be heading in that way and if we need some backup I'll shoot the flair."

"Yes boss," Fredrick said and the two of them moved off to a nearby hill that overlooked the way we would be using to head into town.

"With any luck that road will take us right to the college," Chris said from beside me.

I pulled out the atlas and gave it a look. I found the road I thought we were pointing at and I saw it curved and headed into town about a mile south of the highway we were next to. It looked like it would get us to a spot that would give us the best options on how to approach the college. I nodded my head as I closed the atlas and put it away.

"I think we wait some to hear from Jadee and then use this road to get us closer." I told everyone. We did not have to wait long for Jadee.

"Looks like she has the town up on the screens," Jake said. We all looked at him as he listened. "She's saying the college looks a bit war-torn." He looked up with some alarm. "She said it's looking mostly destroyed. There's two planes crashed in the football stadium." He talked to her and told her we were copying her. He looked up again. "The place is bombed out she's saying. Trucks and all kinds of military vehicles are totaled. It looks like a barricade was put up and that it got taken out." It reminded me of some of the war I had experienced.

"What about the rest of the town?" Quade asked him. Jake asked Jadee.

"Pretty much the same," Jake told us, and you could tell he was repeating her words. "The airfield is overgrown and the buildings there seem to have been burned. Some other buildings are standing around town, but they are looking pretty bad. Everything is basically trashed. Wait! I see a large set of buildings. Looks like a.... yeah, it's a hospital. There's a helicopter landing pad on top."

"Where's that at?" I asked. He asked Jadee.

"East of town," he looked at me and said. I wished for an atlas that would have the breakdown of these large cities.

"Has she seen any sign of movement?" I asked. "Anything moving out there?"

"She's saying no," Jake told me.

"Okay, let's spread out a bit and move down that road there a bit," I said. "Code word is 'plumber' and the response is 'copper'. Plumber." Everyone responded with 'copper'. "Let's ride over to Fredrick and Ray and let them know."

We did that and found them in great spots, looking down over the tree-filled city far-off. They gave me a smile as we rode off down to the road. I looked behind me and saw our party consisted of Quade and Teal who rode behind Davina and I with Jake at our side. Chris, Laura, Shay and Sterling rode behind them, with George and Margie bringing up the tail. I turned back around and as we walked along the road, my mind raced.

It was a paved road, but a secluded one. A few houses were along the way just up ahead and I knew we would soon be surrounded by them. Nothing seemed out of place as we rode on.

The first few houses we came to were boarded up and well-graffiti. It looked like they had once been nice homes on a few acres of ground without buildings that housed all things recreational. Bullet holes covered the homes, though and the boards that were trying to keep out I know not what. Several of them were burned to the ground. We could not tell how recent these things had happened, though there was quite a bit of overgrowth in the driveways and the once well maintained lawns. We rode on.

The homes did not get any better as we neared the curve in the road we were on. The structures got closer together and the land they possessed grew smaller. A few brick houses still stood, though some of their walls had fallen and we could see directly into living rooms or kitchens. It was here we started seeing cars turned sideways on the road and trucks pushed together and acting as some form of road block. It was easy to walk around and leave behind, though the images I still carry with me.

We walked through the ravished neighborhood and finally turned toward the city. We immediately came to a T and saw a gas station on the corner. I say gas station, but it was barely recognizable as such. The cover over the pumps had been torn off and only a small portion of the posts remained. The pumps were smashed and lay in the middle of the street. The building itself was only a little less deformed.

"Looks like the war came through here pretty good," I heard Chris say.

The building had no windows left in it and most of their frames lay hanging inside. I could see the shelves where aisles of snacks would have been sold. They were pushed all in one corner in the back along the cooler. The counter that was in the middle of the store was surprisingly mostly still intact.

"I wonder if they have any sodas left," Chris said.

"Some chocolate would be nice," Teal said. "Maybe they have some lottery tickets." I saw Quade smile at her.

"Doesn't look like much of anything is left around here," Sterling said. "Is Jadee seeing anything?"

"She is still looking over the college," Jake said. "Neil is helping her look around too. They haven't seen any movement."

"Is she saying anything about the college?" I asked him.

"No, they are just amazed at how much rubble is there," Jake said.

"Okay, well let's get moving," I told everyone. "This road hooks up to another one a block ahead. I say we swing by the college and then have a look at the hospital." It sounded easy.

We went straight through the intersection and I could see we were entering another neighborhood. I hoped to see something different than the doomsday structures we had seen so far. It was not to be as the houses there were mostly burned and only part of walls or brick chimneys remained.

I tried to get a hint as to what had happened there. Fighting had obviously been intense in the area as the trees there were mostly broken off and suckers were growing from broken off trunks everywhere. I saw a few military vehicles burned and riddled with bullets. Most of the vehicles there, however, were civilian kinds. I looked harder, but could not see any method to what went on.

"Can Jadee see us moving?" I asked Jake.

"She can see the train and she did see us once," Jake told me. "It's still not light enough for a clear view yet."

"That's far enough, damn you!" I heard from just behind us to our left. I heard movement then to our right.

"We aren't here to cause any trouble," I said aloud. "We're passing through and just seeing what we can scavenge along the way. If this is your area then we'll go another way." I could not see who I was speaking to.

"You saw the signs," I heard a man yell from our right. "I seen ya talking and pointing."

"What signs" I asked. "We aren't from around here and we don't know what to look for."

"Where you all come from?" a nasty female voice growled.

"We come from the north," I lied. "We heard there was a town of military supplies down this way. We figured we'd come check it out."

"Who told you that crock?" the man to our left asked. I turned and tried to see if I could see him. "You just hold still there or we'll cut you down before you can say cold ass winter."

"I just want to see who I'm talking to," I said. "I don't figure we're worth wasting whatever shells you have left."

"We got plenty," the woman yelled.

"We'll all walk out of here if you're up for being reasonable," I said. "Or maybe we all just start blasting holes in everything in sight." I looked around, but still didn't see anyone.

"You'll die mister," the man to our right said.

"Maybe," I said. "But, you better aim well because I already lost a damn good horse the other day and I ain't seeing any around here to replace him."

"You brave for someone in the middle of an ambush," the man to our left said.

"I just ain't up for all the talking," I pushed. "So are we riding on or are we still deciding?"

"I asked you who sent you," the man said again.

"And I said we aren't from around here," I said. "Now we're cold and tired from riding all day yesterday. I got up early and didn't have any coffee. Anyone around here got any food they want to trade?"

"Yeah, we got some stuff," the man to our right said.

"But, we got the drop on em', Cuz," the man to our left said.

"Jadee seeing anything?" I asked Jake softly.

"She can't see where we are," he said. "Too many shadows."

"Tradin's better than dyin'," I said to the hidden assailants. "We're just looking to ride on, unless you have some fresh coffee."

I looked around and saw that we were basically on the weed choked lawn of a burned-down two story house. Several cars were in the street to our left. Logs from broken trees were littered about. Several bomb craters were close by. A pile of rubble lined the street in front of us. It seemed with a coordinated move we could all be in cover with a single motion. These people had planned a poor ambush.

"We can't let you ride that way," the man to our right said.

"Screw that, Cuz, we got 'em dead to rights."

"Turn and ride back the way you came," the man to our right said.

I turned my horse and looked back down the street. I tried to look nonchalantly at where the unreasonable voice was coming from, but I could not tell. There were just too many places he could be hiding.

"Stop right there!" the woman yelled. "We ain't said you could go." I put my hand to my radio.

"If anyone sees a shot take it," I said under my breath. "As soon as that happens everyone jump for cover."

I looked at where the voice was coming from and I saw Chris doing the same thing. Quade was turning his horse around just so as to be able to draw a better line on that side and to move a little closer to a car that was by him and Teal. I moved my horse in front of Davina's.

"Right there," Sterling said and lifting his gun, he shot at something.

We all let loose then and laid down a fire that was un-survivable to anyone that was not behind bulletproof cover. I made sure some of the firing was going left. I swung my horse quickly to the right where Davina was, which was close to a tall, wide log in one of the bomb craters. I did not hear a shot coming at us at all as I saw everyone finding something to hide behind. Our horses ran in different directions, but we made it into the crater as we jumped from the saddle. It seemed we had announced our arrival.

"Sterling, did you get one?" I yelled.

"Yeah, I saw some splatter," he yelled back. "Got him in the throat I think."

"You bastards," I heard the woman saying between sobs. She must have fired as I heard some coming from her basic direction.

"You had the choice," I yelled.

I heard firing some more then and it was not too far away. The aim was not at anyone in particular and I did not hear it ricochet off anything. I did not want to take the chance at her seeing someone and getting a clean shot off, however, so I did not look around to well..

I moved from my cover and ran farther down the street. I stopped behind a car there and saw Quade had the same thought, pulling up behind me. I pointed for him to circle around and outflank the man on our right and pointed to him that I would circle around and take out the woman on our left.

"Be careful," he said. "There may be more of them that kept quiet." I nodded and ran to the rubble of the nearby house.

I picked my way through the rubble of the pushed-over house and saw that a semi-truck had tried to drive right through it. (The truck had fallen into the basement.) I made it to the alleyway behind the house and saw it was blocked off several times with debris of various sorts. I continued through the alley and made it to the back of the house on the next street over. These were in better shape, but still not totally unharmed. I tried to communicate what I was doing with the rest of the group.

I heard more firing as I made it down the next street. I slowed as I got to where I heard the firing coming from. I could tell the woman was using an M16 and listened intently to see if I could get a more precise angle on her. I figured I had it and moved on down the street. Maneuvering in among some rubble, I kept out of site and moved to be able to see where I thought she would be close. Peeking around some torn piece of plywood I saw her there, looking over a dead man on the ground where she squatted.

I watched what she did and readied myself to fire. If she made another attempt to fire on us I would blast her away. She only sat and whimpered over the dead man and took quick looks back where we had been ambushed. Moving with some care to some thicker cover, I moved behind something that would stop a bullet. I peeked out again with my rifle well-aimed.

"Drop that rifle!" I yelled at her.

The woman stood in utter fear and aimed the rifle in my direction. I could see she did not see where I was, but panned around in fright. She shouldered the rifle and took aim at something close to where I had just moved from.

"I see you, you damn bastard," she said and fired. I dropped her before she got off three shots.

I stayed where I was and radioed that I had gotten her. I looked around carefully and moved my head slowly as I did. I was in some great cover all around, but I did not know the terrain. I knew I could easily be in someone's sites.

"I got the man," I heard Quade say. "He gave up."

"Guard from cover," I told him. "He may not be alone."

"Copy that," he said. "He said it was just the three of them. I'm good where I'm at for a few, though."

"Everyone else check in," I said. "Anyone see anything?" Everyone said they did not.

"I'm headed your way," I told Quade.

I moved out of my spot, but kept low and looked around at everything I could think of. I did want to be moving safely, but I also knew that our gunfire could have brought more people heading our way. I got to the house by the street and before I came out I yelled our code. I stepped out with my hands high and immediately saw George aiming at me with a smile.

"Follow me," I told him. Looking, I saw Davina and I saw she was a little upset. "Quade coming to you. Where are you?"

"Greenhouse, west wall on the next street over," he said. "He had taken off. We are about three houses down from where they ambushed us."

I made it there in no time and saw Quade giving the guy instructions. The man had his hands high and was nodding his head in fear with everything Quade said. I yelled to Quade and he waved me over.

"He guarantees there's only the three of them," Quade said.

"What are you protecting down this street then?" I asked the man. He looked at me with pleading eyes. "What is it?"

"It's just us three," he said.

"We better find our horses and get out of here," I told Quade.

"I agree," he said. I grabbed at my radio.

"Set a perimeter and find the horses," I said. "We need to move ASAP!" I got acknowledgement back in return.

"Mister, we were serious on only wanting to pass through," Quade told him.

"I know," he said. "I was going to let you go. I promise, I was."

"I think I saw that," I told him. "And really we are not here for whatever you have down the street there."

"Maybe he can tell us something about the college," George said.

"The college?' the man asked in wonder. "It's been destroyed ever since I've been here."

"How long is that?" I asked him.

"A few years," he said. "There are some damn mean dog packs down there. We eat them sometimes when we can find a few stragglers. Don't get them riled up though. The place is teaming with them. If they get your scent there's no getting far enough away."

"What part of the college are they in?" Quade asked him.

"All over it," he said. "There's some big, frigin,' alpha males there fighting over territory. I've seen 'em. Did you get Aurora?"

"She didn't give me a choice," I told him. I saw the man smile. "What's with the happy face?"

"She's been needing to go for some time," he said.

"Is there another part of your group headed our way?" I asked him.

"No," he said flatly but we could all tell he was lying.

"We should take him for leverage in case we run into some more of them," Quade said. I agreed with him.

"And maybe we send you in first to the college to test out that story of yours," I told the man.

Coming over to him, I handcuffed the man's hands behind him. I led him off as Quade guarded our retreat. George led the way and we were soon back where we had been ambushed. I saw several of our horses under the care of Laura.

"We can't find Shay's horse," Davina told me. "George's, we think, went back to the train."

"I see Shay's," Chris yelled from a pile of rubble. "I'll go get it."

"Stay inside the perimeter," I told him. "We'll gather up and send out a rider under cover."

"It's that way there," Chris pointed.

"Okay, we'll head that way," I told him, seeing it was the way we had come from.

Shay's horse was a little skittish as we neared. It tried eating some grass nervously as we approached, but walked away some as Shay walked up to her. Shay kept trying and finally got within grasp of the reins. With a lunge she grabbed them and fought through a few bucks to calm her down.

"What are we going to do about George's horse?" Chris asked.

"Fredrick just said he saw your horse headed their way," Quade told him. "Looks like you're on foot."

"I guess so," George said. "I can walk Smiley here and use him as a shield if we run into trouble."

"Did they hear the firing?" I asked, though I was sure I knew the answer.

"Yeah, they were heading in actually," Quade said.

"Well, let's get moving south," I said. "We should circle back and then head down."

"Please don't get us too close to the college," the man George pushed in front of him said. "We none will survive it."

"You should be a bit more optimistic," George told him.

We pulled back west out of town and made our way south along some farmer's fields. None of the farm structures were still standing and by the piles we saw, there used to be quite a few of them. We stayed in as much cover as the hills would provide. As we got to where we could easily see the college, we pulled up.

"That Strip Map radar stuff doesn't do the real thing justice," Teal said and those of us who had seen it agreed.

The campus was in fact huge. It covered at least a square mile. A large, once a tall, stone building had been reduced to piles of rubble. It seemed that some large scooping type vehicle had made a fence around the north half of the college with the remains of some of the buildings. Large sections of old brick were in among the piles that made up the fence, adding to the theme that we had seen all morning. The stadium was half missing and I could see that some of the material was added to make a palisade in part of the fortification that was trying to surround the college. It seemed our view from just down from the grassy hillside was the perfect viewpoint. I could see the sun had made it above the horizon.

"How many people do you have with you down there?" I asked the man we had captured. "What's your name anyways?"

Phillip," he said.

"How many, Phillip?" I asked him.

"It's just me," he said flatly.

"Tear his arms off," Chris said in a medieval voice. We all kind of looked at him and he shrugged.

"Anything from Jadee?" I asked Jake.

"She isn't seeing any movement at all," he told me.

"Did you have her look down the street we were just on?" I asked him.

"Yeah, nothing there either," he said.

"Please just let me go," Phillip said.

"Wait, what is that?" Sterling asked, looking through his binoculars. "It's by the gate kind of thing on the side closest to us. Yeah, it's a big, damn dog. There's a couple of them down there."

I looked myself and saw that Sterling was right. There were five of the dogs sniffing around the base of the large smashed gate. One of the dogs looked around as I watched and led the others off where I lost them from view. I looked over at Phillip.

"One set of dogs don't prove your story," I told him. I looked back down at the college. "We need to get down there."

"Why?" Phillip asked. "There's no military hardware down there that I've ever heard of. If there is there is no getting to it."

"With all of that rubble and smashed up military equipment, that has to mean something of them is left," I told him. I truly had no interest in any hardware or equipment. "And if there are packs of dogs down there scaring everyone off, then there probably hasn't been anyone down there rummaging through it."

"How about with a car?" Chris asked. We all looked at him. "I'm thinking zombie-style here. If we go down there in a car or a truck then no dog can get at us. We drive up to the door and walk inside. I've seen a ton of trucks. Maybe we try a few of them."

It sounded like a solid plan if one of the trucks would start. I was not optimistic about that, however. I was not yet convinced that Phillip was totally up front with us either, but I was leaning his way. A car would be nice and if trouble presented itself we could get out of there quickly. It would help to be able to drive in slowly and have a look from something that could get us out of there fast. Trouble was, not everywhere had vehicles full of fuel sitting around and most likely none of them would start with their bad gas and dead batteries. I was not sure about push starting anything, but maybe this guy had an idea just where one might be.

"You have gas around this town?" Quade asked.

"Not since the war, mister," Phillip said kind of sarcastically. "Where are you guys from?"

"That doesn't really matter, I guess," I told him. "Looks like you just drew the short straw. We need to see inside that college. You're going with me down to have a quick look. If you can find a safer way for us to do that, then all the better."

"What, no!" Phillip said and started to stand up. "You have to believe me! I've seen people torn apart by those dogs. There's no way..."

"Wait, hold up!" Jake yelled, standing up and pushing the earpiece of his headset harder onto his ear. "April's calling in! She's saying we have to get out of here, now!"

CHAPTER 22

We all crawled back over the hill, staying low until we were far enough below the crest. Our horses got a little spooked with a full-out rush at them, but in no time we were mostly in the saddle. (Laura rode with Chris and gave George her horse.)

"What is it?" Phillip asked with some fright.

"I can't really get it," Jake said. "There's a lot of noise. Jadee is talking with NASA and April is trying to communicate something."

"We could be running right toward what they are warning us about," I said. "Everyone, form a perimeter. Nothing comes over these hills without us knowing what it is. Jake, get us what we need."

"Yes sir!" he said and turning in the saddle and pulling the radio in front of himself. I watched as he started turning dials.

"Now you," I said pointing at Phillip with my revolver. "You will tell me right this second what is going on in this town, or so help me you will feel all the rounds from this pistol tear through your chest."

"Sir, I don't know what you want," he said, turning so his shoulder was blocking where I was aiming at his chest.

"Where are they coming at us from?" I asked. I saw my group hurrying to the tops of the hills that surrounded the small indent in the landscape we were in.

"Who?" Phillip asked.

"You want to play games with me?" I asked, getting down off my horse and walking over to him. Fear gripped him.

I came up to him quickly, ignoring his pleading eyes. He tried to turn and run, but I was already too close to him for that. I tripped him with a well-placed kick that tangled his two ankles and sent him flying. He landed hard on his chest. I watched as he pulled his face out of the dust.

"Right now, tell me," I told him close to his ear, putting the gun under his chin.

"I don't know," he pleaded. "I promise, I don't know."

"What were you protecting down the street then back there?" I asked.

"My family!" he cried. "I have four children and a wife. We have a small community. We live under the old town square. There are old streets down there. We don't have much food or anything like military stuff you would need. Please don't do anything to us."

"Who else is in town?" I asked, now with a bit more sympathy.

"A few other small groups," he said. "We trade with them sometimes. They wouldn't come after you. No one here is big enough for that."

THE END, AS IT HAPPENS TO THEM

"Hold on!" Jake said. "They found them! I think April is saying they found them!"

"Where are they coming from?" I asked, still holding the back of Phillips neck.

"No, I think they are saying they found where Tara and Olivia are!" Jake said. I dropped the man's head and rushed over to Jake.

"Somewhere here?" I asked.

"No they are getting a signal," he said. "Something April and Tara had been working on before. Sounds like she's talking about a Morse Code kind of thing. NASA is trying to track where it's coming from."

"Somewhere close to us?" I asked.

"It doesn't sound like they know yet," Jake said. The others must have heard as they all came down to Jake. "No, they know it's not around here."

"Can they respond and tell her to ask?" Teal said.

"I don't think they should do that yet," I said. "We don't know what the situation is. It may alert whoever might be with her."

"That's true," she said.

"What exactly is the message saying?" I asked Jake.

"They just got a read on it," Jake said. He looked straight at me. "It's in Cheyenne."

"Wyoming?" Quade asked.

"Yeah, some VA hospital," Jake told him.

"Could it be looped from there, sent from somewhere else?" Chris asked.

Looking back, to see how our prisoner was doing, I saw him on his feet and almost to the top of the hill. He was walking stealthily and looking back over his shoulder. I shook my head to him as a warning, but he took off running. I ran to my horse and jumped into the saddle.

"Let's mount up and get back to the train," I yelled. "I'll get this guy and let him go."

My horse jumped into a full run under me and flew up the small hill. I topped it with some trepidation. I saw our prisoner easily, headed at a full run with hands still cuffed behind his back. He would make it to some shrubs I saw, long before I could catch him.

"I'll let you go if you come back! I'll give you the key to those cuffs," I yelled. "Turns out we are in the wrong city altogether."

I think I saw him start to slow up before he made it into a small patch of shrubs. He jumped back as soon as he got there however and seemed to want to run back toward me. He fell flat on his face again. Two medium sized dogs jumped on his back, one of them tearing at his neck. The scream that came from him was grotesque. Alarm filled me as several dogs sprung from the foliage close to him and started toward me.

"Everyone, move out!" I yelled as I shouldered my AK47.

I aimed at one dog, particular that seemed to be leading the charge. As I saw him explode in a mass of gore I looked for another target, hoping the sight of their fellow being ripped to shreds would turn their minds. It was not so and I found the next target and pulled the trigger, though the others seemed to care little of the fallen comrade.

It was painfully obvious that one gun was not going to stop the charge as a large pack sprang from the shrubs. I grabbed for the reins and yanked them sideways, turning my horse on a dime. He reared up and jumped down the hill as I held tight and kicked his flanks, asking him for more speed.

"Dogs!" I yelled at everyone looking at me with wonder.

They all turned with one accord and we took off at a run. I did not look back just yet, though with my horse already up to speed, I quickly took the lead. I circled a bit as we came to the top of the hill we had come over on the way there. I chanced a look back and saw that the dogs were easily catching those horses in the rear. I saw at least eight large animals. George was going to be the first one to get caught.

As I thought that, a dog lunged at the heels of the horse George was on, causing it to buck with fright. That caused the horse to slow even more and with that, it turned to try and fend off the attack, bucking as it did so. I was surprised to see George still holding on. My heart pounded with fear for him.

Other dogs were still trying to catch up with the rest of us. My turning singled me out and I saw two dogs give me their full attention. Aiming at them, I saw I hit one, which caused it to stop and bite hard at the wound. I saw the other would soon overtake me. Four more joined the chase from our right. I heard firing start from all different areas of our group.

I circled back to help George and my horse did well in the face of the dog that was barreling down on us. I fired at it, but missed entirely as it jumped at the face of my horse. He reared and barely kept it from being able to latch on. With all four feet back on the ground, my horse pawed wildly as I looked for something to aim at.

Everyone else had stopped and were fighting their own battles. Quade had jumped off his horse and having pulled his pipe off his back, was swinging at a dog attacking the heels of his horse. Chris had taken up a quieter position in the middle of us and was slowly aiming and taking out what dogs he could. Laura was trying the same thing, but she was having a harder time of it. I saw Davina close to my side, laying down a line of fire at several new dogs that approached from our left. I did not have time to see what everyone else was doing.

I waited for my horse's movements to allow a clear shot at the dog attacking front our front. As we landed one more time, I shot and saw the dog flip over backward, trying to pull away from the bullets that ripped apart its shoulders. I found other targets as my horse's movements slowed, it waiting for the dog I had killed to attack again. I aimed carefully at a dog coming close to attacking Quade, but I need not have bothered. Quade was in some circling motion that brought his pipe around and smashed that dog's skull. He continued his fluid movements and swung on as I turned my attention elsewhere.

A cloud of smoke was forming around Margie and was beginning to make it hard to see what to aim at there. Margie was still on her horse and was using her legs to tell the horse what to do as she reloaded and continued her rebuke of the ferocious attack. As I watched, she fired on a large Great Dane and blew him back over the top of the hill where he had been standing. With that the dogs seemed to want to regroup.

They started some long howl that seemed to be a signal that they were to pull back. The attack ended in mid-bite and they pulled out from among us as one. They were not however, smart enough to pull back over the hill and find cover. I held my fire, however, wondering if it would provoke another attack if I killed more of their comrades.

We all pulled together at the top of the hill, our horses all wide-eyed and overly skittish. We circled in close, trying to give everyone a spot to fire from, no one directly behind someone else.

"Looks like we could take out a bunch of them right here," Chris said.

"I don't want to start up another attack," I said.

"They could be waiting for reinforcements," Teal said.

"Yeah, it looked like they were coming out of the woodwork there for a minute," Davina said. One of the dogs let out a long howl and it was picked up by the rest of them.

"That's sounding like a call for reinforcements to me," Laura said.

"Okay, let's move as one back toward the train," I said. "Let's start out at a slow walk and see what they do."

We all turned and walked back the way we had come. The dogs watched us and moved along with us, keeping about twenty feet behind us and off to our sides. It seemed they were not totally done with us. I moved us into a small trot and the dogs matched our pace, some moving in closer and a few venturing close enough to try and push between us a little. It was obvious they were looking for a weaknesses. I saw too they were piling up more on our left side.

"I called Wanda and had her start up the train," Quade told me. "Fredrick and Ray are ready to back us up when we get there." I was not aware that Wanda had come.

"Okay, good thinking," I told him. I knew we were still a little ways away from their help.

"Everyone keep an eye out ahead of us," I said. "It looks like they are trying to turn us." I saw a few times the dogs on our left move over and nip towards the horses running on that side.

"You should have them drop the ramps," Chris told him.

"Already told them that," Quade yelled over to him.

I saw the intersection just ahead where we had seen the burned-out gas station. It felt good seeing it, knowing that the closer we got to the train the more likely it was that we would escape this city unharmed. As we got closer, however, the dogs became more aggressive and split up, some running hard to get ahead of us and others trying hard to turn us back toward the neighborhood.

"On three, let's break formation and kill everything we can on our left," I told everyone. "Make a hole for us to get through that street we came in on."

I could see that all of the dogs from our right had vanished; they were obviously trying to get us to go that way. The ranks of the dogs grew four deep on the left and all of their growls were becoming serious. Just up ahead more dogs were pouring in to fill the street we needed to take out of there. I counted quickly to three and everyone fired all they had.

It was a bloody slaughter to say the least. The falling dogs did not seem to affect the other ravenous ones who were bent on turning us at all costs. Several dogs got trampled and the sounds of their yelps were many. I watched as the line, that held their ground in the middle of the street, fall and broke apart. I felt a little bad for the solid brotherhood of the pack as they all moved aside as we rode on through. Looking back, I saw them standing around their fallen fellows and watching us go.

"That could have gone worse," Jake said as we continued to run.

"I'll go with that," I told him and felt the relief in my chest.

"I guess that Phillip guy was right," Sterling said. "I wonder if he'll ever get those cuffs off." I shrugged and rode on.

We made it back to the train without any further trouble. I saw the ramp to our boxcar and slowed as I got close to it. I made it inside and quickly tied my horse to the rail of the pins. I saw all of the others doing similarly.

"Let's get up front and see what exactly going on," I told Jake.

The two of us hurried down the ramp and I did not pay attention to who followed, though, I kept a sharp eye out for any movement around us. Getting to the cabin, I saw Wanda talking into the headphone mic. She tried a smile as we came in, but I was in too serious a mood to try and return it.

"I need to know exactly what's going on," I told her firmly, but as politely as I could muster. "Are they sure it's Tara?"

"Yes, they said April was doing some Morse Code bit with her before all of this happened," she told me. "They were playing some game together on y'all's system. Tara is using that same set of codes to try and reach April now."

"We're ready to move out," I heard Quade tell somebody. I heard Lincoln reply and with a nod from me, the train jerked to life.

"And they said Cheyenne?" I asked "Are they sure?"

"It sounds like they are," Wanda said. "NASA keeps confirming it."

"Okay, where's George?" I asked. I saw George move through the crowd of people that were in the cabin. "I'll need the most direct route there from here, as soon as you can get it to me."

"I'm on it," he told me and melted back into the crowd.

"Is there anything else you can tell me?" I asked Wanda.

"No, but there's a lot going on right now," she said.

"What do you mean?" I asked her.

"I think some guy named McQueen is on his way back from somewhere and wants to head that way," she told me. "Sounds like he is pretty far out, though and couldn't get there until tonight, late."

"I think we can beat that time," I said. "George, I need a time frame." I said loudly.

"Looks like we are going to have to go basically straight back the way we came," George said from somewhere in the cabin. "We'll go straight through these guys' town and head back a little bit. We can go north from there and save a little time."

"Map that for me and give me a time will ya?" I asked.

"I will," he said.

"We can pick up our train on the way through then," George said across the cabin.

"We don't mind driving the whole way," Quade told me.

"Yeah, we're in this now," Teal added her support.

"I just mean if we're headed straight through it may be nice to pick up the train," George told them. "It will be a short pit stop if we fly by. Not that you all can't come, I think it would be best to bring them both."

"I think I wouldn't mind taking a quick look at what we're headed for too," I said. "That radar may not be the greatest, but a quick look couldn't hurt. If we run upstairs when we get there that should give you enough time to warm her up, George."

"We could just pull it along with this rig," Lincoln said. "It won't cost you any fuel that way."

"I think that sounds like a fine idea," George told him.

"I'll have them get it into position for a quick snag," Quade told me and went out to the rear catwalk.

I had not paid attention to where we were headed when we left Hayes. I did notice that we were still headed south and I mentioned that to Lincoln. He told me that there was a loop just ahead that would send us back home. He promised it was quicker that way.

"They're wondering if they should go," Wanda looked back and told me.

"Who?" I asked her.

"A guy named Dan and Vince," she told me. "Sounds like they are a lot closer."

"May I talk with them?" I asked. Wanda nodded with some thanksgiving and moved out of the chair.

I sat down and looked around. I still was not sure what buttons to push, though I had been over it myself a few times. I looked up at Wanda in some frustration and she smiled warmly and flipped several different switches.

"Come in, come in," I said to the mic attached to the headphones.

"This is Axel go ahead," I heard.

"Hey Axel, I was wanting to talk to our compound," I told him.

"Anything I can do?" he asked.

"No, I just heard they are thinking of trying the trip themselves," I told him. "I'm wanting to talk them out of it."

"I think it got brought up, but I'm not sure they're really considering it," he told me. "I can patch you through from here if you want."

"I would like that," I told him.

"Hold on."

"Hey Axel?"

"Yeah, I'm still here."

"Are you able to see what it looks like with that Strip Map Radar?"

"Yeah, we are looking at Cheyenne now," he said with something in his voice. "It looks virtually untouched."

"Anything else?" I asked him.

"No, it's just that the Air Force is close by and Neil is saying there could be a lot of places Kevin could be up in that area. We're trying to look at a lot of them."

"Okay, well I appreciate what you're doing," I told him.

"No trouble," he said softly. "I'll patch you through."

I heard a variety of static sounds and a winding sound that started to get high-pitched. Several clicks later, I heard static again. I waited for some operator to ask me where I needed to go and remembered when I was a kid I used to call them and asked for the time in China.

"Hello?" I heard April asked.

"Yeah, I'm here," I told her. "I hear you all found them."

"We did dad, well Tara at least," she said. "I still hope they're together."

"They should be," I said. "Are you guys looking over the place?"

"Yeah, we have been for some time now. There's nothing really out of place besides the normal gone-through look."

"What do you mean?"

"I just mean the VA Hospital looks a little deserted and overgrown. There are cars still in parking spaces all over, but most with their windows all broken out and the like. No one seems to be around there anywhere. Something ran into it on the north side a little and broke a part of the wall there. It really does look all pretty grown over, though."

"Let's hope that stays the case. I heard some of you are thinking of trying to go?"

"Jadee is kind of losing it," she said a little quietly. "She thinks we can make it in an hour or so."

"If you guys run into any trouble then that definitely won't be the case," I told her. "We don't want to have to worry about finding you guys as well. I'm sure the highway there is not just straight and clear."

"I know, and I think we have her talked into letting you guys handle it. She's a little better now that you all are headed that way."

"I think we have the safest way and if I'm right, it should be about five hours or so," I told her and as I said it, it sounded like a lot. "We are rushing there now. I think we should handle it."

"I think that's the consensus here too," she told me. "I can get them in here if you want."

"No, I was just making sure we were all on the same page. How's NASA helping out?"

"It sounds like McQueen is wanting to be involved," she said. "I'm not sure Mack is quite pushing for that, though. Doesn't sound like the two get along."

"I want my hands on Kevin's throat before they can get to him," I told her.

"I don't blame you for that," she said. I knew my hands would only be there long enough to squeeze the life from him. Well, maybe I would revive him a few times and let others squeeze too.

"Is the message you're getting from Tara saying anything specific?" I asked her.

"No, it was just a game we made up," she told me. "We were trying to get better at Morse Code so she would go down in the Armory and we would play an alphabet game. I know it's her."

"That's okay, I'm sure you do," I told her. "I was just wondering if she told you anything about what was going on."

"No, not yet," she said. "I was wondering if we should write back. Everyone seems to think we shouldn't."

"It might alert Kevin if we do," I told her.

"I know," she said sadly.

"Maybe once we're outside the building up there we can send back a message and see what she has going on," I told her. "Maybe she can help us with a way in."

"I think that sounds great!" she said. "And if Kevin finds out it will be too late for him to get away."

"Agreed," I told her.

"Neil's coming in here," she said.

"Cool, I wouldn't mind talking to him," I said.

"Here he is," she said. "Be really careful, dad."

"I will," I told her.

"Hey Buddy, how you holding up?" I heard Neil's voice ask solemnly.

"I think we're doing okay," I told him. "How's it going there?"

"Not as crappy as you have it, I'm sure," he said.

"It's nothing really," I said. "I'm just glad to finally be heading in the right direction."

"Yeah, I can't wait till you get there," he said. "How long?"

"Don't tell Jadee, but something like five or six hours," I said.

"At least you're heading there, brother," he said.

"Does the signal sound legit?" I asked him.

"You think it may be a decoy?" he asked.

"It happened right after they found out we were working with someone else," I said.

"Think they're pulling you off the scent?"

"Could be, but the way we were headed didn't seem right anyway. At least this one makes more sense and April sounds convinced."

"April said the code had to come from Tara. She said it is exactly what they've been working on."

"Okay, I believe it's from her. Maybe I have to believe it's from her."

"Don't lose hope. This is the one and you'll bring them home."

"Thanks brother. I want you to start thinking of someway safe to answer her signal."

"It could alert Kevin," he said quickly.

"She must have known that," I told him. "Either she's desperate because something serious is happening or somethings changed. I know it could be other stuff, but when we get close we should have something to send back."

"Okay, I'll put some thought into," he said. "I'll get with April and see what Tara might recognize that Kevin won't."

"Good idea," I told him.

"I can't wait to see you guys home safe," he told me. "Be careful."

"We're stopping by this town and picking up our train along the way," I told him. "Then we're barreling there as fast as we can."

"I'll keep an eye on the hospital to see if there are any movements," he promised. "I'm sorry, but I haven't seen anything yet that will tell us if anyone's there. There's some damage to the building, but it all looks old."

"I know you'll do your best," I told him. "We'll call when we get close."

"See ya Buddy," Neil said.

"See ya," I said and took the headphones off. I handed them to Wanda.

"Any news?" George asked and everyone looked at me.

"No, just more of the same," I said. "They are watching the area. Neil is looking into the signal to make sure it's genuine."

"Looks like maybe we could get there in five hours," George said. "It will depend a lot on the rails being lined up and clear. We will lose a tiny bit of time picking up our train."

"I think that will be minimal," Quade said. "It will be ready to go."

"We should only need a quick glance at the radar images to get a good idea of the city," I said.

"Looks like we are ready on our end then," George said. "All's we can do is wait."

I agreed with him and told him so. The cabin seemed to shrink with everyone going quiet. I walked out the backdoor and stood on the catwalk, looking out at the beauty of the Kansas plains. I saw more of the big white, windmills in the far distance. Some of the blades of them were turning and I watched the slow circular motion as long as they were in view. A few herds of cattle dotted the hills and vanished when the grass became the more sparse, coarse type. The warmer wind that had come from somewhere worked to calm me.

I heard the door open and looked to see Davina coming outside. She walked up beside me and leaned over the railing just as I was. We shared a glance and she leaned in to kiss me. I returned it and as she turned to look off the landscape passing by, I kept watching her. She must have felt it as she turned back and furrowed her forehead.

"What is it?" she asked.

"I'm just watching the beautiful scenery," I told her with a smile. She leaned in for another kiss.

"You doing okay?" she asked as we both turned back to the rolling hills.

"Yeah, actually I'm doing okay," I told her. "It feels good to have something to go on. Check in with me later and ask that question if this doesn't turn out to be what it seems like."

"It will," she told me. "Missouri never seemed right."

"I never really felt it either," I told her. "Let's talk about something else."

"What would you like to talk about?"

"How about harvest time back home and Marla's goose casseroles."

"I think I'll be glad to see one of those. Maybe she won't mind if we just look at it."

"I still think I have an overdose," I told her and kind of wanted to change the subject again.

"Looks like our vegetables were doing good, what chance I got to look at them when we were there."

"I wonder if NASA can help with figuring out those systems in the water tanks for you."

"I think I have them almost figured," she said with a hurt look. "I'll be mad if they messed with them while we have been gone."

"I wonder if this is the start of a long relationship with those guys."

"So, they are trying to find a way to come down, right?" she asked.

"Something like that," I said. "I really haven't much cared about what they are thinking about I guess."

"Sorry if I'm interrupting," Quade said. "Looks like home is coming up in about twenty."

"Okay, thanks for the heads up," I told him.

"I love the view out here," he said coming over to where we were.

"So, home must be up northwest there?" I asked, pointing.

"Yeah, a little more west," he said. "The tracks curve a little north of here. I'll leave you all to it."

He walked back inside. We turned back to the landscape and I took my wife's hand. I longed to be done with this and tried to keep my anger at the situation from boiling over. It took a tremendous effort to keep my thoughts from running over.

I checked my weapon and took some time to reload my clips. I tried the mechanisms several times. I felt the strap around my shoulder and did an adjustment that had needed to be done. I looked at everything else and found it all working well. With little thought, I pulled out my butterfly knife and did some long overdue practice on getting it to open and close with the least amount of motion.

Davina took my lead and did all the same things to her gear and armory. She stripped down a little which I appreciated, but which did not help my practicing. I watched her sit and go through everything with meticulous care. I saw she had things there I never knew she carried. I watched with some admiration as she outfitted herself to fully dressed and ready for combat.

I looked then and saw the grain elevators had snuck up on us a bit. They were still several miles away, but coming on fast. I put my knife away and leaned over and kissed my wife. With a smile to her, I wiped my hand down her face. She smiled deeply and I turned and walked back into the cabin, ready again to take on the world.

"Looks like we're right around the corner," Lincoln told me.

"Yeah, I'm ready," I told him. "I think I'm going to head straight upstairs as soon as we get there."

"We'll go with you," Chris said. "I think I'll need to have a look at the city. The topography may come into play and I'd like to know what the highs and lows are."

"No problem," I told him. "Lincoln, do you need any help down here?"

"Maybe just one or two," he said. "I think there will already be hands enough."

"I'll stay here and help," Jake said. "I don't think much up there will matter to me."

"Okay, will that be enough Lincoln?" I asked.

"That will be plenty," he said.

"Ray, you down there?" I heard Quade yell. I saw Ray stick his head through the door that came up through the middle of the cabin.

"Yes boss, we're right here," he said. "Need us out front?"

"No, but we're stopping at town just for a little bit," he told him. "Just stay put and hold down the fort."

"Will do," Ray said and moved his head out of view.

"I'll go with you," Quade said. "I'd like to see the layout myself."

"I'd like to have as many people familiar with the whole area as possible," I told him.

"I'll have a look too," George said. "I'll just take a quick look and come back down. I think I'll ride in the cabin on the way there."

"Me as well," Margie said. "I'll have a look at the map first, though."

"Okay, everyone, but Jake, follow us up," I said. "I want everyone having an eye at what we're walking into. I would like to figure out while we're in front of the radar the best way in and out." Everyone agreed.

I felt us slowing, and it seemed to be significant. I tried not to think of our journey to that place as wasted. We had done what was best at the time and had met some good people in the long run. It was well worth the time spent. I kept myself from the thought that said I hoped that Olivia and Tara would agree.

As the engine came to a stop beside George's Camelback train and cars we all flooded out of the cabin and off the catwalk. We heard music playing from somewhere and Quade said the feast must have already been underway, though it was not quite noon. We walked into the town between the two grain elevators from the other side where there was an exact replica of the one we first came through. It seemed an odd way to see the town. I was turned a little backwards but kept up with Quade.

"Was hoping I'd see you, you bastard!" I heard from our left.

A shot rang out and I jerked around to where I heard the noise, every muscle in my body tense. I saw a small cloud of smoke and looked hard for who in the small crowd I thought could be the shooter. One man stood facing us about a hundred feet away with a snarl on his face.

"They killed my brother and you ain't going to do nothin' about it, you son of a bitch," another man said and pulled his pistol from his hip quicker than I thought possible and fired at Quade.

Gunfire rang out everywhere as the crowd went crazy, some diving to the ground and others looking to see what was happening. A man in a trench coat stepped up beside the man firing at Quade and raised an old Heckler and Koch MP5 machine gun and pulled back the bolt to chamber a round. I am not sure why I did it, but I threw myself onto Quade to knock him out of the way of a sure death. As we landed on the ground I saw my great mistake.

Davina saw in an instant what I was doing. She also saw that I would be throwing myself into the line of fire. Her reaction was as quick as mine. She threw herself in the line of fire for me. I watched as she fell to the ground as the bullets tore at her chest, the vest not helping at all.

Tears ripped from my eyes. I hurled myself off of Quade and scrambled over to her as best as I could. Everything around me melted away and I could see nothing, but my wife struggling to take another breath. Blood came from her mouth. I screamed my agony close to her face and kissed her blood-soaked lips. I saw her tears as she faded, her eyes stuck on me. Her face turned red as she smiled and I felt her hand on my cheek.

"I love you," I told her and I watched her smile and begin to cry. "I love you! I love you!"

I kept telling her as her eyes closed and her head turned to the side. I screamed to the heavens in rage and squeezed her head to my chest. Her body went limp under me and I felt so much pain I wished for a bullet to take my skull apart.

"Shay!" I screamed then for some reason. "Shay!"

I heard the gun battle going on around me then and looked around for Shay. She was kneeling next to me and looked at me with utter sympathy. I could only cry and try to form the words that begged for her to bring Davina back to life. She put down her rifle and came over beside Davina. To my amazement she started doing CPR, smiling at me hopelessly as she did.

"Get back in this fight!" I heard Quade yelling. "Now! Get up right now and fight!"

I turned to see what was going on. Several gunmen were spread out around the town, some behind cover, but most in the middle of the street. Our group was spread out and taking fire. I saw we were trying to return fire, but careful not to hit innocent bystanders. I rose to my feet and looked for the man I saw take down my wife. He had moved over to the side by the porch of the psychic's shop. I walked straight for him.

He did not notice me coming toward him at first. Another gunman did and turned his attention to me. I saved my rage for the one man and kept my step as bullets whizzed past my head and chest. I heard shots coming from our group and heard a scream. The bullets stopped coming in my direction. The battle did not stop, however.

The man I walked for saw me and turned then. He saw me the perfect target and aimed carefully. I walked on and he seemed to get a little nervous. He moved to the side a little, trying to get a smidge more cover before letting go his volley. It took a split second to raise my rifle from under my arm. He jumped a little more to the side and fired, his bullets hitting in the dirt at my feet. I am surprised I noticed them from behind the tears that ran freely down my face.

I pulled the trigger and watch several bullets push his stomach apart. He bent over and grabbed at the pain there, hoping the movement would ease some of the agony. I added to it as I sent more rounds into his right shoulder. He flung himself back and bounced off of the door behind him. He caught himself on all fours and looked at his stomach, trying hard to understand what was happening. As I got close, I emptied my clip as I circled his body. It tore him to shreds. I changed clips and again circled his lifeless body as I screamed at the horror of my loss that I could not get out of my eyes.

I breathed deeply and screamed again as my clip lay empty. I heard the guns firing behind me and turned to see what was going on. I looked at our row of brave fighters, shooting to defend themselves. As I watched, I saw Chris get his left leg, blown clear off, below the knee. He fell and I think I even heard him land with a crash. I am not sure what I thought at this point. I am sure I was numb. The firing went on as Laura jumped down to help Chris, looking desperately to find a way to stop the bleeding. I turned to look and see who shot Chris. I saw a man with a large caliber gun coming through the other gate and taking careful aim at something else. I could only look back at our group and saw Margie planted her front foot and leaning a bit forward, sent a bullet from her musket right through the man's heart. I watched him collapse in a heap.

I remember pulling the clip out of my gun and replacing it with a full one. I aimed several times at armed men and fired, but I am not sure, if I shot any of them. The firing ceased when I saw Allen moving off of his porch at the tattoo shop and finish off a man who was pleading for mercy a short distance from him. His shot to the man's throat was the last one of the battle.

I looked around to see who was hurt, besides the ones I knew of. I was surprised when I saw all of the townspeople had managed to stay out of harm's way. I was surprised to see only eight gunmen on the ground in piles, all quite dead. I looked and saw no one else on our side showing signs of being shot.

Stepping off the porch, I saw Laura had found a tourniquet for Chris's leg. They held each other tightly and Laura tried to give him reassurances. I looked to where Shay was and I could not bring myself to walk there. Tears ran down my face.

CHAPTER 23

I saw Shay still moving and trying to give Davina CPR. Something in me switched on again and I stopped wondering why she would be doing that and ran over to find out. As I got close she yelled for Teal to help her.

"Five pumps, when I tell you," Shay told her. Teal jumped down beside Davina's lifeless body and nodded. "Now." Teal followed the instructions.

"Get Lynn down here, now!" I heard Quade yell to someone.

"Go," I heard Shay say and Teal pumped away. "Let's stay in that rhythm."

I stopped beside Shay and watched her giving Davina mouth-to-mouth. I was desperate to help, but was not sure what to do. I looked on in utter confusion.

"Chris got his leg blown off," I said finally to Shay, for some reason.

"What?" she asked, looking over at where Laura was holding him.

"Laura has a tourniquet on it," I told her flatly.

"I need you to take over here," Shay told me and then bent over to breathe into Davina again. "Right now!"

I bent down and took over the breathing. I think Shay said she would be right back, but I am not sure I remember that right. I just know that I loved the feel of my wife's lips on mine as I breathed air into her lungs.

I tried to concentrate, but I could not. My mind kept going to things we had done together or to her beautiful smile when she pretended to laugh at one of my ill thought-up punch lines. I remembered the time when I asked her to marry me and she had started to cry and I ran to hold her. I remembered the time I had gotten mad at her for driving home on a flat tire.

"I didn't mean to get mad at you," I told her as Teal pumped her chest. "I'm so sorry I did. I didn't mean to." My tears mingled with the blood on her lips as I continued to breathe for her. Teal tried a smile, but I only looked back down at Davina in despair.

I do not remember how long I stayed there breathing for her. It did not seem like long enough as Shay came back and pulled on my shoulder. I remember getting mad at her and brushing her arm away as I bent once more and breathed for my wife. She used some force then and I think I yelled some obscenities at her. I remember then Quade lifting me to my feet and turning me to face him. I do not remember what he told me, but just remember collapsing into his arms as he pulled me in. I much appreciated him doing so.

I watched then as Shay continued to give Davina CPR. I looked at Chris and saw Lynn there working on his leg. Laura was a mess, I could tell, and some woman was holding her as she watched over what was going on there. I turned back to watching the scene at my feet.

"Where's that carrier?" Shay asked.

"It's right here," Quade said. "Hurry!" he yelled at two men coming over.

I saw them carrying a cot and wondered why. They laid it down next to Davina and quickly rolled her to her side. They pushed it under her and lay her back on it. The men lifted her then as Shay and Teal continued CPR. They all moved as one back toward the train yard.

"Where are you taking her?" I asked.

"We need to get her home," Shay told me. "She's fading, but if we get her to our equipment there, then she may hold on for a while."

"That's so far away," I told her as we hurried along.

"I know, but it's worth trying," she said.

"Okay, let's move it then," I told her. Looking back, I saw two men carrying Chris behind us.

We all hurried to where the Camelback train was sitting on the line with the oil tanker and caboose attached behind it. I saw smoke coming from the stack, which meant someone had already started it. George walked out on the catwalk and looked down as we approached.

"We're ready here," he yelled down.

"Let's lay them in the caboose," Shay said. We all moved that way.

We rushed over to the caboose and I helped where I could at getting Davina inside. They laid her in the middle of the floor and continued to work on her. They sat Chris down on one of the beds and put his leg up high under Lynn's instructions.

"Where's my trauma kit?" Lynn asked with some urgency.

"Stan was getting it," one of the men said. "He should be right here."

We waited as Teal and Shay continued to work. Chris seemed in quite a bit of pain and I came and sat beside him. I tried to talk to him and he smiled, but he did not seem to want the company. I knew how he felt.

"Here he comes," Quade said.

A few moments later a man came through the door with a large bag. Lynn hurried to it and quickly grabbed out a large clear, balloon-looking thing and several tubes. Handing it to Shay, I saw her take Davina's pulse.

"I'm getting something faint," Lynn said. "It's not good, but it's something."

I watched Shay shove the tubes down Davina's throat and attach the balloon thing to them. She squeezed and looked over at Lynn. Lynn seemed to be concentrating. She finally looked up at Shay.

"A little better," she told her. "She has broken ribs here and here."

"We need to be moving now!" Shay yelled.

"I'll tell George!" I said and started to run out of the caboose.

"Randy!" Shay said to me in a stern voice. "You need to go get Olivia and Tara."

"No!" I told her. "I'm staying with her!" I pointed to my wife.

"You have to save them," she said softly then. "You are not going to be any good to us here. Don't do this to yourself. You need to get Kevin!"

"I'm getting George moving," I said and left the caboose.

I jumped to the ground and ran toward the engine. Seeing George waiting for a sign, I gave it to him. He nodded and with a thumbs-up, ran back into the cabin. I ran and jumped back onto the caboose. I felt the train start to rumble.

"Go get them, Randy!" Shay told me sternly. "She would want you to."

"Why?" I asked.

"That's who you are," she said. "You're the leader out there and they need you. There's nothing you can do here. I will take care of her."

I knew she was right, but I did not want to admit it. I wanted to be with my wife and never leave her side. I started to think of us together and felt the black pit of where that led open in front of me. I pulled back and looked at Shay. I felt us moving.

"Pulse is steady, but still not great," Lynn said.

I moved beside my wife and bent down to her. I leaned over and rubbed my cheek along hers. It felt warm and I smiled. I grabbed a handful of her hair and wiped it all over my face, smelling her favorite coconut shampoo. Tears flowed onto the strands as I looked at them.

"You can love me more today," I whispered into her ear. Pulling back I stood up. "You okay, son?" I asked, taking a deep breath and looking at Chris.

"Right as rain," he said with a pale, pain-filled grin. "I'll watch over her. You go get that son of a bitch Kevin and bring him home."

I turned then and walked out of the caboose, Quade following behind me. We had not picked up enough speed to make jumping extremely dangerous, but it did not look like an easy dismount was going to be possible. I walked to the end of the ladder close to the ground and saw that Quade took the other side. With a shrug to each other we both jumped. I landed and skidded to a stop. I turned and stood there, watching the caboose move on down the line.

"Time to get moving," Quade said after several moments had passed.

I turned and we took the small sprint back to the grain elevators. We hurried upstairs and saw that Axel and the others were standing at the screens looking at the radar image of Cheyenne. I went there and looked as well, trying to memorize every line where they told me the VA hospital was. I looked over the large city and tried to figure out a good approach to the hospital.

"We're ready to move out when you are," Quade told me.

"I'm ready," I told him. "Do we have the quickest route?"

"George talked to me about it," Eric said from beside me. "We went over it."

"Okay, then I'm ready to move," I told them.

We all hurried down the elevator and I followed Quade as he moved to where the train was waiting. I climbed on board and sat at the window opposite the driver's seat. Eric took up position behind the throttle, and with a nod from Quade, we lurched into motion. He pushed hard on some levers and I heard our wheels grinding. I was sure he would hear about it from Lincoln.

I looked far off and tried not to think of anything, but what lay ahead. I knew I could not do that, but I pushed for it as hard as I could and basically got through the first hour okay. Soon, however, I found nothing worked at keeping myself in check.

"So, anything from NASA?" I asked Jake who was sitting at the radio.

"Jadee reported in and said they were all still watching pretty closely and hadn't found anything odd," he said. "Neil said to tell you the signal has all the criteria of being legit. Sorry, I thought you were sleeping."

"No, I've been admiring the Kansas landscape," I said, feeling a lot calmer for some reason.

"We're in Nebraska now," Quade told me, coming over to stand behind Jake. He looked at Lincoln.

"Yeah, for about twenty minutes now," Lincoln told him. "We'll be turning west here in about thirty minutes. Should be a straight run after that."

"Maybe we should go over some stuff?" Quade asked.

"I think that would be good," I told him. "I think I wouldn't mind a little air first. Mind joining me?"

"Sure," he said, looking at me with a little wonder. He followed me out the back door and we walked along the catwalk to the end. "What's going on?"

"Just thinking about what lies ahead," I told him.

"Yeah, looks like it will be the end of a long road for you guys," he stated plainly and leaned on the rail. I felt it had gotten noticeably colder.

"That's true," I told him. "I've always just wanted for us to be left alone and to survive without everyone having a say in our business."

"I know the feeling."

"It worked for a little bit. We planted and looked ahead to life the way I think it was intended."

"We came out here with the same thoughts. We made a choice to leave rather than stay where trouble was sure to brew."

"Out in Oregon?"

"We helped some people get away from a pretty bad crowd out there and we couldn't stay after that. We had to find a place and so we headed east. We fought a lot along the way. When we got out here and saw it mostly uninhabited, we figured this was the place. I guess we kind of found it mostly unoccupied. There were a few people living in the town and trying to make something of the elevators. We came in and helped them make it what it is today."

"Well, it's pretty great what you've done. A lot of people seem to think of it as home."

"Sure, we settled here and made it home. And I can't see living anywhere else. I love the scenery and the wide-open view as the sun rises. There is nothing better than walking through the plains quail hunting in the early hours of the morning." He seemed to be saying something more.

"I think it's pretty great, Quade," I told him. "I get up early and jog along the river that runs by our compound. It fills a lake a few miles away. It's so still in the morning. There's a pair of foxes that have a den on the far side that no one knows about. Some trees fill a hill and they play in the meadow on the other side. I've sat by a large rock and sketched them several times. It's one of those things that I keep inside and bring around to make myself smile when I need to." I saw Quade looking intently at me.

We stayed quiet then and I felt the wind getting even a little colder. I seemed to feel us getting close to home as we moved through the landscape and me realizing that this could be it. It did something for me, Quade standing by silently and us sharing the view. I am not sure why it breathed life back into me.

"Maybe when this is all over you will never need to have those things stored up inside that you need to draw on to bring you peace," Quade said. "Life will just be what we want from it. That's the dream anyway, I guess."

"No, I think such things can be possible," I told him.

"I think those men today flies in the face of that for me," he told me, running his fingers through his hair.

"It's exactly the opposite," I told him. "It's true, if we let it, the world pushes in and ruins who we are and everything we've built. It steals our lives and pulls us down for sure. But, we can't let it. Times like these are not the norm. If they are, then we've chosen wrong and should move on until we find something that isn't. I admire what you have here, you being part of this new world. Me, I've tried to crawl under a rock and wall people out. I've changed my mind on that in these last several days. I long for us to be more open like you all are. You are the 'them' I forgot about when I gave up on this world and called it worthless. It's amazing what a few bad people can cause inside."

"I will go with that," he said. "My wife, Teal, is the one that pulled us out of my shell. I would never have been able to survive being out here if she hadn't shown me a difference. Now I can't imagine not being here. I know it sounds contrary to the idea with what just happened back there. But really, I think that issue is now forever solved."

"How is that?" I asked.

"Sure you want to talk about it?"

"Yeah, I think I am doing okay. I can't say what will happen five minutes from now." I tried a smile.

"Those guys that attacked us were from New Haven," he told me. I think I figured that much.

"They were the ones you were expecting trouble from, right?" I asked.

"They were," he paused.

"Keep going," I told him. "We're just shooting the breeze here."

"I really wanted them to come," he said, looking at me with some apology on his face. He turned then and looked out over the scenery. "I, of course, didn't want it to turn out like it did. It's just that I knew what lay just over the hill in New Haven. I was always a little worried. Them coming in and causing trouble now and then was a constant reminder that we were never really safe out here."

"I think I understand what you're getting at," I told him.

"I didn't want anything bad to happen to anyone," he said again. "But, I knew those guys were the worthless kind that bully their way around."

"I always think of them as takers," I told him. "They'll take everything you let them; everything they can. They are no good to anyone."

"Exactly!" he said with some emphasis. "You see, those were the only bad ones in New Haven. I've met a lot of them and really they're good quality people. They'll convert you in an instant if you let them, but aside from that, they'll do anything for you."

"So you think by taking out those ones we did, that the rest will be okay?" I asked him.

"Those guys were the disease that plagued New Haven," he said. "I think with them gone we can finally have good neighbors."

"You should probably make a personal visit there soon and reach out," I told him.

"I was thinking the same thing," he said. "I know who will take over there, I think. He's a good guy."

"I hope it works that way, Quade," I told him sincerely. "That's the things we need in life, good neighbors."

"I'm also hoping that you all won't be strangers after all of this," he said. "A few hours away by train is not that bad."

I had not allowed myself to think that far ahead really. It was true that Quade and his people were the kind of friends we all longed for. The life they lived, where they gave back and encouraged each other for new development and growth that promoted one another was a gift in a neighbor. It is the type of brotherhood that I longed to be part of. My heart warmed at the thought.

"I would like nothing more, Quade," I told him. "You may get tired of us."

"We can just disconnect the tracks between us for a while if that happens," he said with a smile. "I'll be excited to see your underground compound."

"I'll be glad to take you for a tour," I told him. "You have to take me on one of those early morning quail hunts, though. We don't have many around us."

"I would love that," he said. "My dog is awesome at pointing them out."

We turned to looking back over the passing scenery. I allowed myself to see an end then. I could see life getting back on track for our compound and the large hunts that would fill our freezers for the winter and seal the bounds between all of us, Dan's compound included. I longed for such and began to ache for it. For some reason, I could not see myself in it yet and figured the recent happenings were holding that back. I saw Quade turn to walk back inside.

"There's just one more thing," I told Quade. He turned slowly.

"What is it?" he asked.

"I was hoping you could be ready to take over command for a while if I need you to," I told him. "I don't want to overreact to something where Kevin is involved."

"Do you think you will?" he asked seriously.

"He took them in order to further his experiments," I told him. "There's no telling what we will find. Quite frankly, we don't know if he met up with some of his friends and he's sitting behind an army up there. Or maybe he's picking apart those girls."

"I think NASA would have seen something if that army thing was the case," Quade told me. "But, I guess we should be ready for that. And I understand your feelings on the other."

"I'm just not sure what we'll find," I told him. "And I'm not sure if what we've just gone through is going to affect my ability when we see whatever's waiting for us."

"I understand what you're saying and I really appreciate you being able to see that and know your responsibility to the team," he told me. "This is still your mission. I'll just help at the front and keep us grounded. How does that sound?"

"Thanks for understanding," I told him. "I'm glad we ran into you, Quade."

"I guess you guys are okay too," he said with a smile and turned, walking back into the cabin.

I sat there then and watched more of what went by. I tried to clear my head and think about what lay ahead. I was glad for the distraction Quade had provided. With some willpower, I stood up and set my jaw. I know we needed this to go off without a hitch. I turned and walked back into the cabin.

"Jake, I need to talk to Neil," I told him. "We need to figure out our approach. You have any ideas on that, Eric?"

"I saw something of a train yard kind of south of the city," he said. "I was thinking we could coast in there and hide among them."

"That sounds like a good idea," I told him.

"It was pretty far south of the hospital," Quade said.

"We may not get a clear line without switching tracks," Lincoln said.

"No, I looked for that," Eric said. "We couldn't make it straight through without moving a few things but this line leads us right in among them."

"Okay then, I think that would work," Lincoln told him.

"The hospital is up north of the city, right?" Sterling asked.

"Just north of the center, yeah," Quade told him.

"I have Neil, sir," Jake told me.

"Ask him if there's any movement," I told Jake. He did.

"He said it's all clear," Jake said. "I got a report on the weather and there are some clouds moving around the area, but nothing that will fill the sky there."

"Okay, good idea," I told him. "Any ideas for an easy way through the city?"

"I looked at the radar for a while," Sterling said. "The city looked mostly intact."

"Some of the buildings on the outskirts were pretty torn up, it looked like," Quade said. "The downtown area seemed perfect, though."

"Neil is saying that big crater east of town is definitely the remains of a huge oil refinery," Jake said.

"I was wondering about that," Quade said.

"Me too," Sterling added. "I was sure it had to be something like that."

"Any activity around it now?" I asked Jake.

"You thinking of circling around it?" Sterling asked. "It's pretty close to the north part where we need to go."

"Neil says no activity," Jake said.

"I think it may be best to hole up just out of town somewhere," I told everyone. "Maybe we pull up to where tracks get close to the remains of that oil refinery. I looked and there were a lot of train cars there still waiting to be filled or whatever. We can hide the train in them. Sorry Sterling, but I'm a little tired of going through the city streets. It looks like it would be better to walk in from there and leave the horses behind."

"I think I can agree with that," he said with a smile. "I hope we don't run into any more of the dogs." Everyone agreed with that.

"You all have a run-in?" Eric asked.

"Yeah, nothing we couldn't handle," Quade told him and gave me a wink.

"I think if we go a bit north from the refinery, we can head pretty much straight west and avoid a lot of houses," Eric said. We all looked at him. "I looked at the radar a little too much. It started looking like faces after a while. But, I think, I memorized it pretty well."

"You're with me out there," I told him. He nodded. "I like the idea of avoiding dense structures, but we will need some cover on our approach and as we move through. We'll have to play it a little by ear."

"I think that's true," Quade said.

"Jake, ask Neil if they've been able to find what part of the hospital the signal is coming from," I said.

"He says no," Jake told me.

"Any idea what section of the hospital he would need to be in?" Margie asked and we all looked at her. "There are many areas to a hospital."

"That's true," Sterling said. "He probably wouldn't be in any of the patient wings."

"He probably wouldn't be in the emergency section or the loading areas," Quade said. He looked to be thinking about something else.

"What is it?" I asked him.

"It's nothing," he said. "It's just I went through a hospital right after the war. It was not a fun time is all."

"You going to be okay?" I asked him.

"No, I'm fine with it," he said. "I just think the loading areas are a good way to go in."

"That's true," Sterling said. "They are probably in an area by themselves."

"Jake, ask Neil to see where at on the buildings the loading docks are," I said.

"North side, in the middle on the opposite side of the main entrance," Jake said.

"I remember a big field being on that side of the hospital," Eric said. "It would be a good way of approaching unseen."

"Okay, let's make that plan A," I said.

"Should we be concerned about alarms going off?" Margie asked. Again, everyone looked at her.

"I would think that the building was a little too abused during the war to still have a working alarm system," Quade said. "I could not imagine an alarm being able to still be effective. Still, I guess he could have control of the system and be trying to barricade himself behind whatever ones do work."

"We should be careful with every door that we open," I said. "I'm hoping this hospital is a little bit broken into so that we can move around without having to worry about that."

"I'm sure it did not survive the war without someone taking it over," Eric said. "Medical supplies were in pretty high demand."

"That's very true," I said. "But, let's cross that bridge when we get to it. We may be able to contact Tara and find out exactly where they are in the hospital and then we will know where to come in at. Once we do that though, we need to be ready to move in quickly. I want everyone with their eyes peeled for any way in that will avoid any detection. I mean an opened door or broken office window might just be all we need to get in without triggering anything."

"Are you thinking about cameras?" Jake asked.

"I think that's just going to be whatever it is," I said. "We may not be able to get close without him having something in place to warn himself. If he does see us, he may run. I don't want him to be able to get away."

"That ain't happening!" Sterling said.

"Okay, so it looks like a northern approach to the buildings with an idea of entering through the dock," I said. "Jake, will you let Neil know?"

"I will," he said.

"Where do you think they will be at inside?" Quade asked. "I mean, I think the labs would be the obvious place."

"Yeah, once we get inside we should look for some type of directory of the place," I said. "Maybe Tara can answer that for us."

"That would be a big help," Quade said.

"Jake, tell Neil that the first thing we need to know is if Kevin has any alarm system in place," I said. "After that we need to know what section of the hospital he's in."

"I'll tell him that information," Jake said and went back to talking on the radio.

"Also, we need him looking with a microscope as we go inside," I told Jake. "We need to know immediately if Kevin tries to run." Jake nodded. "How far out are we?" I asked Lincoln.

"I think about two hours," he told me.

"Will you let everyone know to get ready when we are within twenty?" I asked him.

"I will," he said.

"Anyone got anything they want to add?" I asked. No one said anything. "This will be over in no time. I want to thank all of you for your help here. We couldn't do it without you."

"We weren't doing anything else today," Quade told me with a smile. I returned it.

We all turned to our own things then. I looked at the small pack I carried and found a small bag of instant coffee had fallen to the bottom. I thought about the men down below, and getting up, I told Lincoln I would be down there. I walked down the steps in the middle of the cabin and knocked on the door. I opened the door a little and poked my head in.

"Oh, come on in," Ray said. I came in and closed the door behind me. "I was thinking it was Lincoln again. That man sneaks around. I don't know why, we don't listen to him anyways. You'd figure he would get tired of flapping his gums at us."

"I was wondering if I could take you up on that offer for some coffee," I told him as he moved out of the way so I could walk inside.

"Why yes sir, you can," he said. "We have a little left in the pot. I was just telling Fredrick there that we needed a fresh one."

I felt the warmth of the room as he went and closed the partially-cracked front door. A lantern swung overhead, giving off plenty of light to fill the small area. Ray pulled out a folding chair from somewhere and opening it, offered me a spot at the table. He went then over to the pot of coffee.

"I have a little bag of instant here," I told him. I held up the small baggie.

"Instant?" Fredrick said. "Man, I ain't drinking no instant, not when there's a pot right there."

"You'll have to forgive Fredrick there," Ray said. "He don't have any manners."

"Let me see that baggie," Fredrick said. I handed it to him. "What kind of coffee is this? It looks like Taster's Choice, all light brown and all. It is, isn't it,

Tasters Choice? Now that was some good coffee. Remember those commercials, Ray, where the two English white people were falling in love and they'd only show like half a scene and leave it on this cliffhanger?" He handed me back my coffee.

"Those were French people," Ray said as he poured out the old coffee into a nearby five gallon bucket. He grabbed an old plastic milk jug half full of water and filled the brewing kettle.

"French, white people?" Fredrick said. "No way, those were English folks. You should learn your countries."

"My countries?" Ray said. "I know my countries. You need to learn your countries. I bet you don't even know where England is at."

"What?" Fredrick said, furrowing his forehead. "I know where it be. And I definitely know them people in that commercial was from there. What you say?" He looked at me hard.

"I thought they were Mexicans," I told him with a straight face. They both started laughing.

"Man, shake them bones and we can get on with this game," Fredrick told me, still laughing.

I shuffled the dominoes on the table and everyone took a hand. The bantering went on then and I became part of it. The coffee was soon ready and we all took a cup. Time vanished as we played I am not sure how many hands and emptied a few pots of coffee. I was surprised when Lincoln opened the door and told me we were somewhere close to twenty minutes away.

"Thanks Lincoln," I told him.

"Is that another electric coffee pot," Lincoln asked, pointing to the pot in the corner.

"I don't know," Ray said. "I think that was here." I nodded as did Fredrick.

"We thought you'd put that in here for us, Lincoln," Fredrick said with the most innocent look I had ever seen. "Ray here said you'd never do nothin' nice like that, but I said you was just a good guy like that."

"What?" Ray said. "You the one that said he was some evil lynch man, hating your people and all."

"I never said that there Mr. Lincoln sir," Fredrick said. "What I did say is you don't like no black people. Now I done said that."

"It's alright Fredrick," Lincoln told him. "Just make sure it doesn't fall." Lincoln looked around at us as I tried to hold back my smile and slowly walked back out the door. We watched the door after it had closed.

"Maybe him do like black people," Fredrick said as he looked at us with a straight face and shrugged. We all laughed together.

We finished off the hand of dominoes and I drained my cup. I thanked the two men for the hospitality. They welcomed me back as I left the room, seeing them folding things up and getting themselves ready for what was coming up.

The cabin was transformed when I got there. Bags of gear were spread out and the sounds of weapons being checked and loaded was prevalent. I found my bags and added my noises to the crowd.

We started to slow after a while and I looked out the window. I saw the remains of a huge oil refinery. Two craters covered the entire area with pipes and tubing littering the sloped sides of them. Little stood upright. What did was useless to anyone. I noticed the cabin had grown quiet and looking around, I saw everyone looking outside.

"There must have been a fight here," Quade said.

"Wouldn't have taken much to blow that place sky high," Lincoln added. "I bet the mushroom cloud from it could have been seen for miles."

"I bet," Quade said and got back to storing his gear about his person.

"You see a spot to put us?" I asked Eric.

"Yeah, I think just up ahead there," he said, pointing.

I left him to it and continued to get myself ready. We all checked our radios and found we could communicate with each other. Jake, I saw, was getting the portable radio situated. In only a few minutes we were stopped among some oil cars and ready to leave the cabin.

We all made it to the ground and I was glad to see that Fredrick and Ray would be coming with us. Eric moved up close to me and stood. Making some readjustments, I saw everyone was ready. I turned and led us north through the debris of the exploded oil refinery.

The smell of the place was toxic. It made me cough several times as it did others. Every path we chose was greasy and several times we had to backtrack to make it through. We quickened our pace just to be rid of the area.

We moved through an industrial district, one obviously shut down long before the war. It looked to have been used as a gathering area of some sort during the war as several barricades still remained at key points to restrict access. We moved here with some care, but nothing moved, but a bunch of rabbits.

We turned north at Eric's instruction, trying to come at the hospital from the north and needing to get at a good angle to enter the field that would allow us to do so. He pointed out things often and I followed with the proper movements. Passing at last the large baseball park on our left, we came to the field we had been heading for. We moved low through the tall grass and spread out a little as we came to the edge of it. We bent the grass to the side a little and looked at the large VA hospital just beyond.

"Jake, I need you up here with me," I said softly. He was there in an instant.

"Are we ready to send the signal?" he asked the obvious question. I nodded and he called home.

"With any luck, this will be over in no time," I said aloud, but really was speaking to myself.

"They're sending it," Jake told me.

"Now we wait," Quade said from my other side.

I looked over the hospital then and saw the loading area a short distance to our right. Several brick buildings were in the way of a clear view of the place, but I figured they would only help as we approached the hospital in a few minutes. The hospital itself was also entirely made of brick and was three stories high. We were about in the middle of the huge structure with wings heading in opposite directions. Square areas came off the wings at random spots and made the building anything, but a long rectangle. A bell tower was on the opposite side in the middle of the building and I could see there was no actual bell inside. I saw the usual debris spread throughout the dock area. All of the large garbage containers and recycling bins seemed to be in place along with excess medical equipment of various forms.

The damage to the hospital was something else altogether. Most of the windows were all gone. The large garage-type doors for the two loading docks were missing; I did not even see their remains anywhere close by. A large earthmoving vehicle had smashed through a wall close to the loading area and had crumbled a wall there; a pile of the wall sat on top of the vehicle. It exposed a portion of the hallway that led to the main section of the hospital. It seemed our entrance was secured.

I looked at Jake then and he shook his head. I had hoped that Tara would be waiting at some Morse Code button, ready in an instant to direct us to where she was. I furrowed my forehead and watched the hospital again.

"Is home able to see the hospital with the photograph satellites?" I asked Jake.

"Yeah, and they should be able to stay on us for the next hour," he told me.

"Okay, then let's move over to that loading area and see what we can see from there," I said. "Everyone stay in as much of the cover from those buildings there as you can. Let's assume there are hostiles inside until we prove otherwise." I got acknowledgements all around.

I looked back at the hospital and hoped much. My mind was actually racing, though I was trying to keep it from doing so. It wanted to turn to what was going on at home. I even wondered, for some reason, how George's train was running. I pulled hard to turn from the black abyss that the thoughts on my wife brought. I probably wanted anything else besides having to go inside that hospital and find what could be there. With a deep breath and sheer will, I pushed those things to the side. I stood and crouched over and left the tall grass.

CHAPTER 24

I made it to a large shipping container that was next to a smaller brick building and moved over to the corner of it. Several spools of wiring were leaning up against the container and a stack of orange cones was nearby. A smaller gas powered crane was beyond the container and several stacks of bricks that matched the building were right beside it. Looking back, I saw others leaving the grass and heading in my direction.

Jake came and stood beside me. He shook his head when I looked at him questioningly. When I saw everyone had made it to the container or the building beside it, I ventured a look around the corner. We had quickly cut the distance between us and the hospital in half.

I saw an easy way to stay mostly in cover as we made it the rest of the way. It was clear that some construction had been going on with the buildings before the war as piles of materials were everywhere. It made our job there a lot easier.

I moved along some stacks of metal two-by-fours and held up at a pair of portable toilets. I moved on quickly from there and came to a forklift. I was almost at the docks then and with a couple of short dashes between some wooden crates and another pile of bricks, I grabbed a railing and jumped up to the side of the frame where the loading dock door was missing. I looked inside the hospital.

The place there had been well-graffiti. Emptied cans of spray paint and trash of all kinds littered the place. Large pieces of cardboard were stacked along one wall. I could see the evidence of a long ago fire close to the middle of the floor.

Looking back, I saw everyone waiting for me to enter. I nodded and did so, staying close to the left wall and heading to where I saw the cardboard stacked. I still had not seen a door that led out of there, so I figured to stay in cover until I did. It only took me a few steps before I saw the doorway that led to the interior of the hospital on the far right corner of the room. Seeing the room was clear, I moved there instead.

The door was the swinging type and looked to once have been able to be locked. It hung in one of its hinges, though only mostly closed. Looking back, I saw everyone spreading out inside the loading area, Jake and Quade coming quickly over to me. I turned back and looked as best as I could through the cracks of the door.

All I could see was a wall in front of me beyond the door. I could tell that a hallway went both ways outside the door. I looked, but did not see any other way out of the room.

"Any word?" I asked Jake in a whisper. He shook his head. "Looks like a couple hallways leading in different directions."

"Maybe we should split up," Quade said.

"Okay, keep your radio close," I told him. "Keep me posted if you find a directory."

"Will do," he said. "I'll take left."

"Okay," I told him.

I pointed to Margie, Jake and Sterling and pointed to the right. Quade pointed to the rest and pointed left. Everyone knew their assignment and we turned back to the door.

Quade stood and moved up close to the door. He lifted it an inch off the floor and swung it in just enough for us to be able to get through it. It did not make a sound which surprised me, for some reason. I had expected it to creak like an old haunted mansion's door.

We moved into the hallways beyond, one by one lining them and pushing ourselves close up against the walls. They were lined with doors and each led off for about fifty feet before ending at another hallway. I nodded to Quade and he returned it.

I turned and looked down my hallway and tried to see if any of the doors stood out. Everything was labeled, but we could not see anything, but the first few. They all seemed the same and what we did see did not appear to be what we needed. The end of the hallway ahead grabbed my attention and we walked that way as I shouldered my rifle.

The doors we past were all locked and had no windows. There were names on some and categories on others. I saw one was a maintenance closet. As we got to the end of the hallway, I saw a list of directions on the wall in front of us.

"Looks like that way to 'Laboratories'," Sterling said, looking left. I radioed and told Quade.

"Copy that," I heard him respond softly. "Moving toward a way that says 'Women's Clinic'."

"Copy," I told him. "Will keep you posted."

The hospital was a lot bigger than it looked outside. We turned often and past things that seemed to lead to nowhere, only to go back to make sure and find that they led to entire offshoots unto themselves. We stayed on a constant course toward the labs, but I wanted to clear a little bit of the areas as we went. I felt my nerves beginning to tighten as we moved on.

"Just outside of the 'Women's Clinic'," Quade told me. "Moving inside." I put my hand up to stop everyone. "It looks a little destroyed in here. Office is smashed up. Moving to the rooms. Lights are off. No power in here." It was a full minute before I heard from him again. "No, nothing in here. No way has anything been in here for a while. Hold that thought! I see some stuff has been moved; maybe recently. Sorry, it's hard to tell. There's definitely nothing in here now."

"I copy all that," I told him.

"We'll move on to 'Cardio'," he told me. "It was just down the way from here."

"Okay, we're still headed for the lab," I told him.

"Copy," he said.

The hallways did not stop their winding directions. We ran across an entranceway that was totally smashed and haphazardly refortified. (It did not look like it could withstand much.) We past an exercise area and found it mostly untouched. As we moved around another corner, I saw ahead a large sign by a set of double doors that told us the labs were within. The double doors were wide open.

We moved with some caution up to the entranceway and saw a receiving area with a counter and several metal shelves behind it. Glass doors were off to the left and I was surprised to see them fully intact. A warning told us that only authorized personnel were allowed inside. I went and looked through the glass and saw a long hallway lined with closed doors.

"We should be careful here," Margie told me.

"I agree," I replied. "It won't do to have some alarm going off."

"Maybe we should look through everywhere that's open," Sterling said. "We can save this area for last."

"We would see him for sure if he was in here," I told them.

"There's no power to any of these systems," Sterling said, pulling back from leaning over the counter.

I watched him walk around the counter and look at the computers. I saw Margie try a couple of the switches by the door. None of the lights went on. Thinking back, I had not seen any lights on anywhere.

"I thought this place would be on its own grid," I said.

"Me too," Sterling said.

I saw another set of doors and went and looked through. I saw the same type of hallway behind them. Inside were opened doors with who knew what behind them.

"Here's a bunch of info on infectious disease control," Sterling said. "That's a little ironic."

"Let's think," I said. "Where else could he be doing his work at?"

"I saw signs for 'Extended Care' along the way," Sterling said. "I was thinking about that. This is a Veteran's Hospital. They probably have all kinds of medical equipment he could use all over." I did not like that idea.

I called Quade and told him about the locked doors in the lab. We moved back out into the hallway and looked at all of the signs on the walls, hoping they would tell us where the women were. I went to a broken doorway that led outside and let the cold breeze wash over my face. I tried to think if there was something that we were missing.

"Neil just said that Davina made it home," Jake told me. "Chris is doing fine, but Davina is critical. Shay said to tell you that she's holding on, though." He moved his hand off of his headset. "Sounds like they got her hooked up to the machines in the Med Center. She made it, sir."

I smiled inside, though I am not sure it made it all the way out. I was in mission mode and that was going to be a big distraction. I had tried to push all thoughts about anything else out; hearing that they were coming back in.

"Save those reports for when we find Tara," I told Jake, feeling like the biggest piece of crap in the world. "I can't be thinking of that right now." I only hoped that it would work.

"Yes sir," he told me.

"We need to think," I said. "Where would he have them?"

"How is Tara sending the message?" Margie asked.

"What?" I asked her.

"How is she sending it?" she asked.

"Morse Code is what they said," I told her. "I don't know how she could be sending it. She could be hooking into the hospital com systems. No, that would only get her able to talk to the building."

"There has to be some computer systems running this place," Sterling said. "Where would that be at?"

"Wait!" I said. "How would NASA be reading a signal from this place if there's no power here?"

"Maybe we haven't found where the power is on," Jake said.

"Ask Neil if they are still getting a signal," I told Jake with some alarm. I heard him ask.

"He said 'loud and clear'," Jake told me.

"So where would the power be on at?" I wondered aloud.

I sent the news to Quade and got the same quizzical answer. He told me they were not finding any place with power either. We all wondered what it could mean and I did not like what I was coming up with.

"Ask Shay," I told Jake.

"What?" he asked.

"Ask her," I told him. "She'll know what parts of the hospital could run by themselves."

I listened as Jake asked Neil. We all waited and looked at something interesting on the nearby walls. I saw Jake put his hand back over the earpiece on his headphones and I looked with earnest at him.

"She's saying directors offices would be separate, like where they keep records," Jake started. "Emergency room areas are run separately in case of an overload or panic. She's saying Chemotherapy areas too. They need them separately powered incase the grid goes down, they don't lose containment on radiation rooms or expose the venting systems to those agents. She says the labs will usually be separate too, especially with the worry on keeping their research going. She says that's probably it." Jake looked up at me.

"We've checked the Lab," Margie said.

"We're close to 'Chemotherapy'," Sterling said.

"Quade, I need you to check the 'Emergency Room'," I told my radio. "We're headed for 'Chemotherapy'. Shay said those would be some of the rooms powered separately."

"Copy that," he said. "We'll head that way and give it a full look. We walked right by the hallway that led there."

We headed back the way we had come and soon picked up the signs that directed us to the Chemo area. We still stayed alert on all of the turns and I tried to start keeping better track of all the long hallways and whatever else we past. We soon stood at the end of a long hallway in front of a door that was labeled 'Chemotherapy'.

"Anyway around opening that door?" Sterling asked.

We all came close to the door and looked intently. It was plain white and sterile, without any window; just as most other doors in the hospital were. The knob was there, waiting with the potential of leading us to what we came for, or sounding an alarm that may let it slip through our fingers. I looked at the others and they only shrugged.

"Think this is the only door?" Jake asked and we all looked at him. "Usually they make entrances to chemotherapy a little more inviting."

We walked back down the long hallway and started a little farther on. We turned a few corners and quickly came to a front entrance to the building. All of the arrows on the wall directed us back to the door we had left. We returned with the understanding that we had no choice, but to open the door.

I grabbed the knob and turned it. It was locked which did not surprise me. Getting out my tools, I quickly picked it and pulled the door open a crack, waiting. No alarm sounded.

Everyone got ready and I pulled the door open all the way. I am not sure why I was so wound tight here, but I felt like something was going to spring out at me. As I watched, Margie stepped inside. I rebuked myself and moved in behind her.

We entered a long cement hallway, with tall ceilings to match. Pipes ran the entire length and turned far down the way as did the hallway. I saw a large sign telling us we were entering an area where radiation would be in use. It seemed a very bleak entryway to have someone come through to collect their cure for cancer.

Sterling brought up the rear and put something in the way of the door so that it could not close behind us. He turned then and looked down the long hallway. I had not paid much attention to the end, but as I looked, I saw a single light on at the curve.

"The light at the end of the tunnel maybe," Sterling said. I looked at him and was not sure how to respond.

We walked to the end with some care, each ready in an instant to shoot whatever came around the corner. We made it to the curve without incident. I put up my hand and peeked around the edge which would turn us left.

I saw a set of stairs which ended quickly at a landing. I could see we were going to have to go down at least one flight. I saw more lights along the walls there. I figured at least we were getting closer. I radioed Quade and heard that he was about ready to move on the emergency area. Turning the radio down low, I moved out around the corner and moved to the top of the stairs.

I looked down over the railing and in between the flights of steps. I saw that it was three flights to the bottom. I was not terribly excited about where this was leading us in such a spot, I figured we may lose contact with our other team. I set my jaw, however, and started down, the others following close behind.

We made it to the bottom without incident. We did not see another door the whole way down which surprised me. As we got to the final step we saw a long hallway that told us we were definitely in the bowels of the hospital. We hurried to it and turned several times. Finally, we came to a door on the far wall which stood plainly before us. Another large sign hung on the wall and told us we were entering an area where radiation was in use.

"There is no way this is the entrance to 'Chemotherapy'," Jake said in a whisper, though it sounded quite loud in the box we were in.

I did not like what he was saying for the simple fact that it did not help us at all. If he would have added some explanation or given us another course of action, I would have gladly received it. The sentence he was offering by itself was of little use.

"What exactly does that mean?" Sterling asked before I could, him as annoyed at the statement as I was.

"I'm just saying this can't be where chemo patients come," Jake told us. "Could you imagine them trying to walk up and down those stairs back there and these long hallways after a treatment?" He was making a good point.

"That's very true," Sterling admitted. He looked over at me.

"Why are the arrows leading here?" I asked.

"I'm not sure," Jake said and seemed to try to apologize. "Let's just move and see where this leads."

I agreed with that and was glad that everyone was thinking as we went. It did not help my nerves as I grabbed the knob of the door and felt its cold steel on my palm. I looked back and got a nod from everyone. With one turn, I opened the door to my surprise and looked at what was beyond.

I saw a well-carpeted lobby, complete with a large forest green receptionist's desk. A closed door was on the far side of the desk, but on the opposite wall where chairs were lined, was spaced evenly with a table full of magazines between every third one. On the wall above the chairs was a nice oil painting of an old barn with a pair of pheasants flying off in the foreground. Turning to look to my right, I saw an elevator door, held open by a rollaway bed. Stepping into the room, I saw the wall immediately to my right was also lined with chairs. The room had the smell of fresh carpet.

I walked over to the elevator and looked inside. The bed wore a wrinkled sheet. It rolled easily out of the way of the elevator door. As the bed moved, I was surprised to see the elevator door begin to close. I pushed on the mechanism to make the door reopen. The sounds it was making, with its dings was sending up red flags everywhere in me. I wedged the bed in place and lifted my hands off of it. I was happy to see it staying in place. I turned and saw several worried faces looking at me. We all turned our attention to the door on the far wall.

I tried my radio before I moved away from the elevator and did not get a response from Quade. I moved around a little and still did not get anything. Going inside the elevator did not help. I asked Jake to try his.

"I'm hearing home trying to respond," Jake told me. "It's mostly static."

"Let's see what's going on behind this door here," I told everyone. "Then we should go upstairs and find everyone."

"We could use the elevator for that," Sterling said. I shrugged and figured to think on that later.

We all moved over to the door and this time Margie tried the knob. (I ignored yet another radiation sign which was on the door.) She nodded as she turned it and pulled slightly on the door. We watched it move a little. She looked at me and I gave her the go-ahead. With one movement she pulled it all the way open.

I saw a long carpeted hallway that was lined with doors on the right and only had a couple on the left. I walked to the closest door, which was on my right and opened it. It looked a little like an examining room, but more warm with light brown walls and a fake plant in the corner on a small table. There was a plush reclining type chair almost in the center of the room. Empty bags with tubes hanging out of the bottom were hung from several rolling stainless steel poles.

"This must be where they sit while they get chemo," Sterling said from beside me. We both looked around a little and returned to the hallway.

We tried the next door on our right and found mostly the same thing. We figured the rest on that side to be of equal value to us and turned to looking at the doors on our left. There was only two, both with signs of warning, again of the radiation type.

I pulled on one and found it locked. I picked the lock with ease and as I opened it, I saw a concrete wall facing me about three feet away, with a small passageway that led left. I went in and followed it and saw that the passage turned back right again about ten feet away. It led to another right turn and I took it. At the end it turned again and I could see we were taking a series of passages that was drawing us to some center. After another turn, I found I was correct as the passage opened into a twelve-by-twelve concrete room with a rather uncomfortable looking chair in the center. Several moveable apparatuses hung from the cement ceiling. Looking, I saw a variety of cables and things I did not recognize hanging from the walls

"I guess this is where people come to get radiation treatment," Sterling said. I agreed with him.

"Why all the passageways to get in here?" I wondered.

"Probably has something to do with shielding the radiation," Jake said. "I bet all the walls around here are lined with lead."

"Doesn't look like a fun chair to be in," Sterling said.

"Let's get up top and join up with Quade," I said. "Maybe he's had more luck than us." I was so disappointed at what we had found.

"We should clear the rest of the rooms while we're here," Jake said.

"Okay, but let's make it quick," I told him. "We've already been out of contact for too long."

We went to the next room across and down a little from where we were. It was of course more of the same, complete with comfy chair, though the color was different. We walked farther down and found the next room the same way. I was glad when we got to final door on that side and found little difference again besides the color. Turning around, I saw our last door, it with a radiation sign on it.

"Let's clear it and go," I said with some emphasis.

I tried the door as I was reaching for my lock picking kit, but found it was unlocked. I pulled it open and saw another sterile cement wall there to greet me. The passageway looked the same and turned left as before. We took it and let the door close silently behind us as I led the way.

As we turned again, I saw that this passageway was different. I saw three doors at the end and immediately raised my rifle to my shoulder. They each faced in a different direction, the one at the very end of the passageway was facing us. It reminded me of when we first started looking around our own compound so long ago. There were serious warning signs on the walls here, all telling us we needed authorization to be there, for some reason. Lethal force we were told was authorized. My body tensed.

We moved quickly up to the doors. I read a plaque on the wall to my left first which said 'Radiation Treatment Care and Research'. I tried the door knob there and it turned in my hand. I pushed it in and saw a small room with a long desk on one side. Several computer screens were there as was several panels of dials and odd-looking switches. I saw both screens were on and was alarmed to see one of them was showing the cement room we had been in only a few moments earlier. The other screen showed the 'Windows' logo bouncing around. I moved the mouse that was close by and the screen showed some medical stuff. I wished for Shay to have been there. On a hunch, I felt the chairs, but found them cold.

"Not sure I like that one with the camera on it," Jake said.

"Yeah, maybe we should move along quickly," I said.

We thought to try the one directly across from the room we were in but it was locked. I tried the other door just to see if it would be easier. It was unlocked and

I pushed the door slowly open. I heard a chime as I did so and my heart sank. I hurried through and panned around with my rifle. I saw we had entered a long and wide glass walled area, with much the look of a sophisticated laboratory beyond. The door closed behind us as I saw we were in a clean room, one designed to sterilize the person that came into the area. It separated us from the laboratory.

"I can't believe it!" I heard a speaker say from somewhere overhead in the sterile room we were in. "It's not possible!"

Looking through the glass walls of the room, I moved all around. There was nothing, but the usual laboratory stuff in the direction I was facing. A long metal table did have something being boiled in a clear container. Papers were spread out there and a white coat hung on the back of a chair. I thought I turned quickly, but the scan of the rest of the room seemed to take forever.

As I turned to the left, I saw Kevin with mouth wide-open and fear gripping his face. Behind him was Olivia, unconscious and lying flat on a rollaway hospital bed. Tubes were sticking out of her and monitors were hooked up to her naked chest. I saw a fetal monitor strapped to her stomach. Tara, I saw standing up and looking at us in disbelief. She was somehow tied to the ceiling with a short rope around her neck. Her hands looked to be bound behind her.

"How is that possible?" I heard Kevin's voice again asking loud and clear. I pulled my AK tight against my shoulder and fired straight at Kevin's head.

I saw the bullets stopped by the thick glass, some of them bouncing around us and then landing with a skid and others spinning in a fast circle on the floor. I remember wondering why they did that. I saw Kevin flinch at my reaction and then stand up straight with the realization that he was safe behind this wall of glass. I wondered why so thick glass. He tried on a smile, but it was a nervous one.

"How did you find me?" he asked. He walked toward the other part of the laboratory. He looked over that way and I followed his gaze, but could not see what he was looking at.

I ran to the door of our cage and looked for a way to open it. There was a keypad and no knob. I saw the metal frame of the door was well encased in the bulletproof glass which was quite thick. The rim of the door was flat along the wall. There was no entering the lab without the correct electronic signal. Looking back, I saw the same keypad next to the door we entered through and no knob there but just a handle to pull on.

I watched Kevin looking around the lab some more and finally I saw he was looking at the door on the far right side wall. It was a cement wall with a large sliding metal door. The door there had a window in it and he went there and looked through, scanning frantically what was beyond. He checked the lock and seemed satisfied.

"Where's the rest of you?" he said, still with some worry. I looked at Tara and gave her a reassuring smile.

"Let them go and you'll live," I told him.

"I don't think you understand the predicament you just placed yourself in," he told me. "That's not the only way out of here, you see."

"Jake, are you able to get Quade?" I asked as low as I could.

"I'll try," he told me.

"Don't let him see you trying," I told him.

"Got it," he said softly. "There has to be a way out of here! I hate you Kevin. I should have figured you out a long time ago." he said loudly then, moving to the floor and pretending to look closely at the corners as he turned all around.

"Good luck with that," Kevin told him. "A germ couldn't even make it out of there." He walked up to the glass door. "So, again I ask, where are the rest of you?"

"Roman got shot in the head right in front of me in Kansas," I started, feeling the rage boil inside me. "Davina jumped in front of me and took five rounds to the chest. She must have been turned kind of sideways because her bulletproof vest didn't help her at all. Chris got his leg shot off. They headed back to the compound as fast as George could get them there. Shay is working on Davina right now. I place all of that on you."

"Oh, I guess I deserve that," he said. "You look so serious, I think I may almost believe you." He seemed to have relaxed.

"I think I'm getting through somehow," Jake said quietly. "Keep him talking." I watched as Kevin turned and walked over to Tara.

"So you were sending out a message, huh?" Kevin asked her up close to her face.

He backhanded her so hard that it snapped her head back. She started to fall, but the rope around her neck caught her and she started gagging. She tried desperately to get her feet under her, but she could not seem to find them. I ran to the wall as I watched, hatred boiling in my fists that pounded on the glass. I saw Tara turning purple as Kevin stepped in close to her.

"Come on now, I can't have you doing that," he said and lifted her a bit as she struggled to put her legs under herself. "Well, I guess it really doesn't matter that much does it?" She choked air through her throat and started to regain some color.

"There isn't a place you can go that I won't find you," I told him with as much malice as I could muster.

"I'm pretty sure you will have long since starved to death, here in that very room," he told me. He stopped and looked at me. "You know, I haven't really even thought about it for quite a while. I always wanted to try Belize, though. One ocean the first year, the other ocean the next. Sounds like a great way to retire. Don't tell anyone, though, will ya? I'm keeping that a secret."

He moved over to the long table as he continued to smile to himself. He finally seemed to have lost what was left of his mind, though I did not want to mistake the man once again. (Not like there was much I could do about it anyway.) He typed at the keypad of a laptop for a time and seemed to be thinking about what all to do there. With a shrug he stood up.

"I'm not getting through," Jake told me.

"I guess you kind of forced my hand a bit," Kevin said and circled around the table, coming so close to our glass prison so as almost to touch it.

He went over to the table along the far wall and checked some of the monitors hooked up to Olivia. He checked some of the tubes going into her arm and looked at the bags hanging close to her head. He tapped the top of one of the rolling monitors and shrugged. He said something then that I could not hear. I saw then that he grabbed something off the table.

He put on some gloves and remembering something, walked off a little and pulled a rolling table close to Olivia's bedside. He moved some of the instruments there around a little and gave them a satisfied grin. He picked up a long needle and pulled off a sleeve that covered it.

"What the hell are you doing?" I asked him.

"Oh, you want a commentary?" Kevin said. "I thought it would be obvious. I'm drawing fluids from the baby. I injected her earlier with my own little concoction. I think it's a little soon, but maybe it's just right."

He put the needle down then and grabbed something else. He squirted some fluid on Olivia's stomach and wiped it off with a cloth. He looked over at me and smiled.

"I hate being rushed," he said. "It causes me to forget all kinds of stuff."

"Are you getting anything from Quade?" I asked Jake.

"A minute ago, I thought so, but I haven't gotten him back," he said.

"Did you tell him what door to take to get us out of here?" I asked him.

"I told him, but I'm not sure if he was reading me," Jake said. "I don't think anything could get through these walls. It might just have been static coming in."

"Now, try not to talk during this part if you could," Kevin said. "It's a little tricky."

I turned to watching him and saw that he again had the long needle. He put his fingers on Olivia's stomach and pushed on it. He moved it around and I could see he was feeling for something. With a smile he raised the needle and slowly pushed it in. Moving the angle around once it was a few inches in, I watched as he turned his head and kind of closed one eye, feeling for something with the tip of the needle. Then all of the sudden, he plunged the needle deep. Satisfied, he attached a reservoir to the end of the needle and started drawing out fluid.

"You piece of crap!" I told him. "I'm going to rip your throat out! How do you do such things?"

"It takes a lot of schooling, really," he said with a smile. "I mean, becoming a doctor is a lot of work."

I watched him take the reservoir off of the needle and bring it over to the table. He did something I did not see and was busy at it for a moment. I moved some and tried to see better what was going on, but still could not.

"Oh, just a minute," Kevin said. "I'll bring it up on the screen."

He went to the laptop and turned it to where I could see it. He typed a little and then used the mouse to scroll around. He tapped the keyboard with some satisfaction and I saw a picture come on.

"See this here is the virus," he told me. "Let me zoom in a bit."

He moved the laptop and I saw a microscope. He moved something under the light and looked through the eyepieces. He zoomed in and the picture on the screen became much clearer and seemed to be alive with activity.

"Oh yeah, that's a lot better," he said. Margie walked over to stand beside me. "Wait, I better get this started. I don't think I need to wait. I see plenty of what I want already."

He took the reservoir he had taken off the needle and attached it to some other thing. He pulled up the fluid and put it in several different vials. He then put caps on the vials and put them in the top of a machine. He went to the side of the machine and turned a few different knobs. The vials began to spin and he closed the lid.

"Now, let's take a look while that cooks," he said with some joy. "See these sections here that are moving so much? Those are the clusters of virus. Can you see them really good?"

I saw what he pointed out and it looked just like the virus that I had seen when George showed me all of the footage we found on the pin drive. It was an octopus looking creature with dark green tentacles. It seemed to have the face of a man almost. It moved, sometimes quickly and seemed to be annoyed with anything around it.

"It seems aggressive," I told him.

"That's right!" he said excitedly. "That's what took out the Chinese. It was so funny watching it all happen with no way to stop it, though they tried."

"I'm sure they wouldn't agree with that," I told him.

"Oh, but they would, seriously," Kevin looked at me and said. "That's exactly what they had planned for us. You watched as they found the beginning of our fall amusing." I did see that. "But, it sure turned on them, didn't it?" He chuckled with glee.

"So what's with the spinning vials?" I asked him.

"I am so glad you asked and it brings us to the next part of our demonstration. See this pile of inactivity over here? That is the portion that is the completion of my work. This here is the antibodies that are sticking to the virus. I want you to look carefully at what's left. Let me zoom in again. See this? It's the miracle portion of my creation. The virus died and is letting out the compounds in its tentacles. Technically, they're called something else, but you wouldn't understand."

I saw what he was pointing at and I must say I did not really understand what I was looking at. I did see the octopus type virus bloated and dying. Liquid of different colors where coming from them as though they were defecating some diuretic fluids. The green seemed to come off of their tentacles and flow in rivers and streams and collect in lakes.

"I ain't seeing it," I told him flatly.

"Right there," he said. "All of that is the end. No one has been able to get that to happen. When the virus dies this molecular green fluid changes. I found out the virus, upon its death, breaks down so quickly that the bonds of its cells mix in and change the very essence of these green molecules making them lose all their fantastic charm. We knew it was there, but we were never able to get it in its pure form. It's the reproductive portion of the limbs that gives off that healing molecule. If you cut off one of their limps they'll still live and some of them will even grow back the limb. It's the green stuff, you see. It's all right there. I will diagram it and find where every atom fits. I'll someday know how to live forever and I will give life to whoever I want."

"Is that what this is about," I asked him. "It's about you having some power and feeling like a god?"

"With this knowledge and ability, I'll be god," he told me. "Maybe it's too big for you to understand." He stood up and came over to the glass. "I liked you. You were courageous and it was fun seeing Steve's compound ripped from him. He never thought that would happen, you know. He was so proud of himself. I guess I always knew you couldn't be brought into this. You don't have the right understanding."

"I've been told that before, I think," I told him. "It's always about being on top, isn't it? You have something else someone wants, so you use it to keep yourself above them. It's what destroyed the world, remember?"

"That's one way of looking at it," he said with a shrug. He walked back over to the table.

"So, what's up with the spinning vials over there?" I asked him. He looked back and smiled.

"Well, if you figure out what exact rotation you need and what temperature puts the virus to sleep, if you will, then you can separate what you need into its different forms. Me, I only need the serum, well I guess you would understand that as antibodies. Steve's blood helped with that last part of getting the little creatures to cooperate. Releasing the antibodies back into a patient infected with them, made them ripe to releasing the serum in its pure form without croaking first. It's the green stuff, man." He said that last part as he leaned back and talked in a low-pitched voice. He smiled to himself and went back over to look at Olivia.

"Why don't you just let her go?" I asked him. (I silently wondered if that question ever worked.) "You got everything you need. Sure we'll die here, but they don't have to."

"Oh, they might as well," he said. "I'd rather not be chased to hell and back. You see, I plan on giving a couple of these vials to your NASA friends. That's all they want you know. That way they won't need to bother with me. The problem is, they won't be able to figure it out like I have. They won't know that at first, though. I'll be long gone by then, however, they won't be spending all their time looking for me, right?" He looked around then and came over to the glass and stared into my unblinking eyes. "They'll never be able to return. The virus doesn't work that way. Everyone not constantly exposed to it has no chance at ever finding a cure. The disease is too ravenous. Oh well, NASA." He let out a huge belly laugh and made the 'game over' sound for some video game I could not remember.

He moved around then and collected some papers. He closed up his laptop and set it on the pile. He opened a large box and started organizing some of the papers in there and put the laptop in beside them. He put some different plastic containers with liquid in there and some different instruments. Several needles went in next. He looked around some more and put yet more liquids in the box. Finally, he went to the section over by where Tara was and, pushing her harshly to the side, grabbed something from behind her. Walking over and putting that in the box, he looked around and finally sat down.

"Would it be wrong if I finished my lunch while I waited?" he asked and looked at me. "No? I don't mind if I do."

He pulled a bag over to himself and pulled out some food. He ate some of it and threw the wrapper on the floor, smiling to himself as he did so. He ate more and truly seemed to be enjoying himself.

I spent some time looking around and trying to figure a way out of the situation. I knew there was nothing we could offer Kevin; he was too far gone. I looked harder at the door and only saw frustration all over it. The ceiling was just as sturdy as the rest of the prison. The keypad by the door looked like something to try once Kevin was gone. I looked back and saw him watching me.

"Thinking about the keypad, huh?" he asked. "That's about the only way, I guess. I could tell you how many digits the combo is, but I ain't gonna."

I heard a ding sound and saw Kevin look over to where the machine he had put the vials in was. He got up and went to it, lifting the lid and pulling them out. He looked at them carefully and smiled. I saw they were all about half full of dark green liquid.

"Dead virus, live miracle drug," he said, holding them out to me. "Well, not exactly the way I wanted to be leaving, but if I think about it, there's really no reason to stay. I'm really glad you made it for this. It means a lot, you making the trip and all. Sleep tight."

He walked around with two of the vials and got out a small plastic box of some sort. He put the vials in there and went and grabbed the rest, making five total. Snapping the lid closed on the container, he walked over to the large box and put them inside in some place of honor. With a smile he closed and latched the lid of the box.

He turned to the metal door that he had looked out of earlier. The box he had filled had a long shoulder strap and he hefted it up and adjusted it in place. He looked through the window and, pulling a 9MM out of the back of his beltline, he chambered a round. He aimed it at Tara and looked at me smiling. He shrugged and turned back to the door.

He used an ID card and slid it down some area out of my sight. The door started to open and he looked over at me and smiled. He aimed the gun at me and drew a bead on my head as he waited for his escape hatch to open. His charismatic smile seemed so genuine. I will never forget seeing his head fly sideways as Eric's fist smashed into his temple.

CHAPTER 25

I watched Kevin collapse to the floor and my heart soared with relief. I looked at the door mechanism as though, now without Kevin in the picture, all was well and doors would mysteriously open by themselves. This was, of course, not the case and I looked up to see Quade coming through the door as Eric picked up Kevin's gun and checking the chamber, aimed it at his head.

"Quade, right here," I yelled and waved my arms a bit.

He came over to the glass door and looked for a way of opening it. He did not see one and looked up at me with some question. I looked around for somewhere to send him, but was not sure where.

"Kevin had an ID card he used over there," Margie told him. "Maybe it will work here."

Quade hurried over to Kevin's unconscious body and rolled him over. He looked through his pockets first. He seemed to get more forceful the longer it took him. In the end, he found the card on his belt. He ripped it off with some force.

He brought it over and looked at the mechanism to open the door. He swiped it and it took twice for the door to open. It was however, the greatest sound in the world.

I moved through the door and headed straight for Kevin. I pulled my knife and flipped its blade out. With a looping blow, I came down with the sharp blade aimed at his throat. Quade's strong shoulders pushed up under my forearm and stopped the deathblow that surely would have opened his jugular. I pulled hard in his grip, but he did not let my arm go.

"Maybe we should wait on that until we get out of this place," he told me up close to my face. "No need to rush this. Let's see what's going on over there and give this a second to cool down."

I knew the advice to be good, but I am sure I did not want to hear it. I had seen what he did firsthand. Our computer at home was full of scenes of what he had done. My wife was dying because he was who he was. I tried to pull away a little harder.

"Don't do this," Quade said softly, still holding tight. "You asked for my help and I'm giving it. This here is bigger than just this. NASA being involved means this isn't just about your revenge. Maybe in the end we do this. We need to think ahead for now." He continued to hold me tight, though a look of concern covered his face.

I knew he was right. I hated that he was right. Kevin's blood on my hands would have been the pleasure that would wash away the hurt and satisfy my soul, or so I thought at the time. Still, I knew he was right.

"Okay," I told him. "But keep him on the other side of the room. I don't think I can handle hearing his stupid voice."

"I will," Quade told me and walked with me still in his arms a bit away from Kevin. "Fredrick, you are in charge of Kevin."

"This here guy on the floor?" I heard him ask.

"Yeah, he isn't allowed to talk when he wakes up either, unless asked a specific question," Quade said, letting me go over by the long metal table. "And when he answers we want the short and sweet kind."

"Yes sir, I think I understand just fine," Fredrick told him, moving over to search Kevin and tie his hands behind his back.

With some effort, I turned to the two women. I was heartbroken with what I had seen and I was pained to see it again. These were two members of our family and the thought of what they had been through went deep.

I looked at Tara's face and saw a young woman's smile that was full of relief, but also something else I could not put my finger on. I hurried to her and cut the rope off from around her neck. I walked around behind her and saw duct tape had been used to bind her. It had been rolled into tight cords as she had struggled with it. It did not, however, take long to cut it off. I watched as she moved her arms forward and rotated her shoulders in alleviation.

Turning my attention to Olivia, I saw Eric at her side and looking over her face. He reached up and started removing all of the pieces that held the monitor cables in place. I walked there and helped him. He found the strap that took off the baby monitor. (He threw it against the far wall.) I saw him looking over some of the drip tubes and he turned to me and shrugged.

"How's that piece of crap doing?" I asked Fredrick. "Is he close to waking up?"

"He's moving like he wants to," he said.

"We need him to tell us how exactly to wake up Olivia," I told him.

I watched as he reached down and with one hand lifted him off the floor. He pushed him up against the wall and wedged him there with his forearm. Kevin seemed to want to wake up, but could not.

"How hard did you hit this guy, Eric?" Fredrick asked.

"Sorry," Eric said. "I was just trying to make sure he went down."

"No, I rather that, than being in the middle of a hostage situation," I told him.

"Here, give him some of my water," Margie said and went and splashed some in his face. It did not seem to help.

"Any idea what's keeping her sedated?" I asked Tara.

"Yeah, he keeps filling that bag there," she said and pointed. "She hasn't been awake since."

"She's going to be pretty groggy," Eric said.

"I need to go give Lincoln an update," Quade said. "We left him and Ray upstairs. My radio ain't working in this room."

"Sure, we'll wake her up and then be on our way," I told him.

"I'll be right back," he said and left the room.

"Let's pull that drug out of her arm," I told Eric. "In fact let's pull them all out." I saw there were at least four in her.

Eric pulled gingerly at first and watched Olivia's face as he did so. When she did not move or seem to even notice, he pulled the others out a lot quicker. They started to bleed, so he grabbed some nearby cloth and held it over the spots. He did it all with a lot of care and I much appreciated it.

"Anyone see a wheelchair?" I asked.

We all looked around and did not see one. Tara said she knew where one was and, grabbing the ID card off the table where Quade had left it, she headed through the glass room we had been trapped in. She opened the door we had first come through with the card and disappeared down the hallway as the door closed.

"Let's gather everything we can that has to do with this research," I told everyone then. "Let's take anything and everything."

"Looks like this guy is coming around a little more," Fredrick said. "Yeah, there you are buddy, ain't ya?"

I looked at Kevin and he was able to hold his head up. His eyes still looked far away and his breathing got faster. He looked to be waking up from a long sleep. All of the sudden he jerked his head straight and looked around. I watched as a look of defeat took over his appearance. It was odd how quickly he again began to look like a helpless little man.

"You just stay right there and you may live another minute or two," Fredrick told him. Kevin looked at me and kept his weak-looking eyes focused on my hate-filled face.

I turned and continued to gather whatever looked worthy to be placed in with what Kevin was doing there. As the pile grew, I looked, but did not see any more boxes or bags that would be able to help us carry the stuff we were gathering. I asked Sterling to check around and in no time he came back with several small drawstring bags. I wanted to ask how he found them, but decided not to. He started filling the bags as I gathered more stuff.

Quade returned to the room just as Tara came through the other door, pushing a wheelchair. He gave me a nod as I hurried over to help Tara get the chair through the door. We stopped beside Olivia and looked for the easiest way to get her into it.

Eric took over and lifted her easily into the chair. He got several towels from somewhere and covered her nakedness. He rolled one up and put it around her neck so that it did not lay so much over to the side. She was still totally out of it and Eric walked around and took the handles of the chair.

"You got her?" I asked, but it seemed obvious I did not have to.

"Yeah, I'll pull her up the stairs," he said.

"Looks like we are out of here," Quade said.

"Everything okay up top?" I asked him.

"Yeah, we haven't seen any movement at all," he said. "I'll lead you out. Fredrick, you bring up the end."

"Yes sir," he said.

Sterling and Jake each grabbed one of the bags we had collected. I grabbed the one that Kevin had been leaving with. I looked at him as I passed and had some deep emotions pass through me. I walked out of the door and saw Tara move quickly at my side. I tried to grab her, but I could not.

I saw her jump at Kevin and I heard him cry out in pain. I watched her pull back with her arm and saw a scalpel dripping blood in her hand. She plunged it forward again but Kevin was able to move to the side a little to avoid it. I was there to grab her an instant later.

"Man, that looks like it hurts like a son of a bitch," Fredrick said in Kevin's face, daring him to do anything besides stay there and endure the pain.

I saw she had stabbed him in his upper chest, but could not see through his shirt how bad it was. Blood was already beginning to soak the area and the worry on Kevin's face as he tried to see how bad he was wounded was a little comical. I actually thought about letting Tara go to finish what she started.

Tara yelled some obscenities at Kevin and tried to throw the scalpel at him. I grabbed her hand as it came forward and was able, with some danger to myself, to keep her from getting any force behind it. The scalpel slid along the floor a short distance away. She tried then to kick Keven but instead kicked Fredrick in the butt rather roughly. I was able with some effort to push her through the large metal doorway, she was still yelling her hatred for Kevin.

Quade was hurrying back and saw me struggling to control Tara. He must have thought I had attacked Kevin as I saw relief on his face. He moved out of the way as I continued to push her in front of me.

I don't remember much of what it took us to get out of the basement of the hospital. I remember some concrete stairwell and a few different doors. I do know that it was not the same way we came in and I wondered at that. Getting back to the ground floor of the hospital however, was such a relief that I remember the instant I saw it with clarity.

I saw we were somewhere by the cafeteria and just seeing the word on a sign there made me hungry. I remember the floors there streaked with mud and boot prints that went in every direction. The wall in front of me was collapsed and it looked like the rest of the building in that section was in danger of doing the same thing.

Quade moved past me and led us to the left. I had a lot of questions but knew that none of them pertained to us getting out of there quickly. Ray moved out behind Quade and I moved along with Lincoln down the long hallway. We turned a few times and I looked back, glad to see everyone was there. Eric was moving gently, but quickly, with Olivia, even managing to drift with some care around the final corner of the wide hallway that led to the main exit.

I turned back and saw Quade taking up a position at the doorway. He was surveying the area and Ray was helping him. He pointed something out to him and they both watched the area for a while. After a minute he turned back to me, now up close with Tara and able to see most of what was going on outside.

"Looks good," he told me. "I'll head over to that building there and you all follow one at a time."

I nodded understandingly and Quade turned and ran for cover. Ray followed and Lincoln after that. I held Tara's arm and looked back at Margie. She looked at me and could tell I wanted something from her.

"Stay back and help out with Kevin, will you?" I asked her. She nodded and moved back to stand beside him and Fredrick.

I worried much of the way back to the train, looking everywhere and fully expecting to be set upon now that we were so close to heading home. I had Jake call home and give them a brief update. (It seems NASA came back with a lot of questions which we did not answer just yet.) We tried to find an easier way with Eric pushing the wheelchair and it really was not that different of a way back. The last part got a little difficult but I came back to help and we carried it that last mile or so. I will say we all worked together well and I could hardly believe it when we stepped inside of our boxcar.

Lincoln ran up front with Sterling to the engine, saying they would get us going in the right direction. Fredrick unceremoniously threw Kevin down by the horse pens and told him not to move, adding several descriptions of what he would do to him if he did. Ray walked over and added a few comments to that. I told Eric we could lay Olivia down in my area and Quade pulled back the blankets there as we took her inside and laid her down on the bed. Eric took some care and covered her with some of our blankets. I made sure Tara stayed close to us.

I started to get concerned that Olivia had not woken up yet. She was breathing just fine and I listened to her heart which seemed to be beating just fine, not too fast which is about all I knew to check for. I looked down at her and stood up. Telling Tara to stay close to her, I smiled a little at their both having returned and walked out of our room.

I looked at Kevin, which made Quade a little nervous. I assured him I was over my immediate desire to strangle his neck. They still stayed alert as I moved closer.

I felt the train start to move and noticed we were moving backwards. I had every confidence in the ones driving so I put the direction out of my mind. I was sure Sterling would take care of getting us home in the fastest manner possible. I only wished it would take half the time I knew it would.

"How long is she going to be out of it?" I asked Kevin with some hate dripping off my voice.

"It depends on how her metabolism is doing," he answered softly. I came over and stomped him in the face with my boot heel.

"Now, same question," I told him as blood gushed from his obviously smashed nose.

He could not hold his nose as his hands had been tied behind his back. He tried to push it up against his shoulder but that seemed to cause him more pain. He blinked hard and held his eyes together tight.

"Well, what do you say?" I asked him. "Are we up for some more of this fun trivia game?"

"No, no!" he said. "I really don't know how long. It has different effects. She's been on it for....." He hesitated and I moved in closer which made him stop altogether.

"She's been on it for, what?" I asked him.

"She's been on it for a while so her body might be absorbing it quicker," he said.

"And what exactly does that mean, asshole?" I asked him.

"It should not take much longer," he said. I spit on him as I walked away.

"How long will it take to get to your home from here?" Quade asked me, coming to stand on the other side of the door frame I was leaning against.

"If the tracks lead anywhere straight, then about an hour and a half," I told him.

"That should be no time at all," Quade told me with a smile. "It may not feel like it, though."

"I bet it will," I told him. "I guess I should call home." Quade nodded and looked back outside.

I found Jake sitting by himself. He saw me coming and handed me the radio. I gave him a thumbs-up and he gave me a salute. I knew I needed to work a little harder to get him out of his own head. Walking in to where Olivia lay, I called home.

I got Jadee and she demanded to talk to Tara as we had not allowed it until we got to the train. I heard Jadee crying and sobbing as she heard Tara's voice. They talked a little and it was good to hear. Jadee finally calmed down and I took over. I told her I needed to know how Davina was doing.

"Shay's still in surgery," she told me. "I'm sorry, but I don't know how it's going."

"How's Chris?" I asked trying to stay focused.

"Shay said he would be fine. He's in a room. Laura's with him. NASA keeps asking questions."

"What kind of questions?"

"They are hoping that Kevin is still alive," she told me with her own batch of hatred. "They are asking a lot about exactly where you found him."

"We can give them all that when we get home," I told her. "He is alive, though he's bleeding a lot." I looked over at him and he looked away. "They can go over all of his notes with a fine-toothed comb. We brought everything he had."

"They were wanting to know about that too," she said. "I think that McQueen guy is almost here."

"Why do you say that?" I asked her.

"He was stopping by the college in Fort Collins before he was coming here, just in case Kevin went there," she said. "It sounded like they were almost there when we talked to them an hour ago. When they found out you had Kevin, I think he said he was going to head straight here."

"Okay, well let's see how that plays out," I told her. "Not really looking forward to that conversation."

"Are you going to give them Kevin?" she asked blankly.

"I was thinking that would keep them away from us," I told her. "I ain't going to do anything with him but burn him alive if he stays around too long. I think I got the impression that's all they were going to do with him."

"I'm there for that," Jadee said.

"I'm not sure we let him out of our sight alive," I told her. "I guess I don't want trouble with them is the only reason he's alive now. They are going to have to come up with a pretty good reason for taking him before I let him go."

"I don't think they want him alive," she said. "Mack said they just want to make sure he's dead. Mack has been a big help."

"Maybe we can keep in touch a little, as long as they don't feel they can show up at our door whenever they want."

"It sounds like they are all stationed somewhere out of Florida," Jade said. "Mack keeps saying something about McQueen wanting to get home there. Maybe that means they're too far away to ever come around here again after this."

"That's the hope," I said. "You'll keep me posted on Davina?"

"I will the minute I hear anything," she said. "Want me to go check? Shay wouldn't answer me last time I asked."

"No, let her work," I told her.

"How far away are you?" she asked.

I looked outside and noticed we had changed to moving forward, which I had not remembered doing. I, of course, did not notice anything familiar. I leaned out and looked far ahead.

"I am not exactly sure," I told her. "We left Cheyenne not long ago. I hope an hour at the most."

"I know you are wanting nothing more than to be here. It won't be long."

"I'll call you when we get close," I told her. "I'm glad we found Tara."

"Thank you so much," she said and I could hear her voice breaking.

"Not necessary," I told her. "We're all family. Now we're together again. I'll call you soon."

I walked the radio back over to Jake and he took it with little thought. I sat down beside him and looked out the door on the opposite side of the car. A warm wind moved through at that spot and I could see now why he chose it.

"What's going on?" I asked him.

"Nothing really," he said. "Just glad to be heading back home."

"Yeah, I guess you're excited to get back to your own compound," I told him as seriously as I could.

"No, sir, not at all!" he told me with added emphasis. "I guess I'm just tired is all."

"You've really proven a lot on this trip," I told him. "I'm proud to have had you with us."

"Really sir?" he asked.

"Well yeah, you think I wanted to carry that radio?" I asked him.

I saw him look down and I felt bad for saying that. I thought about how to change it to something else that would be funny, but nothing came to mind. I saw Davina's face then, looking at me with furrowed forehead and scolding me for my behavior. I stood up then and looked down at him.

"You've proven yourself pretty good with that thing. I'll have to talk to Dan, but maybe when we get back we can find a spot for you in our Com Room," I told him. I saw him jerk his head up with some excitement. He got up and did not seem to know what to do with himself.

"Yes sir, I can do whatever you want," he said.

"And if you're going to date my daughter, I'm sure we're going to have to go a few rounds together," I told him. "Maybe you can help me build a ring and we can keep each other in shape." He looked at me then with his mouth wide open. It looked weird him standing there like that. He started shaking his head a little and lowered his eyebrows some. "Or, we can just forget the whole thing."

"No sir!" he said. "It would be my great honor to marry your daughter."

"Now back up a bit there," I told him. "We're going to have to go a lot of rounds before I'm able to get that into my head. Let's just start by building the ring."

"Yes sir!" he said.

I turned back around and started toward the door. I saw Quade trying to erase a smile from his face. I leaned against the door frame and looked over at him.

"What is it?" I asked.

"Not a thing," he said. "Just thinking about some joke someone once told me." I was pretty sure I did not believe him.

I went and checked in on Olivia. She seemed to be breathing about the same. She still was unconscious and I willed us to be home. I sat down next to Eric who had not left the side of her face.

"She's very beautiful, isn't she?" he asked me. I looked at him a little sideways and then nodded.

"Yes she is," I told him. "She's been through a lot too."

"I can see," he said.

"No, I mean she just lost her husband," I told him. "He died right in front of her."

"Wow!" he said. "It's a cruel world to some."

"I'd agree with that," I told him. "Thanks for watching out for her."

"No problem," he said.

I got on my radio and asked Sterling how much longer it would be. He told me about half an hour and I hoped I could keep myself in check that long. I went and told Jake to have home bring the truck to the tracks just down the road so we could get Olivia back. He said he would have them ready.

I went to the box that Kevin had put the vials in and opened it up in front of him. He watched what I did and seemed to understand. I took the plastic container of vials and opened it. I took them all out and threw the container out of the train.

I put two of the vials in the inside pocket of my vest. The other three I handed to Quade who had come over to stand beside me. He nodded to me and put them in different pockets on his person.

"So, you really going to give them that guy?' he asked me.

"Not sure if I can," I said. "They sound intent on getting him, so I'll see how it plays out."

"Sounds like a good way of keeping NASA in good graces," he said. "How about all of the paperwork stuff?"

"I can't think of any use I'd have for it," I told him. "What do you think?"

"Sounded like they needed it more than any of us," he said. "I think it's better that way."

"Think they can do anything with it?" I asked him.

"Maybe we should ask him," he said, pointing to Kevin. I nodded and we both walked over to him.

"What is NASA going to do with you once we give you to them?" I asked him.

"Try to get me to tell them everything I know," he said.

"And when you don't cooperate to the fullest?" Quade said, already seeing the future.

"I'm sure they will try hard," he said. "You have all of my notes there. They won't really need much more from me."

"Why do they need you so bad?" Quade asked.

"They just want the cure so they can come back home," Kevin told him. "It will never work, though. They don't want to believe it, but they are stuck up there forever. I guess, I get to live a boring life of trying to pretend to work it out for them."

"How do you know it won't work?" Quade asked.

"I know everything there is to know about this virus," he said with a little pride. "It does not take to gene manipulation. It's too far beyond that. They just don't know that yet."

"Well, I hope it's a life full of misery for you," I told him. "I would kill you now, slowly, if I thought they didn't want you so badly. But don't worry; I still may get my way."

"Yeah, that's not too hard to figure out," he said. "You might as well. I hear that guy looking for me is not the nicest fellow."

"I hope you're not looking for sympathy," Quade told him.

"No, I know better," he said.

"Looks like your shoulder is still bleeding a lot there, Kevin," I told him.

"Yeah, I think it is," he said. "Maybe I'll bleed to death before we get home." I punched him hard in the face.

"Don't call that place your home," I told him without raising my voice. Blood flowed afresh from his nose. "No, your ability to heal will keep you alive for a long time to come."

"No, not me," he said and looked at me straight.

"What?" I asked him.

"Yeah, why do you think I stuck around Steve for so long?" he asked.

"You mean you never had the healing ability?" I asked him but I already knew the answer. "Of course, that's why you needed to finish your research. It wasn't pride at all. You needed the cure for yourself."

"I'm glad you know," he said.

"Why?" I asked him. "I couldn't care less about you. You won't be thought of a second past the time you leave." It seemed to hurt him a little.

"Ten minutes," I heard Sterling say through my radio.

"Let's be ready to move out fast," I told everyone.

I went to the doorway and saw the town north of our compound coming close into view. We curved and I lost it from view but my heart had leapt at seeing it. I checked my rifle and gathered a lot of what we had taken with Kevin in a pile. I walked back over and stood in the doorway.

"I used to carry one of those," Quade told me. "I used to carry it under my arm like that and everything. I ran out of 7.62s. I think I still have it stashed away somewhere."

"I think I'm getting close myself," I told him. "Thanks for all you've done."

"We ain't done yet it looks like," he said. "Thank me later." I nodded and gave him a smile.

We pulled up to where we were close to the road just down from our compound. I saw my green truck there with Neil standing beside it. My heart warmed and tears filled my eyes. I choked back the emotions and thought about what should come next. As we stopped, I jumped down, followed by Quade and a mixture of movement.

I saw Eric carrying Olivia and walking over to the doorway. Ray jumped to the ground and I watched as Fredrick pushed Kevin off the side with little care as to how he landed. Kevin tried to turn into the motion in order to be able to land on his feet. It did not work and he landed on his side instead, breaking his arm quite grotesquely.

"Oh, my bad, mister," Fredrick said with a smile. Ray lifted him by the broken arm and he screamed in agony.

Neil came up to us then and grabbing me, gave me a big hug. I returned it with pleasure but got back to the business of getting us off the train. Olivia got handed to Quade, but Eric promptly took her back when he got to the ground and let Neil direct him to the truck with her. We all ran over to the truck then, Sterling and Lincoln, bringing up the rear. We piled in and looked ahead to the last leg of our long journey.

We made it to where the gate was open and allowed us access to our compound. As we made the turn, however, Quade pointed farther down the road and looked over at me. Looking, I saw a line of Humvees heading our way.

"Looks like your friends are here to wish you goodbye," I told Kevin. He was still in too much pain to respond.

"Is it them?" Quade asked.

"Yeah, I think so," I told him.

Neil tried to drive carefully which slowed him down a bit. We still bounced around a lot, but it seemed to take longer than necessary to get through the grassy fields to our water tanks. McQueen must have seen us coming and sped up, as I saw before we rounded the hill that he was pulling through the gate with three other vehicles.

"Looks like they're a little serious about whatever they're thinking," Quade told me.

Neil still drove relatively slowly. We finally stopped up the hill close to the horse corrals. We all piled out and looked back the way we came. The Humvees skidded to a stop just down from us and about ten soldiers jumped out, looking ready for however we would react.

"Not sure I like you letting yourself in again," I yelled down to McQueen who got out of the lead vehicle. He stopped and raised his hands.

"It's the end of my mission here," he told me, pointing up to Kevin. "He signals the last of them."

"I hear you had some success on your venture," I told him.

"And I see you had some on yours," he told me.

"Wasn't sure I wanted you to have this here piece of crap," I told him. I did not tell him yet of where the research paperwork was.

"Finally, you pay the price for what you've done," I heard Tara say.

I felt her yank the 9MM out of my side holster and turned in just enough time to see her aiming the gun at the back of Kevin's head. I could not believe it as I saw her pull the trigger. I reacted too late but grabbed her outstretched arm and knocked her sideways. The gun went off again and shot Fredrick in the leg. Two more rounds hit the dirt before Tara stopped and looked at what she had done. She threw the gun down and looked defiantly at the men at the bottom of the hill.

"No way he lives another day," she told them.

I looked down there as well and saw them all shouldering their rifles. We did likewise and I was surprised when I did not feel bullets ripping through me. I kept my aim at McQueen and watched what he would do.

"He wasn't going to cooperate anyway," I told him.

McQueen still did not move. I lowered my rifle and stepped down the hill some. I threw my hands up and just waited for him to decide what he was going to do. He came out from around the door he was standing behind and walked to the front of the vehicle. He told everyone to stand down and walked up the hill a little more. I came down to meet him, surprised this was going the way it was.

"She's one of the women he took?" he asked me when I made it to him.

"Yeah, he had her strung-up," I told him. "She tried to take him out when we were up there. Sorry, we weren't more careful."

"Nothing we can do about that now," he said. "How far did he get up there?"

"We got trapped in a room on the way in," I told him. "He showed me how he was trying to separate the antibodies. He took some fluid out of the other woman. The only reason I'm giving you this is because you helped us find them." I reached in and pulled out a vial from my vest pocket and handed it to him. "Kevin said none of it would help NASA."

"We've all known that for some time, even before they left to go up there," he told me as he took the vial. He dropped it on the ground and smashed it with his boot. "We just needed Kevin and his colleagues to stop pushing forward. The scientists up there know they're doomed to stay. They've been working on that virus longer than any of these guys. They put it to bed a long time ago and accepted their fate. With that man dead on the hill up there, it means I can go home and start living whatever's left for us down here." He reached out his hand and I shook it, shock still filling me. "They said you took all of his paperwork. We'll take it and destroy it. If you give it to us we'll be on our way."

"There's quite a bit of it," I told him.

He called two of the nearby soldiers and they followed me up the hill to the truck. They took the boxes and turned back down the hill. McQueen turned to me and smiled.

"I guess this is goodbye," he told me. "I don't figure on getting this far west again, though I've enjoyed the view of the mountains. Florida will always be the place for me, though."

"It would be nice to visit Disney World," Quade said.

"It got toasted right off," McQueen told him. "But Florida is still good anyway."

I watched him move back down to his Humvee and get into the passenger side. All of the vehicles backed up and sped away. I stood there stunned, knowing it could all have turned out a different way.

I turned when I had seen the last of them and ran up the rest of the way to the water tanks. Quade followed as I went through the door and I quickly made it to the Med Center. I saw Shay and Mary putting dressings on Davina who was still on a bed in the surgical room with tubes hanging all over her and a breathing machine hooked to her face. Teal and Lynn were washing up at the sink nearby. Shay looked up to see me coming to the window.

"How is she?" I asked her. She tried an encouraging look, but it did not work.

"I repaired a lot of damage," she started. "She's still fading. I put a chest tube in, but there's already a lot of drainage." I reached into my vest pocket and pulled out a vial of the serum Kevin had created.

"Give this to her," I told Shay.

"What is it?" she said, changing her look to one of hope.

"Kevin made it," I told her. "It's some of the healing agent."

"Are you sure you want to give that to her?" Quade asked, and then seemed to know that the question was easily answerable.

"Does she have a chance without it?" I asked Shay. She shook her head. "Then give her it right now!"

"Put it through," she said and pointed to a small tray slot in the wall.

I ran over there and opening the door, reached in and put it on the table. Shay came over and looked at it. She took off a glove and picked it up. She looked at me.

"We have to," I told her.

"Okay," she said. "I want you to prepare yourself, though."

I nodded vigorously, anything that would get her to give my wife the ability to get better. I watched Shay move over to a nearby tray and pick up a needle. She took the lid off the vial and drew the liquid out. She looked at me and I continued to nod. I wiped the tears away that started to flow. I watched her put the needle into Davina's arm and inject her with the dark green fluid. We all looked at the monitors, expecting a quick reaction. Nothing at all changed.

"That's okay," Shay told me. "If it's just serum then they may take a few days to work into her tissues."

"I understand," I told her. "She has it in her now. I hope that's enough."

"I'll get her set up in a room," Shay told me. "It will be about twenty minutes." Looking around for my son, I turned back to Shay. "Chris is doing fine," she said.

"Why don't you show me around a bit?" Quade asked.

I agreed to the tour and peeled myself off of the glass of the operating room. I walked around with Quade for a while and I am sure I was not the best tour guide. I do remember him having lots of praises for every room we entered. I saw the rest of the group that had come home, all happy to be back. I was still looking at my watch often and the second twenty minutes passed, I was back in the Med Center. Shay took me to the room where she had put Davina.

Quade stayed with me for a while. He sat down and seemed to be in no rush to leave. I am sorry to him that I was not a better host.

"I best be getting on my way," he said finally, standing up. "I need to get home and make sure things are put to rest with New Haven. I don't want to forget to give these back to you." He handed me the vials Kevin had made.

"I thank you all so much for all you've done," I told him, taking them. "Is there a way we can help with New Haven?"

"No, you've helped enough," he said. "It's a matter of us now working out the relationship with them. Their power is gone so it should go well. Thanks for saving my life at the expense of yours."

We shared a long handshake then and he invited us to come as often as we liked to their town. Teal gave me a hug and a broad smile. I felt really bad as I walked them out. I gave a warm goodbye to Fredrick and Ray as well. Lincoln was still talking to George about a soon trip back so I said a quick, pleasant goodbye to him. As they all moved off I rushed back to the Med Center.

I sat at the head of Davina's bed and listened to the monitors Shay had hooked up to her. Everyone came in and filled the room. I saw Dan and Jessie with his family come in and they stayed for a while before leaving to go home. Shay came in often and checked on her patient, always saying she was about the same.

Olivia finally woke up. I was surprised to hear that Eric stayed to see how she was going to be. We were all relieved when we heard she was fine and we fought past Shay to pay her a small visit. Shay insisted that she stay in the Med Center for a few days.

Everyone came often to visit over the next few days to encourage me as best they could. I visited Chris a lot and we played some cards when there was nothing else to do. It was around the third day that Davina started getting better.

She progressed quickly and healed completely within two days. Shay let her out of the Med Center but said she still wanted to see her every few hours. We walked around the compound and visited everyone, finally able to have some joy spread around.

I had not forgotten Chris who was still in the Med Center. I had given all of the vials of Kevin's potion to Shay and had asked her to use one of them on him as well. She had said she wanted to wait and see how the healing process worked on Davina before giving it to someone else. She was rather strict on that. However, once she saw Davina's recovery, Chris got a dose as well. The wound over the missing leg healed within a few days. Though, I was hoping for more for him, I was glad to see him moving around with a smile on his face, Laura at his side.

I'll put this away now and must say that, though the view from up here on these tanks has not changed, my view of my family and friends and all that has to do with them has. I think differently now on most things and am glad that I was able to stay sane through the transformation. I do not think I will be of need of these pages any more. As I here finish, I will walk down and with a broad smile, put them on top of the rest of the other manuscripts in the bottom drawer of the desk in my office.

EPILOGUE

I had thought to never revisit this again. I came down here to my office to find some good book to tide me over on the long winter that is going on outside. Nothing at all seemed to peak my interest for sitting down with and I thought about this manuscript. I pulled it out and read a bit of the ending. It has been about five months and was just figuring here to add a few things that have been going on since then.

It sounded so up in the air about NASA and truly I was not sure that they would not be back the very next day. To all of our great relief we have seen nothing of them. Jadee still talks to Mack often and they've developed quite a friendship. He helped talk us through some upgrades on our systems. I have been in there late at night and have seen Jadee and him still talking about nothing. It is good seeing a smile on her face. Talk about a long-distance relationship.

We communicated with Quade a few days after they got home. He was gone for a while, it seemed, forming a relationship with the new leadership of New Haven. I am so glad to report that they seem to now be the best of neighbors. I've met quite a few of them and they seem to be a very good sort.

We have traveled back and forth many times to Quade's town. Quade took me on a few of his quail hunts and I think on the last one, before winter hit him hard, that I took four and he only took three. (He's very competitive and I rubbed it in well.) We did a harvest feast with them and our whole compound went there, including some from Dan's place; his sheep pie went over big and I think he found a few people who wanted to start their own herds. Quade did not seem excited about that.

Jake and I finished up the boxing ring and have been out there a few times a week since. We started keeping score and I think I will say here that I am far ahead, whether it is true or not. April and him have been mostly inseparable since we got back and he kind of officially moved here a month later. He is okay at basketball.

Davina and Teal are the very best of friends. They talk all the time and either Davina is over there or Teal is here. It's great seeing such friendship happening. I would be jealous if she did not spend every other second of her life with me.

Vince and Mary did such an awesome job with the gardening inside the water tanks. I think just the other day the final tomato plant dropped its last tomato of the season. They have been in there a lot lately, already moving dirt and getting ready for next year. They have added much to the taste of the food this winter. They have more plans for the outdoor garden this spring, though I thought last year's was good enough. Their other daughter, Vanessa, moved over to Dan's compound last month. It seems she has a lot of friends there and is going to try that for a while.

George and Margie are fitting in more than great. They add a huge variety to everything here. George took up working on restoring some of the train yard over in the city north of us. He's working on some passenger cars that Lincoln found on one of their outings. Come to think of it, I think Lincoln was just here a week ago and left just ahead of the latest storm. I went over there and looked at what they were getting done. It is pretty cool seeing them working together. Margie and Marla are already best friends.

Chris is doing well and he married Laura a few months ago. (Come to think about it, I better write down their anniversary date before I forget.) Lincoln has made Chris a prosthetic leg that seems to be working out well. He promised to make a better one when spring comes around and they can sit down together. Laura is to have our first grandchild very soon.

Tara was a little bolder when she got back. She came out of her shell and has been going with us on every trip to Quade's town that we go on. The last few times we've been there I've seen her hanging out with a certain young man. Quade said he knew him well, but we still decided to have some fun and approached him. We freaked him out by asking what his intentions were. I think he will tread a straight line with her.

Olivia is hugely pregnant now and is expecting any day. We all have a bet on when the baby will arrive and I am sure I am going to win. I did not think it fair that they let some of the other compounds in on it, but I got overruled. Eric has been close to her ever since we got back. She seemed to like him being there and it warms me to see them doing things together.

Sterling and Shay got caught coming out of the same office on a few different occasions. They got caught making out in the gym too. They stopped trying to hide after that and have since moved into the same quarters. I told Dan he owes me, but he says there is no proof about who started it. I threatened to kick Sterling out if he did not tell Dan he gave in first. It did not really work. It does fill me with joy to see Shay falling into his arms every time we return from somewhere.

Neil and I play chess often and I still find him elbow deep in grease in the generator room. I see Marla there more times than not. I do always see a cheerful smile from my friend when I come down.

My awesome wife continues at my side and I am who I am because of it. We do so much together and I have even gotten her to do the early morning jogging with me now that she hardly sleeps. Her smile glows more now than it ever did, if that is possible. Her arms around me is all I will ever need.

It has been a bit over year now since I have last been in this drawer and again I find myself sitting here at my desk. We had an early spring as the snow let up about three weeks ago and the temperatures started to rise. We are all excited about the hunt we have been talking about with Teal and Quade. Looks like the whole town wants to be involved as is our compound. George and Lincoln got the passenger cars up and rolling and looking nice. We took them a few times back and forth at the end of last summer. Boy, were they comfy. Lincoln does not want them to run in winter time as he says it's bad on their older wheel housings.

We did take a trip up north to Cheyenne last summer and dragged home about twenty-five of those oil tankers full of oil that we found at that destroyed oil refinery. It took some doing, but we got them all in a line and brought them here. George said we should not run out again for a while. In the meantime he and Lincoln made a small refinery over at the town up north of us. Seems we do not much need the tankers anymore as George found an oil rig a few hills over and we can get as much crude out of there as we want and now we can refine it. It was worth the time together just going up there, though.

Axel has made leaps and bounds on his computer systems. We talk to them so much and on the big screens that it seems like they are living right outside. His system has changed a lot of the feel of the meaning of neighbors for us.

Quade and I hunted mostly through the winter. We got the ladies to go, though they are not into it as much as we are. Teal and Davina have been fast friends now for a while and I cannot keep up on all that they do together.

Lincoln fixed Chris an awesome leg. I cannot even tell he has it, even when he is running. We go on outings often to hunt or just enjoy being together. He and I started an afternoon jog together which is awesome to me. Laura had her baby son eight months ago. He is about the cutest thing you have ever seen. He will grow up well-spoiled.

Olivia's daughter was born healthy as well, though I heard it was a rough birth. I am glad for Chris's son that the two will grow up young together so that when all else becomes boring they will have each other. Quade won the contest on when she was to be born, even though, I tried to bribe Shay not to tell anyone. Eric is still here by her side.

Tara moved over to Quade's town. Jadee was happier than I thought she would be. She met the young man Tara could not stop talking about. They were married last fall and she is expecting a child now. Jadee is overjoyed.

Jadee still talks often to Mack, if not constantly. I have not heard much about how NASA is doing, but it seems they are surviving well. Jadee does not do much outside of the Control Room.

Vince and Mary did a great job again with the garden last year. They expanded a bit outside and seemed to double their work. They truly seem not to mind it. If I went up there now I am sure to see them happily digging at something. Vanessa is now married to a very nice young sheep farmer and they are expecting a child.

Jake married April a week ago. April is the happiest I have ever seen her. They moved to a section down by the gym, though I told them they could have their own place closer to ours across the hall.

My awesome wife is still keeping up with me on the early morning jogs. We do everything together and my life with her is beyond compare. She smiles my favorite smile often and holds me close.

Wow, five years have passed since I opened this drawer and pulled out this manuscript. Our world here is the forever place that I always hoped it would be. We have those people around us that bring life rich joy and we all experience it every day. The sounds of young children echo down the halls. I think we found out the other day that April's third one is on the way in the spring. Chris and Laura had another one two months ago. Tara and her husband just had her second child. Olivia and Eric finally got married two years ago. They had their first child together last year, though Olivia's daughter knows no one else as father, but Eric.

We are going on our fourth trip into the high mountains to hunt for some elk in a few weeks. Quade and Axel were some of the big takers last time. Dan needs to get a big bull this year or we are all going to make fun of him. Some of the men from New Haven have done well the last few years. Vince actually placed pretty high last year. Chris gave everyone a break and mostly just tracks for us now.

I love watching everyone grow and become more comfortable in the things they have chosen for themselves. I make my rounds and live their lives with them as much as I can. It is a beautiful thing to watch.

I still often sit atop the water tanks and watch the sunsets and my awesome wife still meets me there and wraps her arms around me. I can still see the spot where so long ago we parked our camper and where we first roasted our marshmallows. I look up and see the green-streaked clouds as the sun slowly sets. I know that I will never again need to come to this office and write, as my life is what I have always wanted it to be.

THE END

Randy grew up on the Eastern Plains of Colorado, where he was often found playing in the open grasslands. He now lives in Northern Colorado with his wife and two children. He enjoys camping and hiking in the Rocky Mountains. In his spare time he draws wildlife and paints landscapes. He and his wife like to compete in 'who loves who more'. His wife would like to state for the record, that she remains and always will, loves her husband more no matter what he likes to think or write! They are soulmates and together they have a wonderful life. She looks forward to all the fun and exciting adventures Randy will write up next!

CPSIA information can be obtained
at www.ICGtesting.com
Printed in the USA
LVOW09*1145170717
541605LV00023B/617/P